On the Loose

A Katie Parker Production (Act II)

Jenny B. Jones

On the Loose

Six months into her stay with her foster parents, Katie Parker is finally adjusting to her new family. But after a tornado rips through the town of In Between, nothing is ever the same. When her foster mom, Millie, is diagnosed with cancer, Katie begins to doubt if God really does care. What will happen to Katie? Could she possibly have to leave In Between and the family she's come to depend on? Things spiral even further out of control when Katie juggles a malfunctioning best friend, Spring Break plans, and holding the attention of her own Prince Charming. It's going to take more than a glass slipper and some fairy dust to fix Katie Parker's problems. But will help come in time?

This book is dedicated to my brother, Michael. I love you, and you mean the world to me. We went from screaming, biting, hitting brats to good friends. Life has been crazy, but I would've been insane had I not had a big brother to hold my hand. Or give me noogies.

This book is also dedicated to you because you told me if I didn't acknowledge you, you would tell the world that you are the ghost writer behind all my books.

Once again—I have the last word.

Chapter 1

*A*NOTHER ADVERTISEMENT FOR feminine products. Is it just a universal law that if you sit down to watch TV with a guy, you are guaranteed at least two tampon commercials?

I sigh with relief when *American Idol* comes back on and focus my attention on the contestant.

"Get off the stage! You can't sing. Girl, your mother's been lying to you."

James, my foster dad, rips the remote control out of my hands. He collapses back into his leather recliner and shouts another piece of artistic advice to the contestant on TV. I watch this fifty-five-year-old pastor howling along to an old Kelly Clarkson hit, and wish I had a mute button for his singing voice.

"How did she get into the top ten?" His intense gaze seeks mine. "Have you ever heard anyone so bad?"

Is this a rhetorical question—like when we girls ask if we look fat?

As the painful song ends, James shouts more criticism and comments at the TV. If his congregation could only see him now, preaching his Simon-like truth to the contestants on *American Idol*, they would drop their NIVs and run. It's like the evil spirit of pop, rock, *and* disco takes over his body. *So* not pretty.

I eyeball the remote in his hands, clutched in a death grip. *Ah, remote, we used to be so close. Once upon a time we had such good times together.* So much of my life has changed since coming to live with James and

Millie Scott. Most of it for the good, but their firm control of my viewing habits still totally bites. I'm used to free reign, trolling through the cable channels to my heart's content. I mean my own mother's rules during prime-time viewing hours were that I didn't interrupt her illegal drug sales. She was all for HBO if it kept me occupied. Those days are so over.

"James, are you watching the weather?"

Millie walks into the living room, a frown on her face. She opens the blinds and looks outside.

"Yeah, the weather. Uh-huh." He turns up the volume. "Oh, did you hear that judge? That's exactly what I would've said."

"Honey, switch it to a local channel for a second, would you? Mother just called and said there're some weather alerts."

"Millie, this is the last contestant for the night. We've got to see this. The theme is Justin Timberlake songs, and I've been waiting all week for this."

My foster mom and I freeze. And stare at James.

With a final glance out the window, Millie plops down on the couch beside me. "This is all your fault, Katie. Last night he asked me if he was too old to try out for the show."

James laughs and passes me some popcorn. "I could show Justin a thing or two."

Yes, but we would all need intense therapy afterwards.

Rocky, the family dog, follows the food and parks his large body on my feet. I try to shove him away, but it's no use. Just one of the many things I'm getting used to around here.

"Okay, commercial break. Now flip it over to channel seven." Millie throws a pillow at her husband to get his attention.

"Just a sec." James pulls his cell phone out of his pocket. "We're still going with that voting strategy we talked about at dinner, right?"

My foster dad has a whole system going. He's got spread sheets, bar graphs, and occasionally he even watches *Entertainment Tonight* to get some inside scoop on the singers. I'm just waiting for the day he starts his own *Idol* blog.

Millie lifts herself off the couch and grabs the remote out of James's hand.

"Come on. We're gonna miss the first part of the judge's comments. If you could wait ten more minutes and—"

A loud siren from outside stops James mid-sentence. It sounds like a much angrier version of a school fire alarm. My eyes go wide, and I look back and forth between my foster parents.

"What's that?" The hair on the back of my neck stands on end.

"The tornado siren."

Millie changes the station and a map of our county is on the screen. It's covered in red.

James loses all interest in our TV show, as he grabs his glasses and reads the messages scrolling on the bottom of the television. "A tornado's been spotted. It says we need to take shelter immediately."

The loud wail grows more insistent. Rocky whimpers and buries his nose under the couch.

"Let's get to the bathroom."

Millie grabs the couch cushions and hands me some to carry with us.

I have never been in a tornado before. I'm from Texas, but where I come from, drought is the biggest weather disaster you have to deal with. Living with the Scotts has been one new experience after another, but this is a moment I could definitely do without. Who has a tornado in February, I ask you?

"I'm still calling *American Idol*," James mutters. "Come on, Rocky."

We speed walk into the Scott's master bath. Having a bathroom of my own, I'm never in here, but now is not exactly the time to study the nautical theme Millie has going on in her powder room.

"Get in." Millie steps into the large Jacuzzi tub and holds out her hand. "Put the couch cushion over your head."

Great. So in addition to worrying about being sucked up by a funnel cloud, I'm going to have really bad hair too.

I climb in next to Millie and squat low. The TV blasts the weather report in the other room, and all I can hear is 'Take cover. Go to your safe place.' I scoot closer to my foster mom.

"James, come on. Shut the door." Millie raises the khaki cushion over my head.

Shoving the dog into the bathroom (which is no easy task; that Lab is about as big as a buffalo), James swings his legs over the Jacuzzi and sits on Millie's other side.

"Excuse me." I clear my throat. "Shouldn't I be in the middle? I am the child here. You know, the one you two should be protecting at all costs. My left side is totally unprotected, and—*oomph!*"

Rocky throws his body in to join us, his monstrous frame crashing into my side.

Well, who cares about the tornado? I'm pretty sure I'm gonna die under the weight of this overfed mutt.

"Good boy, Rocky." Millie reaches around and gives her dog a pat. "Feel better, sweetie?"

"Oh, much."

Rocky's whining is louder than both the siren and the TV. His big dog mouth is near my ear, and his breath is more of a natural disaster than any twister. I try to shove the dog off me with an elbow, but he's rock solid.

"Doing okay?" James curls an arm around me and Millie.

My teeth chatter and my body quakes. No, I'm not okay. I'm petrified! I've watched the Discovery Channel. I've seen what random chaos a tornado is capable of. I know perfectly well in a few hours it could be me, a few cows, and a stray toilet stuck in a tree on the other side of town.

"Everything's going to be fine. It's tornado season. Nothing to be afraid of. We're just taking some precautions."

Millie's voice does little to comfort me. Precautions? A precaution is wearing your seatbelt in case you *might* have a wreck. Or carrying an umbrella because it *may* rain. Three people and a dog huddling in a tub with parts of a couch balanced on their heads is not a precaution. It's what you do when the weatherman says a tornado is going to sail over your house and rip through your town.

"I'll pray for us."

With our heads already bowed, James leads us in prayer, asking God for safety and protection.

Even though I'm living with a pastor, and I'm at church a million times a week, I'm not a Christian. Shocking, I know. I'm still on the fence. I'm new to church and God, and I'm only now getting to the point where I can go to the youth services on Wednesday nights without wanting to hide in a broom closet all night. This life of faith the Scotts lead has been a huge adjustment for me.

That being said, I hope we don't get wiped out tonight because I'm just not ready. Should we meet with untimely deaths, I know where the Scotts would go. They'd waltz right into the pearly gates of heaven. Me . . . now that's another matter. *Not tonight, God. I'm not exactly in the believers club yet . . . And besides, I can't die without getting my driver's license. It would be so embarrassing.*

Rocky's ears perk up and he sniffs the air. Maybe he got a whiff of his own breath.

The lights flicker a few times, and James's arm tightens around my shoulders. This is not good.

The trees outside beat on the house, and rain pelts the roof. Isn't it supposed to be really quiet before a tornado? Maybe the threat is over. We'll probably be back in front of the TV in a few minutes.

Then the room goes black.

No lights. No noise from the TV. Nothing but the sound of the wind howling in the rain and the house shaking at the force of it.

The dog growls and paws at the tub.

I scratch his ear. "Rocky, calm down." But who can blame him? I'm about to pee my pants myself.

The walls begin to vibrate, and Rocky catapults out of the bathtub, barking at a new noise.

"Got that cushion over you, Katie?" Millie's voice is higher-pitched than usual, and our huddle gets tighter.

The dog scratches at the door, whining and yelping.

"You shut the door, right?" Millie whispers to her husband. "Rocky, come here. Come on."

An eerie sound like a distant jet plane has me holding my breath in fear.

The door creaks open then crashes against the wall, as the dog frees himself from the bathroom.

"Rocky!" We all call out in unison.

The jet sound grows louder.

And closer.

I can hear things flying against the house. Or maybe it's hail.

"I'll get the dog."

"No, James. Rocky's more likely to come to me. He's got to be under the bed. I'll run out really quick and get him."

"Millie, no."

Ignoring her husband, Millie makes a dash for the door, calling for the dog.

Just as the bedroom window explodes.

My ears fill with the pounding of my pulse. The alarm can no longer be heard, and the jet sound is now more like a train—coming for our house at mach speed.

"Stay here!" James flies into the bedroom, calling his wife's name.

"I'm over here! Just got a little scratched."

I can't see a thing, except for the bedroom occasionally illuminated through the doorway by lightning. My eyes don't leave the door, and I only release my pent-up breath when the shapes of my foster parents are back in front of me.

James shuts us in the bathroom, and we gather close again.

The wind roars, and the Scotts cocoon around me. James is talking, but I can't hear him. Tears slip down my face, and I grit my teeth and bury my head into Millie's shoulder.

The house shakes and sways, as if it's fighting to stay in place. Glass shatters somewhere else in the house. I hold on for dear life.

And then it stops.

My breathing is the loudest thing in the room as the locomotive sounds fade away.

"Is everybody all right?"

The calm timbre of James's voice fills me with relief. We're okay. We made it.

"Katie?" And now Millie's voice.

My body sags against her.

"I'm good." Though my head is spinning. I can't believe I just sat through a tornado. Maybe the Weather Channel will want to interview us.

"I'm going to get a flashlight. Everybody just stay put for now. I think we lost a few windows, so there's probably glass everywhere."

James returns in a moment, the beam of his light illuminating the bathroom. "Millie, you said you were okay."

"I am." She tenses beside me. "Oh . . . I see what you mean."

My eyes follow the path of the light, and I see Millie's white shirt. Covered in blood.

Chapter 2

I DON'T KNOW what smells worse, me or the emergency room. I'm rain-soaked from the run in, I've got Millie's blood on my shirt, and on the way here a wet dog decided he wanted to cuddle.

The clock in the waiting room says it's almost eleven. The Scotts and I sat here for two hours before Millie's name was called. Apparently the tornado really did a number on the town, and there were injuries, some much more serious than Millie's.

I take another sip of my coffee. My foster parents don't like for me to drink the stuff at night, but it's an old habit from my days with my mom. Living with the Scotts, I've learned to appreciate some of the finer things in life, like a safe place to sleep and food in the cabinets. Equally as important, I have developed a taste for mochas and iced lattes, but the courtesy coffee in the waiting room doesn't even include creamer.

I'm holding onto Millie's purse and cell phone. Maxine, Millie's mom, has texted about every five minutes since we've been here.

ANY WORD YET?

Totally bored, I'm grateful for the distraction. I punch in my reply.

NO. STILL WAITING. WILL LET U KNOW.

Just as I hit send, Millie and James come up the hall and enter into the waiting room.

"Do they have to amputate?" I joke.

Millie smiles, but James acts as if he didn't even hear me. It has been a long night though.

"The doctor removed a few small pieces of glass out of my chest. No big deal. A few stitches, some ibuprofen, and I'm good as new." Millie's eyes land on my coffee cup, and she raises an eyebrow.

"What? I was so worried about you, I had to Millie. I didn't want to drink it, really. But in a moment of weakness and despair, the coffee pot called out to me, and I gave in." I bow my head in mock shame. "If you want to send me back to Sunny Haven, I'll understand."

Sunny Haven is the girls home I had the distinct non-pleasure of living in for six months before coming to stay with the Scotts. My mother is doing a little time for her side business—well, OK, her only business—of drug pushing, and here I am.

"All right, our little drama queen, let's go." Millie grabs her purse from the orange vinyl seat next to me. "We need to go check on Mother, then run by the church and the Valiant."

The Scotts own an old historical theater, the Valiant. They completely renovated it last year, and I got to help. But that's a long story.

James looks at his watch. "I'm going to take you ladies home after we look in on Maxine. I'll go to the church and the theater myself. Millie, you should probably be taking it easy so you don't pull some stitches. And Katie needs to be in bed for school tomorrow."

"School?" I trash my coffee and put on my most pitiful face. "James, I have suffered terrible emotional trauma tonight. I sat cheek to cheek in a tub with your dog. I endured a tornado. My foster mother was nearly taken out by a window, and I had to wait in the ER for nearly three hours with only a *National Geographic* from 1992 to read. Don't you think I need a day of recovery?"

Millie laughs and pulls me to her. "I think that calls for a day off.

Given the reports we've heard about the damage in town, there will probably be a lot of kids absent tomorrow."

Elation races through me. Yea! I get to skip school tomorrow! No PE for me!

Then reality sets in. Millie would never agree to me missing school. When I came to In Between High, I was a little behind on the credits, and I'm only now starting to make some good progress. There could be an outbreak of measles, mumps, and scabies, and Millie would still probably force me to go to class.

"Are you sure all the doctor gave you was ibuprofen?" Maybe Millie hit her head, too, and we just don't know it.

A gray-haired man in scrubs walks down the hall, calling out to the Scotts.

"Millie, I forgot to give you this."

He joins us in the waiting area, and hands my foster mom a piece of paper.

"Here's the prescription for pain pills, just in case. I know you said you didn't want to take any, but should you change your mind, I want you to have this."

"Thanks, Dr. Carnegie." Millie hands James her purse, and with her hand at my back, leads us toward the exit, suddenly anxious to leave.

"Don't forget, call my office in the morning, and I'll make sure the clinic gets you in for a mammogram. With your family history, we really need to check that out."

Millie smiles and nods, and as the doctor departs, I put myself in my foster mom's path.

"What? Family history? What is he talking about?"

Millie's gaze travels to her husband, and the two share a look that probably communicates pages of information between them, but leaves me clueless as ever.

"When the doctor was patching me up, he noticed a lump. My sister had breast cancer so he wants to check it out, just to play it safe." Millie shrugs it off. "It's nothing. We'll talk about it later, Katie. Right now, we need to go check on my mom." She grabs James's hand. "And since Katie and I are taking the day off tomorrow, we're going with you to see the church and the theater."

We walk out to the car, the rain now a light mist. Rocky's tail hits the seat, and in his excitement to see us, he barks a welcome.

I push him out of my way and climb in the back.

Millie's words play over and over in my head. Lump? Cancer? What if something happens to her?

What will happen to me?

"IT'S ABOUT TIME you got here. I could've been whisked away to California in that twister, and you people probably wouldn't even have noticed."

Maxine, my seventy-something-year-old foster grandma, is holding open what's left of her door. She's obviously not hurt. She's immaculately put together in a velour jogging suit, perfectly matching nails, and some sporty Pumas. See, Maxine thinks she's my age. Her birth certificate, a document that mysteriously disappeared sometime in the Nixon era, is the only sure proof we have she's a bona fide senior citizen and not a kid. Well, that and her wrinkles.

"Maxine, we called you before and after the storm. I think I've talked to you at least twenty-five times tonight." James walks around surveying the damage. "And not once did you happen to mention part of the roof on your apartment is gone or that your windows were completely blown out."

The Scotts and I take in the trashed apartment in shocked silence while Maxine inspects her daughter.

"Mom, where were you when the tornado hit? In the hall? The bathroom?"

Maxine becomes a flurry of activity, picking up stray clothing and shoes that are scattered everywhere.

"Mom?"

"Oh . . . yes, yes, I was in a hall." Maxine's eyes meet mine, and she silently demands my help.

Millie's dad died a long time ago, and after all these years, Maxine has finally found herself a Mr. Right in Sam Dayberry, the Valiant caretaker. Though it doesn't make much sense (and with Maxine I've learned things rarely do), my foster grandma insists her relationship with Sam is kept hush-hush. So her own daughter doesn't even know she has a honey.

"Well, whose hall were you in?" Millie steps around an upturned lamp.

"You said you were going to a friend's house tonight to watch TV, right?" I chime in. Kind of weak, but it's the best I can do and still be truthful. Maxine was obviously over at Sam's.

"Right. That's definitely what I was doing." Maxine's head bobs a little too eagerly. "Sooo . . . looks like I'll be staying with you guys for a while. I'll go pack my bag."

"Wait a minute." James puts a halting hand up. "I think this is totally fixable. Maybe even for tonight. I'll just grab some duct tape, and—"

"James, there's not a single window left intact. Glass is everywhere, and it's raining in part of the living room. She can't stay here." Millie plants a fist on her hip, a sure sign she's not in the mood for James's funny business.

Maxine waggles her eyebrows at her son-in-law. "Don't worry. You won't even know I'm there. As long as I get breakfast in bed, remote control privileges, and Millie's home-baked cookies every night."

"Our house is kind of a mess too. I would never dream of you being the slightest bit uncomfortable. How about a nice stay at the Coach House Inn?"

Maxine clutches her chest and gasps. "The Roach and Mouse Inn? James, I am hurt . . . I am appalled . . . We're family."

Rolling his eyes, my foster dad picks up a displaced dining room chair and sits down. "Go pack your bags. But pack light. If I have to call in HGTV to fix this place quickly, I will."

Maxine claps her hands in excessive, obnoxious glee. "Come on, girls, you can help me pack. Oh, wait, Katie, just you. Millie's injured."

Great. Nothing like the privilege of folding your foster grandmother's undies.

I follow Maxine down the hall and into her leopard-print bedroom.

"Grab that suitcase there." Maxine points to her closet. "Be careful of the glass."

"Will you be taking the Hello Kitty luggage?"

Maxine mumbles something that sounds like *duh*, and I grab the bag.

"Did Millie tell you everything the doctor told her tonight?" My foster grandma is not known for being tight-lipped, so if I can find out anything else about Millie and the cancer, Maxine's the source. And Millie was talking so quietly on the phone in the car, I couldn't catch all of the conversation.

She grabs some shirts off hangers. "Yeah. I guess. Glass, stitches, and some aspirin, right?"

"The doctor said he found a lump."

Maxine drops a shirt. "What?"

"She didn't tell you that part? Dr. Carnegie says he wants her to come in for some test. A mammogram."

You don't get many quiet moments around Maxine. But this is one of them.

She sits on the bed, despite the fact it's slightly damp from the rain coming through the windows. "She didn't tell me the doctor said that."

I dig for more information. "Do you think Millie—"

"Hey, ladies, we need to get a move on." Millie appears in the doorway. She hesitates and looks at me.

I'm frozen to the spot, knowing I just got busted talking about my foster mom. Millie's a very private lady, and I know somehow I've just broken a rule.

"We still need to go by the church and the Valiant." James enters in behind his wife and closes Maxine's suitcase. "Are we ready?"

The rain has picked up, and we race to the car. Rocky sits between Maxine and me in the backseat. I hold my nose to block out his offensive smell, but Maxine croons to the mutt and scratches his chin all the way to the Valiant.

I drum my fingers on the car door, and anxiety swims through my gut. This theater is really important to me. It's a part of our makeshift family.

Though I was concerned about my foster mom, I'm also worried about the theater. That place has become my home away from home . . . um, away from home. When I'm not at the Scotts, I'm usually there, at the Valiant, working. Last fall I even performed in a play. Most girls my age are crushing on some boy. But me, I'm madly in love with an old stage.

The car can't go fast enough, and my stomach sinks as we pass all the storm damage. Houses with windows out like Maxine's. Roofs ripped apart. Trash and miscellaneous items lining the streets. A car turned on its side. Dogs running loose. A trampoline bent over a fence.

Very little in this town was left alone. I hope the harm is minor to the theater, but our odds aren't good. I slump down in the seat and close my eyes, trying to block out the images in my head, the possibilities for a damaged Valiant.

The car turns the final corner and the theater comes into sight.

There, illuminated by streetlights, is the mighty Valiant, whole and solid, as if the history and love in the old nails and mortar held it together against the wind.

We hop out of the car. James and I walk around the building.

"Not even a shingle out of place." His disbelief mirrors mine.

The Valiant stands in perfect condition. Every window, every door.

My foster dad throws an arm around me. "How do you account for that?"

My eyes travel over every square inch of my beloved theater. I shake my head in awe, and the words tumble out of my mouth before they fully form in my mind. "It has to be God."

Chapter 3

"WELL, GOOD MORNING, Sunshine."

Tying my robe as I enter the kitchen, I shoot daggers at a smiling Maxine. Chirpy, happy morning people really bug me. Especially ones who do it on purpose.

Last night after we checked the church and found it had barely been rattled, we came back home. Tired and drained. And I got a new roommate. Since it was too late to clean out the spare bedroom for Maxine, she spent the night in my room in the extra bed. Yes, just a big ol' sleepover with the grandma.

Except there is no sleeping when Maxine is around. I've heard semi-truck horns that weren't as loud as the sounds coming out of her mouth last night. Between her nighttime Donald Duck impressions and my fretting over Millie and the Big C, I think I slept a grand total of five minutes.

"Looking a little rough today, Dumplin'. How about some of my special juice cocktail?"

With one swollen eye, I regard my foster grandmother. I look like I just walked out of a police lineup, and she couldn't be any more rested and refreshed. Her overly blond hair is tied back in a neat bun, and her pink lipstick matches her sweater set perfectly.

I reach for the juice she's poured and mumble a few syllables that hopefully sound something like thank you.

"Drink up, Sweet Pea." Maxine nods toward the glass. "Does a body good."

So does eight hours of peaceful, uninterrupted sleep.

I toss the glass back as James enters the kitchen. His eyes land on my juice, and he lunges for me. "Katie, no!"

Too late. I swallow the contents. My throat immediately constricts around the slimy concoction.

Gonna. Hurl.

My eyes water, and I run to the sink, gagging all the way. I jerk on the tap and hold my tongue under the faucet like a dog, desperate to wash away the taste.

Wiping my mouth, I turn on Maxine with murder in my eyes.

"What," I growl, "was that?"

"My morning specialty. Prune juice and egg whites."

"Here, drink this." James pops the top on a Diet Dr. Pepper, and I down it in three gulps. Ah, the beverage of champions. My eyes close as I feel the familiar burn that could only belong to a drink capable of dissolving nails.

I pull another can out of the fridge. "That was disgusting. Are you crazy?"

"Is that a rhetorical question?" James's hand goes up. "Because if it's not, I'd like to answer."

Maxine chuckles mischievously. "Woke you up, didn't it?"

I throw a bagel in the toaster, wondering where Millie is. She's usually the first one up and around in the kitchen. "Actually, Maxine, it didn't wake me up. And you want to know why? Because I never *went* to sleep!"

"My, my, aren't we grouchy this morning. When does your charm kick in? Ten a.m.? Noon-ish?" Maxine tweaks my nose.

James unrolls the paper and hunts for the sports section. "Didn't you sleep well, Katie?"

"You mean you didn't hear it?" I ask.

"Hear what?" Maxine's eyes narrow.

I open my mouth and make the loudest, most obnoxious noises I can. I try to duplicate Maxine's snoring, but end up sounding like a choking pig instead.

"I do *not* snore!" Maxine gasps, clutching her chest dramatically.

"Whatever!" James and I yell simultaneously.

I point my finger at Maxine. "You kept me up the entire night."

"I am a refined woman, and I do *not* snore. Take that back!"

"Take that back?" I laugh. "I'll take that back when you *give* me back my eight hours of sleep!"

"Well, I never—" Maxine fans her flushed face with a napkin.

"You may think you never," James interrupts. "But you would be wrong." He looks at me with understanding, like we're united in our pain. "Maxine's gone on some trips with us, and we always make sure our room doesn't adjoin hers. It sounds like that storm last night—only multiplied times one hundred."

Maxine hands me my bagel. "I don't find this topic funny. Occasionally I do have some sinus issues. Perhaps we could talk about something else this morning."

Setting my plate next to James, I poke him in the ribs. "It was like sleeping in a sawmill."

"If she could snore her way into heaven . . ." James shakes his head.

"I don't find this appropriate breakfast time conversation. If I did snore, and I'm *not* saying I do, it is not that loud. Barely a rumble."

"Like the rumble of a Harley-Davidson convention?" I smirk.

"Good morning." Millie shuts the back door, entering the kitchen. She lets the dog off the leash, and Rocky, spying Maxine, runs into the living room.

All teasing stops.

I suddenly feel awkward. Do we talk about Millie's situation? Do we pretend like we're not all thinking about it? What exactly is the breakfast etiquette for potential cancer conversation?

"Where've you been, Mil?" James gets up and takes his wife's jacket.

"Rocky and I went for a walk. I wanted to see some of the damage in the daylight. We better get on over to the church, James. We need to rally our resources and see what people need."

"I need a new roommate," I grumble. "Maxine tried to poison me with prunes this morning."

"Poison you? I did no such thing. The things this girl says."

"I could have died." I look to Millie for support. "From an overdose of . . . fiber."

Maxine's glossy pink lips slip into an innocent smile. "Nonsense. And we're gonna be great roomies. You and me, Katie. We are peas and carrots. Tom and Jerry. Pickles and ice cream."

I tear into the last bite of bagel. "Tom tried to *eat* Jerry."

Maxine clears her throat loudly. "So, Millie. When's that mammogram?"

My eyes bug out of my head. James loses his grip on the paper.

"Well . . . I . . . uh . . . I guess . . ." Millie falters on her way to the fridge. "I haven't made the appointment yet. It's only seven. The doctor's office won't be open for another thirty minutes."

Millie gives her mother a warning look then plants a smile on for me. "Did you know school is closed today? Part of the roof was damaged, and it leaked pretty badly overnight."

"Yes!" I pump my fist in the air. "How bad are we talking here? Like bad as in you need waders to get to class and we'll be out for the next month? Or bad as in enjoy the day off and see you tomorrow?"

Millie smiles. "It doesn't look very serious. I'm sure we'll find out today." She leans down and kisses her mother's cheek. "Did you sleep well?"

"Yes, she did." I answer. "Now when is she moving to the spare bedroom?"

Silence. "James, you didn't tell her?" Millie's eyes soften with sympathy.

My foster dad is suddenly very interested in the classifieds.

"Looking for a job there, James?" I pull the employment section out of his hands and prepare for the bad news.

"Um . . . yes, I was gonna tell you . . . eventually. See . . . we found some leaks in a few rooms. Yup, we've got leaks in the downstairs bathroom, the laundry room, the garage, and . . ."

I sigh. "And the guest bedroom."

Millie pats my hand. "The carpet is pretty wet in there. We're going to have to get the roof replaced and the flooring cleaned and—"

"And Maxine and I are bunkmates." My eyes cut to Maxine, and she waggles her manicured eyebrows at me.

"Katie, it'll be great. You'll see. You'll never even know I'm here."

I accept the inevitable. But not without some ground rules. "You're not gonna play your Sinatra music on my computer."

Maxine bobs her head in agreement. "Frank and I could use some time apart."

"And you're not washing your Spanx out in my sink."

"Well, now, really. I have no need of such things, dear," Maxine says for everyone's benefit. Then in my ear, "You won't see a single scrap of spandex."

"And I'm not getting up and getting you a drink of water every time you ask. Last night was a one-time deal." The woman can really push it.

Maxine catches her daughter's disapproving stare and blushes. "Well, my mouth did get a little parched last night. A few times."

"And you are *not* wearing my shoes."

My foster parents both bend under the table where I know they will see my most recent pair of vintage heels on the feet of one Maxine Simmons.

Millie rises. "Mom, you don't even wear the same shoe size as Katie."

"Roomies are supposed to share things! That's the fun of it." Maxine throws an arm around me. "You share your shoes, maybe a blouse or two, and I'll share my . . . um . . . well, you can wear my . . ."

"Control-top pantyhose?" I throw her arm off and take my plate to the sink. "Fine. Whatever. I'm sure your apartment will be fixed soon anyway."

I look to my foster parents for confirmation. Millie intensely studies her manicure. James's eyes are transfixed on the ceiling. Great.

"Well, then I'm sure your room here will be ready in no time."

Maxine explodes in rusty laughter as she stands beside me. She gives me a smacking kiss on my cheek. "Right. It'll be ready in no time." More laughing. "Don't worry. You won't even know I'm here. This will be fun."

This will be fun. Famous last words. Probably what the Wicked Witch of the West said to all her little monkeys.

Things could not get any worse.

Chapter 4

THINGS JUST GOT worse.

"Let's go camping," James says as soon as I pick up the phone.

My mind races. My foster parents left hours ago when Millie went to get her tests run at the doctor's office. Do they have bad news? Does he feel like this news could best be delivered over burnt hot dogs and bug zappers? Is he wanting a family getaway so we can be together one last time?

"James . . . where are you? What did you find out?"

"We're still at the clinic. I'm in the waiting room. But I did find out your school is closed for repairs. A week's vacation for you Chihuahuas."

No school! Finally something is going in my favor. And yes, our mascot is the mighty Chihuahua. Other schools tremble in fear of us.

"And while I was sitting here flipping through some magazines that have given me way too much information on women's health, I came up with this brilliant idea. We could leave tomorrow morning and camp through Saturday. What do you say?"

I say I'd rather go to school.

I've never been camping. Never wanted to go camping. I'm not a chichi-froufrou type of girl. I don't mind a little dirt or my hair getting messed up, but hanging out in the middle of nowhere without the comforts of home is not my idea of a good time. I like TV. I like being steps away from the refrigerator. I like my wi-fi as strong as my mochas.

"James, it's too early in the year for camping. It's kinda chilly."

"It's never too early to hang out by the water. We'll just bring some jackets for the evenings. Aren't you excited?"

Excited doesn't begin to describe what I'm feeling.

"Did you find out anything about Millie yet?" I take a deep breath. "Do you guys have something to tell me?"

I hear him turn a magazine page. "Wow. Did you know the most popular day for a baby to be born is Tuesday?"

"Focus, James. What did the doctor tell Millie?"

"We don't know anything yet. We'll hear something in a couple of days." James greets someone in the waiting room then continues. "So in the meantime, it's out to the lake for us." His excitement comes through the staticky phone line.

After a few more minutes of listening to James extol the virtues of roughing it, we hang up, and I lay the news on Maxine.

I find her lounging on the couch in the living room watching a talk show.

"Guess what?"

She sips on some iced tea. "You've realized I'm your very best friend?"

"No. Guess again."

"Kelly Ripa is really three hundred pounds in real life, but through the magic of television she only appears that painfully skinny?"

I study the TV. "Pretty unlikely. The big news is we're going camping."

Mad chortling erupts from my foster grandmother. "Correction. *You* are going camping. I am permanently banned from any more family camping trips. During the last outing I *accidentally* fed some raccoons and skunks, so I'm sure I won't be allowed to tag along this time."

Maxine fumbles with the tassels on a throw pillow and returns her attention back to the screen.

"Please go with us."

"I don't think so." She lifts the remote and turns up the volume.

I throw my body next to hers, forcing her to scooch over. My face is close to hers, eye to eye, nose to nose. "This is about Sam isn't it? You won't go with us because you don't want to leave your boyfriend. Your *secret* boyfriend."

She blushes scarlet. "Now, Katie." She clears her throat. "Don't concern yourself in these matters."

"I know you see him every day on the sly. I think you can go without your little rendezvous for a few days. Besides, you owe me."

"Owe you?"

"I'm sharing my room with you."

Maxine rolls her blue eyes and shrugs. "Big deal. You didn't have a choice."

"And . . . I have yet to tell Millie her mother has a boyfriend. A boyfriend you're too chicken to tell people about. I sure hate keeping things from her . . ."

"When do we leave?"

The doorbell chimes, and I race to the front door.

Frances stands on the front porch, balancing a stack of textbooks and magazines. Her glossy black hair hangs loosely in her face, and small tortoiseshell glasses sit crooked on her nose. And yet she still looks stunning and edgy chic—as always. Why she is friends with me, I'll never know. The two of us couldn't be more different.

"I thought we could use the time off from school to brainstorm for our science fair projects." Frances holds a science journal in my face as she walks past me into the living room.

See what I mean? Frances is a genius. She just never turns it off. She makes high school look so easy, juggling fifty million clubs and activities with her four-point-oh. I get a day off from school and what do I want to do? Watch MTV and paint my toenails. Frances's idea of a great day? Reading articles on plant photosynthesis.

Frances's home wasn't touched during the storm, which is kind of sad in a way. Everyone should get to experience sleeping next to a crazy grandma who snores like a man three times her size.

Frances spies Maxine all stretched out and gives her a dutifully polite hello.

"Why, Frances Vega, if you aren't a sight for sore eyes. It's lovely as always to see you, sweet child."

Maxine tends to park herself in the pew that Frances feels is reserved for the teens in church. Every Sunday it's a race to get to pew number forty-seven. Maxine often wins, which infuriates Frances. It's everything Frances can do to be civil to my foster grandmother, which makes Maxine just gush with fake friendliness.

"Let's go up to my room." I pull my friend away from her nemesis and toward the stairs.

"Our room," Maxine calls out after us. "Feel free to make my bed while you're up there!"

"So Maxine really is staying in your room?"

"Um, yeah. Did you think I would joke about something like that?"

We enter my bedroom, the best place in the whole house. I love my room. I guess that's why I was so resistant to share it with Maxine at first. It's this funky pink color, decorated with retro pictures and stark white furniture. It's like living in a Pottery Barn Teen catalog. When I lived with my mom, we moved a lot, so I never really got into decorating too much. Plus we were usually in one-bedroom apartments or tiny trailers. My bedroom frequently was wherever the couch was.

"Can you believe it? No school 'til next week." Frances plops down on my bed, fanning her books in front of her.

"You'll probably have withdrawal. Hey, speaking of zany, wild fun. Want to go camping with us?"

"Who's us?"

"Me, James, Millie . . ." I turn my back and watch a bird out the window. My voice barely a whisper, I add, "And Maxine."

"No, way."

"Come on, Frances! It will be fun. You, me . . ." I pause, trying to think of why camping might be a good time for someone. "The lake. Burgers . . ." Flies, mosquitoes, snakes. "Nature. Getting some sun . . ." Suffocating in a sleeping bag, sunscreen in your eyes, a five-mile hike to the loo.

"It does sound fun." Frances grins, warming up to the idea. "And I had considered researching the Brazilian free-tailed bat for the science fair, so it might be a great opportunity to study their habits over the week and see if it's a project worthy of pursuing."

"Right." I nod. "And I'll study the effects of consuming mass amounts of S'mores."

"So . . . any word on Millie yet?"

I leave my spot at the window and flop onto Maxine's bed. "No. James called earlier, and Millie was still with the doctor. He said it will be a few days before we know anything."

"I'm sure everything will be okay."

"Yeah."

"My whole family is praying for her."

It does make me feel better to think people are praying for Millie. I even had a small conversation with God last night myself. When I wasn't begging him to muffle Maxine's snoring, I asked him to please let Millie be all right. My prayer was pretty short though. I couldn't concentrate with all the noise.

"Are you scared?" Frances shoves aside her science books and focuses on me.

"Nah." I grab a *People* and flip through the first few pages. "I mean . . . I don't know . . . maybe."

"Breast cancer is very treatable, you know. If you'd like, I could gather some research for you. Maybe create a visual presentation with the information."

I laugh. "No, but thanks." I twist my hair around my finger. "It's just . . . what if something does happen to Millie? Where will I go?"

"Why would you go anywhere? You'd stay here."

"I doubt it. I think Iola Smartly would come and get me."

Mrs. Smartly is my caseworker and director of Sunny Haven Home for Girls. I still talk to her all the time. In fact, she makes me write her letters detailing my life with James and Millie. Letters. Not e-mails. She's so outdated.

"Well, then you'd live with me." Frances seems proud of her idea.

But I don't want to live with Frances. I think she's the best friend ever, and it would be great to raid her closet daily, but I'm just now settling into life with James and Millie. I haven't gotten in any major trouble in the last five months. They totally make me walk the line. Without James and Millie, I could go back to my wild ways and end up in jail. Like my mom. And I'd lose my identity. Instead of being called Katie, I'd be something like Inmate 2046.

And . . . I kind of like these people. A lot. They've become like family to me.

Even Maxine.

Frances throws a confetti pink pillow my way. "It's gonna be fine. Really."

It better be. I can't go back to Sunny Haven. Sleeping next to Maxine is nothing compared to bunking next to Trina, who liked to show me her secret knife collection on an all-too-regular basis.

I hang my head. "I don't know, Frances. I feel so lost. So sad." I sniff. "It's like I need some hope, you know? I just wish . . ." I shake my head.

"Yes?" Frances's voice is all concern. "You just wish?"

My head shoots up, and I shoot the pillow across the room at Frances. "I wish my friend would go camping with me!"

And then we're both laughing. And I forget about Millie.

And cancer.

And bears that might eat me in my tent.

Chapter 5

"WE ARE THE world! We are the children!"

Beside me Frances groans in agony. Maxine has been singing eighties hits since we backed out of the driveway. Two hours ago. And there's a reason she's never been asked to join the church choir.

I stretch my left leg out a little, trying to restore some feeling. I'm sitting in the middle of the backseat, Frances on one side, Maxine the diva, on the other. My foster grandmother is taking up more than her fair share of legroom.

"I. H-a-a-a-d. The time of my l-i-i-i-fe—!"

"Maxine, please stop." I rub my throbbing head. "You're upsetting Rocky."

"Nonsense." Maxine scratches the dog under the chin and finishes the rest of her inspirational melody. Rocky knows a lot of tricks, and unfortunately, singing is one of them. When anyone belts out a tune, Rocky will howl along. The first time I heard it, I was convinced it was the Scott's way of driving me out of the house and back to where I came from. And let me tell you, listening to Rocky *and* Maxine wailing some classic Madonna makes for a very long ride.

Millie turns around in her seat. "Mom, knock it off. You're being obnoxious on purpose."

"Yeah, Maxine, you have the next three days to push us over the edge. Pace yourself." James catches my eye in the rearview mirror and winks.

"But I was just getting ready to do my melodic tribute to the nineties." Maxine sighs.

"Save it for the return trip."

"Don't encourage her, James," Millie murmurs.

James turns his black Honda sedan off the highway, and a few minutes later he's stopped at a gatehouse and paying for our campsite.

"We're here!" We weave through the campground, pulling a small trailer between rows and rows of campers, RVs, and tents.

I reach across Frances and lower the window, inhaling the smell of pine trees and barbeque grills. And the occasional odor of dead fish.

"Site number eighty-six. This is us." Millie points to the spot, and James whips the car in.

James begins to set up the tents, as the rest of us unload the car.

I lift a small cooler and place it beneath the covered picnic table. With my hand shielding my eyes from the sun, I scan the perimeter. Trees to the left. Trees to the right. The lake a mere fifty feet in front of us.

Millie comes to stand next to me, her arm wrapping around my shoulders. "It's beautiful, isn't it?"

"Um, yeah." I continue my perusal of the area, hoping my eyes will lock on one particular object of beauty.

"The tall pine trees. The lofty cedars. The lapping of the lake. The hum of a distant boat. The—"

"Flush of a toilet?"

Millie's brows furrow. "What?"

"Where is the bathroom?" These people are out of their minds if they expect me to squat behind a tree.

"Katie, haven't you ever been camping?"

"No."

"Never?" My foster mom laughs and pats me on the back. "You

are going to have such a great time on this trip. You won't even care that the bathrooms are on the other side of the campground or that there's no electricity or hot water."

And then I'm laughing too. "No electricity. That's a good one."

"No, I'm serious."

My face drops. "But how will I watch TV?"

Frances moves in beside us, her binoculars hanging from her neck. "You brought a TV? What for?"

What for? Is everyone a little lightheaded from all the clean air?

"We'll be so busy boating, tubing, eating, and swimming you won't have time to miss your TV," Millie says.

I swat a bug crawling up my arm. "Should I have gotten some shots or anything before I came?"

Frances and Millie leave me standing there, swapping camping stories as they go.

God, if you're up there, I pray I would get a better attitude. We both know this is going to be a long three days, but I have to put on a brave face for Millie's sake. I pray you would keep us safe and bear-free. And Lord . . . when Frances finds her Brazilian bats, I hope I'm nowhere around.

"Hey, Katie! Come help me here." James holds a few poles and motions me over with a jerk of his chin.

With one last slap at something crawling on my arm, I walk over to offer my assistance, enjoying the sound of the rocks crunching beneath my feet. I hand my foster dad some stakes at his command, and watch Frances and Millie setting up lawn chairs. My eyes scan the horizon for Maxine. Where is she?

The three tents go up almost effortlessly (no doubt thanks to all my help holding poles and stakes), and Frances and I pick one and move our stuff inside. I roll out my three sleeping bags—one to sleep in and two for extra cush. I would've brought my bed if they'd let me.

"Want to go for a walk?" I ask Frances, who is jotting down some notes in her science journal.

"Yeah, that'd be great. I can scope out the area for the various wildlife."

"Like cute boys?"

Her pencil stills. "No, like fish species and bird varieties."

I open the flap open, and we step out of the tent.

"Millie, we're going on a walk of the campground. Do you want to go?"

"You girls go ahead. I'm going to get lunch ready."

Frances and I each grab a drink and wander down the road. We pass a cluster of motor homes that make me stop and gawk in appreciation. Satellites, TVs, and air conditioners. These people are probably not going without comfy beds and indoor plumbing.

Frances points to one of the RVs. "It looks like a hotel room on wheels. Ohhh, look at those awesome mountain bikes—"

Coming to a dead stop, Frances is frozen in place, her mouth wide open, her eyes big.

"What is it?"

"*Shhhhh!*" She waves her hands wildly in front of her face. "Don't you recognize that car?" She points to an old Mustang.

"No, not really, I—"

"*Shhhhh!*" Frances tugs on my arm. "Come on. Keep walking."

"Are you gonna tell me whose—"

The front door of the RV flies open and out walks the source of Frances's mental meltdown.

"Well, hello, ladies."

Nash Griffin, a fellow sophomore at In Between High, saunters our way. I take in his vintage Rolling Stones t-shirt, all holey and wrinkled, his long, baggy shorts, the scruffy hair hanging near his chin. He always looks like he just rolled out of bed.

"Ohhh, he's the cutest," Frances whispers out of the side of her mouth.

The cutest what? Cutest dude with bed head? Cutest guy whose clothes have never been touched by an iron? Or maybe most attractive boy in need of a deep conditioner?

"Hey, Nash. What's up?" I give scruffy boy a big smile, my eyes darting to Frances, who has yet to unfreeze.

Nash holds out a fist, and I make one of my own and lightly bump his. He then greets Frances in the same manner.

Frances just stares.

"You gonna leave me hanging?" He tries again.

She blinks.

"OK, how 'bout one of these?" His hand goes up for a high five.

Frances's eyes are glazed over, like she's just seen something shocking. Such as Maxine streaking through the forest.

Our classmate clears his throat. "So what brings you ladies out to the lake? Gonna do some fishing? Some boating? Maybe work on your tans?"

Hysterical laughter bubbles from Frances. "Oh, that's a good one. You're so funny, Nash." More wild giggles.

Oh, no. I have to get her out of here. She must've gotten too much sun already. Maybe she's dehydrated. Or distraught over not making any bat discoveries.

Nash shakes his head then directs the rest of the conversation to me. The one who currently does not sound like a hyena.

"You ladies camping?"

"Yeah, we're here with my foster parents. Gonna stay through Saturday."

"Camping . . ." Frances begins a sentence then spaces out. The giggles start yet again.

I roll my eyes and force a smile. "I think she's inhaled some bad fish or something. We better walk on. See you around?"

His eyes linger on my friend, the one I am currently dragging along beside me. "You know it. I'm here 'til Sunday afternoon, so I'll see you later."

My free hand flaps out in a parting wave. "Later."

We round a corner, and I steer Frances toward a swing set area.

"OK, just take some deep breaths now, Frances." You space cadet.

I push her into a swing and plunk down in one myself.

"What was that all about?"

My friend hangs her head and moans. "Oh, my gosh. I'm gonna die. Seriously, I'm gonna die." She puts her head in her hands. "Please tell me it wasn't as bad as I think it was. Tell me I didn't just make a total idiot of myself."

This gravel sure is interesting. So many different shades of brown here. There's light brown. A few pieces are almost white. Dark brown. Medium beige. Or would these rocks be considered tan?

"Katie!" Frances jerks on my swing chain.

"What?" I laugh. "What do you want me to say? Frances, it was like you were having an out-of-body experience. I'm afraid it was just as ugly as you think it was."

"It was ugly?" she squeaks. "How ugly?"

"Like sumo wrestler ugly."

"Oh, no."

"Like uni-brow ugly."

"You can stop now."

"Mole hair ugly."

"Enough!" Frances's voice echoes through the camp. "Can we go home now? Would James take us back?" Her face is pitiful.

"No. Look, I'm sure Nash didn't think you were being weird." If he hails from a planet in which drooling excessively while repeating the word *camping* over and over are considered normal.

With a big stomp of her feet, Frances puts herself in motion, like she's trying to swing away the last ten minutes. Or maybe she's hoping she'll take to the air and magically fly far, far away.

"Look, I know Nash isn't exactly eye candy, but he's a really nice guy. You could've tried to make some polite conversation with him."

"That's not it."

"I know he's all into the skateboard thing, and there's his whole alternative band he's got going on. But it's not like you to totally clam up and shut down on someone just because you don't hang out in the same social circles."

"That's not it either."

Understanding dawns. "Oh, it's his hair, isn't it? You were so engrossed in the dead ends you couldn't focus on conversation?"

Frances drags her feet in the rocks, her swing slowing to a stop. She inhales loudly. "I have had a crush on Nash Griffin since the first grade." She looks for my reaction.

"And *that's* how you show a guy you like him?" I gesture toward the distant RVs.

Frances wrings her hands. "I'm no good at that stuff."

"What stuff? The acting like a normal human being stuff?"

"Boys," she sighs. "The male species. Gentlemen. Dudes. Hotties."

"Okay, for starters, nobody says hotties anymore."

"See!" Her dark eyebrows disappear in her bangs. "That's what I mean. I'm clueless. Is there a book for this sort of thing? Like a manual?"

Oh, if only. In fact, I wish there was a manual for every aspect of teen life. Guys, zits, school, waxing. Parallel parking.

"I . . . I seriously can't believe you're into . . . Nash."

"I know! He's nothing like me. He's totally not my type. My parents would freak if I brought him home to meet them."

Frances's parents, her dad an overly protective Mexican, and her mother, an ultraconservative woman of a proud Chinese culture, would bar the doors and windows, not letting Frances out 'til she's forty, if they knew she had the hots for Nash. "Well . . . this thing with Nash . . . you'll get over it."

Frances's face crumbles. "I don't want to get over it. Help me, Katie." She grabs my swing and gives it a shake. "Make me cool—somebody the boys will find irresistible. The magnet that attracts all the guys with an invisible force they are powerless to resist."

I turn away, desperate to get my composure and not laugh. *Think of serious things, Katie.* Hunger in Africa. War in the Middle East. Days without my flatiron.

Swiveling back around, my face is stern and composed. "Look, I don't know a whole lot about the men-folk myself. I've only had a couple of boyfriends, and I don't think most of those even count." Like Jesse Cantrell, a boy I briefly dated in the sixth grade just because he would share his Twinkies with me at lunch. "But you are the smartest girl I know. And I think between the two of us, we can have you struttin' it like a Victoria's Secret model."

"Oh, I would never be allowed to wear—"

"With the flair of the girls in the Abercrombie ads."

"My mom says those ladies don't wear enough—"

"With confidence, Frances," I nearly shout. "With confidence. Look at everything else you tackle. You succeed at everything you do, and never have I seen you act unsure of yourself." Until today.

"You're right. I can do this." She smiles for the first time since the incident.

"Sure you can. Now you put that giant brain of yours to work. Start brainstorming some things we can do for damage control, and I'm gonna go right over there and use the bathroom." I point over my shoulder.

"In the shrubs?"

I point further to the left. "The bathrooms."

I lift myself out of the swing, briefly wondering at the way my rear doesn't fit in those things like they did when I was five. As soon as I round the shrubbery and near the concrete bathrooms, the smell hits me.

Lake bathrooms. An aroma like no other.

Pulling my shirt over my nose, I take a giant breath, swing the door open, and enter into the ladies bathroom. Finding the first stall empty, I make a toilet paper wreath around the seat. Okay, here goes nothing.

"And I told you we would tell the family when I was ready."

My ears perk at that voice.

"Well, then I guess I'm not ready . . . What? . . . Well, of course there isn't anyone else. How can you even ask? Have you been inhaling paint fumes again?"

I've just found Maxine. On her cell phone with Sam. On the toilet.

"Awww, I miss you too, sweet muffins." She makes kissie noises into her phone. "No, I miss you more. No, I do. No, I miss you the most."

The breath I'm holding bursts out of my cheeks, as I fail miserably at containing a laugh.

"Who's there? . . . Sam, gotta go." Her voice lowers. "Don't even think of following me out here."

Maxine's stall door is thrown open, banging against the wall, and her head appears below my door.

"Hey! How rude!" Just when I thought lake bathrooms couldn't get any worse.

Her yellow head disappears. "You got five seconds to tinkle, wipe, and flush, little missy, then I want you out here where I can see you."

Five seconds pass.

"Are you gonna go?" she barks.

"Well, now I can't."

"Why not?"

"I can't pee under this kind of pressure." I flush and exit the stall.

"How much did you hear?"

Turning the sink on, I put my hands under the cool stream. "Who cares? Your relationship with Sam is so yesterday." Though I'm proud to say I am instrumental in bringing Sam and Maxine together. "I have a new focus."

She hands me a rough, brown paper towel. "And what might that be?" Her eyes glisten with interest.

"Operation: Get Frances A Boyfriend." I nod at her raised eyebrow. "Are you in?"

She taps a hot pink nail to her lips. "Oh, yes. I'm in."

Chapter 6

AHH . . . THIS IS the life. Frances and I are each sprawled on lounge chairs next to the lake. I'm sunny side up, with one arm over my face, the other holding a paperback. I pull my light jacket closer and shut my eyes. Out here next to the water, with the sun warming my skin, there're no problems. No mom in prison. No foster parent waiting to hear if she has cancer. It's just me and the lake. Birds call overhead. Fish jump in the distance. Boats roar far away. I could get used to this camping stuff.

"Make way for the queen!"

Frances and I sit up, gasping as Maxine throws her lime-green inner tube into the water. She locks her hands into dive position, squats, then launches her body toward her float.

Landing flat on her stomach.

A spray of water covers both Frances and me.

I wipe my face, smearing my sunscreen, and shiver. "Are you crazy? Maxine, that water has to be freezing!"

Maxine adjusts her bathing suit straps and treads toward her tube. "For babies maybe. This builds character. Strength. Separates the wimps from the—"

"Insane lunatics?" I wipe my book off with my jacket.

She flips the raft under her, so she's sitting in the center hole, her legs in the water for all but her freshly painted toes, sticking straight up. "That's a fetching hat you have on there, Frances."

Frances touches her wide brimmed hat. She looks at Maxine, then over to me. At my shrug, Frances regards Maxine again. "Um . . . thank you. I think."

"Yes, when I first met my husband, Mr. Simmons, God rest his soul, I was sporting a beautiful wide-brimmed hat as well. It makes us women look mysterious. Of course I was also in a totally sexy bathing suit. I was dancing at the Circus Circus casino in Vegas, and in between the matinee and evening shows, I had decided to visit the pool." Maxine kicks her legs out. I notice they're covered in goose bumps. "One look at these gams, and it was all over. Yup, sometimes you just have to be willing to show a little leg, you know?"

Frances nods her head slowly. "Sure. Okay." Her eyes close and her head returns to her chair.

"I'm full of tips." Maxine crosses her arms as a breeze ripples the water. "Yes, indeed, I'm a wealth of information on many topics. Dancing . . . fashion . . . dating."

"Dentures."

Maxine gives me the stink eye. "As I was saying, the social graces have always come to me so naturally. But you know, the Lord does not bless everyone with such skills." She clutches her chest. "My heart breaks for you young people today. So many girls these days rely on their outer beauty instead of their inner poise."

Frances sits up so fast her chair buckles, her legs shooting to either side. "Katie Parker! You told her!"

I open my mouth to defend myself, but Maxine beats me to it. "My dear, your secret is safe with me. Katie simply took your little situation to heart and knew to go to the ultimate authority for help. *Moi.*"

"If you tell anyone, Maxine, I will make sure the story of you and Sam is front page news. I'll post it on Facebook, Instagram, Twitter. . . the billboard downtown!" Frances sputters.

"*Tsk, tsk, tsk.* There's no need for the theatrics. I'm here to help."

My friend's eyes narrow. "And in return?"

Maxine waves a careless hand. "Oh. Nothing in return. Well, I guess I would like you and your teenybopper friends to stay out of my church pew, but I don't think that will be a problem, *hmmm*?"

Steam is practically coming out of Frances's ears.

Maxine rubs her hands together. "I do so enjoy a good challenge. This will be fun. The three of us working together . . . to make you datable."

See, I should be feeling badly. Maybe I shouldn't have told Maxine about Frances and Nash, but I know Maxine. She's all talk. All bluff. She's like one of those cats that chase mice to play with, not to swallow whole. While Maxine will enjoy teasing Frances, she would never actually tell anyone about her long-standing crush on Nash Griffin. And we do need some help.

"I don't need your assistance." Frances lifts her chin regally. "But thank you."

"Well, if you change your mind, you know where to . . . oh!"

"What?" I ask, watching Maxine jump.

"The fish. They're biting my tushie." She jumps again.

Frances giggles with satisfaction, but I just roll my eyes. "Well, get out of the water."

Maxine settles back into her float. "I didn't say I minded it."

The roar of a boat motor drowns out any further comments.

James stands at the wheel of a white and aqua striped boat, his hat perched backwards on his head. He cuts the motor and calls out to us. "Ready to hit the waves, ladies?"

"Where'd you get that thing?" I yell back.

"Found it at the dock. Surely no one will miss it." He laughs at his little joke. "It's a renter, so come on. Time's a-wasting. Go get Millie, and let's take a ride."

Fifteen minutes later Millie, Maxine, Frances, Rocky, and I are all suited up in our life jackets, ready to take to the open water.

I tighten the clasp on my vest. "Are you sure you know how to drive this thing?"

James shrugs. "Don't you think preachers and speed boats mix?"

Well, now that you mention it, no.

"This summer we'll come back out and ski. Who's gonna be ready for that? How about you, Maxine?" James puts the boat into motion and pretty soon it feels like we're flying.

"Nope. I am officially retired from skiing. After last summer's debacle at the senior citizen's lake day, I'm through with water sports." She leans in close to my ear, her voice raised over the noise. "Let's just say my top blew off, and I accidentally showed everyone how the Lord has greatly blessed me."

We spend the rest of the afternoon in the boat. We eat the lunch Millie packed and take in the scenery. Maxine, Frances, and I see who can get the most waves from fishermen.

"How many did you get?" Frances asks, her black hair blowing in her face. "I got ten."

I hold up eight fingers.

"Ha! Amateurs. I got fifteen."

I push my hair back. "Well, I guess if we had blown kisses to every boat we'd passed, we'd have gotten fifteen too."

The sun begins to drop in the sky, and James steers us back to the marina. I rest my head on the seat and watch Millie behind the black of my sunglasses. Her curly blonde hair is damp, and she sits next to Captain James. Every once in a while she looks over at each of us and gives a big smile, as if to say, "I'm so glad you're here with me today." That's Millie. She could possibly have a major disease, and she still looks all peaceful and happy. Meanwhile, I'm completely in knots. I want to get home so we can get her test results. How can she stand to be out here? Isn't she desperate to know? How do you just leave home for days at a time when you're waiting to find out if you have cancer?

If Millie has cancer, I wonder if she'll call her daughter. James and Millie have a twenty-five-year-old daughter who is MIA. She's a long story, one I know little about, but apparently their only child Amy is a little cuckoo. At least that's my primary theory. Millie sends her money and stuff, but Amy just continues to ignore her parents. Kind of weird. Amy's an actress, so my other theory involves Tom Cruise, but I'm still working out the details of that one.

After docking the boat, we walk back to the campsite. I'm exhausted, but in a good way. My skin tingles with a little too much wind and sun (despite the fact Millie was coming at me every hour with the sunscreen), and my limbs feel heavy from all the motion. Maybe sleeping on the hard ground won't be so difficult after all.

"Why don't you girls hit the showers up the hill while James and I get the steaks on for dinner."

"I'll go with them," Maxine says in a rush, pushing through us to get to her tent.

Frances and I grab our shower gear and begin our walk.

Maxine catches up to us, her sandals flip-flopping all the way. "Nothing like an invigorating shower to revive us, eh, girls?"

I look over my shoulder. "You just wanted to get out of potato peeling duty."

Maxine pops her bubble gum. "Yeah, that too."

We make it to the bottom of the hill and are ready to start our upward trek, when a familiar voice shouts a hello.

"Hey, girls!" The object of Frances's crush, with a towel wrapped around his neck, strolls our way.

"Hi, Nash." I'm the only one who offers a greeting. Maxine stops to openly stare at him, while Frances makes like a statue, frozen and totally blank.

"If you're headed for the showers, I'm afraid I have some bad news for you." He runs a hand through his wet, sandy-blond hair.

I can almost feel Frances melting.

"The hot water was pretty much nonexistent when I was in there, so be prepared."

"I like water." This from Frances.

Maxine does a double take at my befuddled friend. Then shoots her blue eyes at me.

I shrug as if to say, *I know. I think she's possessed by aliens too.*

Nash only laughs. "Yeah, water is pretty . . . um, cool. Kind of necessary for a shower, I guess." Silence follows his comment—because really, how do you continue this line of conversation? So Nash politely tells us good-bye, and on down the hill he goes.

Frances pivots to watch his every step away from her.

"I did it again," she says.

"Girl, did you hit your head or something before we came?" Maxine shifts her bag on her shoulder and continues walking. "Because that was just pitiful to watch."

Frances falls in behind us, her feet stomping on the pavement. "I know, all right? I don't think you need to point out the obvious. I get tongue-tied when he's around. My brain just malfunctions."

"Don't worry, Frances. We'll help you. We'll have Nash Griffin writing you love sonnets yet." I offer an encouraging smile.

"I don't know that I want love sonnets."

"Okay, sharing his lunchtime tater tots." Now that's something a girl can appreciate.

LATER IN THE evening, after the steaks have been devoured and the dishes cleared away, Frances and I zip ourselves into our tent for the night. Dread settles in my stomach as I look at my sleeping bag. If I put myself in that, it's like I'm a human hotdog, all nicely wrapped up for some grizzly bear's convenience.

I toss and turn for what seems like hours. Despite the padding beneath me, rocks nudge me in the most inconvenient places. On the other side of the tent, Frances sleeps soundly, her mouth slightly open.

Forget it. I can't sleep.

Grabbing my flip-flops and a flashlight, I unzip the tent flap and ease myself out. The campfire is still going strong, and even though it's after one a.m., Maxine, Millie, and James lounge in chairs, still sipping coffee.

"Did we wake you?" Millie wraps her jacket tighter around her.

I slump into a chair. "No. I can't sleep."

"Look, Katie, Bigfoot's only been spotted a few times around here, so there's really nothing to be afraid of. Well, not too much." Maxine hides her wicked grin behind her coffee mug.

"So what were you guys talking about?"

Millie smiles wistfully. "We were just remembering some old camping trips. Amy used to love to come out here."

I nod my head, pretending to be interested. Great. Kooky daughter can handle the outdoor life, but I can't.

"Millie, do you remember the time your father took us to Yellowstone National—"

Maxine's story stops short as a bird calls loudly into the night. *Hooooo! Hoooo-eeee-ewwww!*

She clears her throat and continues. "... The time your father took us to Yellowstone, and I forgot everyone's clothes but mine, and—"

Again the loud warble of a bird. *Hooooo! Hoooo-eeee-ewwww!*

James looks behind him. "That is some birdcall. He must be really close." He turns his attention back to the storyteller. "You were saying ..."

Maxine's beady eyes search the dark campground. "... Um ... I was saying I had forgotten all of ... *hootie, hootie, hoo-hoo*! ... our clothes, and your father was so ..." Her eyes widen in a panic.

"Mother, did you just answer that bird?"

Maxine gasps. "Um ... no, no, I ... um ... Boy, Millie, you gotta cut me off from that *Animal Planet*, eh? No more Discovery Channel for me! Next thing you know I'll be charming snakes." She laughs nervously and gets to her feet. "I think I need to take a walk to the ladies room." Maxine holds up her mug. "I drank way too much coffee. Hard on the bladder."

"Hold it right there." Millie ejects from her seat and blocks Maxine's path. "Do it again."

Maxine swallows. "Do what again, sweetie pie, sugar bunch?"

Millie lifts her chin. "Call that bird."

"Millie, it was an accident. It's like a bird took over my body or something. You know nature does weird things to—"

"Call the bird, Mom."

Maxine nods, cups her mouth and whispers. *"Ca-caw! Tweet-tweet! Chirp-chirp!"*

She makes a show of listening for the bird then shrugs a shoulder. "Well, I guess he's gone, so I'll just be—"

"Hootie, hootie, hoo-hoo!" James's voice echoes in the camp.

Hooooo! Hoooo-eeee-ewwww! comes the reply.

"Do it again, James." Millie shoots her mother an exasperated look, then takes off in the direction of the bird.

"Hootie, hootie, hoo-hoo!"

Hooooo! Hoooo-eeee-ewwww

Millie tears into some shrubbery, James and Maxine both at her heels. I am content to sit back in my chair, awaiting the fun that is sure to unfold.

"Who's there? I see you. Get out here." Then a squeal. "Sam Dayberry! What in the world are you doing skulking about in the bushes?"

I take a sip of Millie's coffee and grin. Nope, I'm definitely not ready for bed.

Chapter 7

THIS MORNING I'VE got bags under my eyes. Bags so big a Hollywood socialite could easily carry a small dog in them.

As if Mondays don't reek anyway, on this particular morning I am suffering from extreme sleep deprivation. Again. Something's gotta give. Last night I had a dream I pushed a snoring Maxine out my second-story window.

To make matters worse, I'm listening to Millie grill her mother about Sam Dayberry for the zillionth time.

"But Mom, I still don't understand how you could hide this from me."

My bagel pops up from the toaster, but Millie pushes it back down again. For the second time.

"Well, actually it was pretty easy. I simply made sure Sam and I—"

"No, I mean how as in *why*. Why did you think deception was the best way to handle this? I just find this situation totally unacceptable." Millie shakes her head.

Maxine slurps out of her coffee mug. "I don't like the word *deception*. I prefer discreet. I am not someone who is interested in becoming the gossip of the town. Unlike some people, I value privacy."

I choke on my juice. "I caught you going through my backpack just last night."

"Stay out of this, cupcake." Maxine glares at me over her java. "I thought I had dropped an earring."

In every zipped compartment of my bag? Um, yeah.

My bagel shoots out again. Totally charred. Millie doesn't even look at it when she retrieves it from the toaster and plops it on my plate.

I pick up the skeletal remains of what once was a cinnamon raisin baked good.

Millie puts her arm on mine. "Not yet. I'll pray for our breakfast."

Too late. It's already dead.

"Dear Heavenly Father . . . thank you for this fine morning. Thank you for a . . . revealing weekend together camping. God, we pray you would forgive us of our sins—sins like deception, lying, sneakiness—"

"Sneakiness is not a sin," Maxine blurts out.

"—I pray you would put a burden on our hearts to walk in your will—your truthful, honest will. Father, we know we disappoint you when we act like idiots . . ."

I lift my eyes to see Maxine's face. She's pinches the bridge of her nose and drums her fire-engine red fingernails on the table.

"We know you look down on our stupid choices and shake your head and . . ." Millie exhales loudly. "And just sigh. Lord, no matter how much we hide our sin—in our hearts, in the bushes . . . wherever—we know you can see it all. I pray for righteousness in this family." She clears her throat. "And I pray that craziness isn't genetic. In Jesus' name, amen."

Maxine purses her lips. "Well, that was . . . inspirational."

Millie hands me the butter. "Eat your breakfast. We have to leave a little earlier for school today."

"Do you think traffic is going to be bad the first day back to school?" I dump globs of jelly out onto my bagel and take a hesitant bite.

"No, I have an appointment this morning."

I swallow the blackened bread in my mouth, its bitter taste leaving a trail down my throat. Under the table I try to hand the rest off to Rocky, my usual food disposal, but he takes one sniff and runs into the living room.

"What kind of appointment? Did you hear from the doctor while we were gone?" Maxine's voice is sharp.

My foster mom hesitates. "Yes. We're just going to discuss the results of the mammogram today." Millie sees my fallen face before I can change my expression. "There's still no reason to worry at this point. Women get mammograms all the time, Katie."

I shove my plate away. I could have had an omelet soufflé or a plate of chocolate donuts in front of me, and I'd still be losing my appetite.

And I feel like I'm being left out. Surely Millie and James know more than they're letting on. Talk to the doctor? About what? And why can't I just ask her? Instead I'm nodding my head like I understand what she's telling me. Like it's all okay. Like I'm not sitting here with black crumbs on my mouth wondering if my foster mother is gonna die.

"Mother, we'll continue this discussion another time. I know you have a karate lesson to get to this morning."

"My study of the martial arts can wait. I'm going with you and James to the appointment."

Millie clears the table, including Maxine's still full coffee cup. "No, you need to go about your normal day. This is just a simple appointment, and there is no reason for you to go."

"I said I was sorry, Millie." Maxine's bottom lip pooches out.

I smile and refill my juice glass. For once the trouble has nothing to do with me. It's a nice feeling, I must say.

The ride to school is a quiet one. Millie makes occasional small talk, but her mind is somewhere else. I want to bring up the C-word, but then again part of me doesn't even want to know.

"So . . . are you nervous about your appointment with the doctor?" *There.* I said it. It's out there.

She looks at me quickly then her focus returns to the road. A slow smile spreads across her face. "I'm not worried. It's all in God's hands. You believe that, don't you?"

Let's say I do believe it. Is that a good thing? Do we want this in God's hands? I personally want this in the hands of some brilliant, Harvard-trained doctor. Some guy who won the Nobel Peace Prize for Medicine. That's who *I* want in charge of this cancer business.

"Katie?" Millie takes one hand from the wheel and rests it on top of mine. "There's nothing to worry about. I'm gonna be okay."

Okay as in I'm gonna be here thirty years from now, or okay as in six months from now I'm gonna be having my morning coffee with John the Baptist and Mother Teresa?

"Do you have any questions, Katie?"

No.

Yes.

I mean, no.

Well, just a million.

I try to talk around the lump in my throat. "I guess I don't get why this is happening." *Katie, do not sound pitiful.*

"Hey, nothing is happening yet." She puts her signal on, then turns into the school parking lot. "But you can pray for me. Will you do that?"

I lift my chin and slowly bob my head in agreement.

"You know what else you need to think about?" Millie puts her car in park and turns toward me.

"No." Like I need one more thing to think about.

"Learning to drive."

I meet Millie's gaze, and we share a smile.

All around me kids are getting out of cars. Their own cars.

"But I like having a personal chauffeur, Millie."

I know. It's weird. I'm sixteen, and I don't drive. No driver's license—is there any greater shame for a sixteen-year-old? I've looked through the driver's manual a few times, though. But that thing is *so* boring. Why can't they spice it up? Maybe Harlequin could rewrite it. *Jackson turned to Avery, kissed her, and said, "Do you know you are the love of my life? And furthermore, when driving in fog you should use your low beams?"*

"Give it some thought. James has upped our collision insurance and is ready to take you driving." Millie winks then gives me a sideways hug. "Have a great day."

My mouth lifts in a grin, and I step outside.

"Oh, and Katie?"

"Yeah?"

"God's in control."

I shut the door and wave as she drives off. God's in control.

Fine. For now, I'll just go along with that. I mean it's totally possible. I'm inclined to believe God saved the Valiant Theater. He knew that theater was valuable to me and the Scotts, and it came out of the tornado with hardly a scratch. And Millie is even more important to me than that building, so she's gotta be okay, too, right?

"Hey, Katie!"

I wave at Frances as she runs across the sidewalk to meet me. We head inside to our lockers, talking about our weekend, and I fill her in on the latest with Maxine.

"Hi, Katie. Hi, Frances."

Hannah Wilkerson, one of the many friends who comes with Frances as a package deal, smiles in greeting. As it is everyday, her brown hair is tied back and waving down her back. When Hannah is doing some deep thinking, she'll twist that ponytail around her fingers.

She taps me on the shoulder. "So did you hear some of the school's roof was blown off? I wonder where it went to." Hannah shrugs. "Since we're back today, I guess they found it."

Okay, so she doesn't do deep thinking often.

Hannah and I walk to English together, while Frances goes the opposite way to her English for Brilliant Kids class. It's not really called that, but it might as well be.

During first hour my eyes are glued on the clock. I'm aware of every instant, every movement of the second hand. I just want this day to be over so I can get home and see what the doctor told Millie. After doing some grammar work (do I really need to know what a gerund phrase is?), some vocab exercises (I must find a way to work the word *verisimilitude* into lunchtime conversation), and reading a short story (it wasn't short enough), the bell finally rings.

I bid farewell to Hannah and meet Frances at the door to history class. A forty-something woman in a denim jumper stands at the front of the room frowning.

"Students, take your seats. I . . . I mean, please . . .

World history is taught by Mr. Patton, a history relic himself. He's so old he belongs in the Smithsonian, right there with the first flag and the Constitution. And his classroom smells like mothballs.

The teacher claps her hands. "I'm Mrs. Vanderhoover. I'm your sub for a few weeks." She smiles weakly and writes her name on the board—dropping the marker twice.

Oh, no. Don't subs know we can smell fear instantly? And some students are like sharks—when they smell the prey, they have no choice but to attack.

Frances takes her seat and up goes her hand. "Where is Mr. Patton?"

The sub raises her voice above the escalating chatter. "Mr. Patton will be out for a while. He has had surgery and will not be back for a few weeks."

"Probably a hip replacement," I whisper to Frances, who sits in front of me.

"Now, take out your history books." A paper airplane goes sailing past the sub. Two more follow.

This is not good.

Mrs. Vanderhoover's voice cracks. "All right, enough of the airplanes. I . . . I . . . now, sir, you need to sit down. What? Well, yes, you may go to the bathroom if it's an emergency."

I flip open my world history book as Wes Gregory, school skipper extraordinaire, charms the sub into a bathroom pass. Five more students leave, complaining of sickness or bathroom issues. Rhonda Darby, co-captain of the cheerleading squad approaches the teacher.

Frances turns in her seat and rolls her eyes. "Here it comes."

"The only girl who enjoys PMS." I watch Rhonda with annoyance.

"Mrs. Vanderhoover, may I go to the restroom, too, please?" The cheerleader pouts artfully.

The sub's beady eyes survey the room. "I think you can wait. Please?"

Rhonda leans in close. "I'm having female problems."

Frances and I swap disgusted looks.

"Er, you may go," Mrs. Vanderpool relents.

"She has cramps every day," Frances mutters.

Mrs. Vanderhoover asks the rest of the class to open our books and begin reading the chapter on the Industrial Revolution. From there, the class dissolves into further chaos.

"Students, if you please. I would like your attention." Her quiet, mousy voice is no match for the roar of twenty totally bored students. "I really need you to . . . um, if you would please listen. The Industrial Revolution can be a fascinating bit of—"

And then Mrs. Vanderpool finally gets our attention.

By throwing herself in her seat, laying her head on the desk, and silently crying. Some people are just *not* cut out to be subs.

We watch this scene for the next few minutes in rapt silence. It's like reality TV, only live. Mrs. Vanderhoover suddenly stands up, grabs her purse, and walks to the door.

"One day you brats will appreciate the Industrial Revolution! Mark my words!"

I'm kind of appreciating it right now.

And then she's gone.

After my next class, Algebra II, comes my favorite time of the day: lunch. When I first got to In Between High, I hated lunch. Being the new kid, it was quite a while before I had people to sit with. I guess there are always people to sit with, but I'm talking the kind you actually want to share your chili pie with.

I sashay through the masses in the cafeteria to what is now my usual table. There Frances sits, surrounded by her friends who have all adopted me. Accepted me.

I unzip my lunch bag, excited to do the one thing at school I know I'm good at—eating. Inside I find the contents of my lunch, lovingly packed by Millie.

My brow furrows. *Hmmm.* Millie's not worried about cancer? Well, the frozen burrito, bag of prunes, salt shaker, and two eggs she packed in my lunch would tell a different tale.

Ew.

"Wasn't history today bizarre?" Frances fills everyone in on our psycho sub. "And then she starts to cry, and while she's wailing she keeps yelling out—" Frances stops.

Oh, here we go again. I've seen that face before. Frances's features are frozen in place.

I catch sight of Nash walking our way. I guess it's to be a day of meltdowns.

"Hey, guys." He gives a friendly smile and carries on small talk with the table. "I saw you girls tearing up the lake this week. Did you have a good time?"

"Totally," I say quickly, hoping Frances will just stay mute and not attempt conversation. "We had a great time out on the boat. Did you happen to see Frances catch that big fish from the dock?"

He looks impressed until his eyes wander to Miss Catch-and-Release herself.

Frances's tilts sideways, and she stares at Nash in awe. With cheese sauce dripping down her chin.

I shove a napkin in her hand and motion to her face. He's never going to ask her out with cheese substitute oozing out her mouth.

"So you like camping, Frances?" Nash, for whatever reason, takes a stab at conversation with her anyway.

"Uh . . . um . . ."

Come on, Frances. You can do it. I'm coaching her with my eyes. I send silent, telepathic messages. Say, *I love to camp. I love to be outdoors where the air is clean and fresh.* (Well, unless you're camped downwind from the bathrooms.)

"Um . . . yeah . . . I like water sports."

I breathe a sigh of relief. Not bad. Her syllables at least formed a sentence this time.

"Cheese fries are good too."

And this concludes the "make sense" portion of the conversation. Ah, well. Maybe next time.

"Yeah, Frances and I like our cheese fries." I hold out her tray. "Want some, Nash?"

With a confused look, he politely declines. His brown eyes light up suddenly. "Hey, I'll be playing at your church this Wednesday. Are all of you gonna be there?"

"You and the band, Nash?" Hannah asks, totally oblivious to Frances's odd behavior.

"Yeah, me and the God Wads. We're helping out with worship." Nash runs his hands through his messy hair. "See you there, dudes. Gotta go get some chow."

As soon as he's gone, Frances turns her radiant smile on me. "That was better, right?"

I nod. "Yeah, I have to admit it was better."

"I was almost smooth."

"Frances?" Her face glows with hope. "You have three fries stuck to your shirt."

Chapter 8

ONE WEEK. OVER one stinking week has crawled by, and still no word from James or Millie on the cancer business. Every day I think, *this* will be the day they level with me about what they know.

I'm driving myself nuts with worry (not to mention I've sprouted a few zits in the process), so I decided last night I would not let James and Millie see how this is bothering me. (When your roommate doesn't let you sleep, you get in *lots* of thinking time. I imagine by the end of the week I'll have a detailed plan for world peace ready.) Instead, I'm gonna devote my energy to Operation: Get Frances A Boyfriend.

"You owe me."

I plant myself in front of Charlie Benson, who looks impressively preppie today in his Abercrombie khakis and button-down. He swivels on his lab stool, and his dark gray eyes assess me warily.

Even though he now goes to my church, one Charles Benson and I have not had a conversation since last fall—around the time I caught him doing the cha-cha with another man. Granted, that man happened to be Maxine's elderly boyfriend Sam. And sure, Charlie was secretly teaching Sam to dance in order to woo Maxine, but still. It makes for good ammunition.

"Excuse me?" His tanned cheeks turn slightly pink, and I know we're both thinking of that infamous moment I first met him.

Charlie is totally not my type, with all his name brand clothes and higher intellect and stuff. But that does not stop me from appreciating the light scent of his cologne creeping my way. But in a science lab that always smells like something dead, I guess anything would smell good to me.

"You heard me." I step in closer to him. Class has yet to start, and we are practically alone in the lab. "You should consider yourself lucky I didn't run to the school newspaper with your little interlude with Sam."

He shrugs an indifferent shoulder. "Like I care."

"Yes, but would your football team?" His eyes widen. "Yeah, I kind of thought they would too." I put on my best smile. "Tell you what I'm gonna do. So we can put this to rest once and for all, I am going to give you my word I will not tell anyone you were doing the *meringue* with . . . a man."

Charlie's eyes narrow. "It was the fox-trot."

"My silence. Forever."

"And what is it you want?" Charlie stands up, now towering over me. Have I ever noticed how tall he is? I mean, I'm a tall girl for my age. Five-nine and a half, to be exact.

I take a step back. Katie Parker does not like her personal space to be invaded.

My eyes dart around the room, checking that no one is within hearing distance. "Look, I'm gonna level with you here, Charlie. My friend Frances is in need of help."

I chew on my lip, uncertain how much to reveal. I can't tell him she likes Nash. He might spread it. "I think Frances and Nash Griffin would make a great couple, but I need some assistance in making that happen."

Charlie leans back against the lab table, looking more relaxed now that he knows I'm not asking for something major in return for my silence. Like a spleen.

"Today in class we'll be partnering up for the science fair. I need you to make sure you and Nash are not partners."

Charlie's eyebrows scrunch together. "What?"

"Since you two sit at the same table, you're always teaming up. But not for this, okay? I need you to convince Nash to be Frances's partner."

"And how do you want me to do that?"

"I don't know." At the first bell, more classmates trickle in. Including Nash. "Figure something out," I hiss and quickly go to my seat at the table behind his.

Nash and Charlie talk for a full minute before Charlie turns around, throws his hands up in the air in surrender and shakes his head. It's a no-go.

Great. I guess I'll have to take care of this myself.

You still owe me, I mouth to Charlie.

Getting up, I put my hand on Nash's shoulder.

"Hey, Katie. How's it going?"

My face is all business. "Look, I have a huge favor." Here goes nothing. "Frances has asked me to be her partner for the science fair, but I really don't want to. I mean, she just asks me because we're friends, but I know my lack of interest in all things science tends to drag her down. I was wondering if maybe you would work with her?"

Nash runs a hand through his wavy hair. "Me?"

Yeah, I know. It's weird, I want to say. But I don't.

"Yeah, see, she is really intent on winning the science competition, but she needs someone with your kind of creativity, you know? Frances has got more than her fair share of brains, but I think what would push her over the top this year is to have more of an artistic touch to the project. What do you think?" *Please don't think I sniffed a bunch of dry-erase markers before class.*

Nash looks at Charlie.

Then I look at Charlie. *Help me, you overstuffed jock.*

"Uh . . . yeah. That would be a great idea." Charlie offers lamely. "Um . . . since Frances is always helping us with our homework, we should help her out. I think . . . I think . . . making sure she wins the science fair would be a great way to pay her back for all her help this year. And with her intelligence and your creativity, Nash, you guys would definitely win." Charlie's desperate face turns to me. "Right?"

"Right. Come on, Nash. I don't want Frances to ask me to work with her out of pity. It's getting old."

"I don't know." Nash looks confused. Of course, he kind of always looks confused.

I go in for the kill. "Did you know she's never made below a ninety-five percent on any assignment?"

"Hey, Frances!"

Nash catches sight of my friend in the doorway and motions her over.

Frances promptly drops her books.

I rush over to help her. And to prepare her. "Nash is going to ask you to be his science fair partner."

She makes a strangled sound in her throat. Panic is written all over her face. In big, bold 3-D letters.

"Listen to me. When he asks you, all you say is yes, okay?" My eyes bore into hers. "Don't try to make conversation. Don't try to be intelligent. Repeat after me: yes."

Frances nods.

I shake her, then catching myself, drop my hands and plaster a smile on my face. "It's one syllable. You can do it." I pull her to our table.

Nash steps closer to her. "So, hey, Frances—"

"Yes," she rasps.

Nash looks at me, but I make a production out of staring at the floor.

"You know we've got this science fair thing coming up—"

"Yes."

"I was wondering if—"

"Yes."

He smiles broadly. "And I was wondering if you'd do my project for me."

"Yes." Frances's black hair sways with her bobbing head.

"Quit saying yes," I whisper behind her.

Nash laughs. "I was just teasing you. But maybe you'd want to be my partner?"

Frances blinks. Then takes a shuddering breath. "I think I'm gonna be sick." And runs out of the room.

Charlie slaps Nash on the back. "I think she's excited."

The tardy bell clangs, and everyone settles in. Mr. Hughes checks the attendance, then steps up to his podium. "As I told you last week, we are picking science fair project partners today. Let's go ahead and get that out of the way before we talk about the project requirements. Select your partner."

Mr. Hughes doesn't believe in seating charts (the only reason I like his class), so everyone is sitting next to a friend. Which makes it really easy for moments like this.

Unless you just partnered your friend up with someone else.

Searching the room, I see no one is left without a partner. Even the kids who are always picked last are paired up.

Except for me.

And Charlie Griffin.

Coming to the same conclusion, Charlie frowns. "I guess that leaves us."

I imagine he's been more excited over athletic physicals.

"Yup. You and me." I swallow disappointment. "Me and you."

There's just something about this guy that rubs me the wrong way. Maybe it's the fact his jeans cost more than my entire last year's school wardrobe. Maybe it's that he exudes all that preppy confidence that only comes from knowing your daddy's the bank president, you're a starting football player, and your name is on at least two credit cards in your wallet.

I don't even have my name on a library card.

Charlie settles onto the lab stool next to mine. "Let's get one thing straight: I take this stuff seriously."

The look he shoots me stops my outburst of laughter. Jock boy takes his science fair seriously? Whatever. His girlfriend probably does his homework.

"My grade is important to me, so if you're not ready to work on this project, then you better tell me now, so I can work by myself."

His words have my cheeks flaming. How dare him! To insinuate that I, Katie Parker, am not a good student.

Granted, my summer is already booked with classes to make up some credits, but I'm a changed woman.

My eyes connect with his. "Look, twinkle toes, if you can't handle being my partner, then say the word. I happen to care about my grade too."

His eyes narrow. "Fine."

"Fine."

"I'll call you tonight so we can start planning."

I grit my teeth. "Can't. Wait."

Biology creeps by slowly. Mr. Hughes believes in lecturing the majority of his ninety minutes of class, so it's hard to stay focused. Coma patients would understand. I doubt Frances got much out of bio today either, as she stared at the back of Nash's head the entire period.

At the sound of the bell, I shoot out of my seat, rudely snubbing my new science fair partner and head to my new favorite class.

Drama I.

I love it. I had no idea I was good at anything but getting into trouble until I came to In Between High. But it just so happens that I am an actress. In the *thee-uh-tuh*, as Mrs. Hall, the drama teacher, would say.

"Take your seats, students! Take your seats!" Mrs. Hall, whose hair color selection for this week appears to be jet black, claps her hands, her gold bangles going off like chimes.

I plop into a front row seat directly in front of the stage. I feel so at home here. The heavy black curtains, the wooden stage floor, the hum of the lights. The gum under my seat.

Ew.

"I have some news. Do you want the good news or the bad news first?" She proceeds without waiting for a response. "The bad news is my husband and I are getting a divorce. He has left me for a younger model who goes by the name of Buffy. I, of course, am a profession-al." Her hands go everywhere when she talks, and her billowy sleeves swoosh around like they're putting on their own show. "This will not interfere with my work here, fellow actors and actresses."

I really like Mrs. Hall, but she's a little too free with the personal info.

She smiles deliberately. "Now onto the good news, which I think you will find *très magnifique!* We all know many parts of our communi-ty were devastated by the tornado last week. I have given this much thought, and I've decided we shall put on a benefit show, the funds going toward families in need."

What a great idea. Except as a lowly Drama I student, I will get relegated to some minor part like Woman Number Four or Student in Crowd. All the upperclassmen will get the plum roles.

"The play will be the night before the annual spring dance." She holds up a hand at the groans. "Now as you know, my advanced drama classes are currently working on *Guys and Dolls*, so this event is going to depend solely on my Drama I students."

A roar of applause fills the theater. Lead role, here I come!

"You will be working with my other two intro classes, so while we will be working on scenes in class some, there will be after school practices. And since this will be a large event, I have scheduled our production in the Valiant Theater."

That's the Scott's theater! This is even better.

Mrs. Hall holds up her hands for attention. "This is a large project to undertake, and we don't have a lot of time, so a couple of senior drama students will be helping me direct." She lists off some students, most of them unknown to me. "And I am pleased to say Trevor Jackson, who will be going to Texas State on a *thee-uh-tuh* scholarship next fall, has agreed not only to play the leading male role in our production, but also to student direct. Students, a warm welcome to Trevor Jackson."

My heart does a little flip as the sound of a seat being vacated ricochets in my ear. I turn around, and there, right behind me is none other than *the* Trevor Jackson.

Sighhhhh.

Our eyes meet briefly as he moves to take the stage next to Mrs. Hall. Did we have a moment there? I think we just had a moment.

He was sitting behind me the whole time, and I didn't even know it?

I suddenly get why Frances drools when she sees Nash.

"Thank you."

Oh. He speaks.

Trevor runs a hand through his dark brown hair. His state champ baseball ring gleams on his finger. This boy is the total package—beautiful, an all-star athlete, and a sensitive, yet talented actor.

Which makes him totally off limits to me. He's so out of my league. I'm meat loaf. He's filet mignon.

"I'm glad to be working with you guys. I hear there's a lot of talent in this particular class."

Did he just look at me? I think he looked at me.

"We will be holding auditions after school next Friday. You can pick up your preview scripts today if you're interested." Trevor smiles, and my eyes are drawn to his perfectly white teeth.

Raising my hand, I'm determined not to be a Frances. I will be confident. "What is the play?" I toss my hair.

Oh, my gosh. Did I just flip my hair? *Noooooo!* Next I'll be giggling and batting my eyelashes. (Which is still better than Frances's drooling.)

His voice is deep and smooth. "We'll be performing *Cinderella*." His mouth lifts easily. "I'll be Prince Charming."

Oh, yeah.

Prince Charming, meet your princess.

Chapter 9

WHEN JAMES PREACHES about hell, I think of PE.

Even though it's a chilly, almost-spring day outside, in this gym of torture, I'm about to bake alive. Sweat drips out of every pore on my body. My hair is wet. And I can smell my own armpits.

"Katie Parker, you're slacking. Pick those knees up!" Coach Nelson blows her ever-present whistle as I run by her. This is my seventeenth lap around the gym.

And this is just the warm-up.

Coach Nelson sports a new hairdo reminiscent of a mullet. Mullets always make me grin, but there's nothing funny about this woman. She's evil. She's a tool of the devil. Coach Nelson is also the mother of Angel (ironic name, no?), somebody who quickly befriended me last semester, only to get me into some major trouble. Angel and I still hiss at each other like old farm cats from time to time, but mostly we've managed to leave each other alone since "the incident." Leaving each other alone can be hard, though. Especially when you're in PE together.

"All right, you sissies. Line up for drills!" *Tweeeeet! Tweeeeet!*

Line drills. What a great way to start a class. I love to begin the period with an activity that can induce puking.

I swipe my arm across my forehead, pulling off as much sweat as I can.

"Go!"

My legs propel my body down the court, stopping long enough to touch the floor and hustle back for more. My side throbs after five minutes of this, but I continue the sprints like I'm a Kardashian being chased by the paparazzi. At the seven-minute mark, girls begin dropping to the ground moaning in pain, grabbing their stomachs or some other injured body part. Ten minutes into the drill, and my guts are on fire. My legs scream for surrender. Three more girls quit, leaving only two of us.

Angel. And me.

Our eyes connect.

Her expression is clear. *I'm gonna run you into the ground.*

I grunt in her general direction. *You gotta catch me first.*

I take the lead, smelling victory (or is it just my b.o.?) and hoping Coach Nelson will blow the whistle to end this. Soon. While I'm still ahead.

I catch sight of Angel's spiky purple hair in my peripheral vision, and I will my legs to push harder. My lungs constrict painfully as I drag in air. Angel's arm shoots out and latches onto mine, then with a jerk, I'm propelled backwards. My nemesis darts in front and touches the floor. Just as the whistle sounds.

I glare at Angel, letting her know without words (like I could speak now anyway) what I think of her cheater tactics. Coming to a stop, I lean over, grabbing my knees. My breathing is ragged and harsh. The little kid in me wants to point my sweaty finger at Angel and ask Coach Nelson if she needs new glasses. Because she would have to be blind to not see her daughter's manhandling of me.

But I shake it off. Like line drills, starting trouble with Angel is pointless.

"Hit the floor, ladies. Time for abs." Coach Nelson forgoes her whistle and opts for yelling instead. "Move it!" It's a nice variation.

I grab a mat and settle in next to Hannah. She and I have gotten closer, sharing in the pain and agony of PE. Initially Hannah was too goody-goody for me. Too sweet and syrupy. And, honestly, too dense. But she's grown on me a lot. And she leaves her overly kind nature in the locker room in PE. Nobody—not even Hannah—can endure this class and still come out smiling.

"Give me one hundred crunches, and I want to hear you count!"

I scoot closer to Hannah. "Wow, Coach Nelson's new mullet is making her nicer. Normally it's a hundred and fifty crunches."

"My stomach is already killing me," she groans.

Hannah is a little on the plump side. Just one of the many reasons I've grown to like her. A lot of the girls around here are into the Hollywood anorexic look, but I know I can depend on Hannah to share a pint of Ben and Jerry's with me.

At the coach's next bark, we turn over onto all fours and do planks, which basically means you hold the push-up position until your arms start shaking and your shoulders and abs burn like someone's holding a blowtorch to them.

"Now I want to see tricep dips from the floor. As soon as you get to one hundred, you can hit the showers. Count it!"

My body hurts so bad I could cry. This class should be illegal. I push through the pain, though, and set my mind on hurrying. The first one to the locker room gets the shower with the curtain that doesn't have black mold and peep holes.

"Ninety-eight. Ninety-nine." I heave myself up one . . . last . . . time. "One hundred." And collapse onto the floor, my body quivering.

I drag myself up, throwing my mat into a stack and shuffle into the locker room.

The rough spray of the shower is a welcome rest, and I take a moment to just let the water work its magic.

The sweat washes away as I stand there, lost in thought.

Last night Millie acted weird. When I showed them my preview script for *Cinderella* and told them about auditions, it was like they were forcing their enthusiasm. I know they are really into my drama efforts, so it was totally out of place. What if they got news yesterday? News they didn't share with me. When I first arrived in their home, they were very secretive about their MIA daughter. Maybe Millie got bad news, and they're hiding that from me too.

"Where are my shoes?"

Rinsing off the last of the soap, I stick my head out the shower.

Angel tosses things out of her locker. Shirts and shorts fly everywhere. Her face is red from class. And from anger.

"Somebody in here took my shoes!" She turns on Hannah. "Have you seen them? The ones I had on earlier?"

Hannah collapses onto a bench. She mutely shakes her head.

I towel off as Angel confronts every girl in the locker room. My t-shirt slides on just as Angel plants herself in front of me.

"You." Her nostrils flare.

I stare at her for a few seconds. My face is totally blank. I will not let her think she is intimidating me.

Which she is.

"Do you know anything about the whereabouts of my shoes? My brown leather ones?"

"Nope." I grab my socks and take a seat.

"They were here at the beginning of class, and now they're gone." Perspiration still clings to her skin.

I concentrate on tying my shoelaces and don't bother making eye contact with Angel. "Haven't seen them."

She picks up a gym bag and throws it against the wall. Its contents spill out. "One of you lifted my shoes. I will find out who did it." Angel's eyes scan the room before her gaze lands on me. "And you will be sorry."

The cool air outside is like a big Band-Aid to my aching bones. James waves at me from his truck in the school parking lot. That's odd. Millie usually picks me up.

"Hey. How was your day?"

I collapse into the passenger seat. "It was a PE day. Need I say more?" James smiles in response, but his attention seems elsewhere. Something is up.

"I brought you some clothes. I'm gonna take you over to Frances's house. You can study and eat dinner at her house, then ride with her family to church."

"Where's Millie?"

James hesitates. "We ... ah, had a doctor's appointment this morning. She had a little in-patient surgery." He sees my thunderous expression. "It's okay, Katie. She had a biopsy so we can get a better idea of what's going on."

"Why didn't you tell me? She had surgery and you just forgot to mention it?"

"No, we didn't forget. We didn't want to upset you."

"That plan worked well."

He rests his hand on my arm. "It was a quick procedure. She's been home all afternoon. Even been baking cookies—well, with Maxine's 'help.'"

I turn away from him and look out the window. "When will you find anything out?" *Or have you already, and you're just keeping me in the dark? Again.*

"Soon."

"I could've gotten a ride with Frances, you know." Unlike me, Frances is in the elite club of student drivers.

"Millie sent your makeup because she knew you'd want it after PE." He turns down Frances's street. "And I wanted you to have your Bible."

"I do like to be hot and holy." No, stop talking! I'm supposed to be mad. James and Millie are shutting me out of all of this, and I *cannot* act like it's OK.

James stops in the Vega driveway. "We'll see you at church. And Katie ..." James gives my hair a little tug. "Everything's gonna be fine."

My foster dad drops me off with a wave. His cell phone is to his ear before he's out of the driveway.

What if he's talking to Iola Smartly? Saying, hey, Millie's got cancer, so come get this girl off our hands.

No, think positive. Millie is one of the nicest, godliest people I know. God's not gonna mess with someone like her. How totally unfair would that be? To her. To me.

I walk past the small koi pond and as soon as I'm on the porch, Frances swings the door open.

"Hey!" Her hair is piled on top of her head, anchored by some hand painted hair sticks her grandmother sent her from China.

"Guess you're stuck with me tonight."

"Where did James and Millie have to go?" Frances's dog takes advantage of the open door and shoots outside. "Ming Yu, get the dog!"

"I don't know." I watch her twelve-year-old brother chase their cocker spaniel into the neighbor's yard. "Millie had a biopsy today." My friend's mouth drops. "Yeah, I know. They didn't even tell me about it." I shake my head. This is *not* sounding good.

I follow Frances inside. I have yet to adjust to the zoo that her house is. It's like a circus sideshow. People would pay money to step inside this home. Her father, a pediatrician, is from Mexico. Frances's mother, a tiny woman with a loud voice, is from China. Together they over-decorate, overcook, and overdo the home with their dual cultures. It makes Frances miserable. The walls are covered with cultural art, historical photos, and generations of family portraits. There is no space left untouched.

"Hello, Katie!" Ling Vega enters the living room, carrying baby Maria on her hip. "Are you hungry? Tonight we're having an old recipe handed down to me from my great-grandmother." Mrs. Vega's black eyes sparkle.

"Oh, yeah. I'm starved. I could eat anything."

"Tonight I'm preparing spicy fish and cabbage soup."

Anything but that. I force an enthusiastic smile, but Frances sees right through it.

"Mom, you're the only one who likes that. I bet great-great-Grandmother didn't even eat it. Why can't we have burgers? Grill some hotdogs?" She throws her hands in the air and heads upstairs. "Steaks? Something normal for once."

"Zhen Mei Vega, there are children starving in the world!" Mrs. Vega calls out after us. "Most of your friends are probably eating frozen chicken nuggets tonight! Or bologna!"

Frances grumbles all the way up the staircase.

"So what's the latest? Did you see Nash after lunch today?" I flop myself into Frances's lime-green beanbag chair.

Frances shuts her door and sighs. "No."

"What did we talk about on the phone last night? Strategic hall placement."

"I know! But after lunch he was talking to some friends. And then after seventh hour he disappeared into the boys' bathroom." She grabs her biology book. "I didn't think I should follow him in there." It comes out like a question.

"No! Of course you don't follow him into the john." Where has this girl's brain gone?

"So where do we start? What do I do?"

I grab a pen and notebook out of my backpack. Time to make a list. "You're gonna continue to work on strategic placement in the hallways. Drop a book near his locker. Speak to people in his proximity. Be in his path."

"Right."

"Step two. It's time for you to ask Nash to get together and work on the science fair project. You need to talk to him in biology tomorrow." I scribble this down.

Frances hangs her head. Strands of her black hair escape from her knot. "I can't, Katie."

"Frances, sometimes we do things we don't want to do." Oh, my gosh. Did Millie just jump into my body? I sounded like an . . . adult.

"Can't you help me with that?" Oh, how the mighty have fallen. This brainy, future fashion model/nuclear physicist has gone from happy and confident to melodramatic and suffering from an inferiority complex. It's driving me nuts. I have bigger things to worry about.

"*Hmmm . . .*" I tap my pen to my chin, trying to focus. "What about we see if Nash and Charlie want to meet us at the public library after school tomorrow to get started on our projects? I'll ask them both." This could work.

Frances throws herself onto her bed and covers her face with a white and black comforter. "I don't know!"

"Frances."

Her face reappears.

"Do you like Nash or not?"

Her eyes go all dreamy. "Yes. Nash is . . . is . . . awesome." She sighs.

"Well, then you can do—"

Suddenly Luis, Frances's six-year-old brother, rockets out from under her bed. "Nash is awesome! Nash is awesome!" He flies out of the room. "*Mawwww-Meeee! Frances has a boyfriennnnnd!*"

Frances makes a grab for her brother, but it's too late. Frances has just been outed.

"Maybe your mom didn't hear." I offer weakly. With Luis's volume, I think Nash himself possibly could've heard it.

Frances and I spend the next hour and a half rehearsing how she will act tomorrow in biology. We make a list of safe topics for her to discuss with Nash and possible replies. Mrs. Vega calls us to dinner, but before we go downstairs, I make Frances pinkie-swear she will practice.

It's at step ten that it hits me. The smell of stew. Fish stew at that. Wow. Potent.

"Hello, girls!" Mr. Vega, newly home from work, kisses his daughter's cheek and gives me a big bear hug. I'm not much of a hugger, but these I've gotten used to. There's something very comforting and genuine about this family's enthusiasm for me. Like I'm an extension of their household.

After grace, we pass the food one dish at a time.

Mrs. Vega hands Frances some bread. "Do you have something to tell us?"

"We're the only people I know who put cod in liquid, drown it in cabbage, and call it dinner?" Frances hands me the bread basket.

Mr. Vega chuckles. He's all about international cooking, too, though. When it comes from Mexico. "See, I told you we should have eaten the *carne asada* tonight."

Mrs. Vega swats at her husband with her napkin then returns her attention to Frances. "Do you have a boyfriend, Zeng Mai?" Only Frances's parents call her by her first two names. Like all things cultural or fishy, Frances rejects it.

"Luis! Don't you ever step foot in my room again!" Frances bestows her best evil eye on her little brother. Who promptly opens his mouth and shows her his chewed food.

"Zeng Mai, you have a boyfriend, and you did not tell us?" Cesar Vega's smile disappears. "You know you must ask permission to date anyone. Why have we not been introduced to this young man?" He looks to his wife who only shrugs.

"Nash is awesome! Nash is awesome!"

"Luis, be quiet! Mom, tell him to be quiet!"

"So Nash is this young man's name?" Mrs. Vega ladles out soup for herself.

"I don't have a boyfriend, okay? I'm boyfriendless. Totally without a boyfriend. *Sans* boy. *No tengo un novio.* There? Are you happy?"

The soup goes to Frances. Who passes it to me. I drop some in my bowl, not wanting to be rude. *Ugh.* Stin-kee.

"Do you like this boy then?" Mr. Vega tears his bread in two.

"He's my science fair partner, Dad. No big deal."

"Katie is not your science fair partner? Don't you both have biology?"

"Well, Mrs. Vega, I wanted to work with someone else." It's kind of true.

The rest of the meal passes by with the Vegas quizzing Frances about Nash. The more they ask, the madder she gets. Eventually I tune them all out as thoughts of Millie consume me. They don't just do a biopsy for the fun of it. They must suspect it's cancer.

After dinner Frances and I do the dishes, then we follow the family into the minivan and head to church.

Target Teen is the Wednesday night church service for junior high and high schoolers. Initially it was punishment for me to come here, but now it's not too bad. The youth pastor, Mike, is a pretty funny guy, and I find myself sucked into his lessons. But it's the music that always speaks to me and has me coming back for more. There's a full band, made up of fellow Chihuahuas who go to our church, and it's like MTV meets Jesus. Electric guitars, drums, dimmed lights, rockin' harmonies. It's the best.

"Hey, Katie. Hey, Frances." Charlie, who has recently started coming on Wednesday nights, greets us in the doorway, flanked by his girlfriend Chelsea.

Two words about Chelsea: Total. Snob.

Seriously, she's tall and blonde, and she just screams out "I'm simply lost without a boyfriend." She's the type who's had a boyfriend every day since kindergarten. Her dad works for some major corporation, so she's loaded. Like dripping with money. She carries a Prada bag. And I don't mean the kind that upon closer inspection really says *Rada*.

"Hi, Charlie. Hey, Chelsea." Frances, having calmed down some, is back to her old polite self.

"Hey, guys." I try not to notice Chelsea's jeans look just like the pair I saw in *InStyle* magazine this week.

In the uncomfortable silence that follows, Charlie makes at attempt at conversation. "Katie is my partner for the science fair."

"Great." Chelsea looks me up and down before finally dismissing me as both harmless and useless.

"Hey, Chels, why don't you stay here with Katie and Frances while I go talk to the guys?"

Chelsea's shiny pink lips pucker. "You're not gonna leave me . . . here, are you?" She clings to his arm.

I can't stand clingers.

Charlie says good-bye sheepishly and pulls his girlfriend along with him to greet some other people.

"Take your seats everybody." Pastor Mike takes the stage. His diamond earring blinks in the spotlight. "We're gonna open up with prayer then we have a special treat for you tonight. The God Wads are here to lead worship. So make them feel welcome."

Pastor Mike prays over us then introduces the band. "Give it up for the God Wads!"

Frances and I pick a seat next to Hannah and some other girls from school. "Oh, my gosh. Oh, my gosh. There he is."

I follow the path of Frances's laser stare. Right to Nash, bass guitar player for the Wads.

"Don't do anything crazy like throw your bra onstage."

The band pounds into their opening number, and everyone jumps to their feet. Hands go up, some sing along. Frances drools. I stand there and watch the whole scene, still feeling a bit like an outsider. What's it like to just throw your hands in the air and become one with the music? To totally worship and not care what anyone thinks? At what point does this all get comfortable?

After six or seven songs, the God Wads exit the stage. Frances leans over my way to watch them go. She's all but in my lap.

Pastor Mike grabs a microphone as the lights come up some.

"I have a brief announcement. The spring break mission trip to Florida has been cancelled."

A chorus of "Awwwws" drowns out whatever he's saying next.

Frances and I exchange pained looks. I was gonna get to go too. That totally blows. I've never been to Florida.

Stupid tornado.

"I know, it stinks. But listen." Pastor Mike pauses until the room quiets again. "Why drive for over seventeen hours to do mission work when we have people who could use our help right here? Guys, I've prayed about it a lot, and I know the right thing to do is stay in In Between. I'll bring you more details later, but you better believe it will still be fun. You know I'm gonna make sure of that."

He's echoed by a few hoots and hollers. Most of us remain quiet, watching our dreams of sandy beaches and clam bakes disappear. And yes, I know that's not what the mission trip is about, but it sure was a nice bonus. Helping a poor neighborhood *and* getting a tan.

"All right, more on that later. Let's go ahead and dive into the Word."

Pastor Mike has a student pray for us (I would *die* if he ever picked me) then opens his worn Bible.

"Guys, tonight we're gonna talk about faith. Who here has got some faith?"

Hands shoot to the ceiling.

"I mean real faith." Pastor Mike's bald head glistens in the dimmed lights. "It's easy to have faith when things are going well. But what about when a boyfriend dumps you? What about when a parent leaves? What about when someone you love is sick?"

My ears perk at that. He's on staff here. Does he know something about Millie?

"Hebrews 11:1 says faith is the substance of things hoped for, the evidence of things not seen. If I was a betting person, I would put in some serious cash and bet many of you are hoping for something. Are you strong enough to believe it?" His eyes sweep over the crowd. "Are you willing to let this go and allow God to be in control?"

As the pastor gets into some examples, my mind once again goes back to Millie.

God, I'm not totally there yet. I just need some more time. I do know you're real though. But God, Millie needs you. She's a total believer.

She's a sold-out, fish-sticker-on-her-car Christian. She can't have cancer. It's not fair. Give it to someone who deserves it. Give it to someone who doesn't have a foster kid. Until my mom gets her stuff straight—if ever—I need James and Millie. You can't just drop me here and then toss me right back out.

"We're gonna make a commitment here tonight." Pastor Mike puts down his Bible. "Whatever it is that's on your heart. Whatever it is you're struggling with, that you're praying for. Give it up. Let God have it. And have faith." A candle sputters beside the pastor. "Right now, where you're at. Let's take a moment and pray silently. Ask God to take this issue over for you."

Heads drop. No one stirs.

All right, God. I'm trusting you to take care of Millie. No cancer, all right? I can't handle anymore craziness. Can't handle any more disappointments. I am stepping out on faith tonight. And believing that Millie is cancer-free.

Chapter 10

THURSDAY'S ARE GREAT, aren't they? By the time Thursday rolls around, you can say to yourself, yes, I can do this. Because when I get through this day, it will be Friday.

I'm standing next to Frances's locker waiting for the 7:55 bell to ring for biology. Frances's locker is unfortunately located next to Chelsea's. As in Charlie's Chelsea.

Chelsea currently has her arms roaming up Charlie's chest toward his neck. Who needs police officers on security duty at this school? What we need is some PDA police. Maybe I should make a citizen's arrest.

To his credit, Charlie intercepts Chelsea's predator hands and holds them in his own.

"Katie? Hello?" Frances waves her hand in front of my face.

"What?"

"You're staring," she whispers.

I shake my head to clear the images. "Sorry. Gross displays of affection (hey, they should be called GDA!) are like car wrecks. They're so heinous; it's hard to turn away sometimes."

"Hey, guys!" Hannah limps toward us, her ponytail swishing behind her.

"What's up with the leg?" I ask.

Hannah shrugs. "PE injury."

We all nod in total understanding.

"Hi, Charlie. Hey, Chelsea." Hannah waves happily.

Their cocoon of love now disturbed, the couple moves apart. "Hey, guys. Didn't see you there." Charlie smiles warmly.

Yeah, I'll bet you didn't. You were too busy making out with Handsy McHands-A-Lot.

Chelsea snaps her gum a few times. Her look of disdain reminds me of Angel. "Hi." Her attention goes back to Charlie.

"Did you enjoy church last night, Chelsea?" Frances asks, her eyes already going all dreamy. No doubt remembering Nash playing his heart out.

Chelsea does a partial eye roll. The type that is so small she could deny it, but it's there all the same. "Yeah. The band was . . . okay."

"Okay?" Frances slams her locker shut. "The band was fabulous. The band was out of this world." She sucks in air. "The band was . . . was the best of any band I have ever seen on that stage."

"Sure. Whatever." Chelsea grabs Charlie's hand and leads him down the hall. Much like one would lead a cow.

"How can he stand that girl?" I ask when the duo is absorbed by the masses.

"I think she's nice."

I pat Hannah on the back. "You think everyone is nice."

"That's not true!"

Frances pulls a breakfast bar out of her backpack. "Hannah, last week you said you felt sorry for the Al-Qaeda."

"Well, I just think they need some love and understanding." She pinches off a bite of Frances's breakfast. "And maybe some fiber in their diet."

I shut my own locker, and that's when I see Nash. "Frances! Where are you supposed to be?"

Her brows lower in thought. "Biology class?"

"No! Strategic hall placement! Remember?" Ugh! All my efforts are being wasted!

Frances shoves the rest of the breakfast bar in her mouth, her eyes wide with fear. Or too much granola.

"You missed your chance. Here he comes. You were supposed to be near his locker this morning."

Frances squares her shoulders. "Not too late." She continues to chew. "Ah can do dis."

Oh, no. Here we go. "You have a giant granola bar in your mouth, for Pete's sake. Stop while you can and don't do this. This is not in our plan."

"Ha, Nosh." *Smack, smack.*

Part of me wants to turn away so I don't have to look at this.

"Hey, Frances." Nash takes off his hat and bows like he's a knight in the queen's service. "Ladies." He rises with a wicked grin.

"We saw you at church last night. Great job." Maybe if I dominate conversation, Frances won't be able to get a word in.

"Tota-wee awthome."

Mini chocolate chips shoot out my friend's mouth.

Hannah wipes her cheek. "Ew."

Nash frowns. "Thanks."

"Wadda wook on our scieths far projeck?"

My eyes implore Frances to give it up. *Abort mission! Abort mission!*

"Huh?" Nash shakes his head.

I move in front of my friend, who now has oats hanging from her upper lip. "She said we'll see you in biology!" A Chelsea-like giggle bubbles out of my mouth. *Tee. Hee.* Yes, so, so funny. We all smile like cheerleaders until Nash is gone.

"Wow. I didn't know you liked . . ." Hannah twists her hair with a ringed finger. "Granola bars."

I grab Frances and lead her to biology class. "What happened to sticking with the plan?"

"I'm giving up, Katie. Seriously. It's over."

"What's over?" Someone's breath tickles my neck.

I settle my backpack on the lab table and turn around.

Charlie Benson.

What's over? Your girlfriend's lipstick—all over your face.

Okay, it's really not.

As if I care anyway.

"What's over?" He sits on his own lab stool and crosses his arms, patiently waiting for our story like he's Dr. Phil.

"Your ego, Charlie. It's overrated."

"I think you mean overinflated."

He has the nerve to smirk.

"Whatever." I turn my back to him.

"What's not working is your scheme to hook up Frances and Nash."

Frances gasps.

"Yeah, I saw you in the hall." Charlie grimaces. "Train wreck."

"Frances is doing just fine, thanks." If I were Pinocchio, my nose would be in the next county.

Charlie lifts his muscled frame from his lab stool. The leather of his letterman's jacket squeaks as he leans onto our table. "I think I can help you."

I sniff with disdain. And get a nose full of his woodsy cologne. "You can take your offer of help and stick it where the quarterbacks don't—"

"We'll take it," Frances interrupts. "Your help, that is."

"Wait a minute." I am so onto him. "What do you want in return?"

Charlie runs a hand through his honey-colored hair. "Well, you see—"

"Whatever it is, we'll do it." Frances's words come out in a rush. Her eyes nervously skitter across the classroom, checking for the absent Nash.

"So it's a deal?" Charlie extends his hand out to Frances.

Before I can throw myself between them, their hands connect, and Frances shakes on it.

"It's a deal."

Great. Über–good girl Frances just made a deal. With the devil. Probably his help in exchange for her beating heart.

"What do you want, Charlie?" I cannot believe he took advantage of my friend. In her most vulnerable state.

Charlie hesitates then moves in closer. "I need you to be Chelsea's friend."

My obnoxious laughter has the class swiveling in their seats. "Whew! That's a good one." I wipe the tears from my eyes. "Yeah, we'll go hang out with her at cheerleading practice today after school. And then maybe this weekend we can go shopping for eight-hundred-dollar handbags together." Oh, the jokes this guy tells.

Charlie frowns. "I'm serious. And you have the wrong idea about Chelsea. There's more to her than that."

Yes, but the fact that she's a good kisser and has no need for Wonder Bras still does not redeem her.

"What did you have in mind?" Frances is totally serious. She grabs a pen to take notes.

"I need you to hang out with her at church. Show her around. Introduce her to people. She's so shy—"

My cheeks make fart noises as the contained laughter bursts out. "Oh, you gotta stop. Seriously."

"Can you focus?" Frances jabs me in the ribs. She scribbles something in her notebook.

Probably coming up with chemical formula for a personality transplant for Chelsea. If that girl's shy then I'm the Chihuahua valedictorian.

"I thought if she felt more welcome at church then . . ." Charlie glances at the door as Nash walks in. Mr. Hughes shuts the door behind him.

"Good morning, class. Let's get started."

"We'll talk about this later."

"Get Nash and meet us at the public library after school. We'll talk about our projects then." I groan. "And Chelsea."

"I don't know if I can." He ambles back to his seat.

"Make it happen, Benson." I jab my finger towards him. "Or no deal."

IN DRAMA CLASS I sink into a plush theater seat. And openly stare at Trevor. He's onstage chatting with Mrs. Hall, whose whole body is in the conversation. Sometimes I don't know if she's talking. Or doing an interpretive dance.

The russet tones (natural, of course) in Trevor's dark hair shine under the spotlight. Today he's sporting some faded jeans, a button-down polo, and his totally hot smile.

Very nice.

"Actors! Actresses!" Mrs. Hall claps her hands. "Today I have two things to tell you." With a black-polished finger she swabs some lipstick off her teeth. "Number one, my soon-to-be ex-husband is a lying snake who has moved in with his girlfriend Buffy." She leans in toward her audience. "For future reference, never let your husband hire a secretary named after a color of fingernail polish."

Trevor looks out into the audience. He absently winks toward the crowd. Three girls beside me sigh.

"Item number two, today we are going to practice scenes from *Cinderella*. This is to prepare you for auditions, which are tomorrow. I know it's soon, but Trevor will be helping you with these vignettes and will be on hand to answer any remaining questions you have about audition procedures."

More giggling from behind.

Mrs. Hall throws her orange silk scarf across her neck. "Trevor will specifically be working with those trying out for the part of Cinderella. Raise your hand if this applies to you."

Hands go to the ceiling like a church revival.

Great. Look at all my competition. All my simpering, giggling, too cute for words competition. And that's just this class. There are still two other classes of Drama I that I'll be auditioning with.

As the girls rush the stage and fight for Trevor's attention, I hang back, choosing instead to work with my friend Jeremy.

Jeremy's pretty cool. When I came into this class after bombing a few other electives, he was my first friend. On day one I discovered we both love the movie *The Princess Bride* and neither one of us gets mime. *And* Jeremy has connections. His third cousin's sister has a boyfriend whose stepsister's aunt knows the neighbor of Reese Witherspoon. He's hoping to meet her one day. (Reese, that is.)

I help Jeremy with his scenes for the first forty-five minutes. He wants to be the king. The male roles are pretty limited in this play. It's either the prince, king, or guys who blow bugles.

"Now it's your turn. We've practiced so much I have the king's lines memorized."

"Memorized already? That's really good, Jeremy."

His face falls. "There are only five lines."

"But you get to wear a crown."

His smile returns.

I give *Cinderella* my best for the next thirty minutes. Jeremy and I are waltzing (more like swaying with an occasional leg spasm movement), and I'm practicing my "Oh, no it's midnight" face, when I feel a tap on my shoulder.

"May I cut in?"

I know that voice. I hear it in my dreams.

I swallow hard. And turn around.

Nodding weakly, I am swept into the arms of Trevor Jackson, the fairest guy in all the land.

At my look of dismay Trevor laughs. "I thought you might want to learn how to waltz." His eyes meet mine. "The right way."

I plaster a smile on my face, trying to buy some time until I can find my tongue.

"How . . . how do you know how to waltz?" Is this just a pre-req for guys at In Between?

His grin reveals brilliantly white teeth. *Mmm* . . . and fresh, minty breath too. "Drama II. You'll learn it next year." He pulls me closer. "But why wait 'til then when you can learn now?"

Sighhh.

Only Trevor Jackson can make words like "one, two, three" sound romantic as he teaches me the waltz. Tucked close to his chest, the rest of the class period flies. By the time the bell rings I've stepped on his feet six times, tripped myself twice, actually achieved witty banter three times, and been tempted to hand him my heart about one hundred times.

I look at the clock just to make sure it's really three. It is.

Trevor lifts my hand. "As an Elizabethan gentleman, this is where I bow over your hand." And he does. He really does. "And you curtsy." His smile sends butterflies rappelling off my stomach. "But remember . . . Cinderella is totally captured by Prince Charming. So when she curtsies, her eyes never leave his."

At Trevor's nod, I sweep into a low curtsey. Just like I saw on *Pride and Prejudice* last weekend. Yes, okay, I was watching public television with Maxine.

When my hand is released, I cradle it to my chest.

"Take care, Katie. I'll see you tomorrow."

He'll see me tomorrow? Trevor plans to see me? When? Why? I need to get my hair done!

He winks. At me. "At auditions."

Oh, right. I knew that. Auditions.

I didn't think he was asking me out or anything. Noooo.

Well.

Maybe for a second.

Chapter 11

MEET AT MY *house after school. CU there.*

This was the text message Frances and I got from Charlie during eighth period.

After a call to Millie, in which I assured her of my safety and promised not to do anything stupid, I hopped in the car with Frances. Frances drives a station wagon. And aside from the fact she calls it Sally Ann (for no apparent reason), there is nothing cool about it. Her mom says if Frances is gonna drive, it's going to be something that can haul all three of her siblings. This wagon could probably carry all the siblings in the state of Texas.

My car door creaks shut, and Sally Ann sputters to life.

"What's our strategy?" Frances's knuckles are white on the steering wheel.

"Does it matter?" I fasten my seatbelt. "You've totally ignored every strategic plan we've had."

"No! Don't give up on me. I need more strategy. Strategy is the only way."

"Fine," I say on a sigh. "Here's what I think we should do. We'll all have some small talk for a few minutes. I assume Charlie will probably get us something to drink or eat. This will probably take about fifteen minutes. You can handle that. Charlie and I will be there for interference. Then I'll suggest we break up into our respective partners so we can work on our projects."

"Uh-huh, okay, yeah." A drop of sweat beads on Frances's brow. Not a good sign.

"So then you will suggest to Nash that the two of you adjourn to the dining room. Charlie and I will take the living room."

"Why do you get the living room?"

"Because if you get the living room then you'll seat yourself as far away from Nash as you can get. I know you."

Frances nods rapidly, her eyes glued to the road.

"So you'll go to the dining room. Let Nash sit down first, and then you will sit directly across from him."

Frances chews on a fingernail. "What will we talk about?"

I open my mouth to respond, but Frances's squealing muzzles my thoughts.

She grabs my hand. "Oh, my gosh. We're here. What do we talk about? Help me, Katie!"

I grab my stuff and open the door. "In this order: compliment his performance at church, discuss today's disgusting meat loaf casserole in the cafeteria, and ask him where he's going for Spring Break. If there's any time left, declare your undying devotion and break out into Whitney Houston's 'I Will Always Love You.'"

"Hey, girls. Welcome to the *casa*."

Charlie walks out to greet us, and I look right through him to the house. *Casa?* More like El Mansion.

It's gigantic. It looks like the White House or something.

What am I doing here? And why do I have Richie Rich for my science fair partner?

"Frances," I whisper, ducking my head back into the car, "if you need help the code will be 'I'd like a glass of water.' Can you remember that?"

Her smile wobbles on her face as she faces our host. "*Hola*, Charlie."

I follow the two into Charlie's foyer. He has an entire room just for the front door. A giant chandelier hangs overhead. I take a step to my left. I've seen enough scary movies to know what can happen to teenage girls directly beneath giant light fixtures with spiky glass things hanging down.

"Come on in. Nash is in the kitchen."

Yeah, he's probably in there hanging out with the maid and butler.

Charlie escorts us into his kitchen, which is surprisingly . . . cozy. The walls are a sunny yellow and remind me of Millie's favorite Italian restaurant. Dark brown cabinets surround the walls and ceramic roosters perch on the counter tops.

The smell of chocolate chip cookies attacks my senses, and I immediately quit my decorative analysis and scan the room for the baked goods.

A short, plump woman enters the kitchen. "Hello! Come on in. I have some cookies that will be coming out of the oven in about five minutes." Her cheeks are pink with color, and her oversized mouth is pulled into a smile.

"I'm Donna." She holds out a hand for me to shake.

I take in her simple white t-shirt and khaki pants, which have seen better days.

"Are you the maid?" I ask, picturing Charlie's mom upstairs, reclining on a chaise lounge eating bonbons.

Donna's smile vanishes. "What?"

"Katie, this is my mom."

Somewhere in the kitchen a clock ticks.

"Would you like a glass of water?" Frances whispers behind me.

"It's quite all right, dear. I do look a mess. I've been outside all day mowing."

Charlie's mom puts her arm around my shoulders. Her stubby fingernails are in serious need of a manicure.

"I'm so sorry." And I thought Frances was going to be the one to blow it today.

"I guess in a way, I am the maid. This one," she points to Charlie, "refuses to pick his underwear off the floor."

Ew. Okay, things I don't need to know about Charlie Benson.

"Now, you kids go on into the living room, and I'll bring you some cookies and fresh lemonade in a few minutes."

Are you the maid? I am such an idiot. She'll probably spit in my lemonade.

I land on an oversized couch, propping my feet up on a matching ottoman. Frances parks herself right beside me. As in cheek to cheek.

I shoot her a look, but she's too busy chewing her thumbnail to notice my glare or the fact that her butt is crossing some boundary lines.

Nash sits in a chair, playing the drums on his knees. He does this a lot. It's like he can't sit still.

Charlie grabs the remote and turns it to some music channel. "So I thought we could discuss our science fair projects. I figured it would be more fun if we hung out together . . . when we did discuss our projects."

Maybe Frances and Charlie should be a couple. They both are so eloquent in times like these.

"Nash, would you dining room like to go with me?"

I shake my head violently at Frances. No! Not yet. She's going off-script.

She tries again. "I mean would the dining room like to work on the science fair project. No, what I mean to say is—"

"Cookies are served!" Charlie's mom carries in a tray loaded down with frosty lemonade and a small mountain of chocolate chip cookies.

With quick hands, I make the universal signal for "zip your lip" and hand Frances a glass.

Charlie and Nash share a laugh over the day's math class then segue into discussing fantasy football, which leads to a lengthy conversation on ESPN.

Frances and I are left with nothing to do but eat cookies. Which isn't such a bad predicament to be in. But it doesn't get Frances any closer to a date with Nash.

"So I guess we should get started on our projects." At my declaration Frances freezes mid-bite. "We'd probably get more done if we went to separate rooms."

Take your cue, Frances.

She takes another cookie instead.

Must I do everything? "So Charlie and I will stay in here, and Nash, you and Frances can talk shop in the dining room."

Frances's only response is a croaking noise.

"Sounds good to me." Nash stands up.

"Water . . . need glass of water." Frances tugs on the collar of her vintage eighties t-shirt.

"You want a glass of water?" Charlie jumps to his feet.

"No. She doesn't."

Charlie eyeballs me with confusion. "Katie, if she wants some water, it's not a problem."

Frances nods her head frantically.

"She's fine. Aren't you, Frances? I don't think you need any water . . . yet."

"Hey, I think she's choking." Nash nearly trips over his own baggy pants as he hurdles the ottoman and grabs Frances. "Can you breathe?"

My friend makes wheezing noises and clutches her throat. Nash's arms snake around her and he locks a fist under her chest. He clutches Frances tightly, and gives two forceful pushes on her stomach.

A wad of cookie the size of a golf ball shoots out of her mouth and across the room. On Charlie.

Frances collapses against Nash, sucking in air like she's been held underwater.

"Oh, my gosh! Frances, are you okay?" I shove Nash aside and move closer to my friend.

Her breath is labored, but her color is going back to normal. "I said I wanted water."

"But choking really wasn't covered under the code," I mumble.

Frances leans in close to my ear. "Maybe next time you can go over the exceptions *before* I'm forced to call my own ambulance?"

The next ten minutes are spent making sure Frances is well enough to proceed with our science work. It also gives me time for my heart to slide from my throat back down to my chest. I have Frances recite the preamble from the Constitution to double check that all her systems are go.

Charlie finally pitches in and helps by escorting Frances and Nash into the dining room down the hall.

When Charlie returns I'm checking out his expansive DVD collection in the entertainment center. His family seems to enjoy a broad range of flicks from VeggieTales to *Scarface*.

"Do you and Chelsea watch movies a lot?" *Augh!* Where did that come from?

He collapses into the couch, opposite end of where I was sitting. "Sometimes. But if it doesn't have Tatum Channing in it, she's not too interested."

I turn my face to hide a smirk. In the months I've spent in church, I've learned we're supposed to live like Christ and be good and kind. And not trash someone's shallow girlfriend.

I fail on a regular basis.

Charlie and I had a text conversation a few nights ago about our project, so we really don't have anything significant to discuss.

"Now about Chelsea . . ." Charlie begins.

Like I said, nothing significant to discuss.

Oh, behave, Katie. Be kind, be kind, be kind. Think positive.

Blessed are the merciful, for they will be shown mercy. Blessed are the pure in heart, for they will see God. Blessed are the . . .

Charlie's hand lands on my shoulder. "Katie, did you hear me?"

What in the world? Is that *supposed* to happen? How did I remember that? Did I know I knew that verse? Oh, my gosh. What if this is a sign of insanity? I must Google spiritual overexposure when I get home.

"Katie?"

"What?" My voice comes out too loud. Resuming my seat on the couch, I take a deep breath and contort my face into a look of serenity. I will be calm. I will not scare my classmate.

"So you were saying about Chelsea . . .?"

Charlie closes some distance between us, and I fight the urge to jump into a nearby leather recliner.

"I just don't understand why the girls at church ignore her."

I study his tan face. Yup, he's serious.

"Well . . . um . . ." How do I put this? "She's a little—"

"Shy. Yeah, I know."

Shy wasn't what I was going for. "I don't know, Charlie. I'll do all I can, but the reality is I'm still pretty new to Target Teen myself. It's not like I have an inside track into all things cool at church."

"But you'll start hanging out with her on Wednesday nights, right? I mean, that was the deal? And when you girls get together for church socials, you'll ask her?"

My eye twitches spastically as I ponder the many joys of hanging out with Chelsea.

"Katie, you agreed to help me in return for helping Frances."

"Now, wait a minute," I protest. "Frances agreed. I never agreed to this. I stand to gain nothing here."

"I did make a one hundred and two percent on my science project last year."

Well, now you're talking.

When I came to In Between, let's just say I didn't come with the prettiest scholastic record you've ever seen. Until I got here, I never cared. But good grades must be like what drugs were to my mom— once you taste it, you want more.

"Can you assure me we'll make at least an A on this project?" The sigh that escapes is beyond dramatic.

Charlie grins. "At least a ninety-five."

My eyes are drawn to the dimple that appears on his left cheek. Does Trevor have a dimple?

"Fine. I will welcome her next Wednesday night like she's my long-lost sister."

"And you'll talk to the other girls at church?"

"We'll be her new best friends." I suddenly feel a little queasy.

"Great. Thank you." Charlie runs a hand through his toffee-colored hair. "It's really important to me that Chelsea likes church."

"Because you only date church girls?"

He shrugs. "I only date Christians."

"And Chelsea is a Christian?" Is there a denomination for snobs?

"Well, yeah." Charlie reaches for his lemonade. But he's frowning.

"Are you sure?"

He takes a drink. "Are you? A Christian?"

I now hear the NIV translation in my head. Does that count for anything?

"I guess . . . not . . . yet." At his look of disappointment, my words come out in a rush. "But I do believe in God, and I understand about Jesus, and though sometimes I'm overwhelmed by all these rules you have, and some Sundays I really do enjoy church, except for when Hannah's great-grandmother sings solos because she's tone-deaf, but no one has ever told her, but I kind of think that's deceitful, and she sings the same verse over and over and—"

Slam!

I stop mid-rant, leap up, and race to the front door. "What was that?"

Nash scratches his head and looking out toward the front yard. "That . . . was Frances."

"What happened?" I stick my finger in Nash's grunge t-shirt covered chest.

"I think she just asked me out."

Chapter 12

"FRANCES! FRANCES, WHERE are you?"

No response. I search the yard for an annoying three minutes until I finally get the idea to pull out my phone and call her.

Her ringtone, the school fight song, plays loudly from the direction of the station wagon.

By the time it gets to the trumpet solo, I'm staring at my friend, who is lying down in the backseat. On the floor.

I open the car door and peer down.

"Oh, hey, Katie." Frances chews on her lip. "What's new?" She then promptly bursts into tears. "Oh, my gosh! Can you believe I just ran out of the house? I'm freaking out here." She pulls a stray napkin off of the floor and blows her nose. "And when I meant to say, 'Want to study the effects of soy beans on s-s-skin health,'" instead . . . instead I said, 'Do you want go with me to . . .'"

The rest of her sentence is indecipherable due to much sniveling and some unladylike nose blowing.

"Did you ask him out?"

Frances responds by covering her face and howling.

I pat her leg. "This is fixable."

"My dad." Sniff. "He's gonna kill me."

"No, he's not."

"Well, then he'll lock me up in my room and never let me come out until I'm really, really old. Like twenty-five."

"What exactly did you say to Nash?"

"I think I asked him to my cousin Esther's *quinceañera*." Frances hits her head against the door a few times. "My father is going to flip when he hears I asked a boy out. Girls don't do that. Not in my house."

I flick a stale cookie off the seat and gather my thoughts. "So . . . how can we use this?"

"Huh?"

"Frances, I think you should tell Nash you want him to accompany you to your cousin's birthday party in order to do research for the project."

She sits up. "Katie, that's brilliant. Why didn't I think of that?"

"Because you were too busy hiding in the car."

"And how do I explain running out of there?"

I chance a smile. "Invisible killer bees?"

SO HOW DO you cover up these psycho moments in life we all have?

Easy. You get someone else to do it.

I send one final text, mostly satisfied with the results. I simply asked Charlie to take care of the matter. After all, he's close friends with Nash. And if I'm going to suffer through being Chelsea's new BFF at church, then her boyfriend can start helping.

"Should I wear the pink stilettos or the black ones?"

Maxine preens and primps in front of the full-length mirror in my bedroom. *Our* bedroom.

I assess the outfit she's modeling. "This is a simple family dinner at home. Not *Sex in the City*. What's wrong with the jeans and flip-flops you had on earlier?"

It's reckoning time at the Scott house. James and Millie are cooking dinner for Maxine and Sam Dayberry. It should be interesting. Because I don't think Sam's been asked over so my foster parents can praise his bird calling abilities.

And my roommate is nervous. Like throw yourself in the station wagon floorboard nervous.

Maxine grabs a bottle of perfume and sprays it until I start choking.

"What is that stuff? *Ick*. Haven't you ever heard less is more?"

"Sweets, when you're my age all you've got is more. Now . . ." Maxine applies a tart red lipstick. "Do we need to go over hand signals again?"

I turn the next page in my algebra book. "No. For the last time, I've got it."

She turns her attention on me. "When I pick my teeth?"

"I'm to change the subject."

"And if I run a hand through my hair?"

"I'm to provide a distraction."

"Put the book down and focus. There are more important things in life than homework."

Normally I would agree.

"Final challenge, so pay attention. If I wiggle in my seat and raise my eyebrows it means . . .?"

"You ate too many beans at dinner?"

"No! It means that—"

"It means I'm supposed to ask God for a holy miracle, such as stopping time or a call for Armageddon so you will not have to endure another moment of your daughter's disrespectful . . ." I search my memory for the rest of Maxine's command.

"My daughter's disrespectful inquisition into her mother's personal affairs." Maxine nods in satisfaction. She does a full turn in front of the mirror, and her short, black skirt swings around her. "How do I look?"

"Like you belong on *America's Next Top Model*."

Maxine holds my chin and smiles into my face. "Good answer. I think I'll keep you."

"Keep *me*? Um, need I remind you that you are currently residing in *my* room?"

The doorbell announces Sam's arrival, and Maxine gives herself one final look-over. "If I do say so myself, I've still got it."

"Brain rot?"

"Good looks. Now be a dear and go downstairs with me." The beauty queen makes a grab for my hand and hoists me off my bed. "Now, you go first, and when you get down there, I want you to call me down to dinner."

I look at my foster grandmother like she's crazy. It's a facial expression I've come to call "The Maxine."

She grits her teeth and pushes me towards the stairs. "Just do it."

When my feet hit the last step, I make sure everyone, including Sam, is in the kitchen.

My eyes nearly roll back into my head. "Hey, Maxine," I droll.

From the top of the stairs comes a loud throat clearing.

"Oh, Maxine, if you would be so kind as to grace us with your stunningly beautiful presence, I do believe it's time for dinner." I smile at James, but he only shakes his head.

With all the expertise of a practiced Vegas showgirl, Maxine floats down the stairs, her pink spike heels leading the way. "Oh, did you call? I was just upstairs doing a little light reading." Her eyes meet Sam's. "I just finished reading *The Iliad* and *The Odyssey*. I so enjoy a good book when I have a free moment."

James puts a hand on my shoulder and murmurs near my ear. "Maybe she could shovel out some of the manure in here—when she's done reading her classics."

"Maxine, you look lovely," Sam says in reverent awe. "And that dress . . . It makes you look like Penelope."

Maxine scowls. "Who in the world is Penelope?"

"It's Odysseus's wife." Millie says tightly.

With a shrug, Maxine enters the kitchen. "I must've skipped that page."

There is a moment of awkward silence in which no one knows

what to do. Since they're outed, can Sam hug his girlfriend? Does Millie use this time to tell Sam how disappointed she is in her theater caretaker? Should James ask Sam what his intentions are?

"Frances asked a boy out today."

I'm sorry. The tension was getting to me.

I explain the story in detail as we move to the dining room, a room that is rarely used around here.

The table is set with brown tapestry placemats and fine china. The Scotts didn't break out the china when I came to live with them. In fact, I think they hid it.

"If everyone will take their seats, I'll serve dinner." Millie wipes her hands on a towel. "Katie, could you help me in the kitchen?"

Maxine pulls on her ear. What does that mean? She didn't go over that one.

"Um, sure, Millie. I'll be right there."

Sam pulls out a chair for Maxine, seating her to my left.

"What's the ear tug?" I whisper.

She takes a gulp of water, leans over and crunches ice near my cheek. "It means if you leave me alone for too long you will wake up tomorrow with all your bras in the freezer."

I think about this for a moment. "I'll be quick."

Following Millie into the kitchen, I grab dishes like I'm a server at Applebee's. In my right arm I balance a basket of bread, a giant salad bowl, and two bottles of salad dressing. My left arm cradles a bowl of steaming hot French green beans and an overly full serving dish of corn. I want to ask Millie the hundreds of questions I have for her, but I don't.

"Katie, what are you doing? I didn't mean for you to bring in everything." Millie's voice is all concerned, but her face says *Girl, if you drop my dinner, you will be eating off-brand cereal for the next month.*

Channeling my inner Cirque du Soleil acrobat, I manage to race back to the dining room without losing a single bean. Behind me Millie carries a platter of roast beef.

I still marvel at the food in this house. Growing up with my mom, a gourmet dinner consisted of one of those discount frozen dinners. You know, one of those entrees that was covered in gravy, consisted of four thousand calories, and tasted like Alpo.

But Millie cooks like Martha Stewart. When she's not helping out at the church or the Valiant Theater (or dodging my questions), Millie watches the Food Channel in her spare time. I personally find watching cooking shows about as interesting as watching C-SPAN, but James and I both reap the benefits of Millie's odd viewing habits.

"Let's pray." James clears his throat and opens his mouth to begin grace.

"I'll do it." All eyes shift to Millie. "I'll pray tonight."

No one dares to argue. Maxine elbows me beneath the table.

"Our gracious, Heavenly Father. Lord, thank you for this meal. Thank you for this time together. We are grateful for safety, food, and . . . the opportunity to live an honest life in this great country. Lord, we ask that you forgive our sins. Every single one of them. We pray your Holy Spirit would burden our hearts with the need for honesty, and that we would always come to this table and to you with clean hearts. Dear God, we ask you convict us of—"

"Dear Lord, this is Maxine talking." My head snaps up as my tablemate interrupts. "Father, you and I go way back. Let's face it. I've known you longer than . . . others here. God, I pray you would remind us of your command to honor our parents. Teach us to honor our elders with respect and all the reverence they are due. Lord, I have been maligned lately and—"

Millie butts in, her voice strong and loud. "God, I pray you would give us discernment. Because Lord we all know we are to honor Biblical truths and not *parental* truths. Now Jesus, you understand hurt. And you tell us you hurt when we hurt, so Lord, I know you carry a daughter's burden. You know how a child of God would feel if her mother was answering clandestine birdcalls in the woods. Hidden by the shrubs and—"

"Enough!" James waits until he has every eye on him. "You two should be ashamed of yourselves. This is a time of prayer. This is not how we talk to God and ask him to bless our food. Is this the godly example you want Katie to witness?"

The ladies drop their heads, leaving James, Sam, and I to stare at one another. We all share an eye roll and then James continues.

"I will now say grace. And then we will discuss this issue like adults. Godly adults."

James prays over our food, and we hesitantly begin dinner. Almost wordlessly dishes are passed and food is served.

"I would like to say something." Sam's deep voice is like a bullhorn amidst the near silence.

Millie opens her mouth, but James rests his hand on hers, halting any interruption.

"Millie, I know you've been avoiding the theater lately, so I think it's time you heard my heart. And then you can decide if you want me to remain as caretaker of the Valiant or not." Sam tips back his water glass like he's trying to sip out courage. "I have loved your mother for quite some time now. Even before she knew I existed. She is a woman full of life, faith, and integrity."

Millie crosses her arms and snorts.

"When your mother finally decided to honor me with her company, she thought it would be upsetting to you."

"Why? Why would I care if my mother was dating someone?"

Sam shifts uncomfortably in his seat. "Well, I asked Maxine that many times myself. I, uh, believe she felt like she was protecting you. She's never dated anyone since your father died."

"That was fifteen years ago." Millie says.

Sam tugs at his shirt collar. "Yes. Well, you don't have to tell me that. Maxine, would you like to shed some light on this?"

Maxine helps herself to her third serving of roast beef. "Nah. You're doing good, sweetie. Keep going." She smacks her red lips. "Katie, hand me the gravy bowl."

Sam's helpless looks are lost on Maxine. "So, *ahem*, as I was saying. Your mother felt it was in your best interests if we did not socialize in public and if we didn't tell you of our, um, friendship."

"Friendship?" Millie repeats.

"Fine." My foster grandmother waves a hand. "Our smokin' hot love connection." Sam refills his water glass. Twice. "Millie, I want to make it very clear." He sends Maxine a dagger-like glance. "That your mother and I have acted honorably and godly."

"Yes, fine, so back to why you two couldn't bother to tell anyone about your relationship?" Millie rubs her forehead like it hurts to sort it all out.

Don't try to make sense of it, Millie, I want to say. Maxine defies logic. She's the cost of gasoline. There's no explaining it. You just try and survive it.

Maxine runs a hand through her hair. Her elbow jabs my side. Again. I'm so enthralled in this mess, I completely ignore her. I had no idea normal families had crazy fights too. This is awesome. This argument sounds like it's straight from my old trailer park.

"Oh, for crying out loud, Millie." Maxine sticks her thumb in my direction. "You had a new child in your house. Then there was that fiasco with trying to track down Amy a few months ago. You should be thanking me instead of spitting in my mashed potatoes. I was only thinking of you. Trying to protect you."

"Maybe we should just move on from here." James uses his most preachery voice.

"Oh, eat your corn, James. Sam and my mother owe us an apology."

I flinch as Maxine waves her hand in front of my face. "I'm picking my teeth," she says slowly.

"Then get a toothpick." I shoo her hand away.

"Maxine, your daughter is right. We owe this family an apology. We should have trusted them to want us to be happy. You and I should have been open and honest about all of this . . . Maxine?"

"Oh, all right! Fine. I'm sorry." Maxine throws down her napkin. "I'm sorry, Millie, I am. I do worry about you, though. The last thing I want to do is stress you out even more. I know I can sometimes be a small source of concern anyway."

James and I lock eyes and share a small grin. Maxine has been known to ride her bicycle into chicken trucks. People in town call her Mad Maxine. She is no *small* source of concern. She's a natural disaster. She makes global warming look insignificant.

"Mom, I want you to be happy. What kind of daughter would I be if I didn't want that for you? I feel like you don't even know me if you think I couldn't handle the idea of you and Sam together."

Maxine stretches her arm across the table and interlocks her hand with Millie's. "Aw, sweetie, I know this is going to come as a surprise, but sometimes . . . I don't do the right thing."

James's body convulses in coughs. I look to the ceiling and wait for lightning to strike.

"I made a mistake, and I'm sorry. Sam and I are both sorry. But we would like to begin dating again with your blessing."

Millie's face softens. "Of course you have my blessing. I love you."

Rising from her chair, Millie wraps her arms around her mom and kisses her on the cheek. I guess that's the difference between this family and where I come from. In this instance we have a happy ending. In my family this evening probably would've ended in yelling, a few beer cans thrown, and my mom slamming the door on her way out for more cigs.

"Who's ready for dessert? We have apple pie tonight—with your choice of whipped cream or ice cream." Millie, now a paragon of peacefulness, backs her way toward the kitchen, taking everyone's orders.

I push away from the table. "I'm stuffed. I think I'll get dessert later." Frankly, I need a break from these loons.

"I'm going to wait on pie too." James stands next to his chair and points at me. "Why don't you and I go outside for a bit?"

"Why? Is there going to be more hugging?"

James shrugs. "Probably." His hand disappears into his shirt pocket only to come right back out. With car keys. "Tonight we're going to start your first driving lesson."

Chapter 13

DRIVING? NOW?

I swallow. "Tonight? But it's late! It's dark!"

"The sun hasn't even set yet. Come on. Driving lesson number one begins in two minutes."

I do not return James's big grin. I don't want to drive. I'm perfectly happy being chauffeured by Frances right now.

"You're never gonna catch a dude if you can't even get a driver's license," Maxine drawls.

I snatch the keys and walk out the front door to the family sedan. With much grumbling I open the car and climb in. James sticks his head in the other side.

"Hey, Katie?"

"Yeah?"

"You're on the wrong side. The driver's side is over here."

"I thought I would just take notes tonight." I tap my head. "Mental notes. You know, study the road." I gesture to the steering wheel. "Go ahead. Get in."

"That's not how it works." James holds the driver's side door open and stands there patiently. Tapping his foot.

"Oh, you wanted me to drive tonight. As in take the wheel. Master the road. Sorry, I guess we have different approaches to learning. See, I prefer to observe, James. I feel that much can be gleaned from—"

"Katie?"

"Yes?"

"Get in this seat."

"Yes, sir."

After we are both buckled in and I've adjusted the rearview mirror a half dozen times, I put the keys in the ignition. The car roars in response.

"Is the car always that loud? Maybe something's wrong with it. We should probably try this some other time."

"So the left pedal is the brake. Put your right foot on it."

All out of stalling tactics, I obey.

"Now the other pedal is the gas, of course. I want you to put the car in reverse, keeping your foot on the brake. When I tell you to, you're going to give it a little gas."

"Maybe we should let Maxine try this. She's good at giving a little gas."

James barely cracks a smile at my attempt at levity. He's in teacher mode and nothing is going to interfere. "Got it in reverse? Now slowly let your foot off the brake and then lightly touch the gas pedal. With that same foot, Katie."

I have two feet! Why can't I use both of them? What's my other foot supposed to do? Just hang out? Maybe when I'm really good I can rest it on the dash.

"There now, you're backing out. Good job. Turn the wheel slightly. Check your rearview mirror and see how you're doing. Keep turning. Great." James smiles and pats me on the back.

I jerk back. Don't touch me, man. I'm driving here. I'm driving! I navigate the car away from the house and down the long gravel driveway. I guess this isn't so bad. I hope I'm not speeding though. I check the speedometer.

Five miles per hour.

"You're doing great. I knew you'd be a pro at this. All right, now you're going to take us out of the driveway. Slowly turn left."

The wheel slips out of my hand, and I jerk it back. The car lurches my way and gravel flies everywhere.

"Easy there. You're doing fine. Just straighten it up a bit."

My foot slips off the gas. I look down to make sure I'm putting it back on the right pedal.

"Katie, watch where you're going." James grabs the wheel and steers us back toward the right side of the road. "Much better. Okay, now you're going to drive us down Smith Street here. Use the blinker. This is a smooth road. Very little traffic."

My hands relax on the steering wheel, and I ease back into the seat a bit. I can do this. I'm actually driving.

I drive us up and down some streets, using my blinker with skill and precision. Well, actually I use the windshield wipers with skill. I have yet to find the blinker on the first try. But our windshield is nice and clean.

The sun rests at the bottom of the horizon, ready to let the moon take over. The In Between sky around me is a springtime mix of violets and blues.

"Super job, Kiddo. I suppose we better wheel her on back home. Why don't we try one last challenge before we go. See that driveway on up there with the gnomes around it?"

I nod my head and study the circular drive at the end of the road.

"I want you to pull into that drive and back out of it. Think you can handle that?"

I smile, now more confident with this driving business. "Sure." Besides, what's the worst that could happen? I take out a few gnomes and their property value goes up?

I drive slowly toward our destination. Feeling brave, I reach over and turn on some driving tunes.

"Katie, there's something I want to talk to you about before we head back." James lowers the volume. "Lighten up on the gas there. Good. Now you're going to ease into the driveway."

My hair hangs loose in my face, and I shove it behind my ears. I think I could do this driving stuff. If I never went any direction but forward.

I check my side mirrors to make sure I'm not destroying any tacky ceramic elves. Turning the wheel slightly I maneuver the car into the driveway. Just about got it. There. I'm in! I did it!

"Nice work, Katie. Now back out of the drive. Bring the car back onto the road. Katie . . . you know how Millie and I have been going to all of these appointments lately?"

"Uh-huh." My focus on the road is like a sniper on his prey. I am relentless. My efficiency knows no bounds. James's voice is barely a buzz in my ear.

"Millie and I have been talking to some doctors, you know. Had quite a few tests."

Just a bit more and I'm in the road. Nothing's coming. Side mirror check—all clear. Rearview mirror check—excellent. Here I go, ready to get back on the street. Just gonna reach for the gear shift and get ready to put it in drive. I'll put my foot on the brake and . . .

What? What did he just say?

". . . so while the news isn't the best, we are hopeful, Katie. We know God's in control." James's eyes are intent on mine. "Are you okay with this? Do you have any questions?"

The houses around me become a blur as I focus on my foster dad. "What did you just say?"

He clears his throat. "I said Millie has cancer."

My head explodes. Or maybe it's my heart. Suddenly I feel nauseous and trapped. Trapped in this car. Must get us back home. No. This is not happening.

"Hey, Katie, put it in park and let me drive us home."

I'm vaguely aware of James's hand on my shoulder. What is it I'm supposed to be doing? Backing out into the street, right? Right. Okay, almost there. Just a few more minutes and I'll be home. Where Millie is. Millie and her cancer.

"Let me drive. Katie?"

Agh, my head. I can't think. Just gonna apply the brake a bit and—

"Hit the brake! Hit the brake! Watch out for the—"

Crash!

"Light pole."

"MILLIE? MILLIE!"

Slamming the front door, I sidestep Rocky and search through the house for my foster mom. I cruise through the living room, the dining room, and kitchen, coming to a halt in the breakfast nook, where Millie sits alone drinking coffee.

"Why didn't you tell me? How long have you known? What did the doctors say?"

My words come out in a jumbled-up mess.

Millie rests her mug on the table. "What happened to your face? There's a huge red mark on your forehead."

Absently I rub the spot above my left eye. "I hit the steering wheel. Millie, I don't understand why—"

"You hit the steering wheel?" Millie is out of her chair in an instant. She wears her mom face now, and her hands grab my cheeks as she looks me over.

"You have to tell me everything you know about the cancer." I jerk my head out of her grasp and take a step back.

James enters the kitchen looking a little disheveled.

"What in the world happened?" Millie shoves me in front of her for James to see. Like he didn't have a front row seat to my little vehicular disaster. "You said you were going to start with the basics tonight, James. Not a lesson on how to deploy the airbags."

I love it when Millie gets motherly. Except for moments like these, when I'm trying to get her to focus on the matter at hand.

"I might've put a little dent in your car." I risk a look at Millie. She winces. Yup, Millie, I wrecked your car. Just my way of saying, *Sorry you have cancer.* Most kids probably would've gone with a Hallmark.

James pours himself a cup of coffee. He inhales the aroma like he's trying to breathe in some strength. "I told Katie about the cancer." He swallows down some java. "Right when she was backing out."

Millie puts a hand to her hip. "And?"

"And Smith Street is short one light pole tonight." James forces a smile.

"Are you okay? Does your head hurt? Did you black out or anything? James, did she black out?"

I grab Millie's hands. "No. I'm fine. Your car isn't, but I'm fine. The issue here is you. What's going on?" I swallow back a lump in my throat. "You have cancer."

Her head nods once. "Yes."

I drop my eyes and focus on the tile floor. "What does this mean?"

Millie's soft hand rests on my shoulder. "It means I'm going to have surgery soon to remove it. They've found three lumps. So they'll go in and remove the breast, the cancer, and then they'll go ahead and do some reconstructive surgery while I'm out. Later I'll take some treatments—some chemo, radiation. It's going to be fine."

I move my shoulder and her hand falls. "Don't say that. It's going to be fine? How do you know? It's not fine." I look at both of them. They don't get it. "Do I have to go home?"

Millie moves in to hug me, but my hands go in the air and I shake my head.

"You're not going anywhere," James says.

"Have you talked to Iola Smartly?"

A look is swapped between my foster parents before Millie answers. "No."

"So you don't know if I have to go back to Sunny Haven yet." I turn away from them both and stand in front of the bay window in the breakfast nook. A single hot tear slips down my face. I brush it away as quickly as it drops.

"There is no reason to think Mrs. Smartly will want you to return to the girls' home. Nothing's changed. James and I still want you here. With us."

Another tear. *Keep it together, Katie. Do not fall apart right now.*

I wrap my arms around myself and sniff. "How bad is the cancer?"

Millie clears her throat. "Things are going to be fine."

"Are you gonna die?"

"No." Millie smiles. "That was one of my first questions. It is serious, but Katie, we know God is in control, right?"

"Are you kidding me?" I swipe my hand over my nose. "How can you think that? Things could not be anymore *out* of control. You have cancer, Millie. Where is God in that? When I was praying and asking God for you to be healthy and not have cancer, where was he then? Because he sure wasn't listening to me."

James closes some distance between us. "Katie, you're new to the faith. I know things don't make a whole lot of sense right now, but God doesn't promise us that we get whatever we want when we pray. And he doesn't guarantee bad things won't happen to us."

"This is just so typical. This is *so* my life. Things were going good. I should have known it wouldn't last."

"Honey, things are going to be all right. This is treatable." Millie tucks a piece of hair behind my ear. "I know it's scary. But I'm going to be depending on you more now."

"I just ran your car into a phone pole." Newsflash! I'm not the one you want to trust with anything important. Like a bumper.

"The car can be fixed." Millie thinks for a moment. "Right? It *can* be fixed, can't it?" At her husband's nod, Millie continues. "We're still going to teach you to drive. You are still going to audition for that play tomorrow. And life will go on. I'm simply going to rely on you a little more in the next few months."

"Whatever you need, Millie. My bone marrow, my blood, you name it."

"I was thinking more along the lines of walking the dog and getting Mom to fold her own underwear."

"Oh." I can do that, too.

My foster mother folds me into a hug. James scoots in and pulls us both to his chest. We stay like this for a full minute. I lean into these two and think about how far we've come. How far I've come. Six months ago I wouldn't have let them lay a hand on me, but now I'm one of them. Aren't I? And I know I need these people. I've come to depend on them. Trust them. But there's really nothing they can do to protect me from this. My reality is that Millie is sick, and I'm going to have to watch her suffer through that. And if the cancer is stronger than her, I'll lose the closest thing I've had to a mom.

"As long as we're here together, why don't we pray?"

James's idea is like a Gatorade shower on our happy huddle. Prayer? Whatever. We've already prayed about this. And God said no. End of story. I really don't have anything more to say to the Big G right now.

"Make room for the matriarch!" Maxine, now dressed in her red silk pajamas, enters the kitchen and butts into our circle. As we bow our heads, James's voice becomes a hum in my brain. Instead of hearing his words to God, I concentrate on the floor. And the Sponge Bob slippers on Maxine's feet.

Chapter 14

Dear Mrs. Smartly,

Thanks for the last letter. Twelve whole lines. Wow, I think that's a new record. When you're as close as we are, I guess words aren't necessary.

Nothing new here. Things are great. Perfect. I'm going to church, learning to drive, Millie has cancer, and I'm auditioning for a play.

Since things are so fabulous here, I see no reason for a case worker to drop by anytime soon. Plus I saw Rocky drooling this morning. I wouldn't want to risk your caseworker's health in case that dog is mad with rabies.

Look, here's the deal. If you jerk me out of this home, I'm telling the world about your secret crush on David Hasselhoff. I mean business. You don't want to cross me on this. I happen to know for a fact you even have some of his old cds. As in the ones you can only get in Germany and other countries where they don't speak English.

Millie has some serious cancer, Mrs. Smartly. They need me. We both know I bring sunshine and boundless happiness into their lives. I am the spring in their step. The color on their cheeks. The reason they get out of bed in the morning. To take me out of this home could jeopardize Millie's health, and I know you don't want that on your polyester-clad shoulders.

And no, I still haven't heard from my mom. But I'm okay with it. I have better things to worry about. Like global warming, the decline in quality reality TV, and you preparing a spot for me at Sunny.

Tell the girls hello for me.

I love you, Miss Hannigan,

Katie Parker

Chapter 15

THE DAY IS here. Friday. My audition. I unscrew the lid on a bottle of diet pop and chug it until I feel the comforting burn on my throat. I like to think that's the caffeine doing its magic. More than likely it's the acid eating my trachea, but whatever. I'm too tired to care. I lay awake all night. When I wasn't worrying about Millie, I was imagining myself having to share a room with eight other girls again. Eight new strangers at Sunny Haven. Maxine obviously wasn't too worried to fall asleep. She snored better than ever.

Frances and Hannah follow me down the hall to the theater. Frances has not stopped with the motivational pep talk. My head is so crammed full of positivity, it's crowding out all the lines I memorized.

The three of us stop at the main doors to the theater. Only those auditioning are allowed in.

Frances pushes her glasses up on her nose. "You're gonna be great. I know you're gonna nail this part. And you've totally been in my prayers."

"Prayers-schmayers."

Frances does a double take. "What?"

"Nothing." Nothing at all. Oh, yeah, except for the fact that I fired God last night. Here's your pink slip, Jesus. Things just weren't working out between us. But probably not something I need to share with Frances. She definitely wouldn't understand.

"I guess I better go in there." My stomach quivers.

Frances gives me a quick hug. "Break a leg!"

Hannah gasps. "Oh, my gosh! That's the meanest thing ever, Frances. I mean, sure, she took out a light pole last night and half of Smith Street was plunged into darkness, but I don't think that's any reason to . . . Ohhhh . . . Here comes Trevor Jackson."

Any lines I have memorized take a flying leap out of my head as Prince Charming himself saunters our way.

"Hey, ladies."

His smile is dazzling. His voice is smoother than a sax in the Chihuahua marching band. "Hey, Katie."

And then the most incredible thing happens. Trevor Jackson—*the* Trevor Jackson—winks at me. Yes, I saw it. His left eyelid closed for a brief second. His left cheek lifted in a smooth grin just for me.

Sighhhhh.

If I have to do someone bodily harm in order to get the part, I will be Cinderella. My foot *so* belongs in that slipper.

I shake my head and try to get some composure. "Hi, Trevor. Are you ready for auditions?" *Don't giggle. Don't blush. Keep a steady gaze.*

Trevor grabs the door handle, and his football ring sparkles under the fluorescent lights. "Oh, I'm ready." He winks again. "I'm always ready. The question is, Katie Parker, are you ready?"

Oh, my gosh. He knows my name. *He knows my name!*

The giggle erupts. *Oh, no. Stop it!* Now is not the time for the Frances in me to emerge. "I'm ready."

Ready for auditions. Ready to go out on a date with you. Ready to spend my life as Mrs. Trevor Jackson.

"Great. See you in there. I'm pulling for you."

And with those beautiful, parting words, Trevor enters the theater. His spicy cologne lingers, and I close my eyes and breathe it in. *Sooo* nice.

Frances grabs my arm and jerks me back to reality. "Katie, that was Trevor Jackson."

I smile in the direction of the stage door. "Yeah. I know."

"I think he was flirting with you. Hannah, did you see that? Was that total flirtage or what?"

Hannah pops her gum. "Frances, what kind of friend tells someone to break her leg?"

"It's a figure of speech," Frances says. It's a drama thing. Break your leg means good luck."

"So wishing this really horrible thing on Katie is actually wishing her luck."

"Yes. Do you get it?" Frances checks her watch. "You better go, Katie." She gives me a quick hug. "Good, er, I mean break a leg."

"Yeah, Katie, I hope you break both of your legs. And an arm!" Hannah slaps me on the back. "While you're at it, break a nail." She looks at Frances. "What? What's worse than breaking a nail? That's gotta be some major good luck I just wished on her."

"Hannah, that's not . . . never mind." Grabbing the door, I give it a pull and step inside. "Thanks for the support, guys. See you later."

Everyone is piled into the first four rows in the theater. Mrs. Hall, garbed in a shocking pink ensemble and matching platforms, chats with Trevor onstage. Her hand shoots out mid-sentence and a prop from *Guys and Dolls* crashes to the floor.

My eyes scan the perimeter like I'm a lion on the hunt. I size up my prey. Many are harmless, but there are a few girls who could easily be a princess.

I sign in and check the list for those auditioning for *Cinderella*. The names take up two full pages. Apparently word traveled fast that Trevor was the leading male. Great. Now every girl at In Between High wants to be an actress.

A heat rushes over me, and suddenly I'm ticked. That's right, I'm mad. I care about this play. If the role goes to some two-bit Barbie doll just because she looks better in a tiara, I am gonna go postal.

I. Am. An. Actress.

This is more than just wanting to be partnered up with the hottest, finest, yummiest boy in school. What if this is the last play Millie gets to see me in? I don't want to be third ballroom dancer from the right. I want to be Cinderella!

Fine. Look out all you primpy, overstuffed, oversprayed, swooning girls. Katie Parker is in the house, and I am not letting you bat your eyelashes all the way to my role. This is war.

"Students! Take your seats please. We are about to get started." Mrs. Hall crosses to center stage, her platforms clicking on the hardwood floor. "As you know Drama I is going to perform *Cinderella* for the community. I am very excited to see you all here. It seems we have many Cinderella candidates. It's time to get serious and focus on the roles you are auditioning for. Do we all have our motivation?"

Oh, I've got my mine.

"Cinderella is a hardworking girl living a tragic life." Mrs. Hall throws her hands to the ceiling. "She gets a chance to go to the ball and meets her Prince Charming. Our prince, of course, will be played by Trevor Jackson."

Sighs and ill-contained giggles ricochet throughout the theater.

Mrs. Hall narrows her eyes. "As I was saying, Cinderella is introduced to her prince. And even though she's dumb enough to fall for his good looks and smooth dance moves, she does eventually get that happy ending." She clutches her heart and laughs bitterly. "Cinderella naively thinks he will always love her. Well, he won't, Cinderella, he won't. Pretty soon he'll trade in the horse and carriage for a Miata convertible and a gym membership. And just when a little gray starts to show in your hair and you've given your last miniskirt to Goodwill, in walks Prince Charming's new secretary. Well, fine! Who needs your stupid glass slipper—"

"Mrs. Hall?"

"Yes, dear?"

"I have to be at baseball practice by six."

Mrs. Hall tugs on her electric pink collar. "Right. Let's get started.

Actors and actresses, I need your attention. We will begin with the reading for Cinderella since that seems to be where the most interest is. You will read a scene with Trevor, your prince. When I call your name please meet go center stage with him."

Sighhh. I would go anywhere with Trevor Jackson. Center stage, stage left, and definitely offstage.

The drama teacher calls girls out alphabetically. Since my last name begins with a P, I have quite a wait. As each Cinderella wannabe recites her lines, I scrutinize every word, every gesture, every vocal inflection. I must be better than the best here. I was born to be Cinderella. I mean, let's think about this. Cinderella comes from a poor background. I do too! Cinderella wasn't used to fine things. Me neither, Cindy. Cinderella is destined to find true love with the prince, who happens to be Trevor. What a coincidence—so am I. The play might as well be titled *Katie.*

An hour slugs by. And then, "Miss. Parker, you are next."

The air whooshes out of my lungs at Mrs. Hall's announcement. Now? Already? If I wasn't giving God the cold shoulder, I would totally be asking for some help. But I'm through with that, so it's all up to me. I am gonna blow these people out of the water.

My legs carry me up the steps and to center stage. Trevor's easy grin gives me a small sense of comfort. The sight of forty girls glaring back at me does not.

Okay. Shoulders back, deep breath.

Hold on to your *thee-uh-tuh* seats because I am here to dominate.

"Katie, are you ready, dear? Begin reading from page thirty-seven."

I face Trevor. Oh, my. He has the best teeth. How does a guy get his teeth so pearly white? They look like an actor's teeth, so perfect and—

"Get on with it, dear." Mrs. Hall makes a grand gesture with her bangled arm.

Right. I take one last look at the script then put it down.

Mrs. Hall shakes her head. "No, dear, this doesn't have to be memorized. Don't you need your script?"

"No." My eyes lock on Trevor's.

With my muse right before me, I grab his hand and recreate the scene in which the prince dances with Cinderella. There is no In Between, there is no Katie or Trevor. On this stage stands Cinderella and her prince. Two people on the path to love, happiness, and some really good costumes.

"And when I dance with you, it's like all my cares float away. I will never forget this evening." I am so smooth.

"Good lady, you must give me your name. I beg of you." Trevor's deep voice sends a chill down my spine.

"My name is of no matter. This dance is all that . . . What is that? I must go. No, I must leave you. Good-bye." And I tear myself from Trevor's arms, fleeing to stage right.

I'm not sure, but I think I might've just achieved brilliance. Mrs. Hall's face is beaming. She nods her head in appreciation.

"It's in the bag." Trevor stands next to me and whispers low.

"I don't know." I shrug innocently. "I just went out there and did what I could. I know it's nothing you're used to working with. I'm new to drama."

"You were awesome." One hand goes on my shoulder. "I'll call you if I hear anything. But you know who I'm pulling for."

I laugh softly. "Thanks." My fingers rest on his briefly before he returns to center stage. That's right, I just dared a hand touch. Score.

If Trevor wants me to be the lead, then that will seal the deal.

My heart filled with glee and giddiness, I skip off the stage.

"Chelsea Blake."

And nearly trip down the last step. What? Who?

"Chelsea, please take the stage."

No! That glee spontaneously combusts as I see Charlie's girlfriend approaching the stage. Where did she come from? She's in a Drama I class? How did I not know this? Ugh. She's everything I'm not. Sun-kissed blonde hair, legs that scream supermodel, and pouty lips that are never without shimmery gloss. I can't even remember to apply the occasional ChapStick.

My lunch threatens to climb back up my throat. I can't stay here. I will not watch that girl violate the laws of good acting by whining and posing through the audition.

God, I would just like to take a break from ignoring you to say this is not fair. You made Chelsea blonde and beautiful. And a boy-magnet. I get the stage. Is that too much to ask for? Have I ever said, God, can I have a C cup? No. Acting is my thing. Let her stick to what she's meant for. Like boys. And filing her nails.

Grabbing my backpack, I hustle it out of the theater and into the auditorium lobby. I fling open my purse, grab my phone, and punch in Millie's number.

No answer. How am I supposed to get home?

Ten minutes later I'm pressing redial for the millionth time. Where is my foster mom?

The theater doors sail open, and I turn my head. Trevor.

"Hey, Katie, are you waiting on a ride?"

"It seems my ride is MIA." It takes everything within me not to quiz Trevor about Chelsea's performance. Surely it was bad though. She fails at *acting* nice on a regular basis.

Trevor holds up his keys with a jangle. "How about I take you home?"

Gulp. How about it? On one hand, it gives me the chance to show Trevor how I could be the planet orbiting his sun. And what if something is wrong with Millie that she isn't answering her phone? I definitely need to get home. On the other hand, Millie will flip out if a boy brings me home without permission. She's all strict like that.

"Uh . . ."

Trevor takes a step closer to me. "What's the matter, Katie?" He smiles. "Don't you like me?"

Like you? Hello, you say the word and your name is carved onto every notebook I own.

"Yeah." I stare into his Hershey brown eyes. "I'd like a ride."

I float behind him toward the parking lot.

Trevor stops and studies me. "You didn't tell me whether or not you liked me."

Be cool. The school parking lot (especially next to the overflowing trashcan) is not the place to confess my undying love. What did that teen magazine I read last month say? To act slightly aloof. Mysterious.

"I might like you, Trevor." Insert alluring smile here. "I haven't decided yet."

"TAKE THIS NEXT right."

My ride is almost over. I run my hand over the leather interior of Trevor's Hummer. Yes, the boy drives a Hummer. Mostly I don't get the draw of these vehicles. I'm sure a tank of a truck comes in handy sometime. Like when you need to reorganize some mountains. Or if Trevor gets called to war, he can just drive on into the battlefield. Crush some small countries with his enormous tires.

Regretting the ride has reached its conclusion, I point Trevor into the Scotts' long drive.

"Well, have a good practice." Was that lame? I think that might've been lame.

Trevor puts the gear in park. "I guess I'll see you at our first rehearsal—Monday, after school." His arm travels to my seat rest. "Catch ya later, Cinderella."

"Whatever. I'll probably get a backstage role. Girl who hangs up costumes."

Millie appears on the front porch. I can see her frown from the car.

"I better go. Thanks for the ride." I open the door.

And fall out.

"Oh!"

"You okay?" Trevor calls out.

I jump up. "I'm good!" A little further down than I thought. "Guess I need to work on my dismount." And bandage my pride while I'm at it. Sixteen-year-old girl dies in driveway. Cause of death? Total embarrassment.

I shut the massive door and wave good-bye to Prince Charming.

"Katie, who was that?"

I jump at Millie's voice.

"Oh, hey, Millie." My ankle throbs.

"Who was that boy?"

"Trevor Jackson. He's directing our play. And he's in it."

Millie's eyebrows rise. "You were not to leave the school until I picked you up. You know my expectations."

I catch the full force of her attitude, and I feel the old Katie Parker threatening to come out. The me from six months ago would've said something smart and walked off about now.

"I called you, Millie. I called you a dozen times." I try to keep my voice even. But really, what is this inquisition for? It's not like I've been out causing trouble with this guy. And it's not like this family is into full disclosure.

"I told you I would pick you up."

"You didn't answer your phone."

"Mother changed my ringtone again. When I heard the rap song going off twenty minutes ago, I thought it was her phone. I'm sorry. But I don't want you riding around with people I don't know. I've never met that kid."

"I said his name is—"

"Trevor. Yes, I heard you. But do I know him? No." Millie flails an arm like Mrs. Hall. "Do I know it's safe for you to be in a car with him? No. And do I feel comfortable with you being alone with boys—especially without my permission? Absolutely not."

My face burns. And it's not from the fading sun.

"Look, I called. Just like you told me to. And you were nowhere to be found. I just wanted to get home. For your information, I was worried about you." Okay, that's only part of the reason I left with Trevor. "What if you were sick and couldn't get to your phone?"

Millie frowns. "Why would I be sick?"

"Because you have *cancer*? Excuse me for being concerned and wanting to rush home and see if you were lying on the floor unconscious!"

Cluck-cluck! Squaaaawk!

My head jerks at the noise. "What was that?"

Millie inhales loudly. "It's nothing. You know, cancer doesn't really work that way."

I come at her with full volume. "Well, how would I know? You haven't told me anything. *Nada!* Nothing!"

Cluck-cluck! Squaaaawk!

"I'm not sick. I'm perfectly fine right now, and you shouldn't worry about me. I'm not concerned in the least."

"Millie?"

"Katie, the point is . . . What?"

"What," I point. "is that?"

Cluck-cluck! Squaaaawk!

Millie looks behind her. "Oh, that's a chicken. Listen, do you understand we have rules here and when you—"

"Why is there a chicken in the yard?"

"Pipe down out here. There's a noise ordinance in this town, for crying out loud." The screen door slams as Maxine comes onto the porch. She plants her hands on her hips. "And there's not *a* chicken in the yard. There're four of them. Think of them as our new pets." Maxine circles a finger near her head then points at Millie.

I slowly nod, feeling like I'm missing the punch line. "Pets. And what are we calling them?"

Maxine smiles. "Dinner."

"They're free-range chickens. I bought them today."

"Millie," I say. "It's understandable you're stressed, but most people shop for purses or shoes when they're overwhelmed. Not poultry."

"She's on a health kick." Maxine consults her watch. "Started about two o'clock."

Millie rolls her eyes. "I've decided we're going to eat healthier, that's all. More natural."

My eyebrows lift. "And we're doing this because . . .?"

"Because," Millie's voice drops to a mumble, "there's medical evidence a natural diet can help . . . Well, that it can be good for you. Hey, who's ready for dinner?"

"Ew!" I stare at the red and gold fluff ball pecking at the ground.

"No, the chickens are for eggs." Millie casts her mother a warning glare. "Not for dinner."

"I had a great audition, by the way." So obviously Millie is completely preoccupied with the cancer, but she could at least take five seconds to ask about my day.

Millie pulls me to her in a hug. "Oh, honey, I prayed for you all day. I knew you'd be wonderful." She pats my back. "But from now on I want to know where you are at all times. And with whom. And no going anywhere with anybody unless you have my permission."

"Woo! That boy was hot." Maxine slaps her knee. "If I were thirty years younger . . ."

Millie snorts. "They'd arrest you."

Chapter 16

"YOUR COUSIN IS really pretty." My eyes are glued to Esther, who is currently in the middle of a dance number with her partner and about fourteen other couples her age. The group waltzes in perfect time across the country club ballroom to a melody played by a string quartet. Yes, In Between doesn't have a single McDonalds, but they have two golf courses and a country club. That's some messed-up priorities if you ask me.

"Yeah, she's beautiful," Frances grumbles and checks the door one more time for her science partner to arrive. So far, no Nash. And no Charlie.

"How long did they work on that dance?" I ask in awe. "Everyone is doing the same thing at the same time." It's like watching ballroom dancing on ESPN2.

Frances forces a laugh. "Only the best for Cousin Esther. Her parents hired a choreographer." She sees my look of disbelief. "*Quinceañeras* are a big deal to my father's family."

"Yes, but not to this one." Mr. Vega butts into our conversation, jerking his chin in Frances's direction. "We could've had her *quinceañera* at the White House, and Frances would not have cared. Would not have been grateful. See how Esther smiles? *She* embraces her culture. *She* isn't embarrassed by it."

"Katie, pass the beanie weenies. My dad wants me to embrace our culture. Like Esther." Frances ladles some onto her plate and takes a bite. *"Mmmm.* Taste the homeland."

Mr. Vega crosses his arms and glares. "There is nothing wrong with your cousin's food choices. Katie is not ashamed to enjoy our culture."

All eyes at the table turn to me as I'm shoving a chip overloaded with guacamole into my mouth. I look at Frances, my mouth full of dip. "You gotta try this."

My leg receives a sharp kick beneath the table. *"Ow.* Sorry."

"No," she whispers. "Look. Nash and Charlie are here." Frances curls her lip. "I hope Esther doesn't see them. She's always trying to one-up me. If Nash gets one look at her in her dress and tiara, it's over."

Nash and Charlie stop at the entrance and survey the scene. Frances abruptly stands up and waves her arms to get their attention.

"Frances, watch out, you—"

Down goes a waiter, clothes-lined by Frances's arm.

"Oops, oh, my, um . . . I'm sorry, sir. Here, let me help you up."

"No," the waiter protests. "That's okay, I've got it. No, really, miss, please don't—"

Crash! Frances looses her grip on the waiter's hand and lands right on top of him and his serving tray.

By this time, a small crowd has gathered. The celebratory waltz is no longer the main event.

I launch out of my seat and heave Frances off the poor waiter just as Nash and Charlie arrive at our table.

A short, elderly woman punches Mr. Vega's shoulder *"Qué es éste ruido? Tú estás aruinando la quinceañera de mi Esther."*

Frances translates in my ear. "What's this noise? You are ruining my Esther's *quinceañera.*"

"Ah, mama. Just a little accident. It's all taken care of." Mr. Vega kisses the woman on both of her wrinkled cheeks.

Frances whispers, "That's my grandma. She's mean. Esther's her favorite."

The woman glares at Frances. She waddles around the Vega family table, pinching every family member on the cheek and muttering in Spanish.

Grandma Vega stops when she gets to me.

I look at Frances. Then back at her grandma. "Hi there." She stares at me for a full minute. Do I have tamales in my teeth again?

Grandma Vega smiles tightly then clenches my cheeks.

"En ese vestido pareces una campesina."

I return her smile. "What did she say?" I think she likes me.

Mrs. Vega pipes up. "She says you are lovely."

Frances takes a long swig of punch. "She says your dress makes you look like a village peasant."

I remove my face from the woman's grip.

With one last evil eye for Frances, Grandma Vega departs for another table.

Mr. Vega stands. "Welcome, Nash and Charlie." His words are polite, but his voice is curt. "We are glad to have you here. Please, sit. The father-daughter dance is about to begin."

We all take our seats and focus on Esther. Her father meets her in the middle of the dance floor. He carries a pillow with a pair of high heels on it.

"What is that?" Nash asks.

Frances sighs. "Her father is presenting her with a pair of high heels. She'll take off her flats and wear the new shoes. It's a sign she is a woman now and not a child." Frances leans in, "She's still a total child. High heels are so not gonna help her."

Wow, so far this has been a really cool experience. This girl has raked in the presents, too. And she gets a new pair of shoes? Sign me up. I want a *quinceañera.*

"So, Nash, you are my daughter's science fair partner?"

Uh, oh. Here we go. Mr. Vega is so protective of his daughter.

The waiter brings Nash and Charlie plates full of tamales, salad, rice, and something called roast pork *carnitas.*

"Yeah, we're working on . . . er, what did you say our project was again?" Nash glances at Frances.

Frances stares back, like Nash's eyes are holding her captive in a trance. I give her a solid elbow to the ribs.

"Oh, right, our science fair project. We are effecting the various ethical diets of our study. I mean, we are ethicating the dietecting studies of our various effects." Frances grabs her punch glass and drains it.

Mrs. Vega puts down his fork. "I thought you said you were studying the effects of various ethnic diets."

"Exactly what I just said."

Mrs. Vega balances the baby in her lap. "And you, Katie? What are you and Charlie researching?"

I reach into my oversized purse and pull out two small potted ferns. "We are collecting data on the effects of sound on plants. According to Charlie, Leafy and Spiky here are going everywhere with us for the next two weeks." I slide one near Charlie's plate. "Here, you can at least take one of them. That way we both look like dorks. I don't want to keep all the fun for myself."

The slow song ends and Esther's father spins her under his arm. Everyone claps and *oooohhhs* and *ahhhhs*. Everyone but Frances. The DJ, set up in a far corner, announces the dance floor is open. A pop hit pounds through the room.

My friend catches my eye and whispers, "Meet me under the table." Her head ducks under the tablecloth.

You have got to be kidding me. She slaps my knee.

Fine. I turn to Charlie. "I'll be right back. Don't let anything happen to Leafy while I'm gone." And under I go.

"Katie, I can't do this. You have to help me. I'm making a fool of myself in front of Nash." Her eyes go wide. "Again."

Ugh, there's an entire gum collection under here. "Ask him to dance."

"No! Are you crazy?"

"Am *I* crazy? Who's the one asking for a conference under a table? Not me."

"I can't ask him to dance!"

"Yes, you can. And you will. Get him out on the floor, then talk about your science project. I'm going up. See you topside."

My head breaks the surface. Frances's parents are too busy with the other children to have noticed our absence, but Charlie and Nash have both frozen mid-fork at my reappearance.

I clear my throat. "She thought she lost a contact."

From a shrill voice behind me comes, "Frances doesn't wear contacts."

Slowly I turn around. Esther, in all of her gossamer gown glory. Her long, pink formal poufs out like a ballerina's tutu. I wonder if she'd let me borrow that gown for the play. Probably not. I have a feeling this girl doesn't share much.

After bumping her head, Frances makes it back up for air. "Oh. Hi, Esther."

"Did you see what Grandma Vega got me for my birthday?" Esther holds up the diamond cross around her neck. "Isn't it the best?"

Frances rolls her eyes. "No, actually I think the dictionary set she got me for my *quinceañera* was the best. And every time I come across a word like *expurgation,* I cherish it all the more."

"Who are your friends?" Esther runs her manicured hand over the top of Nash's chair. "You know, the dance floor is open. I might be persuaded to dance with you. I don't want to leave out a single guest." She eyes Nash like I was eyeing the cake earlier.

"He's dancing with me." Frances lurches out of her chair, grabs Nash's hand, and drags him all the way to the dance floor.

Esther's dark eyes caress Charlie.

"Great party." He smiles nervously at the she-cat. Then his hand finds mine. "Katie, this is my favorite song. Come on."

Charlie doesn't let go until we are in the center of the dance floor, surrounded by other people getting down with their bad selves. He lets go of my hand only to grab my waist and pull me closer.

"You're an actress. Act like you like me."

Reluctantly, I slide my arms around his neck. We start moving to the beat of a very old slow song.

Desperate to take the awkward out of the moment, I look into his face and smirk. "So . . . Britney Spears's 'I'm Not a Girl' is your favorite song? I had no idea. Is there anything else I should know?"

His eyes are on Esther, making sure she is a safe distance away. "No, I don't think so."

"Nothing? Like maybe you enjoy wearing pink underwear on the weekends? Or besides listening to Britney ballads, you also enjoy songs from your Celine Dion collection?"

Charlie tears his gaze from Esther and focuses on me. The impact of his smile catches me off guard, and my heel lands on his foot. "Oops, sorry. You know, we should probably be charting Leafy and Spiky's reaction to this song. Unlike you, they're probably real men and don't go for this sort of tune."

"Leafy and Spiky are men? Since when?"

"Since now." I watch my hand in Charlie's.

Charlie smiles and spins me around. I come back into his arms like we've practiced the move a hundred times. Aside from some junior high PE classes, I don't have a whole lot of ballroom experience.

I search the masses for Nash and Frances. I locate them dancing near the DJ. Or Nash is dancing. Frances sways in a zombielike fashion. It's not pretty. But they're out there. And they're together. And she hasn't thrown up on him yet. I do believe this is progress.

"So are you going to the spring dance?" Charlie asks.

I have heard about this yearly March event, but haven't given it much thought. Who's to say I'll still be here in March? "Oh, yeah. I just have to decide which boyfriend I'm going with. Which hearts I'll break."

And did I mention I've never been to a school dance? Yeah, I know—shocking. But dances require dresses, and until I lived with the Scotts, I didn't have a lot of clothing options. And though it's not a prom or anything, this dance requires a formal. The only formal dress I've ever owned was a twenty-five-year-old prom dress my mom found for me for Halloween one time when I went as an eighties Madonna.

Charlie's eyes narrow on something across the room. "Smile at me. Like you mean it."

I think of Reese Witherspoon the moment she enters Tiffany's in *Sweet Home Alabama*. I look at Charlie like he's the only one in the room. He pulls me closer.

"I saw you riding through town with Trevor yesterday."

Cut scene. Smile over.

"So?" I don't believe I like his tone. "We're both in *Cinderella* together. Well, that is if I get a part." And I will.

We move across the floor in silence. I take the moment to appreciate his clothing choices. Charlie Benson can dress. Not in a really deliberate I-spent-two-hours-picking-out-this-outfit way, but in a style that looks like he just threw some stuff together and ended up looking like an *American Eagle* model. His khakis fit nicely on his football player body. The shirt I'm leaning against is a button-down, decorated in a small, trendy pattern. And he doesn't even wear athletic socks with his dress shoes.

Then I notice his frown.

"You should be careful with Trevor Jackson."

He swings me out and reels me back in. Charlie is quite an accomplished ballroom dancer. It took me falling out of a tree last semester to find that out.

"What do you mean? I'm not dating him. We're in a play together."

"He's a total player. That's all." Charlie's voice is kind and caring, but it sends my blood to boiling.

"Yeah, when Trevor took me home when I was stranded at school without a ride, I thought, that guy's such slime. How could he not think I wouldn't see through his ploy? Because a real gentleman would've let me walk home."

"That's not what I meant, I just—"

"Forget it," I snap. "I can take care of myself. And the day Trevor Jackson is interested in me is the day I run across campus naked."

"Well, of course, he could be interested in you. You're smart, you're funny, you're pretty—never mind. Just keep an eye out. The dude's ruthless."

I'm smart? And funny? Charlie Benson thinks I'm all of that? My head spins.

Why didn't he say I was a good actress?

Oh, well. Take what you can get.

"So . . . are you saved yet?"

My bubble of temporary happiness bursts. "Ever heard of a little tact? Who just comes out and asks that?"

Charlie smiles. "I do."

"No, I'm not there yet. I'll text you when I do."

"You wanna talk about it?"

"No." The song fades and a fast paced beat begins. I step away from smooth moves Charlie. "I'm gonna check on Frances then monitor our plants. I want to make sure they survived that last song."

"What if Esther comes back?"

"Tell her you've got a girlfriend." And it's not me.

I weave in and out of dancers, but Frances and Nash are nowhere to be found. They're not at any of the tables either. Probably outrunning Esther. Or Grandma Vega.

Taking my search into the hall, I see a familiar blur go by.

"Trevor?" It's like I conjured him up.

He hoists a golf club bag on his shoulder and turns around. "Well, hello there. What are you doing here?"

"A party. And you?"

"Just hitting a few today before the sun sets."

He's a country club member. Reason number 496 why this guy would *never* be interested in me. He'll probably grow up and marry someone with the last name of Hilton or Hilfiger.

His golf attire is adorable. Most people look like dorks in golf-wear. Not Trevor. He could wear a trash bag and still look totally hot.

He smiles and his eyelids drop a bit as he comes closer. "Katie, you did a great job during your audition."

Now this is a man who appreciates art. Who knows talent. Who would never allow Chelsea Blake to slip her perfectly pedicured foot into my glass slipper. "Really? I don't know. I have so much to learn."

"I did notice there are a few things you need to work on, just to take it to the next level."

Was that suggestive? Because coming out of his mouth, it sounded totally hot.

"Like what?" I ask.

"Maybe we should get together sometime. Work on a few things."

My head is about to explode. Did Trevor Jackson just say we needed to get together? Is this my life? This stuff does *not* happen to me!

I shake my head to make sure I'm not dreaming. Nope, he's still there. Looking gorgeous. And watching me. I want to get my phone out and take a picture of this moment.

"Um . . ." I giggle. "Yeah. That would be great. Anytime."

With a single finger he taps my nose. "I'll call you."

I stand there in a Frances-like stupor as he struts away. Oh, my. I think I'm having a hot flash.

"See what I mean? Total parasite."

I wheel around. And find Charlie.

"How long have you been standing there?" My face flushes. How dare he ruin this perfect moment?

"Long enough." He shakes his head. "Frances needs you. If you can tear yourself away from Trevor long enough to help her out."

I bite my tongue. "What's wrong?"

"She passed out."

"Where is she?"

"On Esther's cake."

Chapter 17

"I**T WASN'T A** total disaster." I try to console Frances at church Sunday morning. It's not working.

"My grandmother says I've ruined Esther's entire fifteenth year."

I think Esther's lack of personality will ruin her year before an absence of cake does her in. "Frances, really, I wouldn't give it another thought."

"One day later, and I'm still blowing pink icing out my nose."

"Maybe Nash would find that sort of thing hot. I mean a girl who can produce icing on command? What's not to like?" My eyes are on the door, as I watch all the teens filing in for the pre-church youth service. These Christians—sometimes I just don't get it. We have church. Then we go to the sanctuary and have some more church. From what I hear, our youth service is better than Sunday School. Frankly, how could anything with the word *school* attached to it be holy? Or the least bit interesting.

"It was really sweet the way Nash tried to help you up."

"Yeah, it was. Until my dad got all possessive and pulled that fork on him." Frances groans and lays her head down on the aluminum seat in front of her. "My life is over. My dad's never going to let me date. Nash won't ever want to be seen with me again." She bangs her head on the chair. "My own grandmother doesn't even like me. If only life were as easy as a calculus test."

Yes. If only.

"Maybe I could talk my dad into moving."

"Frances, nobody but Charlie and Nash even know about it. Let it go."

"Hey, Frances! Get all that icing out of your hair?" Hannah bellows across the room, heralding her arrival.

"Nobody knows?" Frances whines. "The video footage is probably all over YouTube, titled "Girl Falls In Cake. Loses One Earring and All Her Self-Respect."

"Hello, girls. I like your shoes, Katie."

Frances lifts her head in bewilderment. I turn around to be sure my ears aren't deceiving me. Because that sounded like Chelsea Blake. In fact, it sounded like Chelsea being nice.

"Um . . . hi, Chelsea." Or girl who looks like Chelsea. Her boyfriend stands by her side. His eyes flit to me before he smiles warmly at Frances.

"Great party Saturday, Frances. Thanks for letting us work on our projects there," Charlie says.

"Yeah, I heard about your little tumble." Chelsea awkwardly pats Frances's shoulder. "These things happen to all of us."

"Really?" Frances grits her teeth. "You've done a whole body belly flop into a five-tier cake? You've sent the cake and the table it's on crashing into the ground? Did you single-handedly cause a cake to explode under your impact, covering every person within a ten-foot radius, including your grandmother, with strawberry icing?"

Chelsea attempts a smile. "Well, no."

"Charlie, where is Spiky?" I notice my science partner does not have the other plant. "I brought Leafy this morning. I thought we agreed we would take them with us everywhere."

His girlfriend laughs. "I wasn't going to let him bring that silly plant with him to church. Come on, Katie. You were just kidding about that, right?"

I glare at Charlie.

Chelsea continues. "Actually, I was talking to Charlie, and I really don't know if your project is up to his caliber. I think you're underestimating Charlie's ability if your idea of an experiment involves him toting around a fern all day." She laughs like there was a punch line.

"We came up with the idea together." My eyes shoot daggers—no, machetes—at Chelsea's brilliant boyfriend.

"Well, maybe you should come up with something else," Chelsea purrs. "Charlie is in the running for valedictorian. He doesn't need you bringing his grade down."

"Now, wait a minute, I—"

"Katie," Charlie's hand on my shoulder cuts me off. "Why don't you show me how your plant is doing. I could get a comparison."

I close my mouth. And glare. "Fine. I'll take you to Leafy." We walk toward the stage. "But I don't want your girlfriend's negativity anywhere near my plant."

We walk next to a giant speaker upstage where I have placed Leafy. "He seems to really like music. I wanted him to be close."

Charlie nods. "Yeah. That's great. Just write down your data."

"Are you not going to say anything?"

He lifts up the plant and inspects a frond. "Say what?"

I grab my plant back. "Like you're sorry?"

"Sorry? For telling you to watch out for Trevor?"

"What? No. For Chelsea totally insulting me. Insulting our plant." I hold Leafy to my chest. "And get off Trevor's back. It's getting annoying."

"Chelsea's just looking out for me. She can be a bit much."

A Rottweiler with rabies is a bit much. Chelsea is beyond bearable. "If I'm holding you back, Charlie, then do your science project on your own." My cheeks burn red. Am I too stupid to be this guy's partner? At least I'm not dumb enough to date someone like her.

"No, of course you're not holding me back. Forget what she said. We have a good project, and we need to stick with it." Charlie runs his fingers through his hair. "Hand me the plant so I can check it out."

"You're not touching him. You weren't responsible enough to bring his brother. If Chelsea really wants the truth, *you're* the one not pulling your weight in this project."

"And you're not holding up your end of our bargain by hanging out with Chelsea."

"I'm not . . ." I shake my head. "You say I haven't . . ." My brain is about to explode with horrible, mean things. "First of all," I spit out, "your girlfriend is . . . is . . ."

"She has nobody here. No girls to hang out with anyway. Why aren't you helping?"

"You haven't helped Frances." And your girlfriend's a shrew!

"Whatever. I got Nash to Esther's party, didn't I?"

I jab my finger into his chest. "I need more output from you."

"Fine," Charlie frowns, then looks away. "Just help Chelsea this morning. Please?"

The only thing that's gonna help her is a personality transplant.

"Do it." His voice is bitter in my ear.

"Why are you acting like you're mad at *me*?"

Charlie's eyes finally focus on mine. "I just . . . I . . . I'm not mad at you. It's just—"

"Hey, guys, take your seats. We have lots to talk about today." Pastor Mike jumps on the stage, dissolving my conversation with Charlie.

"Try and be her friend, okay?" Charlie takes Leafy from my hands and places him back on the floor next to the speaker.

Charlie and I walk back to where we left Frances and Chelsea. Frances doesn't bother to hide her relief at our return.

"Chelsea was just telling me she's thinking of spending Spring Break with our youth group," Frances says with forced enthusiasm.

Charlie catches my eye and inclines his head toward Chelsea.

"Wow. That's . . . um, great. You know we're doing mission work that week, right?"

Chelsea flips her golden hair. "Well, of course. I bought some new Coach luggage. I can't wait for everyone to see it."

I take my seat. "Yeah, that will look great. I'm sure all the homeless people will love your designer bags."

Pastor Mike sets his Bible down. His bald head shines under the stage lights, but he doesn't wear his usual pirate grin. He looks tired and worn.

"Welcome, everyone. Guys," the pastor runs a hand down his face. "I have a lot to share with you today." The room quiets, as his intensity has everyone's attention. "Last night we got a phone call. My wife's father was killed in a car wreck. She flew out at midnight to be with her family in Memphis. And I'll be leaving this afternoon."

My heart clenches. Tears sting the back of my eyes. I may be on a permanent hiatus from God, but I like Pastor Mike. And his wife. I feel terrible for her. Yet another example of God not stepping in. Why did this guy have to die? Where was God? He wasn't too busy healing Millie, that's for sure.

Pastor Mike swabs at his eyes. "Right now, I just want to pray for my wife, her family, pray for all of us."

We bow our heads. I stare at my lap, not wanting to close my eyes. Not wanting to make that full connection with the G-Man.

"Dear Heavenly Father, I come to you tonight shaken and saddened. Lord, I pray for my wife, for my mother-in-law, and family. I ask for strength and comfort in this horrible time. God, I don't have any answers here."

That makes two of us.

"I don't know why this happened. I do know when we hurt, you hurt."

Whatever.

"Hebrews tell us faith is the substance of things hoped for, the evidence of things not seen. I sure can't see the sense in any of this. All my family is seeing is pain, and all we have are questions."

Preach it, brother. I totally understand.

"But we will rely on you. Put our trust fully in you."

Whoa, no. Where are you going with this?

"Lord, there are others here tonight who are also hurting. They have problems that seem much bigger than you. Questions that don't have answers. Situations that don't make sense."

I can testify to that.

"Maybe their parents are getting a divorce. Maybe someone is sick. Maybe every day at school is torture. I know there are needs in this room. There are doubts. There are people mad at you, God."

Try furious.

"And this morning I ask your Holy Spirit go to work on these kids. Let them know your love is constant. And even though life is unpredictable, your love is never changing. You care more for us than we do. There's a person sitting here right now who feels like you've turned your back on him. Or her."

I lift my eyes to see if the pastor is looking at me, but his head is down. His full concentration is on this prayer.

"There is a person here tonight who thinks you don't exist. You can't be real."

Now this is just creepy. Do I have a sign over my head or something?

"God, we know those are doubts Satan has placed in this person's heart. And it takes a stronger person to not listen to that. It takes a stronger person to run to you even when things don't make sense. When we're hurting. When there is no happy ending."

Warm tears slowly slip down my cheeks. Pictures of Millie, James, and my time with them pass through my mind like a slide show. Millie cooking dinner. Millie taking me shopping for a new wardrobe when I first came to stay with them. My bedroom—decorated by Millie.

God, I don't want to lose Millie. I don't want to be taken away from this family. Where are you? Why are you doing this? How can you just let these things happen? Death. Cancer. My life before the Scotts.

I just don't know. I was so close to buying all of this—to believing in you. And then everything stopped making sense. And now Laura's dad? Is Millie next? You didn't protect her father. Why should I believe you're going to save Millie?

"You don't promise us you'll make sense. You only promise us you're in control. And you will take care of us. If anyone knows sacrifice, it's you. If anyone knows the pain of watching a loved one suffer, it's you. Deal with our doubts. Help us get past those fears. So we can run into your waiting arms."

Pastor Mike closes up his prayer amidst a symphony of sniffles and broken cries. I wipe my own eyes, desperately wanting to erase all traces of a reaction. Silly, I know. The whole room is sniveling, but I don't want to be a part of that. I want to be dry-eyed. Unaffected.

The pastor opens up the area in front of the stage like an altar. The band begins to play softly as people pray individually and in small groups.

"Katie?" Frances whispers beside me. "Do you want us to pray with you? For Millie?"

It's like the room stops. The noise all fades away. Charlie and Chelsea lean in for my answer. I feel like God himself holds his breath, waiting for my response.

"No." I look away. "No, I don't think so."

"Well, I'm gonna pray for her anyway." Frances scoots past me. "And for you."

Embarrassed at Frances's not-so-subtle display of faith, I cross my arms and silently watch my friend pray. On one hand, I want to grab Frances and tell her she's wasting her time. But yet I wonder what it feels like to be that secure in something. To have that much faith, that much conviction. There are a million reasons why I shouldn't believe God is gonna heal my foster mom. And right now Frances isn't letting a single one of those reasons hold her back.

The music winds down as Pastor Mike grabs the microphone again. "Guys, I appreciate the prayers. Keep 'em up. My family's really gonna need them. Speaking of families in need, it's time to talk about spring break. We have the details ironed out. Are you ready?"

Oh, can't wait. He's already told us our trip to Florida is cancelled and we're staying in In Between.

"There's a lot of work to be done in this town. The tornado wreaked havoc on a lot of neighborhoods around here. You guys know the area churches have been housing families in any way they could. The local apartments are full. Our church even has families staying in our gym. You guys are gonna get your socks blessed off in two weeks. We are going to show these families what Christ looks like."

I'd like to know what Christ looks like. Maybe he could stop by my house and *heal Millie*!

"We'll camp out on the church grounds. During the day we'll help rebuild homes." Rebuild? Um, I was gonna have to practice my sand castles before I went to Florida. There's no way I can do actual house construction. "In the evening we'll cook for the displaced families and have church services for them. It's gonna be great." His eyes twinkle with enthusiasm as I let go of my vision of sunbathing on the Florida beaches. "There will be four people to a tent, so choose wisely. Pick your friends who smell the least."

The mood lightens a bit, and the room fills with Spring Break chatter.

"Four in a tent," Frances says. "That's you, Hannah, and me . . ."

"Guess you're gonna need another person." Charlie's eyes bore into mine.

I force the words out of my mouth. "Chelsea, would you like to be in our tent?"

A smile spreads across Charlie's tanned face. I wait for Chelsea's own joyful display.

"I don't know." She pops her gum. "I'll let you know."

Before I get the chance to tell Chelsea where she can pitch her tent, Charlie stops me. "Hey, congratulations on your role in

Cinderella."

"What?"

"Yeah, Mrs. Hall posted the cast list on the school website right before we left for church."

My heart pounds. "I . . . I got the part?"

Charlie nods. "Yeah, good job."

I grab Frances and pull her into a fierce hug. We share a moment of senseless, high-pitched girl shrieks.

"I got it!" I yell. "I'm Cinderella." Frances and I jump up and down.

"Cinderella?" Charlie shakes his head anxiously. "Katie, no."

No more squealing.

No more jumping.

"What do you mean no? You said I got the part."

Charlie clears his throat; his face glows red. "The part of Drizella."

"Drizella? The *ugly stepsister?*" Can't. Breathe. I think I'm gonna be sick. I can't be the ugly sibling of Cinderella. I'm supposed to be Cinderella. There has to be a mistake.

Frances moves in close. "Who's Cinderella?"

Chelsea twines her arm around Charlie's and smiles. "That would be me." Her blue eyes laugh at me. "I'm sorry you didn't get the part, Katie. Maybe you just need some more practice. I could help you sometime."

I grab my Bible, desperate to escape. "I'll let you know."

Chapter 18

"MAXINE, GET OUT of the shower!"

I bang on the door with my fist. From the other side of the bathroom door comes the shrill off-pitch warbling of my foster grandmother. She's butchering a country song—something about a rhinestone cowboy—and my head is about to split open.

I think I slept a total of five minutes last night. And I woke up furious. I cannot believe I am Drizella, Ugly Stepsister Number One. The sister whose name nearly rhymes with Godzilla. I'm not even the sister that has a bit of kindness. I'm the full-on hag sister. Where am I going to find the inspiration for that?

"What do you want?" The door swings open, and Maxine pokes her turbaned head out.

"I want a shower." And the role I deserve. And something strong to drink—like a Diet Dr. Pepper. And some fairness. Can I have a thimbleful of fairness? A smidgeon? Just a skootch?

"Somebody woke up on the wrong side of the bed this morning." She unwraps her towel and blots her hair.

"I woke up thirty minutes ago. And that's exactly how long I've been waiting for you to get out of the shower."

"Guess you better start getting up earlier if you want to shower first."

I push my way into the bathroom. "You have all day to do nothing. I, on the other hand, have school. A schedule to keep. Places to be."

"*Hmph.* I do nothing? Today, little missy, I have ballroom dancing at noon, bridge at two, and snorkeling lessons at four. Come talk to me when you can compete with *that.*"

Mutely, I stare at Maxine in the mirror.

She smirks. "That's what I thought."

I quickly shower and blow-dry my hair. I skip makeup. I figure it's the ugly stepsister thing to do.

"There's our girl." Millie greets me with a smile the size of Texas as I slink off the last step and into the kitchen. "I made you a special breakfast today."

Joining Maxine at the table in the breakfast nook, I watch Millie proudly set a plate in front of me. She rips off the napkin draped over it.

"Ta-dah!" A stack of pancakes with strawberries arranged in a smiley face. "Made with all organic ingredients," Millie says.

"She's still got her knickers in a knot. Guess I'll have to eat her pancakes."

I smack Maxine's outstretched hand with a fork. "Touch my pancakes and you'll draw back a nub."

With Rocky at her heels, Millie brings me fresh orange juice. "Katie, I know you're still upset about the play, but honey, we're really proud of you."

I drown my misery and pancakes in syrup. "But I don't want to be the stepsister. I want to be Cinderella." My whiny voices makes the dog's ears twitch.

Millie sits next to me, sipping hot tea. "I think it's great you got a part. Not everyone did, right?"

I nod my head. "I was born to be Cinderella."

"I always thought I was born to be Brad Pitt's next wife." Maxine pours her own juice. "Reality's a bitter pill, isn't it?"

With a frown at my plate, Millie pulls the syrup bottle out of my reach. "Katie, I know it's not what you wanted. But you're going to be great in that role. And I'll be seeing you in the afternoons at the Valiant Theater."

"And I'll see you there—when I drop by and visit Sam."

I glare at Maxine. "Perfect. I was just thinking we don't get to spend nearly enough time together."

"Millie, I think Katie's juice must be bad. As in *bitter.*"

"Maybe if my new roommate wouldn't wake me up at five in the morning singing disco hits and—"

"Disco hits? Disco hits? I'll have you know today's selection was a medley of commercial jingles." Maxine swabs her lip with a napkin. "And that constipation ditty was just for you."

"I am so tired of waiting an hour for you to get out of the shower. And then to be subjected to your nasally, out of tune—"

"Nasally? You wouldn't know quality music if it hit you in the—"

"Mother! Katie!" Millie stands up. "Please."

I just want to go back to bed. And dream pretty, glass-slippery dreams.

"Now that I have your attention, I have a bit of news." Millie blows on her tea, her eyes thoughtful. "I'll be having my surgery Wednesday morning—the mastectomy, the reconstruction, and I'll be as good as new."

I shove my plate away. "Why are you just now telling us?"

Maxine crosses her arms. "That's what I'd like to know."

"James and I didn't feel like there was any need to tell you sooner—just so you'd worry sooner."

"I would have liked to have known," I say. "And what is reconstruction?"

"Millie gets a new booby." Maxine slurps her coffee.

A corner of Millie's mouth lifts. "Now, I'll be staying a few nights at the hospital after the surgery, so you can either spend the night with Frances." She looks doubtfully at her mother. "Or stay here with Mom."

Maxine wiggles her eyebrows. "We could have a wild party. Think of it, Katie—dancing, loud music, a keg of Metamucil."

Millie ignores her mother. "You'll need to have Frances pick you up after school. Sam has offered to drive you and Mother to the hospital after he gets off at the theater."

"What?" My temper, which was already on simmer, is climbing towards boiling. "I'm not going to school Wednesday."

"Yes," Millie says evenly. "You are."

"I want to be at the hospital."

"Give it up, Sweet Pea. I've already lost this argument. We'll have Sam take us Wednesday evening." Maxine's face is calm and serene. She must be up to something.

"I don't want to go that night. I want to be there during the surgery. Why can't I?"

Millie sets her tea down and begins clearing the table. "Because you'll get behind in school. And there's nothing for you to do at the hospital. This isn't up for debate. I will rest better knowing you are at school."

What if something happens and I'm not there? I need to be at the hospital.

"Am I not family enough to be there?" My voice quivers.

Millie flinches. "Of course you're family."

"Then quit treating me like a houseguest. Is that all I am? This is a big deal, and you're expecting me to treat it like another day. Like this doesn't matter to me."

Millie exhales deeply. "You're making a big deal out of nothing. I'm going in for a surgery, I'm spending two nights, and then I'll be back home. And you are going to school." She throws the last fork in the sink. It lands with a clank. "End of discussion."

My mind races with a fury. I'm desperate for some profound, cutting words. "Whatever." I toss my napkin on the table and run up the stairs. I'll be profound later.

A few hours later I'm sitting in history class. Still furious. My brain still buzzing with things I could've said. Should've said.

"Class, I'm Miss Smeltzer. The lesson plans Mr. Patton left say we are having a test. Clear your desks." The sub swipes at her face where sweat is pooling.

Test? Aw, man. I totally forgot about the history test. Who needs to know about ancient Chinese rulers anyway? I can barely remember the name of America's vice president. I am so gonna flunk this.

And what is up with today's sub? She calls herself "Miss," but I don't know many ladies with fully developed side burns and chin stubble.

On tree trunk legs Miss Smeltzer walks by me and tosses a test on my desk. She reeks of cigarette smoke. Not oh-I-just-had-a-quick-cig-before-I-came-to-school, but the kind of smell that belongs to someone who's smoked a few packs a day her whole life, and her every pore emits a nicotine odor.

She smells like my mom.

But my mom doesn't have a five o'clock shadow.

My hand inches toward the exam. I scan the first page and see few questions I know. I flip to the second page. Third page. Fourth page. Sixth page.

I raise my hand. "Can I go to the nurse?"

"No." The sub's voice is deeper than James's.

She's gonna be sorry if I puke.

How does one make oneself throw up? I know. I'll think gross thoughts. I think of being trapped in a coffin of insects. Eating live roaches on *Survivor*. Drinking out of Rocky's water bowl.

Oh, it's no use.

I answer as many of the questions as I can. And fill in C for the rest. It's possible ninety percent of the answers are C. Looking down at my bubbled answer sheet, I see a shape taking form.

A tiara.

If you turn the paper sideways it's a tiara of penciled in bubbles. My body slumps in the seat, and I rest my chin on my desk.

God, this is so unfair. Yes, I know I've said the word unfair *like a million times in the last week. But seriously, am I living a joke? I don't get the part, Charlie is acting all weird, his snob girlfriend gets my role, Millie has cancer, I'm not allowed to go to the hospital, and now I'm about to turn in a test that will make my history grade take a dramatic leap south.*

Are you there?

Do you even see me? Hear me?

"Are you done?"

My head shoots off my desk. "Huh? What?"

The stinky sub reaches for my test. "I said are you done?"

"Yes." I slowly nod. "I'm finished."

COACH NELSON BLOWS her whistle until her cheeks balloon and her eyes bulge.

"Listen up! Today we're starting something new. I think you're gonna like it. It's current. It's trendy. And it's popular."

Hannah and I exchange a hopeful look. Pilates? Yoga? Hip-hop aerobics?

"Wrestling."

Everyone groans. Coach lays on the whistle again. "Stop your complaining. This is going to be fun."

That's what she said about water polo last semester. I'm just lucky I wasn't one of the fifteen girls who got sent to the ER for stitches or broken bones.

"First I will go over some basics. Next I will be pairing you off by size." Coach Nelson rubs her hands together. "Then we'll have some matches."

Just when I thought my day couldn't get worse. If she asks us to buy spandex outfits and go by names like Shazaam or Electra, I am so out of this class.

Coach Nelson explains a few moves. I tune her out until I hear the words *crotch lift*. Um, there better not be any lifting of my crotch.

"So, in review, you can use the following moves today: the grapevine, the pin, the crotch lift, the cradle, and the gut wrench. The three important parts of the match are the takedown, breakdown, and, finally, the pin. Any questions?"

The class stares blankly.

"I need two volunteers." She searches the class for a few willing victims. As usual, she finds none. "Parker, Angel, front and center."

No way.

Hannah pats me on the back. I roll my shoulders, take a deep breath, and try to muster up some courage.

"Break a leg," Hannah says, her smile weak.

"Hannah . . . Never mind. Thanks."

"Let's go, Parker. On the mat."

As I stand, I meet Angel's stare. She doesn't try to disguise her hatred for me. Any lingering fears I have evaporate, leaving me ticked and insulted by Angel's attitude. What does she have to be mad about? I'm the one with real problems.

I stand next to her, perhaps a little too close. Oh, let's see what you've got, Angel. Because you're not the only one who woke up angry today. You don't have the exclusive rights to being mad at the world. There's a new bad attitude in town.

And it belongs to me.

"When I blow my whistle, begin. Ready?"

Angel nods once, already in attack mode.

Tweeeeeeet!

My heart gallops in my chest as my opponent moves in closer. We circle each other, Angel out of pursuit, and me out of a sheer lack of creativity. I wasn't exactly paying close attention during the tutorial.

Angel lunges for my shoulders. Her fingernails pierce my skin. Now that can't be legal.

I check for Coach Nelson, but the rest of the girls have circled around the mat to get a closer look. Coach Nelson stands behind them talking into a cell phone. Great. We're about to have bloodshed, and she's probably on the phone with Dominos.

"Get your fingernails out of my arms." I try to wrench myself out of Angel's grip.

"Whatsa matter? Are you gonna cry?" Angel's voice is songlike.

I see red.

With all of Angel's concentration on ripping my arms off, I take the opportunity to hook my leg around one of hers and give it a good pull.

She falls like a house of cards.

I don't bother to hide my triumphant smile. The crowd roars in approval.

A hand latches onto my ankle and before I can step back, Angel jerks me flat onto my backside. My tailbone throbs.

Angel and I both spring into action, leaping onto one another. We become a tangled unit of arms, legs, and claws. I can't see a thing, all I can do is strike out, desperate to pin her down. She's like a fish, squirming and impossible to hold in one place.

My neck snaps back as Angel latches onto a handful of my hair.

"Hey! Let go." Hair pulling has got to be illegal.

"Aw, poor baby. Did I mess up your salon style?"

I manage to flip her some and gain the upper hand. I am seconds away from pinning her.

Angel grunts. "You think you're so much better than everyone else. You and all your new friends."

My arms are shaking. I've almost got her flat on the ground. "Get over it, Angel. Find someone new to obsess over."

My ear fills with her primal cry, and Angel knees me in the stomach.

And I go down, releasing my hold.

Pain. All I see is pain. All I taste is pain. I think I'm gonna be sick.

"You don't want to mess with me, Katie Parker. You'll regret it, I promise you that."

I can't even talk. I would hold onto my gut, but her hands are pinning mine to the mat.

No, I gotta recover. I can't let her beat me.

Dear God, please give me strength.
Strength to beat the living snot out of her.

I rock my legs up and under Angel. My stomach rebels, but I push her off with a herculean effort.

The other girls are chanting now. Totally absorbed in our TV-worthy smackdown.

Angel tucks and rolls, springing back to her feet. She grabs me by the hand, hoists me up, and her fist punches into the right side of my face.

I stumble back in shock. In pain.

And now I'm mad.

Taking a few steps back, I get a running start and torpedo myself toward Angel.

Like a linebacker, I plow into her stomach. With my head.

Angel gets slammed into the floor.

And me? Well, I get detention.

Chapter 19

"THANKS FOR THE ride."

Frances stops the car at the Valiant. "Sure, anytime."

With her daughter sprawled on the gym floor, Coach Nelson finally decided to get off the phone during PE. She sent both of us to the office. I insisted on taking Hannah, my witness.

Angel got three days suspension. I got two afternoons of after-school detention. And Coach Nelson got her wrestling mats taken away.

Frances chews on a fingernail. "What are you going to tell the Scotts?"

I shrug. "Why should I tell them anything? I'll serve detention, and they'll never know about the fight."

"Katie, your eye is the size of a small orange. A bright purple orange."

Yeah, it does hurt like crazy. I'd flip down her visor and take a look, but my injured eye is swollen shut. I don't want to overwork my good eye. I'm gonna need it for practice.

With a wave goodbye to Frances, I fling open the door to the Valiant, and with my Cyclops eye, search for Millie. I don't see her. Hopefully she's not working at the theater today.

Inside, practice is well underway.

The creaking of the giant entry door gets Mrs. Hall's attention.

"Ms. Parker," she calls. "Nice of you to join us. I suppose you have an excuse for—oh, ewww."

All eyes roam my way. Including Trevor Jackson's.

"Sorry I'm late. I had a little . . . accident." As in someone's fist accidentally found its way into my eye socket.

"Well, yes, yes, I see that. So sorry, dear. Come on down here. We're reading through our lines in small groups. Join your group." The drama teacher motions me over to Trevor. I smile weakly and mumble a hello to everyone. My group consists of Trevor, Chelsea, and Jeremy, who plays the part of the other wicked stepsister. In drag. That's right. Mrs. Hall's idea of two ugly women? A boy in drag and me. Such a confidence booster.

"Katie, what happened to your eye?" Jeremy's voice is so loud it echoes in the theater.

I want to slither into the orchestra pit and never come out.

"Are you okay?" Trevor touches my shoulder, his face drawn with curiosity and concern.

"I'm fine. Really. I just thought I'd get into character. A little early." I laugh. Alone.

"Let's get started. We're already on page fifteen, but I guess we can start back at the beginning." Chelsea's concern is touching. Seriously, I'm about to shed a tear over her genuine warmth. I glare at her with my one good eye.

We continue our read-through for another hour, stopping at the sound of Mrs. Hall clapping.

"Actors and actresses! Your attention, please!" Today Mrs. Hall is decked out in a billowy skirt of eggplant purple. A silver vest covers a frilly lavender blouse. I like this teacher a lot, but one day the fashion police are going to taze and hog-tie her.

"If you have noticed, there are a few roles we did not cast with students. As I mentioned weeks ago, these roles will be open to the public. Community involvement will mean more ticket sales." Mrs. Hall paces the stage. "Now, we need an onstage orchestra for the ball.

Does anyone have any family members who would be interested?"

Mrs. Hall jots down the names that are called out.

"And we have the plumb role of the fairy godmother. I see an older, more mature woman for this character. Do any of you have gifted grandmothers?"

A throat clears behind me.

Mrs. Hall continues. "A great aunt, perhaps?"

"*A-H-H-H-E-M!*"

The teacher jots down more names. "I feel the part calls for someone who's ethereal and radiating joy."

"I've got the joy, joy, joy, joy down in my heart? Where? Down in my heart? Where? I've got the joy, joy, joy, joy—"

My head does a one-eighty and there behind me stands Maxine, belting it out for all to hear.

"What are you doing?" I hiss.

Mrs. Hall frowns, but continues. "This person would need to have a nurturing, mother-like aura."

Maxine steps out from behind me. "Cookies? I have some home-baked cookies for everyone!"

"No!" I grab her basket of baked goods. Everyone takes their eyes off Maxine and stares at me. "Believe me. It's for your own good."

"Introduce me to your teacher," Maxine whispers.

I sigh. "Mrs. Hall, this is Maxine Simmons. She was just leaving."

Maxine pokes me in the ribs, her voice low. "Nice shiner, you little scrapper. I've got some heavy-duty makeup that will cover that right up. You know, *hide* it."

"Mrs. Hall, Maxine would make a great choice for the fairy godmother." I can't believe this is coming out of my mouth. "She has a lot of stage experience." She was a showgirl in Vegas. She wore feathers and a leotard. "She is very . . . motherly." She hasn't smothered me with a pillow yet. "And we could probably learn a lot from her." My foster grandmother can burp the Spanish alphabet.

Mrs. Hall studies Maxine from her viewpoint onstage. "Very nice that you could drop by our practice, Mrs. Simmons. Do you always travel with a wand?"

Maxine pulls out a star-topped wand sticking from her purse and waves it. Glitter flies everywhere. "I sing too. Tell them I can sing, Katie."

I bite my lip. "Oh, she can sing all right." She belongs on an out-take of *American Idol.*

Maxine graces everyone with a granny-like smile. "My daughter and son-in-law own this theater. And my friend Sam is the theater caretaker. I'm here all the time."

I snort.

The sales pitch continues. "My apartment was devastated by the tornado. I'm lucky enough to live with my family temporarily." Maxine's arm slinks around me, and she draws me to her side. "I would love to help those less fortunate, those without homes."

Should I start humming the "Star-Spangled Banner"?

Mrs. Hall grins. "We would be delighted for you to read for the part of the fairy godmother. Just come with me, and we'll do a quick audition. Students, any protests?"

Maxine's arm around me tightens. "One word, and I'm taking pictures of your shiner and sending them to Millie."

I close my eyes in defeat and watch my foster grandmother flitter and flounce away.

"Hey, cool lady." Trevor breaks the silence in our group.

"Yeah," I mutter. "She's just nifty."

Chelsea grabs her designer purse. "I'm out of here. See you all later." She lowers her lashes. "Bye, Trev."

'Bye, *Trev*?' What was that?

Jeremy gathers his stuff. "I gotta go too. I hope your face is better tomorrow." *Call me*, he mouths. I watch my red-headed friend walk away.

This leaves me and Trevor. Alone.

If this were a movie, the cameras would be coming in for the close-up.

Say something witty, Katie.

"So how's the baseball team looking this season?" Sports. Always a good topic with boys.

Trevor frowns. "The season ended last night. We lost."

Oh, right. And this is where I exit.

"So what did happen to your eye?" He moves in closer. One single theater seat separates us.

"It was. . . nothing."

"You ran into a door?"

I return his smile. "Fell off my bike."

His laugh is better than all the ibuprofen I took. "Hey, I'm really sorry you didn't get the role you wanted. I did not see that coming."

"Yeah. I guess I can work on my range with the stepsister part. Being mean will be a stretch for me."

His eyes rove to my swollen face. "I think you're on the right track."

We share in the laugh this time, and I feel one more link added to our connection.

"So what are you doing this weekend?"

My heart quickens at his question. Where is he going with this? Is he going to ask me—

"Because some people are having a little get-together, and I wanted to know if you'd like to go."

Play it cool. Don't start shrieking until you get outside to the parking lot. This may not be a date. He may just mean this in a friendly sort of way. Not in a will-you-wear-my-letterman-jacket sort of way.

"Um . . . yeah. That sounds great." The Scotts may totally disagree. "What time?"

He scribbles something on a piece of paper. His dark hair catches the stage lights. "Eight. Here's the address."

Oh, okay. Not a date. Exactly. "I'll meet you there."

"See you tomorrow at rehearsal."

I hold the paper tightly. "See you then."

"And Katie?"

"Yeah?"

"Don't run into any more doors."

Chapter 20

CLANG! CLANG! CLANG!

Wednesday morning I shoot out of bed, yelling. My pulse pounds.

The fog clears, and I realize I'm in my room. In my own bed.

But a crazy woman stands over me, a copper pot in one hand. A wooden spoon in the other.

"What are you doing?" I shout. "Are you trying to kill me?" I clutch my racing heart.

Maxine laughs. "You look funny when you sleep. Your mouth hangs open like this." She opens her mouth like a rhinoceros. "And your nose twitches like—"

"Maxine, what are you doing?" I check the alarm clock. Ten 'til seven.

She throws her kitchenware on the bed. "James and Millie left for the hospital about thirty minutes ago. Her surgery is in two hours. That gives you an hour to get ready and one hour for us to get there."

"Get where?"

"To the hospital, *Señorita* Sleepy Pants."

And now I'm awake. "Millie banned us from the hospital today."

"James and Millie are gone. And I am in charge. And I say we're going to St. Mary's Hospital."

I brush my bedhead out of my eyes. I always wake up looking like I battled a wind storm all night.

"How are we gonna get there?"

Maxine throws me my pink, fluffy robe. "Meet me in the conference room at oh-seven-hundred hours. You will be debriefed."

She walks out the door, Rocky at her heels.

"I'll be *what?*" I call.

"Meet me in the kitchen in ten minutes! I'll fill you in!" And she skips down the stairs, beating her pot like a drunk percussionist.

Minutes later I step into the kitchen. "What is that smell?"

Maxine closes the oven and wipes her hands on a gingham apron. "Breakfast."

My stomach quirks at the strong aroma. "Sure doesn't smell like Millie's waffles."

"Bah! That's sissy food. What we need is the breakfast of champions."

"Wheaties?"

"My special triple-decker pizza. It's not quite done."

"What exactly are you up to?" I'm afraid to ask. The answer always gets me grounded.

She opens the freezer while humming a chirpy little tune. "This morning calls for a good stiff drink." Maxine pours something into a frosty mug. Next she plops ice cream into the drink.

"A root beer float?"

"Yup. Drink up." She slides one across the table, and I catch it in both hands. "Cheers."

She clinks my glass with hers and guzzles her root beer down. "Must go check the pizza."

"Maxine, you know I can't drive us to the hospital. I've only had one driving lesson."

She cuts the pizza into sections. "Well, of *course* you're not gonna drive. We don't have time to knock down any power lines."

My foster grandmother serves me a plate of the biggest, cheesiest, meat-loaded pizza this side of Italy. "Are these green beans on here?"

Maxine shrugs. "I thought we could use the protein. Let me pray for our food." She clears her throat. "Dear Precious Lord, you know I try hard to be obedient. Well, today is not a good day. Okay, neither was yesterday. Or the day before. Anyway, today we will be visiting Millie. Katie will be skipping school. I will be skipping my *Days of Our Lives*. And Lord, about Marlena—"

"Get on with it, Maxine."

"*Ahem.* Right. So, God, we ask forgiveness for disobeying, but we will be doing it anyway. Please be with the doctors. We ask for healing for Millie and strength for the family. And we pray the wind won't be against us as we bike our little hearts out. For our dear Millie. In Jesus' name we pray, amen."

"I am not getting on your bicycle, Maxine."

"We leave in forty-five minutes. Ginger Rogers is waiting."

"Oh, no. No way." Ginger is Maxine's bicycle built for two. The last time I took a ride, I ended up falling twenty feet and belly flopping into a pool. Owned by Charlie's grandmother.

"Look, Katie Parker, here's the deal. If you go with me, you're in trouble. If you let me go alone, you're in trouble. Either way, you're facing some serious doggy-doo. Now I helped you camouflage that black eye Monday night, so you owe me. And I say we're riding Ginger Rogers to the hospital."

"It's an hours' ride at least."

Maxine smiles. "Then you better eat up." And she hums the rest of her happy melody.

"I CAN'T GO much further. I'm not gonna make it. You're going to have to pedal alone."

Maxine whips around, smacks me in the forehead with her gloved hand, and continues to pedal. "I did not raise you to be a quitter!"

I huff and puff air, pushing the pedals to climb the hill. "You didn't raise me at all."

"And there's our problem. Now keep pedaling."

Through the insulation of my bike helmet, I hear a sound like tin foil. Something being unwrapped. And then I notice Maxine's feet are propped up on her bike. "Maxine!" I growl. "Are you eating?"

"Nuh-uh."

"I smell food."

"Iths jus pitha." I can see her jaws moving as she chews.

My legs have moved past throbbing to numb. My lungs burn for air. And Maxine's kicked back, having an appetizer.

But I'm too tired to be mad.

We cross one more busy highway, our last before the hospital. Only two cars honk as Maxine steers us into traffic. She honks back with her squishy horn tacked to the handle bars. I'm sure the Lexus was very intimidated.

Maxine signals with her hand, and we turn into St. Mary's parking lot. She steers us around the building and motions for me to stop.

"Um, Maxine?"

She rips off her helmet and shakes her golden hair. "Yeah?"

"This is the plastic surgery wing." The Walter C. Monroe Cosmetic Surgery Center, a sign says.

"Oh." She pats her face. "Habit, I guess."

And we pedal to the next entrance.

Sliding doors *whoosh* open as we walk through the surgery center lobby. I walk behind Maxine. If we get in any trouble (which we will), I want her to walk through the fire first.

We shuffle down the hall and into a large waiting room.

An empty waiting room.

"Katie?"

I jump and spin around.

James. Holding a cup of coffee and a newspaper. "What are you doing?"

"Uh . . . uh . . . uh . . ." I grab Maxine and shove her in front of me. "It was her!"

"Katie, you were specifically told to go to school." James's frown deepens.

"I tried to tell her, James. She wouldn't listen." Maxine settles her purse into a chair. "You know kids these days."

"And you, Maxine. I am ashamed of you. I have enough to concern myself with without worrying about you pedaling all over the county."

I think of my overworked legs. "I wouldn't worry about her pedaling."

James consults his watch. "Ladies, I'm calling Sam. Katie, he will be instructed to drop you off at school. And Maxine, he can drop you off—"

Maxine throws up a hand. "Careful now. Remember you're a preacher."

James sighs. "He can drop you off at the house."

"This was not my idea," I mumble.

"James, we rode a long way here. We're tired. And Katie and I both deserve the opportunity to sit here with you as a family. And I see there's a TV, so I can be a pillar of strength to you *and* catch up on Salem all at the same time." Maxine plunks into an ugly orange chair and grabs a magazine.

"Please don't call Sam. Let us stay. You know I'm gonna be worthless at school today anyway."

James removes his glasses and massages the bridge of his nose. "We will discuss this when we get home. Is that clear?"

"Yes, sir."

"It's going to be hours before you can see Millie."

"I just want to wait with you." Let me stay. Let me be sit here and pretend I'm part of this family. I'll imagine you want me here. And that Millie is going to be fine.

James shakes his head. "Millie is not going to be happy." But he pulls me into a loose hug anyway.

I settle in a chair beside Maxine, who reads a copy of *Seventeen*.

Maxine turns a page. "Got a pen on you?"

"Why?"

"I want to take this quiz. Ten ways to tell if you're old enough to have a boyfriend."

I bite my lip. "Sounds like a waste of ink."

The lobby doors open, letting in sunlight and two familiar faces. Pastor Mike and Laura. I haven't seen them since her father died. Ugh. What do I say? *Sorry your dad died, and welcome to our cancer party?*

"Hey, guys. Have you heard anything yet?" Pastor Mike puts an arm on James's shoulder.

"No, it's gonna be hours." My foster dad forces a smile. "How are you, Laura?"

Laura nods. "Day by day, you know? It's just going to take some time—for all of us."

LAURA SITS ON a coffee table in front of me. "Katie, how are you holding up?"

I nod and smile. "Great. Thanks." I'm a mess. It's not even nine a.m., and I need some caffeine. And I have helmet hair. "Couldn't be better."

She moves in closer. Her eyes scrutinizing. "Is that . . .? Do you have a black eye?"

Laughter comes from behind Maxine's magazine.

"It's nothing." I didn't cake on nearly enough makeup this morning. "I'm going to go get something to drink. I'll be right back." Diet Dr. Pepper. Need it now.

Laura stands up "I'll show you where it is."

I sling my purse over my arm and follow my pastor's wife down the hall.

"So . . . um . . . sorry about your dad dying." That sounded just as stupid as I thought it would.

"Thanks. I know the youth group was praying hard for us, and I appreciate that."

Instead of answering, I study the tile beneath my feet. It's just like the kind in Sunny Haven, the girls home I came from. The home I would return to if something happens to Millie.

"Here we are." Laura guides us into a small room, wall to wall with vending machines. "I'll buy." She digs into her purse. "I insist."

We each get a drink. Laura pulls out a chair at a table, and taking her cue, I do likewise. Though I really just want to go back upstairs and wait with everyone else.

"Katie, I can tell you're upset about all of this."

I take a long drink. And shrug.

"It's okay to be afraid, you know." Laura puts her hand on mine. "And it's normal to wonder what God's up to. But I hope you know he is in control. He's on the job."

I set my bottle down. A smart remark dances on the tip of my tongue, but I swallow it back. "Laura, I think there is a God. I know that. But as far as being a Christian . . . well, I really don't see the point these days." There. I said it.

Laura twirls her wedding band around her finger. "What's changed for you?"

"Come on. What do people really get out of it? Look at Millie. She's a pastor's wife, she's nearly perfect. And she gets cancer. And then there's you."

She frowns. "What about me?"

"You're this amazing Christian, totally nice person. And look at what you're going through."

"God doesn't promise us this easy life."

"It's just not fair. That's all I'm saying. And Millie deserves more than this. Why isn't God taking care of her?"

"No, it's definitely not fair. But you were headed in the right direction. And now you're just totally through with God? Is *that* fair?"

I grab my drink and stand up. "Fair? Nothing in my life has ever been fair. But was it fair your dad died? Is it fair my foster mom has cancer and could die? I don't see the purpose in any of this. It's so pointless."

"But it's not pointless. I know it's hard to understand. But God's gonna be with Millie through all of this. And you too." Laura rises from her chair, her eyes intense. "I know you're hurting, and I hate that you look at the things that have happened recently as reasons not to trust in Him."

I throw my bottle away. Meeting over. "I think I better go back to the lobby. I want to be there when we get news about Millie."

Laura's hand stops me. "Before we go, I just want to pray for us. Pray for Millie."

No. I don't want to pray. I'm sick of talking to God. He's obviously not listening. He has his holy earplugs in whenever I speak. How do I tell my pastor's wife that praying is a total waste of time?

"Thanks, but I really don't want to—"

"Laura! Katie!"

My head snaps toward the door.

Pastor Mike runs into the room. "Ladies, come quick. You would not believe what's happened."

My heart plunges. "Is it Millie?"

His mouth spreads into a grin. "No," he says. "It's Amy. She's in the lobby." The pastor grabs my hand and tugs me toward the door. "The Scott's daughter has come home."

Chapter 21

THE THREE OF us—Pastor Mike, Laura, and I—speed walk down the hall. I round the corner, the lobby in sight. James stands in the middle of the room, his arms tightly wrapped around a young woman. Amy. His daughter. His real daughter.

I'm an evil person! How is it I'm standing here, and I'm sad? For me. The Scott's only child, who hasn't been home in years, has finally returned, and I'm . . . I'm . . . jealous.

They needed a daughter. And I filled that spot. I got to play that role. What if they don't need me anymore? All because that deserter came back.

"Katie." James sees me standing near. "Come here. I want you to meet my daughter."

James has tears in his eyes.

And I do too. Something about the way he said *my daughter* slices through me. I can't explain it. I repeat: I'm evil. That's the only explanation. I should be happy for him. I should be so glad Amy is safe and the Scotts can quit worrying.

But I'm not.

I close the distance between us, step by slow step. "Hey."

James wipes at his eyes. "Amy, this is our foster daughter Katie."

Yeah, I know. Your real daughter. Hi, I'm the fake one.

She's wine, and I'm grape juice. Amy is a diamond. And I'm a dull cubic zirconium. She's mink. And I'm just a fuzzy substitute.

I stick out my hand and clasp Amy's. Her hand is small, smaller than Millie's. I shake it, but hardly squeeze for fear of shattering it in my light grip.

Everything about the Scott's daughter is fragile. Her light brown hair hangs loose and unkempt around her face, like she hasn't slept in a few days. The sweatshirt she wears swallows her body, like she's lost somewhere in her own clothes.

Amy smiles at me, but her eyes don't meet mine. Or anyone's.

She's uncomfortable. How ironic that this is her family, and she's uncomfortable.

"Amy, honey, how did you know about your mom's surgery? We decided we wouldn't upset you and tell you about it until it was over."

"I told her." Maxine puts her magazine down. "I knew she would want to know."

James pulls his daughter to him again and kisses her on her head. "Thank God. I'm so glad you're here."

"Dad . . ." The long-lost daughter speaks. Her voice slow and distracted. "I'm pretty tired. It was a long bus ride."

Maxine tilts her head, thoughtful. "I sent money for a plane ticket."

Amy smiles at her grandmother. "I'm here, right?"

"Right. And that's the important thing," James says. "I'm afraid to take my eyes off of you. Afraid you'll disappear. You'll stay a few days, right?"

You can tell James doesn't want to push it. His eyes glisten with excitement and questions, both of which are firmly in check.

I walk around the reunited father and daughter and plop into a seat next to Maxine. She pats my leg, her eyes staring straight ahead.

"I don't know about staying. I have a job back in Miami."

James lowers his voice. "Why haven't you called us? Written to us?"

Amy shakes her head and forces a laugh. "Not now, Dad. Gimme a break, okay?"

"I think it's a fair question." Maxine pulls a fingernail file out of her bag. "The only reason we knew you were in Miami this month was because you needed money."

"Maxine, that's enough." James glares at his mother-in-law. "Amy, we love you. Your mom and I want you to stay as long as you can. Forever if you want." He smiles.

My heart splits in two. If James offers her my room, I'm walking back to Sunny Haven.

"Slow down. I'm here to see Mom. Let's not make this a big deal."

The hands on the clock barely move as I'm forced to listen to the Scott family reunion. A solid hour of James lavishing Amy with praise, Amy dodging questions, and me staring at the ceiling. Pastor Mike and Laura try to engage me in conversation, but I'm too busy try to act like I'm not listening to Amy to say anything too intelligent.

The youth pastor tries again. "So, Katie, are you excited for the spring break mission work?"

I shift in my seat. "I'm not going."

All conversation stops.

For the first time in an hour, James looks at me. "What? Of course you're going."

I shake my head. "No. I've decided not to go."

"When did you decide this?" Maxine asks.

Three seconds ago. "I dunno. It's been a while."

"It's going to be a great time." Pastor Mike stares at me like I'm an alien. "You don't want to help the people of In Between? People who lost their homes? Everything they own?"

I grab a magazine and open it to a random page. "I have a science fair project due about that time. And then there's the play after spring break. I think it would be best if I stayed home and worked on that." Whoa, some of the stuff in *National Geographic* should have warning labels.

James crosses his legs at the ankle and pins me with his eyes.

"Katie's just a little stressed with school and the play right now. I'm sure she'll be ready to tackle the mission project by Spring Break."

No. I'm not going. What's the point? Go serve soup and sandwiches to some down and out In Betweenies and tell them how great God is? Hey, folks, sorry your house blew away, but I would like to tell you that God loves you. I don't think so.

Hours later I wake up from a cat nap as Millie's surgeon shuffles into the lobby.

"Mr. Scott?"

I study this man's face—every line, twitch, and blink. Does he have good news? Bad news? Or maybe he just came out to weigh in on the mission project issue like everyone else.

"Mr. Scott, Millie's out of surgery and in recovery. We removed the three tumors with no problem."

With one eye on Amy, I sigh with relief. The Scott's daughter doesn't move a muscle. No reaction at all. This chick is so weird.

"There was some node involvement, so it is a bit more extensive than we'd hoped. We'll talk about this more later. But she did well."

Yes, of course they'll discuss it later—when I'm not around. And I know from my research lately that lymph node involvement is not good. Not good at all.

"You can see Mrs. Scott in about an hour when she's transferred to a room."

James thanks the doctor and shakes his hand.

The Price is Right blares on the wall. While someone screams for joy over winning a sports car, six people in a hospital lobby are mute, silent. Exhausted and worried.

Thoughts circle through my brain like NASCAR drivers, one idea chasing another. What if they didn't get it all today? What if I have to go back to Sunny Haven? What if I get sent to live with a different family?

James manages a small smile. "I think we have a lot to be thankful for today. Why don't we thank God for Millie's surgery going well?"

We gather around James, everyone taking hands. I stand between Laura and Maxine.

My head bows as my foster father offers up a prayer to God. The God of cancer. The God of abandoned kids. The God of druggie moms.

". . . And Lord we ask for healing for Millie. We pray you would lay your hands on her and . . ."

My eyes focus on the floor. I examine Amy's shoes. A ragged pair of boots. Brown, scratched. Ugly. I continue my inspection all the way up to her sweatshirt.

And my eyes meet hers. I jerk my gaze back to the floor, but curiosity draws me back to her face.

How dare she stare at me! How rude.

"Amen."

Pastor Mike and Laura give a round of hugs to everyone. When it's her turn, Amy steps back.

I'm soon cocooned in a three-way bear hug with my youth pastor and his wife. Their words hit my ears. But not my heart.

"God is on the job, Katie. You'll see."

"Hang in there, girl. We're praying for you too."

I cling to them for an extra second, then step away. Saying nothing, I watch them leave. I'm all out of words. All out of hope. Life just kicks me in the gut everywhere I go.

James puts one arm around me and another around Amy. Maxine leans into her granddaughter. Stand next to me! Did Amy pedal for a solid hour to get to the hospital? No. Did Amy have to stomach your atomic pizza this morning? No, I did! What about me?

"Anyone up for a late breakfast? We can grab a bite before they take Millie to her room." James hugs me in closer.

"I'm not hungry." I step out of his embrace and return to my seat.

"I think I'll catch a quick nap." Amy steps over my legs and settles onto the couch.

"Maxine? Care to join me in the downstairs cafeteria?"

Maxine grabs her purse. "I'm starved. I've hardly had a thing to eat all morning."

I pick up my *National Geographic* again and flip through the pages. Ten pages of ancient Egypt. Mummies—you've seen one, you've seen them all. I throw it on a nearby table.

"How long are you staying?" Amy's voice breaks the silence.

I look up, checking to make sure she's actually talking to me. "I. . .I don't know. I guess until my mom gets straightened out."

Amy picks at her fingernail. "What's up with your mom?"

Where is Maxine's *Seventeen* magazine? I could use a good quiz right now.

"I said, what's up with your—"

"I heard you." I shrug an indifferent shoulder. "Drugs. Prison."

Amy sits up. "She got busted for doing drugs?"

"No. Selling."

She considers this. "What kind of drugs?"

"Cough drops." My head bobs to the back of the chair. I want to go home.

"What are you so mad about?" She chews on a nail.

"I'm not mad. I'm just worried about your mom." Unlike you, I happen to care about your parents. "How long are you staying?"

Amy pulls her finger out of her mouth. "Not long. Gotta get back."

"They worry about you all the time. They've been waiting for you to see the Valiant."

"Yeah, well, I don't have time to see their theater."

"They restored that old theater for you, Amy. Did you know that?" Heat spikes through me. "Last fall they worked day and night on that building. Hoping you would be there opening night. They looked for you the entire night."

She lifts a shoulder. "I was busy."

"Don't you even care? You've got two parents who love you, and you don't even care. Do you know how much I would give to have parents who cared about me? Or how many times I've wished I had been born into this family?"

Amy laughs, shoving her brown hair out of her eyes. "I *wasn't* born into this family."

I rewind the words in my head. "What?"

"Didn't they tell you?" She stands up, grabs her jacket and brushes past me. "I'm adopted."

"Wait—"

Amy pivots, facing me. "I've never been good enough. Never could be what they wanted me to be. And they're treating you the same way. I can't believe you don't see that."

I shake my head. "The Scotts . . . they're great parents."

"Tell me, Katie, do you go to church because you want to? Or because they make you? Do they pressure you into things like, oh, I don't know, mission projects? Yeah, they're great parents. As long as you fit the mold—a good little Christian girl, who makes good grades and never gets into trouble. As long as you're perfect."

My hands are clenched, shaking. "They don't expect me to be perfect." I stab my chest. "I get in trouble all the time," I say like a badge of honor. "The Scotts love you." Even though you're psycho.

A shadow falls across Amy's face. "They love the idea of who they want me to be. Think about it. Because I'm betting it's the same for you." She steps toward the door. "Tell Dad I'm at home. I gotta get out of here."

The doors close.

And I'm left alone.

Utterly, miserably, pathetically alone.

Chapter 22

I SIT IN a chair next to James. The sea foam walls of Millie's hospital room do nothing to soothe my fried nerves. Maxine continues to file her nails, and if Millie doesn't wake up soon, Maxine's bound to break out the fingernail polish.

I twist the string of my hoodie round and round my finger. Is now a good time to tell James his daughter is a total freak? Would it be appropriate to use this moment to ask why nobody told me Psycho Daughter was adopted? Why does this family keep everything from me?

Maybe they even adopted Maxine.

My foster grandmother yawns loudly then catches my eye. "Huevos Rancheros make me gassy."

I see a small movement of feet under Millie's sheet. Then an arm shifts. And finally, two eyes struggle to gain focus of the room.

James shoots out of his seat and settles on the bed next to his wife. "Hey, hon." He smoothes her blonde hair away from her pale face. "How are you feeling?"

Millie's eyes travel across the room then settle on James. Her head bobs in a nod. "Not . . . bad." Her voice is low and weak.

My foster mom gives a sluggish smile toward me. "How's school today?"

Maxine coughs twice.

"Well, I kind of didn't go."

Millie frowns. Nice to know in her drugged-out stupor she can still put her mom face on.

Her manicure complete, Maxine walks to the other side of the bed. "About time you woke up. I wanted to turn the TV on, but James wouldn't let me. He said the citizens of Salem could get along without me for one day." She snorts in disbelief.

"Why's Katie not in school?"

"Oh, don't you worry about that." Maxine picks up Millie's hand on the bed. "James, tell Millie who's here."

James pours Millie a cup of water and holds the straw to her mouth. "Amy's here. Or was here. Er, I guess is here."

Millie tries to sit up.

"No, no, lay back down." James puts a hand on her shoulder. "You have plenty of time to see her." His mouth curves. "She looks good. A little thin, but good."

Amy looks like she hasn't eaten in a year. Her hair is sprouting split ends and crying out for a trim. And she shakes like a car antenna. Yeah, she looks real good.

Millie pushes the water away. "Where is she?" Her words slur. "Where is she, James?"

"She'll be back soon. She went to the house. To rest."

Or to steal my laptop. I do not trust that girl.

Millie lays her head back, a smile on her lips. "My baby's home."

"THANKS AGAIN FOR picking me up."

I press my back into Frances's passenger seat and close my eyes. So tired. Worn to the bone.

"You didn't miss anything at school today. Well, except a quiz in history. Oh, and Nash kissing me."

Nap over. "What?"

"Yeah, at lunch. He put his greasy corndog down, wiped off his milk mustache, and said, 'I can't properly digest. My brain is filled with no other thought than I love you, Frances.' And then he grabbed my face and—"

"You know your left ear twitches when you're lying, right?"

Frances scowls and turns onto my street. "It could happen."

"Yeah, when Justin Bieber is in the White House."

She puts the car in park. "I'm coming in with you. I want to see the Scott's daughter."

Doesn't everyone?

Earlier in the afternoon I had called Frances to give her the update on Millie. And to beg her to pick me up from the hospital. I needed a break. A Trevor break. She kindly offered to take me to play rehearsals. I mean, they can't have a decent rehearsal without Drizella, Ugly Step-sister Number One.

Walking up the sidewalk, I catch a blur out of the corner of my eye. "Rocky!" The giant dog leaps on me, his elephant-sized paws settling on my shoulder. "No, Rocky! Get down. Ew, mud!" I heave the dog off, pushing with all my strength. He lays low to the ground and licks my shoes, like he can't get enough of me. At least someone appreciates me today.

"What are you doing out here, boy?" I look around for Amy and grab Rocky by the collar. "Come on. In you go."

Standing on the front porch, I start to put the key in the lock, but the front door stands open. "Hello?" I call out. Frances stays with the dog in the entryway, and I grab a towel for his muddy paws. If only fixing his dog breath were that easy.

Peering into the den on my way to the laundry room, I see Amy, sprawled out on the couch watching a talk show.

"I brought the dog in." I stand there until she acknowledges me.

"Uh-huh."

"You left him outside."

She picks up the remote, the volume inching up a notch. "He wanted to go out."

"Yeah, but you can't just let him loose. He eats Old Man Potter's ferns, and the neighbor kids OD on dog tongue."

Amy ignores me.

Frances and I wipe Rocky down, his paws still brown, but not bad enough to stain anything.

We head to my bedroom.

Where I find clothes strung everywhere and a stained, worn suitcase on my bed.

Frances wrinkles her nose. "Is Amy sleeping in your room?"

"Actually, it's my room" My non-sister pushes past the door and steps in. "This used to be my room." She walks around. "Not much left of mine. I can tell they really missed me."

Girl is ticking me off. "You're twenty-five. I don't think the Scotts are bad parents because they packed up your Barbies and 'N Sync posters." And where am I supposed to sleep? I cannot believe this.

Amy pulls a cigarette out of nowhere and lights up.

"Are you kidding me? Put that out! This is my room!" I rip the cigarette out of her mouth and run into the bathroom. I take a few deep breaths and watch it swirl down the toilet.

"Calm down. You're just like them."

Amy plops herself onto my twin bed, and I jerk the *People* from under her foot. "They are your parents. And I like them. And aside from the gray hair, if I could be anything like them, I would jump for joy."

She fluffs my pillow and sticks it behind her head. "Since this is my room, I'll be sleeping here. Where are you gonna sleep?" And then she laughs. Like she's just remembered the funniest joke. The high pitched sound razors my nerves.

"Are you sure you're feeling okay?" I ask. And please don't breathe your crazy germs on my bed.

She winds it down to a giggle. "Oh, I'm really good. But Dad said for you to stay with your friend here for a few days so he and Mom could spend time with me—their daughter."

I open my mouth then clamp it shut. My brain shuffles through every foul word and vile name I know (and there are many). A particularly creative insult comes to mind, and I load it for blast off. "You—"

"Is that what he told you?" Frances butts in, but I tuck the curse away for future use. "James said Katie was to go home with me?"

Amy settles into the bed, wiggling her nasty boots all over my hot pink comforter. "Yup." She closes her bloodshot eyes and flops a hand over her face. "Nighty-night, kiddies. Turn the light out on your way out."

I march to the closet and stuff some clothes in a bag. "The other bed belongs to Maxine." I heave the duffle over my shoulder and smile. "And she's had a lot of huevos rancheros today. Sweet dreams."

Frances and I stomp downstairs and pile into the station wagon.

"She's not anything like I thought she would be," Frances says, pulling out of the driveway.

"No. She's worse." I must be wearing a Kick Me sign today. Because the hits just keep coming.

I punch in James's cell phone number. No answer. His voice mail greets me with cheer and blessings. Yeah, well you know what you can do with your Christian goodness, James?

Beep!

"Hey, it's Katie. Frances is taking me to rehearsal, then I'm spending the night at her house. But I guess you already know that." *Click.* Pastor Jerk-face.

"I'm really sorry." Frances turns in the direction of the Valiant theater. Going her normal five miles under the speed limit.

"Thanks." I look out the window. Random spots of In Between still lies in pieces from the tornado. "But it's no big deal. It's not like I care."

"Yeah, we'll have fun tonight. Maybe we can talk mom into ordering pizza." Frances huffs. "Who am I kidding? Heaven forbid my family honor the Italian culture. I just hope it's not squid stew night."

The car squeaks to a stop in front of the theater. Frances grabs her backpack and opens the door.

"You're staying? We'll be rehearsing for a few hours."

"I'll just hang out here. That way I can see you practice and work on my next strategy to get Nash to beg me to go out with him."

Er, right.

I swing open the doors of the theater and gain some comfort. Like knowing you have a friend saving you a seat at lunch, the Valiant is familiar and welcoming to me. Makes me happy. Its Art Deco style still fascinates me, even though my own sweat went behind almost every brushstroke.

We sail through the lobby and the black lacquer doors that lead into the theater.

"Katie? Frances?"

I manage a half-smile for Sam Dayberry. "Hey."

"I thought I was gonna pick up you and Maxine and take you to the hospital after rehearsal." He takes his cap off and wipes his head with a handkerchief.

"Change of plans."

His eyes narrow. "Who changed 'em?"

"That would be Maxine."

"Don't tell me . . ."

I nod. "Ginger Rogers. Yup, rode all the way to the hospital."

He mumbles something about insanity. "Heard the news about Millie. I'm praying for her. Life will be good again. Hang in there." He pats me on the shoulder.

"Right."

"You okay?"

"Amy's here." That strung-out cow.

Sam's face splits into a grin. "That's wonderful. Praise the Lord."

"You do that." I leave him and Frances standing there.

I'm so ticked I can hardly appreciate the totally hot aura surrounding Trevor Jackson. He's head to head in conversation with

Chelsea, yet another person whose fan club I will never be joining.

I approach the couple just as Chelsea lays her hand on Trevor's arm and laughs.

"Oh, Trev!" She flips her golden princess locks. "That's so hilarious!"

Trevor says something back, his voice deep and low. I can't hear him, but Chelsea's eyes light up. His hand moves closer to hers. Closer . . .

"Hey, Katie." And Jeremy blocks my view. I stretch my neck, peering around him.

I step to the left of Jeremy. In time to see Chelsea and Trevor, standing miles apart. Surely he didn't put his hand on hers. Would he?

"Hi." My fake smile hangs crooked on my face.

Trevor catches my eye and winks. At me.

I lift a single eyebrow then give Jeremy my attention. Well, most of it. Okay, a small percentage of it.

"I was wondering if you wanted to discuss our wardrobe." He reaches into his coat pocket. "And here. I found these backstage at school." My fellow stepsister shoves a giant plastic nose on my face. "Perfect!"

Chelsea explodes into giggles. Again.

I wrench the pointy schnoz from my own nose. "I am *not* wearing this thing."

"I think it looks great." Trevor steps between me and Jeremy. "For the character, that is. Your acting skills are top-notch, so shouldn't your costume be just as professional?" He flashes me his white teeth.

My acting skills are top-notch? *Sighhhh.* "Um . . . yeah." I take the nose back. For Trevor I would wear anything. A suit of armor. The butt-end of a donkey costume. Anything.

Mrs. Hall claps her hands at center stage. "All right students, are we all here? Let's get to work. I have a six o'clock appointment with a divorce attorney. He's the best in the county, so I don't want to keep him waiting. Mr. Hall won't know what hit him. Did I tell you about the letters I found in his top drawer yesterday? Well, I was going through some—"

"Mrs. Hall?" Trevor rolls his beautiful brown eyes.

Our teacher blinks. "Yes, dear?"

"Can we start now?"

She clears her throat. "I believe that's what I was saying. Now, if I may continue. Let's start from the top. We'll do a very informal run-through of the script. No staging or blocking today. But we will be onstage. Just move where the script takes you."

She claps her hands and Leslie Traylor, Cinderella's stepmother, and Chelsea take the stage for the first scene.

Jeremy and I sit in the front row. I'm totally ready to tear Chelsea's performance apart. Should've been my role. Instead I get a glue-on nose.

Jeremy pulls some pictures out of his backpack. "So, I was thinking we could wear long, brown wigs. Maybe have them braided. I've been doing a little research on the time period, and—"

"Didn't see you at school today." Trevor takes the seat on my other side.

My heart kicks it into overdrive. Somewhere in my head I'm aware of Jeremy still speaking. But all I know is Trevor.

He noticed I wasn't there! Not only does Trevor know I exist, but he was looking for me. I just want to tattoo his words on the inside of my eyelids, so I can see them every time I blink. Or sleep in class.

"I was at the hospital." I give him breadcrumbs of my day. "My foster mom has cancer. She had surgery today."

Trevor puts an arm around the back of my chair. "I'm sorry. How are you holding up?" He leans in to whisper, and I catch myself sniffing him. *Mmmm.* Spicy, woodsy. Hotsy.

"I've had better days. It's good to be here though. Take my mind off things." I stare at my hands, wishing I was brave enough— Chelsea enough—to stare into his eyes right now.

His hand moves to my shoulder and squeezes lightly. "I'm really sorry. I guess you're not gonna be in the partying mood Friday night, are you?"

The party. How could I forget about that? I guess because I knew the Scotts would sooner let me hitchhike cross-country before they would allow me go to a party.

But now? Who cares. I'm out of a home, I've got demon-possessed Amy taking my bed, and nobody in the Scott family even knows I exist right now. So they sure won't notice if I'm gone a few hours Friday night.

"I'd love to go to the party." I bravely raise my eyes to his. "But things are a little mixed up at my house right now, so I don't have a ride there. Know anyone who could pick me up?" Anyone tall, dark, and all Prince Charming?

He hesitates. Not good. *So* not good.

And then he slowly nods. "Yeah, I can pick you up. No problem." He pauses again. "And you're sure your foster parents won't care?

I think of Amy. "No, they don't care at all."

Chapter 23

FRIDAY SPINS MY brain. I go to all eight classes for forty-five minutes each. Just enough time for each teacher to give a pop quiz and assign a pathetic amount of homework.

With my bag full of books and my neck in a crick from sleeping over again at Frances's, I slither into my seat in biology and lay my head down on the cool lab table. Yesterday I skipped drama rehearsal and made Frances take me to the hospital to see Millie. It seemed like I couldn't get a word in for the Scotts playing catch up with crazy Amy. When your daughter ignores you for years and lives in a different state every week, I guess you have a lot to talk about.

And the Scotts didn't say a word about kicking me out of my room. I came *so* close to asking them about it, but what could I say? *So, Millie, I know you have cancer and all, but did you know your daughter belongs in the circus?* Or *moving Amy into my room was such a funny joke. Hysterical. Believe me when I say, I laughed so hard, I cried.* Why can't I just ask them about it?

"Katie?"

"*Hmmm?*" I keep my eyes shut tight, but recognize the voice as Charlie's.

"You okay?"

Lots of people asking that question. But does anybody *really* care about the answer?

"Great. Fine. Couldn't be better."

And to add to all my grief, the vending machines are no longer carrying mini chocolate donuts due to some board member's idea to make us all healthy. I needed a sugar and chocolate fix, and all the machine offered me was roasted peanuts and whole wheat crackers. I'm depressed, and I'm mad. Is *now* really the time to remove all chocolate from the building?

Charlie pulls his stool next to mine. Unlike Trevor, he doesn't smell like cologne. Just smells like Charlie today. Clean with a touch of fabric softener.

"Chelsea is spending the weekend with her sister in Dallas. I was wondering if you wanted to get together tonight and work on our science fair project. You know, reunite our plants."

My plant. Amy Scott, daughter of the year, is probably using it as an ash tray right now.

I prop my head up on a fist and face Charlie. "I'm kinda busy tonight."

"Oh. You and Frances hanging out?"

I study the graffiti on the table. How did my phone number get on here? "No." Erase, erase, erase. "I'm going to a party."

Charlie frowns. "The party at Trevor Jackson's?"

"Yeah." I sit up. "So?"

"Katie, Trevor is not the type of guy you need to be hanging out with."

"He's been very nice to me."

"Well, of course he has."

My eyes narrow. "What is that supposed to mean?"

"Trevor Jackson runs through girls like Chelsea goes through makeup."

"Look, Charlie, I'm not going in hopes he'll propose. I've had a really bad week, and I deserve a night off from all the crap."

Charlie nudges my hand. "Do the Scotts know you're going?"

"I . . ."

"Hey, guys." Frances bounces into the seat next to mine. "What's up?" Her eyes become a GPS system, tracking the nearest distance to Nash, who's at another table talking to friends.

Charlie gets my look of death. My look that says *You say a word about this party, and I will run your underwear up the nearest flagpole.* Not that I have access to his underwear, of course. But it's still a threatening face I'm making here.

"Nothing." I flip my biology book open. "Nothing at all."

FRIED FRIDAY IN PE. It's a great way to end the day. Forty minutes of line drills, push-ups, pull-ups, speed drills on the jump ropes, and sprints. And if we're lucky (or still upright and breathing without medical assistance), we get five whole minutes to shower and change.

"Get those knees up. Swing that rope. Faster! Faster!"

Coach Nelson yells above the slapping of thirty jump ropes. Jumping rope was so much fun for me as a little kid. Why does she have to go and taint it like this?

I swing my rope and trip as it comes back around. So. Tired.

I didn't catch a lot of Zs last night. James called to check on me after play rehearsal. I didn't have much to say to him. He asked if I didn't want to stay home with Maxine and Amy. Whatever. Like he wanted me at home. It had sounded believable though.

"Drop the ropes and give me twenty-five push-ups!"

I throw my rope down and prop my body on the floor, nose to the ground.

One.

Two.

Should I wear my new jeans tonight? Maybe with the cute little heels?

Three. Or was that four?

I wonder if I should bring a jacket? What if we're outside some? But if I don't take a jacket, then Trevor will have to offer me his if I get cold.

Seven. Ugh. How many more? My arms are jelly.

"Finish it up and hit the showers. You sissies stink!"

I peel myself off the floor and get a whiff of my armpits. I do reek.

Hannah limps my way, and we walk to the dressing room. I fling open my locker and grab my shower gear.

"Hey! Where're my shoes?" Hannah digs through her locker and searches all around her. "My shoes are gone."

I sort through her stuff, pulling out her backpack, digging through her giant purse. No shoes.

"Who's got Hannah's shoes?" I yell.

Angel slams her locker closed. "That's it. Somebody in here is a thief." She looks at each one of us. "And we're gonna find out who it is."

She and a black-haired friend attack every locker, pushing the few protesting girls out of the way and springing the doors open wide.

Though I have nothing to hide in my cubby, I do not want Angel's grubby hands on my stuff. When she stands in front of my locker, I remain in place. Guarding my space.

"Move it, Parker."

I shake my head. "I don't think so, Nelson. I'm really glad you're helping Hannah look for her shoes, but I don't have them. And you're not touching anything of mine."

Angel smirks. "If you got nothing to hide, then there's no problem."

"You're currently my only problem. Now I'm gonna take a shower. And I don't want to see you near my things. Are we clear? Because I would hate for you to get suspended again."

Angel plants her face so close to mine I can smell her afternoon breath. "Open the locker."

"Outta my face, Angel."

She turns to her friend. "I think she's got something to hide."

Hannah steps between us. "She doesn't have anything to hide. We don't even wear the same shoe size."

"Open your locker," Angel growls. Her eyes carry a variety of threats.

"Nope."

Angel puts her fists up. "I've been practicing my wrestling lately. You either show us you don't have the shoes, or I'll show you my latest move called the punching bag."

My shower bag plops to the floor. I stretch my arms out. I am so not in the mood for another black eye.

"Well, Parker?"

"Katie, don't do this. It's not worth it. This is the last thing your foster mom needs." Hannah's voice nails through some of the choking anger.

Millie.

If I stress her out, I would be the lowest of the low. What kind of person upsets a cancer patient?

I pick up my stuff again. Shoving past Angel, my shoulder rams into hers. "Have at it. But if you take anything, I will hunt you down."

The spray of the shower beats into my skin. Walking around with raw fury burning in your gut makes for a long day. I want to turn back the clock. Go back to a month ago when things were nearly perfect. No cancer. No Amy. No Angel picking fights on a regular basis.

No knowledge of what really goes into the cafeteria goulash.

"Parker! Parker!"

The fifth time I hear my name, I shut off the spray and poke my head out the curtain. "What is it, sweetie?" My giant grin matches my syrupy tone.

Angel stomps to my shower and holds up a pair of shoes. Hannah's shoes. "Do these look familiar to you?"

Water drips down my face. "Glad you found them."

"Found them in *your* locker."

A draft shoots under the shower curtain and blows across my

cold skin. "What?" I look for Hannah, who stands behind Angel, twisting her ponytail.

"I didn't take her shoes, Angel. Hannah knows I would never do that."

"And what do these shoes tell you?" Black combat boots dangle from Angel's other hand.

"They say 'My owner has really bad taste, and I wish someone would put me out of my misery.'"

Angel throws the shoes to the concrete floor. "Cute. You think you're just real cute, don't you?"

I pull the curtain tighter around my face. "Right now I think I'm wet and freezing. Now can I dry off or are you going to get to your point?"

I edge my arm out and grab my towel hanging on a hook.

"My shoes were in your gym locker. Hannah's shoes were in your gym locker. Is this becoming clearer?"

"Stop it, Angel. You know Katie didn't steal anything."

Is that doubt I hear in Hannah's voice?

I wrap the towel around me and step out. "I did not take anything."

"I opened your locker, dug under your bag and some clothes, and found your hidden stash of shoes."

Gripping my towel, I close the distance between me and Angel. "I do not steal. You did that. You put that in my locker, Angel Nelson. How pathetic can you get?"

"I think the proof is in your locker here. Everyone witnessed it. I didn't pull those shoes out of my sleeve. They came from your locker."

Angel and I stand in the center of the dressing room. Everyone stands around us, their eyes glued to me. I look around. Doubtful stares everywhere.

"Come on. It's me. I've been in this class all year. Why would I take anything now?" Did that sound a bit desperate? "Look, I don't know how those shoes ended up in my locker, but I did not take them. End of discussion."

I bust through the circle and pull out my clothes. I jerk my shirt over my head.

"Don't walk away from me. You can't just steal from us and think we're not gonna do anything about it."

Fear tugs on my gut. "You do whatever you need to, Angel. But you and I both know I wasn't in anyone else's locker. Maybe the janitor put them in there. I don't know."

Hannah chews on her bottom lip.

"Hannah, you believe me, right?"

"Sure, Katie." She clutches her flats in her non-twisting hand. And drops her gaze as I walk by.

"I don't know what you're up to, Angel. But you've picked the wrong girl to mess with." I shove past my accuser.

Thirty girls watch me leave. Their faces the same—doubtful, accusing.

Walking out, I carry my gym bag and my backpack.

And what's left of my dignity.

Chapter 24

"**Y**ou're sure you don't want to spend the night again?"

Frances parks her beastly station wagon in the Scott's driveway.

"Yeah. I'll just stay here."

"What if Amy's taken over your room?"

My door opens with a painful creak. "I'll kick her out. That's my room, my bed. And she and her cigarettes can take the couch." I'm done playing nice. I have no doubt something else hideous is going to happen to me. I want to at least face it from the comfort of my own bedroom.

"Oh, hey, Hannah and I are going to the movies with some of the Target Teens. Are you in?"

Images of PE burn in my brain. "No. I'm just gonna hang out."

"With Maxine and Amy?"

I sling my belongings over my shoulder. "Sure . . . for a little while."

Frances clicks the radio off, silencing some classic Gwen Stefani. "I know that face. You're up to something."

I blast her with an eye roll. "I'm going to Trevor Jackson's party tonight. He invited me."

Frances catapults out of her seat, only to be jerked back by the seat belt. "What? Katie, no." Her black hair dances as she shakes her head. "This is not good."

"Yes, it is. Finally something in my life that *is* good." I drop one bag and lean on her door. "Haven't you ever felt like the world was against you?"

"Is this about the shoes again? I told you Hannah was cool with that."

"It's not about the shoes. Forget the shoes." Not that I could. "It's everything!"

Frances tilts her head. "Do you want me to pray for you right now?"

"No! No, I don't want you to pray for me. I want . . . I want . . ."

"Yes?"

"Forget it. Thanks for the ride."

"Wait! Katie—"

I slam the door.

Frances rolls the window down and yells. "Do the Scotts know you're going to Trevor's party?"

"You sound like Charlie. Just get off my back."

Her brows furrow. "You think that hurts my feelings, but it doesn't. Right now you are acting out of your own pain. You are taking your fears and anxieties and projecting them onto me. By deceiving the Scotts and attending this social function, you are reciprocating your own inner punishment."

I blink. "Huh?"

"Don't go to the party. This isn't about you and Trevor. This is about the fact you're mad, so you're purposely disobeying your family."

"No, it's definitely about me and Trevor." I turn around, my eyes narrowing at the sight of the front door. "Bye, Frances."

"If you call me from jail, I won't pick you up!"

I wave as I make my way up the sidewalk.

Frances sticks her head out of the wagon. "Friends don't let friends drink and drive! Give hugs not drugs! Alcohol is the most commonly used drug among teenagers! Fifty-two percent of all—"

I close the door behind me and stop. And listen.

"Hello?"

Heavy pounding comes from overhead. Is that in my room? That girl better not be messing with my bedroom. I have had it!

The bags crash to the floor, and I sprint up the stairs.

With a curse on my lips, I explode into the room, armed and ready to do battle. "Get outta my—"

Maxine stands on her bed, two nails dangling from her glossy lips. Rocky, drooling on my bean bag, opens one eye.

"My, how I've missed your sweet hollering."

"Hello to you, too," I say.

"Hold this up so I can see where I want it."

Maxine lifts a picture, and tragedy closes in on me once again.

"That is the ugliest, most hideous thing I have ever seen."

In her arms Maxine cradles a velvet print of Jesus and his disciples. They sit at café tables sipping mochas.

"Are you ashamed of Jesus, our Lord and Savior?"

"When he's in neon? Yes." I grab the nails on the bed. "Take it down. You are not putting that in my room."

"Talked to the contractor today about my apartment. Those people are so backed up. Looks like I'll be here another month or two. Thought I'd personalize my space with some art. What's the problem?"

"Art is neither fuzzy nor does it glow in the dark. Take it down. And what is that smell?"

"Sorry." Maxine grimaces. "Beans for lunch."

"No." I tour the room, kicking Amy's clothes out of my path. "Don't you smell that?"

She sniffs. "Did you forget to put your gym socks in the laundry again?"

Things are starting to click. "Does Amy do drugs?"

The bed gives as Maxine sits down. "What are you thinking?"

"That a typhoon hit my room for one thing. And I'm staying here tonight. I don't care what James and Millie say. I'm sleeping in my own bed tonight."

"Well, where else would James and Millie want you?" She raises an eyebrow. "What makes you think Amy's on drugs?"

"Duh. Basic health class information here. She's got all the signs." I take my arm and rake more of Amy's junk off my bed. This calls for clean sheets.

"So she's a little eccentric. Nothing wrong with that."

"My mom was a dealer. I saw people like Amy all the time."

"Well, I think you're wrong." She fluffs a throw pillow.

"Do you?"

My foster grandmother sighs. Her face, for once, serious. "Yeah . . . I've had my suspicions too. I'm just afraid to say anything. Afraid to rock the boat and upset Millie and James. Now is not a good time, you know?"

"Amy needs help though."

"Katie, Amy's had help all her life. She's been in and out of every kind of treatment center from here to Canada. James and Millie have gone above and beyond to help that girl." Maxine gives a weak shrug. "I love her, but I can't reach her. She's gonna have to fall on her face for once. Rely on the G-O-G, baby. The G-O-G."

I smile. "The grace of God."

"You know it."

Do I know it? Do I really believe God can pick you up, when you're at your lowest, most disgusting point and dust you off and make it all better? And why should I believe that? I've yet to see it.

Time for a topic change. "So . . . are we going to the hospital to see Millie?"

"No. I've already been. They're coming home tomorrow morning. They said for Sam not to bring you out."

A karate kick in the stomach would not hurt more. "Why?" My voice is detestably whiny. "We could take Ginger Rogers."

"No, toots, not this time. Millie said she didn't want you hanging out with a sick lady on a Friday night."

"I want to hang out with a sick lady." I rip the sheets off my bed.

"Aw, come on. You and I can stay up really late tonight. Watch some old movies, pop popcorn. Short-sheet James and Millie's bed."

I turn my head and stop a tear. "Nah. I've . . . um . . . gotta study."

Maxine cackles. "Study? Is that code for text some hot guy?"

"No. I have a science fair project. My partner is picking me up to go work on it." Oh, I'm a liar. A rotten, stinky liar. And to Maxine of all people. But I've got to get out of here and go to that party. Trevor Jackson wants to see me. Do I need any more motivation? And if I do, how about the fact my foster parents are right now having family cuddle time with Amy and don't want me there. If they don't want to be around me, why should I feel guilty about making my own plans?

"Is this your plant experiment you've been working on?" Maxine asks.

"Yep, that's the one. Trevor Jackson is picking me up tonight, and we're gonna . . ." Declare our undying love for each other, decide to date exclusively, and practice our good-night kiss. "We're gonna swap data." Or spit. Whatever.

Maxine scratches her chin. "Sounds totally dull."

"That's me." I force a smile. "I'm all about the homework, you know."

Nearby the dog begins to snore.

"Rocky, get out. What is that mutt doing in my room?" I nudge the oversized fur ball awake and shoo him out. He stares blankly, refusing to move.

Maxine rises from the bed. "Well, I'm sure you have some notes to review. Some data to check. I'll let you get ready for your . . . science fair project." She snaps her fingers. "Come on, Rocky."

The dog doesn't move a muscle.

"Want Grandma to make us a banana split?"

Rocky races Maxine downstairs.

I spend a good two hours sanitizing the room. Amy's belongings stack neatly in a corner. I have sprayed the room with deodorizer until it smells like a Hawaiian tropical rainforest.

And now on to the portion of the evening in which I get beautiful. Or at least passably mediocre.

Aside from Target Teen events, this is my first party in In Between. What should I wear? I skip to my closet and twirl around. I need an outfit that says, "I'm available, but not in a slutty sort of way." Or "I'm a good time. But not *that* kind of a good time." Or "Though I have nothing in common with you preps, I've got A-list potential."

I decide on a slim-fitting pair of jeans, distressed in all the right places, and a black, long-sleeved t-shirt, decorated with the emblem of a vintage punk-rock band. I slip into my favorite pair of Cons, stretched out from Maxine "borrowing" them. And of course, my favorite turbo-padded bra.

In the bathroom, I retouch my makeup, going a little heavier with the smoky eyeliner for evening. I fluff my hair, then give it a good shellac of spray. A little perfume. A little gloss.

And then I sit. For hours. Afraid to move or blink. I grab a magazine and flip through it to see if there are any last-minute tips I can use, but that only makes me more nervous. I want Trevor to like me. I want his friends to like me. God owes me this moment, I think. Kind of like a reward after my horrendous day. Like Millie gives Rocky a bone when he needs a treat. I need this night to go well.

I should've got my ends trimmed.

I shouldn't have lied to Maxine. What am I doing going to this party?

I'm just dropping in at the party. Not staying long. It will be fine.

Trouble won't possibly have time to find me.

Chapter 25

"**M**AXINE! WHAT ARE you doing?" I leap off the last few stairs and speed into the living room.

Trevor, right on time at eight o'clock, sits in a leather wingback chair.

Maxine skewers him to the seat, holding a broomstick to his chest. "Just thought Trevor and I would get to know one another."

He looks to me for help.

"All right, back away from him." My voice resonates with calmness. Like on those cop shoes when the investigators talk to insane lunatics holding bomb detonators. "Drop the broom nice and slow."

While I might be going to the party, my dignity will no longer be joining us.

"Please." For the love.

She eases up on the broom. "I just wanted a closer look at the boy."

"Then get your bifocals."

Maxine chokes. "I do not wear bifocals." She smiles at Trevor. "Silly girl. She's so funny. Always making me laugh."

I mouth an apology to Trevor, who has yet to move a single, beautiful muscle.

"Maxine, this is Trevor Jackson."

"Your science partner?"

"We gotta go." With my eyes, I plead with Trevor to play along.

"So, Mr. Jackson . . ." Maxine runs a hand through her hair. "Are you looking forward to the science fair?"

He startles. "I . . . yes. Love the science fair. Just can't get enough . . . science."

Behind Maxine I nod my approval.

"Well, I think your topic is simply fascinating." Maxine takes a seat in the matching wingback, a mere foot away from Trevor. "Tell me, what progress have you made this week? Any discoveries? Interesting observations?"

Why did Trevor have to come to the door? Couldn't he have waited out in the car and laid on the horn like any other guy? It's all caving in on me. I'm so stupid. Stupid, stupid, stupid.

The object of my affection flashes Maxine a smile with all the brilliance of a Fourth of July sparkler. "Ma'am, I would love to share my latest data with you, but then you wouldn't have any reason to come to the science fair." He stands and props a lazy arm on the chair. "And I'm going to enjoy counting the days until I see you there."

Maxine twists a strand of golden hair around her finger. "Well . . . my, my, my."

"We gotta be going. See you in a few hours." I sling my purse over my shoulder. "And if Amy comes back, tell her to sleep in her parents' room. There's no vacancy in my bed."

My hand latches onto Trevor's bicep, and I lead him out the door. The door clicks shut behind us. *Whew.*

Reluctantly I release my grip on Trevor. "Sorry about that. She's a little kooky. If she knew I was going to a party, she'd demand her own invitation."

I walk beside Trevor, very aware of how lucky I am in this moment to be with him.

Until the door crashes open, rattling the house.

I jump and turn around.

"Oh, Katie, dear?" Maxine sashays outside, her hair glowing under the porch lights.

I swallow. "Um . . . yes?"

"Did you really think I would just let you leave?"

Gulp. "I guess I was hoping." I am so busted.

"Now what kind of foster grandmother would I be if I let you two go—"

"Maxine, I'm sorry, I thought—"

"—without this." She shoves my plant toward me.

With trembling hands I take it. ". . . Thanks?" I tuck it under my arm.

Not until I close the Hummer door do I realize I haven't taken a breath in at least a minute. I sag into the chair, limp with relief.

"Your grandma's a trip." Trevor buckles up and starts the engine.

Just drive, Pretty Boy. Get us away from here as fast as you can.

During my long wait for this not-exactly-a-date date, I made a mental list of various conversational topics. Sports (I watched ESPN for a whole fifteen minutes for this guy), school (Principal Wayman— toupee or real hair?), his future plans (Will you be coming back to In Between often?), and the play (Is it just me, or did I totally get the shaft?).

I should have used that time to study lines or catch up on algebra because Trevor grabs his phone as soon as we're out of the driveway and talks all the way to his house.

The giant SUV weaves through town until we come to a gate-house. The In Between golf course? *This* is where Trevor lives? He throws two fingers up in greeting to the attendant, and the security gate opens.

He pulls the Hummer through, now making his fourth phone call, as far as I can count, and we pass by the country club, then rows and rows of upscale homes with their sprawling golf-course backyard.

I clutch my plant and suppress a whimper. I am so out of my league. If my mom could see me now, she'd laugh. That is if she still remembers I exist.

Trevor pulls into the driveway of a two-story brick home. The garage door rises, and the Hummer comes to a rest in one of the empty spaces. Right next to a red BMW.

He ends his call, and I blurt out a quick "Thank you for the ride" just as he fires off a text. Does he even remember I'm here?

"Yeah, glad you're here. Hope you have a good time." He jumps out.

I open my door and grip my way down to the floor, a hiker making her way back down Everest.

The walls of the garage shake and bump with the loud music from inside. I recognize a familiar rap song.

"Katie, you know, this is my party, so I probably won't see you around much. I need to make the rounds, talk to everyone. Keep the glasses flowing."

I grin and bob my head. "Oh, yeah, sure. Totally understand."

With one hand on the doorknob, Trevor stops. I stop. He turns around and steps closer to me. We are toe to toe. A breath apart.

"I'll still be watching you all night though." His tanned face draws nearer. His mouth parts, his hand claims a spot in my shoulder. My eyelids flutter closed.

"Trevor!" A quarterback-sized guy hangs out the door.

Trevor steps away so fast, I lose my balance and bump into the wall.

"Dude, did you get the other keg?"

Trevor hands the guy his keys. "It's in the back. You and Jennings wanna bring it in?"

Like Rocky gripping my nightshirt with his teeth, something tugs on my conscience. But I let it go. Just a few hours of fun. That's all I'm asking for.

Trevor follows the party noises into the house. And I follow Trevor.

He high-fives a few people, bumps knuckles with some guys from his baseball team, and stops to talk to the captain of the cheerleading squad.

I fade into the scene and do what any party loner would do. Find the food.

My foot taps in time to the music as I fill my plate with cold pizza rolls and crackers.

Trevor swaggers in my direction, juggling four bags of chips and a cup of beer dangling from his teeth. He drops the chips on the table and grabs his cup.

He returns with another cup and places it in my hand. Guilt squeezes my chest. A horrid image of Pastor Mike flashes in front of me. What would he say if he walked into this party? Or Millie? Or Frances?

But it's not like I'm doing anything. I'm holding a cup for crying out loud. No crime there.

"Great party." I am so lame. Who says "great party?" Only total dorks who never get invited to these types of things.

"Thanks." He smiles and plants a hand on the table.

I step into the space between us. "Did I mention I need to be home in a few hours?"

"But you're not Cinderella." He takes a drink and winks.

This guy could pick his nose, and I'd find something hot about it. And normally his sly winks send my heart into orbit. But just now? Not so cute. I'm sure it's just my bad mood.

"See that guy over there?" Trevor points to another jock. "He'll be wearing a lampshade within thirty minutes. Four beers and he's toast."

"Oh, wow. Four? That's so weak." And I laugh. Because he's Trevor.

"You better drink up. I like a girl with some stamina in her."

I live with Maxine. You'd need less stamina to run the New York Marathon *and* the Iron Man.

"So . . . about that ride . . ."

"Katie, we just got here. Relax. Eat. Drink. Be merry." His hand reaches for the hair hanging artfully in my face and tucks it behind my ear. "Gotta get a refill and make some rounds. See ya in a few."

I wiggle my fingers good-bye.

"He's something, isn't he?"

Turning around, I see the voice belongs to an upperclassman from In Between High. Pretty. Painfully skinny. Brunette. Expertly dressed. I dislike her immediately.

"Yeah, he's nice." My eyes follow Trevor throughout the living room. A room the size of the Scott's entire downstairs.

"I wouldn't get too attached." She selects a chip and takes a measured bite.

She even eats pretty.

"Oh, we're just friends." I smile ferociously, implying more. "We're in—"

"The play together. Yeah, I know."

"How do you know?" Has Trevor been talking about me? That would be totally amazing.

Her copper highlights shimmer as she laughs. "Because that's where he picks up all his little conquests."

I choke on a glob of bean dip. "What? I'm not one of his conquests. Look, I think Trevor really gets a bum rap. People just don't understand him sometimes, you know?"

"Yeah, people like you."

I focus on my phone like I've just gotten a text. "It's been nice talking to you—"

"Monica. I'm Monica Blake."

Why does that name sound familiar?

"As in Chelsea Blake's sister."

Oh, well, I see the lack-of-personality disorder runs in the family. "I'm Katie."

"I know. And my friendly advice to you is to stay away from Trevor if you're smart." She breaks off a piece of another chip and sticks it in her mouth.

"Doesn't sound very friendly to me." Leaving my plate there, I go in search of friendlier territory.

I swirl my beer around as I peruse the crowd. What's stopping me from drinking it? This is a party. And I should be partying.

I lift up my cup and sip.

Nope. I can't do it.

I swallow it down but pour the rest out in a nearby ficus tree. Where's a trash can?

Probably in the kitchen. Wherever that is. Has to be close. I wish Trevor would come back and talk to me. I don't know any of these people. This is so not cool.

I push through a crowd of people flocked around guys playing a video game.

"Kill him! Bullet in the head! Yeah!"

Ugh. Why can't they play some nice games? Like Monopoly or Jenga? You know, the kind that don't involve giant body counts.

Weaving through the living room, I walk down a short hall and find the kitchen, a restaurant-sized room painted in a fierce red with creamy white accents.

And I find Trevor.

With his arm around some girl.

My feet trip over a crushed beer can in the floor.

Trevor jerks his arm away. "Hey, Katie."

"Hey." I stare his friend down, my focus blurred by the smoke coming from another room and my own jealousy. "Just looking for the trash."

"Oh, yeah, I need to get some garbage bags going huh? Last time I forgot, everyone decided to throw their trash in the pool. My dad was furious."

"See ya later, Trev." The miniskirted girl slinks out of the kitchen.

I sit my cup on the counter and step toward the doorway.

"Whoa, wait." His arm reaches out and grabs my wrist. He gently pulls me back to him. "What's up? Who spit in *your* beer?"

I shake my head, concentrating on a spot on the floor. "Nobody. I'm fine." Monica Blake's words replay in my head.

"That was a good friend of mine. She's having a rough time. She doesn't have many people to talk to right now." He tips my chin up with is hand. My eyes meet his. "Don't be mad. I didn't think you were like that. You seem to really have it together, you know? Not like a lot of these girls around here."

"I didn't say I was mad." I shrug. "Why would I be mad? I'm glad you could be there for your friend."

Trevor smiles. "You're different. It's what I like about you."

His arms circle around me, and his face hovers over mine. I lean into his warmth, and once again close my eyes as his mouth draws closer to mine, like two magnets surging towards one another.

Trevor's lips brush mine, and I move my hands up his polo-covered chest.

He deepens the kiss. My brain is on overdrive. Can't think. Room is spinning.

Somebody get a fire extinguisher. Because this is about to get hot.

Woo-woo-woo! Woo-woo-woo!

So hot I hear sirens in my head. That's right, sound the alarm because Trevor Jackson has got his lips on mine.

Trevor raises his head. "What is that?"

I pull him back to me. "Nothing." Isn't that sweet? He hears it too.

Woo-woo-woo! Woo-woo-woo!

The fog in my head disappears, and I'm snapped back to reality at the noise. That's not in my head. That's coming from outside!

"What is that? Is that the police?" I clutch Trevor's shirt. If I get hauled downtown again, I am gonna die. Just drop to the floor and die.

"Nah, can't be." Trevor runs out of the kitchen into the living room.

The music volume drops.

"Open up!" A voice calls from outside, magnified and loud.

Except for a few whispers and the voices coming from the game, the house falls silent.

I stay in the kitchen, searching for somewhere to hide. The pantry will probably work. It could hold five of me. Plus I'd have unlimited amounts of mac-n-cheese.

"Katie Parker! Front and center!" *Squawwwk! Beeeep!*

My heart stops.

I know that voice.

I run to the living room, peel back curtains, and peek through the blinds.

Maxine. Standing in the front lawn in her Sponge Bob house shoes and her hair covered in curlers. Holding a megaphone.

"You send Katie Parker outside, or I'm calling the cops and busting this party!" The megaphone screeches.

My face flames with heat as every partygoer looks at me, their glares pinning me to the spot. Unable to move. To think. I'm drowning in humiliation.

Knock! Knock!

I jump back from the blinds. "Don't answer that!"

The knock turns into banging.

I hear the megaphone squawk to life again. "It doesn't take long to dial nine-one-one! Here I go. I'm calling . . . Nine . . ."

Running to Trevor, I grab his collar. "It's my foster grandmother. Tell her I'm not here. Tell her my friend Frances picked me up."

"One . . ."

Trevor shakes his head, his eyes wide. "If she calls the cops, we're all dead meat."

"Two!"

Trevor rips the door open. "Don't call!"

Maxine stands in the opening. "Well, hello, Mr. Jackson." With her mud-mask covered face, she gazes up at the stars. "Lovely evening for underage drinking, isn't it?"

She lands an elbow to his chest and shoves past him. The megaphone rises to her mouth. "All right, you brats, clear out. I know who you are. I know your parents. I know your parents' parents. You have five minutes to clear out of here and get home. Don't make me call the po-po. I'll do it."

I hang my head. I will never recover from this. I'll be a hundred years old and people in this town will still hate me for this. I'll have to move. Go to a private school. Change my name. My face.

"You." Maxine points a French-manicured finger at me. "Get outside. Ginger awaits."

Rambling nonstop apologies to everyone I pass, I shuffle out the door behind Maxine.

Trevor holds the door open.

"I'm sorry," I offer weakly. A few minutes ago he was kissing me senseless. Now he looks like he wants to shove me under the wheels of his Hummer.

His glare shrivels my heart. "Just go."

My eyes fill with tears. "Trevor," I sniff. "I need to ask you just one thing."

His chest expands with his deep exhale. "What?"

"Can I get my plant?"

Slam!

Chapter 26

"**A**ND YOU WILL address me as Maxine, the most beautiful woman you know. And you will start watching Hallmark movies with me every week. And you will eat any green vegetable Millie puts on *my* plate. You will hold my hand every time I get my eyebrows waxed. And—"

"Okay, Maxine."

"Excuse me?"

"Okay, Maxine, the most beautiful woman I know, I get it. I'm in your debt."

My foster grandmother and I sit on opposite beds in my room. Her nasty velvet rendition of Jesus at Starbucks now hangs on the wall above her head. I can't seem to look away from the thing. Stephen King should write a book about it. It's that horrific.

"And you will let me put my hot pink bedspread back on."

I grimace. "The plaid one with the white pom-poms? No, that's so ugly and—"

Maxine picks up her cell phone like she's going to call someone— like James and Millie—to tell them of my horrible deeds. And get me grounded for life.

"Okay! Fine. I love the plaid bedspread. Wish I had one just like it." To suffocate myself in. Seriously, my life is over. I will either collapse under all of Maxine's demands or confess all my crimes to the Scotts just to get it over with.

"I am so disappointed in you, little missy." Her hands rip at the curlers.

"I know."

"You lied to me." Maxine shucks out of her daisy print robe and grabs her red silk one in its place. "I thought we were buddies."

For the second time tonight, tears fall freely down my face. "We are."

My breath catches at Maxine's expression. I see hurt and disappointment. Like I've stolen something from her. Like I've crossed a line, and I can't return.

"Friends don't lie to one another."

I grab a Kleenex and blow.

"I mean sure, I may have stretched the truth when you asked about my age."

I nod my head.

"And I may not have been completely honest when I told you I got Botox injections last month because the clinic was having a clearance sale."

"Uh-huh."

"But still, Katie." Maxine's voice is almost a hush. "I trusted you. And you abused that privilege. Of course I did know you were lying."

"You did?"

Maxine sticks a thumb in her chest. "You gotta get up pretty early in the morning to trick this girl."

"Did Frances rat me out?"

"No, your real science partner called."

"Charlie called? When? Why? What did he say?"

Maxine arches a perfectly shaped brow. "Interested, are we?"

Am I?

"No. I'm not. Of course not. In fact, the jerk knew I was going to the party. He called here to get me in trouble."

"Well, it worked."

"And where did you get the siren on your bicycle?"

"Nice touch, wasn't it? Got that baby on eBay." Maxine settles at the foot of my bed. "What's going on with you? You haven't been yourself lately."

Rocky's nose appears in the crack of the door. He nudges it open and trots in. He stands in front of me and whines. Dogs have it so easy. What do they have to worry about? Sleep, get up, eat kibbles, chew on a shoe, sleep, drool on someone, go back to sleep.

"Answer me, Katie."

I lean back on the bed and throw my hands over my face. Rocky chooses this moment to leap onto the bed and snuggles in beside me.

"Get out." I shove at the dog, who refuses to budge. "Get off this bed." His nose burrows under my knee. "Your new artwork is scaring him."

Maxine crosses her arms and her brow furrows. "Get on with it."

"I don't know." How do I explain that my whole world is crashing? A giant, flaming ball of destruction. "Nothing's going right."

"Such as?"

"Millie has cancer."

"That is tough." Maxine nods. "But how does that affect you?"

"See, that's the whole point. It does affect me. But no one around here acts like it does. I'm the last one to know anything. And then James and Millie treat me like I don't care about any of this. Like today, I didn't get to go to the hospital."

"I knew you'd be madder than a wet cat. Honestly, they thought they were protecting you. James and Millie are trying to do everything they can to not upset you. They wanted you to go out with your friends, though not of the keg party variety, and have fun. Millie said she didn't want you thinking you had to wait around at the hospital all night."

"But I wanted to. Doesn't anybody care what I want?"

"I stuck curlers in my hair and painted my face with a peach mud mask. Would I humiliate myself for just anyone? I care about you, kid." She shakes her head. "Get a clue, yo."

"Have you been watching MTV again?"

She shrugs. "So what if I have? I had to do something while babysitting Amy these past few days."

"And that's another thing. Amy."

"What about her?"

"Amy comes home, which is great. Fabulous." Not really. "And I get kicked out of my room. Do you know how that made me feel? Fine, so this was her room. But this has been my home, *my* room for over six months." I swipe at my eyes. "How do you think I felt when I'm told to go stay at Frances's house?"

Maxine's eyes narrow. "Who told you to do that?"

I sniff. "Amy did."

"That little—"

"She said her parents wanted to spend time with just her, you know, like a family, and I was to stay at Frances's."

Maxine sits next to me. "You listen to me, and you listen good. *You* are this family." She pulls me close, smashing my head against her bosom. "You are one of us. Do you understand?"

I need windshield wipers for these tears.

"I don't know who that woman is, but she's not our Amy. I'm sorry she's been hurtful to you. But she's not herself." Maxine pats my head, and I spill the story about Angel and the shoes. "I'm sorry you're had a bad week. Believe *me*, I know it's hard to sleep when you're not in your own bed."

"Yes, I can tell from your eight hours straight of snoring every night that it's disturbing your beauty rest."

Maxine smiles. "And I'm sorry you've felt left out lately."

I nod.

"And I'm sorry you've apparently had your brains sucked out by aliens. Because that is the only excuse for what you pulled tonight."

I push my foster grandmother away. "But you're not going to tell James and Millie?"

"I said I wouldn't." She holds up a finger. "If my conditions are met. But if you do something like that again, or if you fail to eat one single lima bean off my plate or miss one day of my chicken feeding duty, I'll spill my guts like Texas road kill."

"Well, isn't this cozy?"

Rocky's head snaps up as Amy walks through the door.

"Hello, Amy, dear." Maxine goes to hug her granddaughter. Amy turns her head at Maxine's kiss.

"Where's my stuff?"

"I cleaned up a little. It's stacked over there." I point to her suitcase in the corner.

Amy smirks. "How nice of you. But I was perfectly comfortable the way it was."

Maxine resumes her seat beside me. "This is Katie's room now. And you had it completely trashed."

Amy stumbles over to her things and tears open the suitcase. "So?" Her red eyes transmit loathing and disgust. Angel could take lessons from this woman.

"You can sleep in your parents' room tonight. It has a much more comfortable bed anyway. One of those space age mattresses you know." Maxine drops her voice. "Excellent for jumping on, Rocky and I have discovered."

"I don't want to sleep in there." She smiles at Maxine. "You sleep in there, Grandma. Katie and I can bunk in here. Like a big slumber party."

Maxine reaches into my nightstand without turning away from Amy. She pulls out a stick of gum and pops it in her mouth. I narrow my eyes. Can't get anything by that woman. Not even my secret gum stash.

"Katie will sleep in her bed. I will sleep in mine. And you will sleep in your parents'."

Amy stomps her booted foot. Dried mud sprinkles on the wood floor. "I don't want to! You take their bed."

"Nope." Maxine pops her gum. "Now get ready for bed, Amy. You look like you haven't slept in weeks."

"Like you care."

"That didn't work when you were thirteen, and it sure doesn't fly now."

Amy grabs some clothes from her suitcase. "I'm outta here."

"Where are you going?" Maxine throws up an arm and halts her granddaughter.

"Back off!" Amy yells. "I'm sick of the questions! I'm sick of being told what to do. Nothing ever changes!"

"Are those your mother's keys?" Maxine asks.

"My rental's out of gas."

Maxine holds out her hand. "Hand them over now."

"No!" Amy shoves past her grandmother and bolts out the bedroom door, slamming it shut.

Maxine and I run after her. I hurdle the stairs, but by the time I race onto the porch, Amy is backing the car out. I sprint down the driveway, but it's no use.

Maxine calls from the front steps. "Come back, Katie. You can't catch her."

"What do we do?" I yell.

She holds up her cell phone. "We call the police."

Small lights on either side of the drive illuminate my steps. "And what do we tell them?"

"That Amy's driving under the influence." Maxine holds the door open. "See, Katie, you keep sneaking out to those parties, and *that's* what happens to you. First it's cigarettes. Then it's alcohol. Then it's drugs. And then you're just another Amy. Cracked out, washed up, and skinnier than a starved supermodel."

"Yes, Maxine."

"Excuse me, Sweet Pea?"

"Yes, Maxine, the most beautiful woman I know."

We each take an end on the living room couch, and I turn on a Hallmark movie. While Maxine places a call to the In Between police department.

"This is Maxine Simmons. I want to report a major disturbance." She sighs into the receiver. "Her name is Amy Scott."

Chapter 27

WHEN I ROLL over and look at the clock Saturday morning it says eleven. I think I can count this day a success already.

The next thing I notice is Maxine standing in front of the mirror, a pink hat on top of her head, with salmon colored feathers sticking out in every direction.

She catches me looking at her. "Well, hello, sleeping beauty. You like?"

"It looks like the butt-end of a flamingo." I rub my eyes and throw my feet over the side of the bed.

"Well, then you don't have to wear it. You can wear another one."

"Why would I wear a stupid hat?"

Maxine moves away from the mirror and stands over me. "Because you will be attending my ladies tea this afternoon."

A bubble of laughter escapes. "What? I don't *even* think so."

Maxine glares. "James and Millie are home. Downstairs, in fact. Would you like to explain to them why you were at Trevor Jackson's house or should I?"

"There better be cookies at this tea party." I jerk my arms into my robe and cinch it tight. "How long has Millie been home?"

Maxine smiles. "A couple of hours."

"Why didn't you wake me up?"

"Because I would've missed this." She holds up her cell phone. On the screen in brilliant color is a picture of my face. Mouth wide open. Troll-like hair.

Maxine's cackle follows me all the way downstairs.

"Good morning, Katie." James intercepts me on the bottom step and pulls me into a fierce hug. "We missed you, kid."

"Right back atcha." I step away. "Where's Millie?"

"She's in the living room."

I find Millie curled up on the couch in some new lime-green pajamas with Rocky keeping a close watch.

"Hi, sweetie!" My foster mom's pale face brightens. "Come sit next to me for a while. I've missed you."

I cuddle in beside Mille, who rests her arm across my legs. I lean into her shoulder, careful not to put too much weight on her.

"I'm glad you're back," I whisper. "Things aren't the same without you." *I'm* not the same without you. "Did Maxine tell you about Amy leaving last night?"

"Yes, she did. She also told me Amy led you to believe we didn't want you in the house while she was here."

My eyes drop to the floor.

"Katie, that is not true. You belong here, with us. I would never kick you out of your own bed."

"That's right." James sits on a leather ottoman. "Surely you know if I kicked anyone out of her bed it would be Maxine."

"But why wouldn't I believe her?" I look at both foster parents. "A lot of stuff has happened lately that has made it clear I'm not really a part of this family."

Millie's hand flies to her chest. "Well, of course you are!"

"How can you think that?" James asks.

"You left me in the dark about the cancer. You didn't want me at the hospital during the surgery. And Friday I wasn't allowed to come see you at all. Like the only person you wanted to see was Amy." Did that sound as pitiful as I think it did?

James scoots in closer. "Katie . . ." He removes his glasses and rubs the bridge of his nose. "You've been through a lot. Even before you came to live with us. Our goal has always been to provide the best possible home for you."

"By making me feel like an outsider?"

"No," James continues. "By protecting you from any further hurt."

"We just wanted to do everything to keep you happy. Nothing we did was with the intention of leaving you out. I didn't want my cancer to stop you from having a fun weekend."

Oh, I wish it had.

My foster dad pats my knee. "We can see we made a few giant mistakes. We seem to be doing a lot of that lately." He looks at his wife, who wears a matching expression of worry.

"If I could bear hug you right now, I would. We don't want you to ever doubt your place in this family." Millie stretches a smile across her face. "We love you, Katie."

James nods. "We certainly do."

My heart swells, but my brain freezes. I know I should say something here, but I can't. Words pound in my head trying to break free, but I can't seem to grab hold of any of them.

"How precious."

The spell of the moment breaks as Amy appears in the room.

James stands to his feet. "Where have you been? We've been worried sick about you."

"Where are my car keys?" Millie holds out her hand.

"Your car is fine. That *is* what you've been so worried about, right?" The keys jangle as Amy tosses them to her dad. "Maybe I should've given them to Katie. My new replacement."

I place one foot on the floor, ready to make my exit and leave them alone to fight.

"Stay, Katie," James says. "This is a family discussion. Besides, you need to stick around for Amy's apology."

Amy laughs. "Apologize? For what? Your little brat here kicked me out of my own room last night. And Grandma just let her."

"That's her bed. Her room. You should thank her for sharing it with you the past two nights," Millie says.

"You know, since you told her we didn't want her around." James crosses his arms.

Amy opens her mouth, but her mother holds up a hand and stops her.

"We purchased a plane ticket for you back to Miami. Your plane leaves at three o'clock. Your bags are packed and in the rental car. Your father put gas in it for you this morning."

Amy's red eyes tear up as she stares at her mom. "So you're kicking me out?"

James runs a hand over his clean-shaven face. "There's a list in your suitcase. Pastors I know in Florida. A list of treatment centers."

"For what?"

"You need help, Amy."

"I'm not on drugs anymore."

I bite my lip. *And I'm on the cover of Vogue.*

Amy makes a strangled sound, puts her hands over eyes and sobs. "I've never been good enough for you! Admit it."

"That's not true." Millie's voice catches.

"All my life I've tried to please you. It was never enough. My grades weren't high enough, my clothes weren't right, I didn't love church enough. Why can't you just love me for me?"

"How can you say that?" James thunders. "You can't possibly believe that. We've given you everything. Love, home, our support. But we will always want more for you. We will never stop believing you could do more with your life. That you can build a good life."

"A life that looks like yours? Fits your idea for me?"

"We want you to be healthy and safe. And a functioning member of society. Is that really too much to hope for our child?"

"So kicking me out is how you're gonna help me?"

Is now a good time to offer a certain neon velvet print as a parting gift?

"We've played this game for years." Millie says.

Her husband nods. "We're done. Every time we bail you out, we're just making it easier for you to live like you do. Easier for you to sink further into your addiction. We realized this weekend it has to stop. It's time we let you fall on your face."

"Thanks," Amy sneers. "Thanks a lot."

"We love you," Millie whispers. "And you will always have a place in this family and in this home. When you get clean."

"When you're ready to try, all you have to do is call. Call us. Call any of those numbers I've given you."

Millie sniffs and rubs a hand over her running nose. "We're here for you when you're ready. And we're praying for you. We know God can heal this situation."

"God? I don't care about God. He's been shoved down my throat all my life!" Amy holds her arms out. "Where is God in all of this? Where is he when I can't go a day without something to get me through? Where is he when I can't get a job?"

Amy continues to rant, and I feel some of my animosity toward her deflating. This girl is just sad.

"Where is your God when I get kicked out of one more apartment?"

"I'll go with you to the airport this afternoon," James says. "If you leave us a number, I'll call you with your mom's test results."

"Don't bother. I'm done with this." Amy storms out of the living room. The three of us follow her. She stops at the front door. "I'm your daughter," she says through her tears. "Your daughter."

The door slams.

Nobody moves.

Amy's car starts up and roars out of the drive.

"Who's ready for a tea party?" Maxine glides down the stairs. A feather boa drapes her neck and floats behind her.

No one answers.

"What?" She pops a pink bubble. "Did I miss something?"

"I TALKED TO Nash today." Frances kicks off her shoes and lounges on Maxine's bed.

"You called him?"

"Yes. My cover story was that I needed to talk to him about our project."

"Frances, I'm shocked." I grin. "And totally proud. How did it go?"

"Terrible. First of all, I got nervous. And I just started spewing out whatever was in my head. And when I'm nervous, I usually try to think of random facts and trivia . . . So that's what came out."

"I'm sure he didn't notice. It was a good reminder for him how smart you are."

"Yes, because who wouldn't want to date a girl who calls you and says, 'A cow squirts about 200,000 glasses of milk in her lifetime.' Or 'Seven hundred million people have blood sucking hookworms and don't even know it.'"

Maybe that's Maxine's problem.

"And that's not even the worst of it. Do you want to know the worst part?"

"I would love to." I smile, content for now things are somewhat back to normal. Millie and James are home. Maxine is in the den watching her DVR'd soaps. Amy's gone, and Frances is . . . well, Frances.

"He said . . ." She looks to the ceiling, like she's about to call on God for help. "He said he couldn't talk to me, that he had band practice."

"So?"

"So? So! The band was practicing because they have a new member. A girl. It's Jessi White. She's in my Pre-AP English class. She's tall, skinny, dark hair, perfect skin."

"So she's basically your twin?"

"Are you kidding? She's like viper hot. The girl dresses like a biker chick. Wears these grungy, nasty old t-shirts." Frances shakes her head. "She's so cool."

I sigh. Frances's life would be so much easier if she'd choose someone else to like. One of her math club nerds, for instance. "So this girl's in his band. That doesn't mean they're making out in between sessions."

"Don't you get it? *I* could've been in his band. I could've been their ultra-cool band chick."

I laugh so hard I snort. "Frances, come on. You play the flute."

"Are you saying I can't totally rock out?"

"Yes."

Maxine explodes into the room. "Good news, ladies!"

I watch the dog tromp in behind her. "The circus is leaving town, and they want you to go with them?"

"Very funny. I am here to inform you the tea party will begin in forty-five minutes. Everything is set. The silver is polished. The china is waiting. The tea is brewing. And James and Millie have taken a long Saturday drive." Maxine squints at Frances. "What's wrong with you? Did you make an A-minus at school last week?"

My friend rolls her eyes. "No. Boy troubles."

With eyes aglow, Maxine settles next to me. "Do tell."

Frances relays the chronicles of Nash while my foster grand-mother nods at all the right moments and inserts the occasional, "Yes, yes, I see."

"I'm not making any progress," Frances concludes.

Maxine studies my friend. "I said I would help you, and help I will. I know just what you need to do."

I smell the trouble like week old bean burritos, but Frances walks right into it. "What should I do?"

Kneeling on the floor, Maxine sticks a hand under her bed, rum-mages around, and produces the second ugliest hat I've seen today.

"You drink tea!" She plops the monstrosity on Frances's head.

"She's not going to your tea party, Maxine." Especially with something dead riding on top of her head.

Maxine quirks an eyebrow. "Frances, here's the situation. What you are doing isn't working. In a little over thirty minutes, the living room will be filled with ten ladies of distinction. Of experience. Ladies who have lived full lives. Who have been around the block."

"In their walkers," I mumble.

"Zip it!" Maxine puts a hand over my mouth and pulls me toward her. "As I was saying, what do you have to lose?" Her hand tightens. "Believe me, we know men."

I break loose. "I think you meant to say, 'We know Depends.'"

Frances considers her invitation. "I don't know . . ."

Maxine levels me with her evil eye. "Katie's going. Tell her how much fun it's going to be, snookums." At my silence she adds, "Katie loves tea parties. In fact she loves all sorts of *parties*, don't you, Sweet Pea?"

"It will be loads of fun." My teeth are going to snap from clenching so tight. "You should go."

"Well, of course she's going!" Maxine pats Frances on both cheeks. "Now I'll just lay out some hats, and you two can pick the ones you want to wear. Dress code is hats, gloves, and no pants of any sort." She smiles and I feel my blood boil under my skin. "We'll let you get by without the gloves. This once."

Thirty minutes later Frances and I stand in front of my dresser mirror. We both wear similar looks of shock and disgust.

"I think I look like a pilgrim," Frances mutters.

"My hat looks like an Easter bunny threw up all over it."

"Thanks for letting me borrow your skirt." Frances's hem nearly drags the floor. I have a good five inches on her. "You ready?"

My cell phone chirps. Text message from Maxine.

GET UR BUNS DOWN HERE NOW.

"Let's go," I say. "We've stalled all we can."

Our heels click on the hardwood floor as we enter the living room. Maxine, dressed in a frilly pink concoction, rises from her seat.

"Ladies! Attention, please. I would like to introduce you to the girls I was telling you about. This is Katie." I force a smile. "And this, my dears, is the lovelorn Frances Vega."

The silver headed crowd erupts in a singular, sympathetic *ooohhh*.

"Take a seat, girls. I will bring you your tea and scones."

I nudge Frances. "Scones?"

Maxine returns bearing china cups of hot tea. I should've told her to put Diet Coke in mine. The dainty cups rest in saucers rimmed with Oreos.

"I was fresh out of scones today." Maxine says when I bite into a cookie.

The elderly ladies chat amongst themselves for a few minutes. Rocky is nowhere to be found, I note. Probably scared away by all the fashion violations in this room.

Maxine shushes the room. "All rightie, let's get started, shall we? Today's topic of discussion is romance."

The women nod in appreciation.

"Specifically, Frances Vega wants some romance in her life, but the object of her affection is not cooperating. Though I have no experience with that, I'm sure all the rest of you ladies can relate to her pain." Maxine paces the length of the living room. "Now here's the skinny. Frances likes this boy. He's in a band." The women nod again. One gives Frances a thumbs up. "They go to school together and are partners for the science fair."

A woman in lilac raises her hand. "How about a project on kissing?"

Frances blushes. "Um . . . um, er, uh, no. We—we already have our project. But thank you." She looks to me for help. I cross my arms and shrug. I could've told her this would be painful.

"Let's start with the basics." Maxine ticks each item off on her hand. "Interests, lingo, and clothing. First item, interests. Who wants to take this one? Marge?"

A plump woman with jet black hair (minus the two-inch white roots) speaks up. "Interests. You need to determine his interests. If he likes to fish, then you learn about fishing. If he likes to whittle, then you buy a knife. If your man likes to sit on the porch, then you buy yourself a rocking chair."

I cover my grin with my tea cup.

Maxine nods. "Simple as that. All right, next is lingo. How 'bout it, Betty Lou?"

"Lingo is indeed important." Betty Lou pats her scalp-tight perm. "You gotta learn to speak their language, young lady. If he says he's too tired to go to the mall, then that means there's a ballgame on. When your man says he's going to get some milk, that means he's headed strait for Gus's Getcher Gas to have coffee and donuts with the boys. And if he says his arthritis is acting up, then that means call the neighbor boy, 'cause he ain't gonna mow the lawn."

Maxine pats her friend. "Wise words, Betty Lou. Wise words. Now, let us discuss clothing, a very important aspect in attracting one of the opposite sex. Who shall take this one?"

"Ew! Me! Me!"

"Um . . . All right, Mabel. Sure, you give us your best pointers on clothing."

Mabel, the shortest woman I have ever laid eyes on, stands up and straightens the folds of her yellow and green plaid skirt. It is a horrific contrast to her blue silk blouse.

Maxine coughs into her hand. "*Ahem*! Color blind. *Ahem*!"

"Your clothing choices are so important." Mabel's volume could wake the dead. "You have got to glam it up, young lady. A man likes a woman in hosiery." Mabel raises her skirt to show her knee highs, ten shades darker than her skin tone and drooping toward her ankles. "And wear quality clothing. I myself like a nice polyester with an expandable elastic waistband."

Frances looks like she's ready to cry. I eat another cookie and press my ear into the side of the chair to give it a break from Mabel's yelling.

"And jewelry. I like to color coordinate, of course. If I'm wearing purple, as I am today, I will wear purple beads." Mabel holds up her necklace, a stand of multiple shades of brown. "Boys notice the details, you know. And finally, your crowning jewel."

"My hair?" Frances asks.

"No, your shoes." Again, Mabel hoists up a leg. "If you're going to be chasing that boy all day long, you gotta have shoes that can keep up."

Frances looks down. "Orthopedic comfort shoes?"

Mabel nods. "With Velcro closure. That's important."

Beside me, Frances sighs.

And Maxine sneaks a smile. "Excellent information, ladies. Bravo. I think Frances has a lot to ponder, a lot to absorb from all your wisdom." She bites into a cookie, black crumbs hanging on her lip. "Or. . . you could just try being yourself."

Frances shakes her head. "That only works in Disney movies."

"All right, then we'll continue. Gladys. You said you had something to add?"

A nearly bald woman holds up a bright orange. "We will now move on to the kissing lesson."

Chapter 28

"**Y**OU CAN GET up now. We're here."

From my slumped position in Frances's car, I close my eyes and groan. "I can't face them yet. All those people will know I ruined their party. It will be all over school. Katie Parker is a party ruiner. Invite her and watch her psycho granny single handedly destroy the evening."

Frances shrugs. "Yup. Probably so."

Wow. Thanks for the sympathy. Why don't you just sky write *I told you so*, so there will be no doubt how you really feel.

She opens her door and steps out. "You can't hide on my floorboard forever. Besides, there's that history quiz you gotta make up. And then you have play rehearsals."

"No. I'm quitting the play. Then I'm dropping out of school. I think I'll work at McDonald's the rest of my life. I'll be the invisible voice you hear in the drive-thru."

"Whatever. Oh, hey, Charlie. Hey, Chelsea."

Just when you think it couldn't get any worse.

"Is that Katie down there?" Though my head is now covered, I hear Charlie loud and clear. "What are you doing?"

I lift my head. "Praying?"

He sticks his face in Frances's open door. "Very holy."

I slink back into a sitting position and grab my backpack. "I just wanted some reflection time."

"Oh, time to reflect on the party you invited your foster grandmother to this weekend?" Chelsea's snooty voice sings.

I get out and slam my door shut. "I did *not* invite Maxine."

Charlie levels his eyes on me. "Guess you shouldn't have been at the party in the first place."

Frances sniffs. "I totally agree."

"Well, thanks. Thanks for your support." I heave my backpack over my shoulder and fall into step behind them. "Frances, could you move over a little to the left? Thanks." Gotta make sure I'm totally covered and out of sight.

I shuffle behind them through the front doors and into the main hall. Almost to the lockers. A little bit further . . .

"Hey, Trev." And Chelsea splits from the group huddle and leaves me wide open. For all to see.

Trevor stands with a group of guys. They all smile at Chelsea.

Then Trevor spots me. And so do his friends.

"Hey, it's the girl who brought her granny to the party. Check it out, Trevor."

"Hey, Katie, can I get my money back on that keg I paid for?"

"Yeah, I need a ride after school today. Do you know anyone who could pick me up—on a bicycle?"

Soon the hall is filled with Katie jokes, peppered with some name-calling and insults. I speed away from Frances's side and make a beeline for the bathroom. I hear Frances call out for me, but I just keep running down the hall.

I round the corner and shove my way past the door. Three girls at the mirrors stop mid-lipstick and stare.

I fling open a stall. "Yes, I'm the girl whose grandma crashed the party." And I slam the door shut and take a seat. I think this is the bathroom where I had lunch on my first day of school. Nothing like a special bond with a toilet.

Ten minutes pass. I sit Indian-style with my chin resting in my hands. How much longer 'til the tardy bell? When it rings, I'll go get my books and go to class. But not until then.

The bathroom door opens again. This sure is a high-traffic room.

"Katie?"

Oh, no. Frances.

"I know you're in here."

I watch her feet pace the length of the stalls. She pauses to search under each one. She comes to the last stall, where I sit. Her head pops under the door.

"Hey."

"Can't a girl get some privacy?"

Frances's face smiles back at me. "You can't stay in here forever."

"I'm ruined. I'm the joke of the school. You heard those guys. Trevor didn't even take up for me."

"No, but Charlie did."

"What?"

"Yeah, he warned them all to quit harassing you. Then one of Trevor's friends said, 'You and what army?' And Charlie said, 'No army. Just the football team.' And that pretty much took care of it."

He did that? For me?

"It really doesn't change anything." I bang my head against the metal wall. "This is a disaster."

"You don't need somebody like Trevor."

"Frances?"

"Yeah?"

"Do you think he'll still might ask me to the spring dance?"

I SOMEHOW SURVIVE English class and with a binder covering my face, I walk to history. I slink into my desk in front of Frances.

The tardy bell rings, and an older guy shuts the door. Another day of history, another sub. Can't wait to see what this guy's issues are.

The man stands up at the podium. His too-dark hair is neatly parted to the side. He wears a creased pair of khakis with some trendy leather lace-up shoes.

Wait a minute . . . Is that? I squeeze my eyes shut and open them again.

Mr. Patton?

"Good morning, students. So good to return to class today. I took a small medical leave, but I hope education continued in my absence." Mr. Patton, his pink skin pulled taut, smiles. For once I can see his eyes, no longer hidden by saggy lids. His grin reveals new pearly white teeth, all shaped to perfection.

Frances taps me on the shoulder. "Somebody had a little vacation at the plastic surgeons."

I turn around. "He looks twenty years younger. Well, minus the bad dye job. But the goatee is a nice touch. He's a totally different person."

At that moment my ears fill with the familiar high-pitched whine of two hearing aids.

Frances laughs. "Well, maybe not *completely* different."

Next to me a trio of girls giggle loudly. Thinking they're finding the nipped and tucked Mr. Patton amusing as well, I turn my head towards them, my face stretched in a smile.

But they're not looking at our history teacher. They're looking at me. And pointing.

I hate my life. The only bright spot to this day is that it couldn't possibly get worse.

"Katie Parker to the office. Katie Parker to the office."

The overhead intercom blasts my name for all the school to hear. Great, what now? Does the principal want to see me so he can laugh in my face too? Maybe give me detention for tackiest party moment ever?

I shrug my shoulders at Frances, gather my stuff, and head out the door.

I hope everything's okay. What if Millie's sick and they need me to come home? What if Maxine got pulled over for disturbing the peace with her bike horn again?

In the office the front desk secretary stuffs envelopes while smacking on gum. "Take a seat, hon." She continues to stuff without even sparing me a glance.

"Um . . . I was called to the office. I'm Katie Parker." Loser Extraordinaire. Most Unpopular. Least Likely to Get a Future Prom Date.

"Principal Wayman will be with you in a bit. He's busy yelling at someone right now."

Oh. How nice. Glad I caught him on a good day.

Ten minutes later (just enough time for me to imagine every possible horrible reason for being here), a lanky junior boy leaves Mr. Wayman's office, followed by the principal himself.

"Katie Parker?"

I swallow. "Yes."

The principal runs a hand under his tie then crooks a finger. "In my office."

That was not a happy face. Apparently I am not here to receive the coveted student-of-the-month award.

I step into the man's office with heavy dread resting on my gut. The interior does nothing to soothe my stomach. Total time warp. I think I just walked into 1985. Nice cracked "wood" paneling. The metal office furniture has more dents in it than my mom's last car. And the peach and country-blue rug under his desk is the *pièce de résistance*. He just needs a Prince poster to hang on the wall.

Mrs. Whipple, the counselor, sits under a mallard duck print. She is the last person who should be in the position to help and advise people. I think she eats kids for dinner.

Mr. Wayman gestures toward the chair next to the counselor. "Take a seat."

"I like your vest," I say to the gray-headed woman. Her collection of quilted vests and matching denim skirts is beyond compare.

"We're not here to trade niceties." She holds up a pair of shoes. Angel's. "Do you want to explain to us how these got into your gym locker?"

My heart beats triple time as I realize I am being accused of stealing. All because of Angel. Somehow, some way, she did this.

The principal's chair squeaks as he shifts his weight to lean over his desk. "We're waiting."

"I . . . I . . . um." Stop sounding guilty! I didn't do anything. "I didn't take those shoes."

"Really?" Mrs. Whipple smirks. Did I mention she's Angel's aunt? Yes, she and Coach Nelson are sisters. I assume their dad goes by the name of Lucifer. "So these shoes just magically appeared in your locker?"

"I don't know how they got there."

"Do you really expect us to believe you had no idea they were in your locker?" Mr. Wayman's face screams doubt.

"Yes."

"Miss. Parker," the counselor drawls. "These shoes, as well as Hannah Wilkerson's, had been locked in each girl's respective gym locker."

I nod my head. Each locker has a built-in lock, and if the locker is shut, it can only be opened with the combination.

"And how is it you think I got into their lockers?"

Mrs. Whipple snorts and points a stubby finger. "You're a smart girl, Katie Parker. And we know from your history you're also a troublemaker."

My mouth drops. "That isn't fair. I'm not a—"

"Be quiet, Katie," the principal warns. "Last semester there was some trouble between you and Angel Nelson, and she believes you've been harassing her."

I jump to my feet. "That girl gave me a black eye in PE. Are you *kidding* me?"

"Sit down." Mrs. Whipple glares above her bifocals.

The pressure of tears pushes at my eyeballs once again. "Angel Nelson is a coward and a bully. If anyone has been harassed here, it's me."

"Well, Miss. Parker, it's not Angel Nelson who had the shoes in her locker, now is it?" The principal's thick southern accent shreds my last nerve.

"What about Hannah? She's one of my closest friends. Why would I steal anything of hers? And why would I leave the stuff in my locker?"

The counselor clucks her tongue. "Honestly, I've never been able to understand the mind of a thief."

"I'm *not* a thief!"

"We are sending you home for the rest of the day." The principal pulls out a form from his desk drawer and scribbles his name on it. "We want you to think about this situation for as long as is takes."

"As long as it takes to fess up to something I didn't do?" My hands tremble on my lap. "This makes no sense."

The principal hands me a slip of paper. "Disciplinary Suspension" it reads.

I crumble it up and hold it in my clenched hand. "This is *not* fair."

"Your foster parents have been called. Mr. Scott should be here anytime."

I stand again. Shocked. Frozen. Outraged. "That's it?"

The principal nods. "That's all."

"But know," the counselors hisses, "we will be watching you."

Mr. Wayman frowns. "One mistake, one more stolen item found in your possession, and we will punish to the fullest extent. We will not tolerate thievery." He straightens in his leather chair. "Chihuahuas do not steal."

With my suspension notice in hand, I grab my stuff and bolt out of the office. Deciding to wait for James in the parking lot, I bypass the front office waiting area, and cruise right into the hall.

And smack into Charlie Benson.

"Oh, hey, Katie, I—"

I jerk myself out of his grip and give him a slight nudge to get him out of my way. I gotta get out of this place. Now.

"What is your deal?"

I hear his voice, but I'm not stopping for him. Who cares about him? Who cares about this school?

"Fine. Be mad. I was just trying to look out for you Friday night."

That stops me. I pivot and turn to face the jerk. "What?" With five good stomps I close the distance between us. "Are you serious? Do you really think I care what you have to say to me right now? Because I don't. I don't want to talk to you; I don't want you to talk to me. In fact," I poke my finger in his chest. "I don't even want my plant anywhere near you."

"Going to that party was really stupid."

"Yeah, well you know what? Calling my house Friday night was really stupid. Because of you, my cover was blown, and Maxine stopped by the party and ruined my life."

"You shouldn't have been there in the first place."

"That's not for you to say, is it?"

"Excuse me for caring about you."

"Did I ask you to?"

"No, but that's what friends do."

"Friends? I've had better treatment from Angel."

"Oh, really? If I remember correctly, Angel gets you into trouble. I was trying to make sure you stayed out of it."

"Well, maybe you should mind your own business. Why don't you keep an eye on Chelsea, your girlfriend?"

"What is that supposed to mean?"

"Haven't you noticed how cozy she is with Trevor?" In some distant part of my brain, I immediately regret saying that. But the majority of my head doesn't care a bit. I just got accused of stealing. I just got *suspended*, for crying out loud. I can say whatever I want.

He huffs. "Now you're just trying to start crap."

"They're awful friendly with each other. I would think it would be a better use of your time to keep an eye on her rather than where I'm at during the weekend."

"Whatever."

"Right. Whatever." Is there steam coming out of my ears yet?

"I just don't want to see you get in trouble. Or get hurt. Is that so terrible?"

"But I *did* get in trouble. And I got humiliated. So thank you. What a great thing for a *friend* to do."

"I meant *real* trouble. The police could've busted that party. Or someone could've gotten hurt. Or . . ." He runs a hand through his hair. "Forget it."

"Wouldn't I like to."

"I'm sorry I messed everything up." He shakes his head.

"No, hey, no problem. Who needs dignity?" I laugh bitterly. "If you hadn't jerked my somewhat-redeemed reputation out from under me, then *this* would have anyway." I wave the suspension notice in his face.

"What is that?" He snatches it out of my hand. "You're suspended?"

My face burns crimson. "Yup."

"For what?" His eyes scan the paper. "Stealing?"

"Yeah. Stealing. So now I'm a party-ruiner *and* a criminal." I turn to walk away, but his hand on my wrist halts my attempt. "Let go of me, Charlie." *Before I start clinging to your shirt and bawling.*

"Tell me what happened."

I pull on my arm, but he doesn't let go. "It doesn't matter. Just back off, okay? I gotta go." I try not to, but I can't stop myself. I search his face for disappointment, revulsion. For any sign he believes I would do what that slip of paper says. I see only a blank expression.

With a final tug, I free my arm and turn away. "Forget it."

"Tell me." He moves in front of me.

I run a shaking hand through my hair. "Angel set me up. I don't know how she did it, but she did. She planted some stuff in my locker." And I tell Charlie, the boy I am totally furious with, the entire story.

He raises a thoughtful eyebrow, as his steely gray eyes meet mine. "I think I can help."

My raw attitude flares again. "Look where your help got me Friday night. Just leave me alone and mind your own business."

"Don't be mad, Katie." He tilts his head. "I said I was sorry."

I stare at him and shake my head.

"You don't need to be hanging around Trevor. I told you he was trouble."

And you don't need to be hanging around your Gucci-snot girlfriend, but do I butt in and tell you that? Um, no.

"I gotta go."

"You still mad?"

"Yes, Charlie, I am."

"And there's nothing I can do to fix it?"

Shaking my head, I walk away. Leaving him standing in the middle of the hall.

"Nothing?" he yells.

I shuffle toward the main exit. "I don't ever want to talk to you, Charlie Benson. Nothing you can say is going to change my mind."

His voice calls out as I put my hand on the door. "I can prove you didn't steal the shoes."

My hand stills. "Well . . . now that changes everything."

Chapter 29

JAMES SLAMS THE car door. "I never could stand that principal."

"So you talked to him?" When James arrived at school, I waited in the car while he went in and spoke with the twins of terror, Mr. Wayman and Mrs. Whipple.

"Yes, for all the good it did. He didn't hear a word I said."

I study his face. "So you believe me?"

He rips his glasses off. "What kind of question is that? Of course I believe you."

If relief were a blanket, I'd wrap myself in it and snuggle deep. I wasn't sure how James would react—what he would believe. Despite the sheer hideousness of the day, I smile.

"Well, you deserve a day off anyway. You've been working really hard. Your grades are good, and you have a big part in a very important play." He pats my knee and then starts the car. "Not to mention, you've had to put up with Maxine for a roommate."

He's right on the last part. Someone should nominate me for sainthood. Except for the fact I went to a party last weekend without my foster parents' permission. The guilt of that little deception still gnaws at me.

I sigh. "Let's just get out of here."

James puts the car in reverse. Stops, and shifts it back into park. "You can drive."

"Oh, no. No way. Remember—light poll? Crash? Many unhappy

In Betweenies on Smith Street?"

He opens his car door and slides out. "Get in." He notices I'm not budging. "You can do it."

We switch places, and I settle into the driver's seat. I adjust the rearview mirror, the side mirrors, the seat, check my lip gloss, my seatbelt, and finally change the radio station.

"Any day now."

I shoot my foster dad a withering look and finally back the car out of the parking spot.

Dear God, if I hit a car before we get out of here, please don't let it be an expensive foreign import. How about a nice, banged-up farm truck? Plenty to choose from here.

Though it takes us nearly twenty-five minutes to get there, I pull us safely into the Scott's driveway.

"I did it." I beam with pride. "I really did it! And I did a good job, huh?"

James opens the car door. "Yes, great job. Though you know at some point you're going to have to drive faster than ten miles per hour."

I level him with a frown. "Kinda ruining the moment here."

Together we walk to the front porch.

Where three chickens wait for us.

"Chandler, Joey, and Ross are out again." I step over one and head inside the house. Where I'm greeted by slow melodic violin strains piping from the surround sound speakers. Millie, in another new pair of fancy pajamas, sits cross-legged in the middle of the living room, eyes closed, hands resting on her knees.

James shuts the door and finds me staring at his wife. He shakes his head and rolls his eyes. "She's meditating."

I notice the dog flopped over beside her, and Millie opens one eye. "I'm just being quiet and still." She closes her eye. "You should try it."

"Oh, thanks," I whisper. "But I think I'll just go on up to my room."

"It wasn't a question. Sit down."

James shakes his head and leaves me to *Señora* Serenity. I settle into the same position next to her on the floor.

"Why are we doing this?"

"Shhhhh. Are your eyes closed?"

"Well, Millie, since your eyes aren't open, I could say yes here, and it really wouldn't—"

"Shut them."

I snap them closed.

"Stress makes people unhealthy. Did you know that, Katie?"

I believe it. I totally feel sick now, maxed out on my share of stress.

We sit through five more violin concertos. Millie breathes in and out like she's being graded on volume, and I'm so busy trying hard not to laugh, I am nowhere near relaxed. Plus, it's hard to be all at peace when you're suspended.

She slowly rises from the hardwood floor. "Come on, I'll fix you something special for lunch."

I join my foster mom in the kitchen. After James hands Millie a skillet and a few other items, he sits at the bar drinking coffee. We discuss the day, and I fill them in on my recent encounters with Angel.

Millie throws some stuff I don't recognize in a frying pan. I hope that's not the main course.

James puts his mug down. "Why didn't you tell us Angel had gotten aggressive with you in PE?"

I shrug. "I dunno. I didn't want to upset you guys. I thought you had enough to deal with."

Millie slices into an onion. "Is there anything else we need to know?"

Oh, like I lied to Maxine and told her I was working on my science fair project, but actually I was going to a party without your permission? Or that there was underage drinking at this event? Or that my foster grandmother showed up and busted the party in her Sponge Bob house shoes? Oh, and PS, I'm the laughingstock of the school.

"Nope. Can't think of a thing."

We talk more over an appetizer of cheese and crackers in the breakfast nook.

"All right. Lunch is served."

Millie plops a burger on my plate. I pick a sesame seed off the top of the bun and pop it in my mouth. "Can I have some mayo?"

My foster mom shakes her head. "No more mayonnaise for us. I threw it out. You won't even miss it."

"Well, a burger sounds good. Should hit the spot after the morning I've had." I open wide and sink my teeth in.

And promptly spit it out.

"Ugh. What *is* this?" I chug down some water. "That's no hamburger."

James lifts his bun and inspects the contents.

"I didn't say it was a hamburger. It's a tofu burger." Millie tears into hers. "Things are gonna change around here. We're gonna get healthy."

James pushes his plate away. "Or die trying."

"I have an idea."

"Does it involve more tofu?" Because these new ideas of Millie's are *not* working for me.

Millie's eyes sparkle. "It involves shopping."

"Shopping?" *So* much better than meat substitutes.

"You mentioned the spring dance the other day. James can take us to the mall. You're going to need a formal. What do you say?"

I say I totally don't deserve a new dress! I'm a rule-breaking, deceitful loser.

"I can see you in something full-length. A soft pink to complement your strawberry-blonde hair."

I'm the sludge on Spam. I'm the permanent ring in the school toilet bowls.

"Strapless? Maybe with a gauzy sash. Very old Hollywood."

No. Must resist. "Are you up to it, Millie?" So weak . . .

"I can't wait to find out. I think I'm good for a few hours." She smiles then points to my plate. "Eat that burger and we'll even get new shoes."

I rip into it. "*Mmmm.*"

THOUGH I'M SUSPENDED, I decide to go to play rehearsal after shopping. It's at the Valiant, so it's not like I'm going to be on school property. Shopping was . . . heaven. I got the works—a fitted yet flowy dress, like something you'd have seen on the red carpet circa 1950. And these shoes that sparkle when they catch the light with a cool vintage heel. And when I tried them on, I felt like a princess.

James drops me off at the door, and I know he'll probably hit the couch after his afternoon in the mall.

"Hi, Katie! How are ya?" Sam polishes the brass trim on the concession counter. His hat perches crooked on his head, and he wears his typical uniform of overalls.

"Hey, Sam." I give him a quick hug. "Things are all right." I mean, I guess things could be worse. Like I could be dead. "How's it going with Maxine?"

"Hot date tonight." He raises his eyebrows. "Gonna take her to Ida Mae's House of Vittles and buy her the best chicken-fried steak in town."

"Sounds very romantic." I stare at the theater doors. "Well . . . I guess I better get in there." Time to face Trevor Jackson.

With a heavy heart, I pull open the door and ease my way downstage.

"Hey, Sweet Pea." Maxine's voice stops me at row three.

I do a double take. "What are you doing here?" Maxine wears a powder pink tutu and a rhinestone crown.

"I got the part of the fairy godmother. Didn't you hear?"

My eyes search for Trevor, and I locate him onstage, running lines with Sydney Mason, the girl who plays the prince's mother. Has he seen Maxine? I stand in front of her, trying to shield my cast-mates from the sight of her.

"This isn't a dress rehearsal!"

"I'm into character. I guess I'm more serious about this than you."

"Yeah, seriously deranged." I look her up and down, from her flouncy tulle tutu to her ballet slippers, criss-crossed on her white tights. "You look like Miss Havisham in toe shoes." I jerk my head toward Trevor. "Do *not* say anything to him. Please?"

Maxine adjusts her sparkly crown. "What on earth would I have left to say to him?"

I nod slowly. "Good." And I walk past her downstage.

"Especially since I've already had a nice, long chat with him just a few minutes ago."

I turn around and pin Maxine with the meanest, maddest, baddest dirty look I've got. She waves her wand at me and cackles.

I take a seat on the front row next to Jeremy, my fellow ugly step-sister.

He smiles around a mouthful of braces. "Can you believe the play's in less than three weeks? Today's the last day we can use our scripts."

I nod and mumble my agreement. But my focus is on Trevor. And the blonde onstage with him.

I nudge Jeremy. "Should a mother and son be that close? This isn't incestuous Cinderella."

"They're just going over lines. Trevor's a pro. I've seen him in dozens of plays." He moves closer to me. "Are you jealous?"

"No, definitely not. I just want this show to be perfect, you know?"

Jeremy grins and shakes a finger in my face. "You're jealous. Is there something going on between you and Jackson?"

If there was, it was killed the night Maxine broke out her bull-horn. "No. I guess we were talking for a while, but I'm pretty sure that's as far as it's gonna go."

"Awww. Katie got her heart broken." Jeremy pats me on the shoulder.

"No, I didn't," I snap. "We were just friends. No big deal." I watch the blonde giggle and toss her hair. I thought I was different. That maybe he really liked me. Sure he has a total player past, but I could've changed all that.

At least I don't have any scenes with him today. My goal is to get out of this practice without talking to him. Not that he *would* talk to me anyway. But he does still have my plant.

A few minutes later Chelsea shows up in all her designer denim glory. At the sight of Trevor onstage her eyes narrow. "Should he be that close to her?"

"Hi, Chelsea." A blush spreads on Jeremy's cheeks. "You look nice today."

She spares him a glance. "Thanks. Hey, Katie, we missed you at school today. And I just want you to know, I will be keeping my purse with me at all times. So don't get any ideas." She clutches her Coach handbag and sashays off toward Mrs. Hall.

I turn to Jeremy, my eyes stinging. "See, I got accused of stealing these shoes, but I—"

"I know. Anyone who knows you doesn't believe you did it."

I sniff. "Thanks, Jeremy. That means a lot to me. Hey, you should come hang out with us at church sometime." I swallow a gasp. Did I really just invite someone to church? What is *wrong* with me? God and I are *so* not getting along. I can't invite people to church. They'll think I'm . . . a believer. And I've got it together. Girls who get suspended definitely do not have it together.

"Yeah, I might try that. Chelsea goes, too, right? To your church, I mean."

Oh, boys are sooo stupid. Number one, she's totally out of his league. And number two, his league is so much better than hers. That girl is a witch. Had she gotten the part of the evil stepmother, there would be zero acting necessary.

"Yeah, she goes sometimes." It's my turn to pat his arm. "As do a lot of other girls from In Between." Girls with personalities. *Girls who won't squash you like a bug between their French manicured fingernails.* Oh, well, the invitation is already out. No sense in taking it back. "Just think about it and let me know. We meet this Wednesday night." *And if you have any Jesus questions, you'll have to ask Frances because I sure don't know the answers.*

"I can't this Wednesday." Jeremy's face falls. "Our house got pretty messed up last month in the tornado. We're moving from our grandma's place into a shelter."

The shock and pity registers on my face before I can catch it.

"No, it's okay. We were renting the house that got trashed, and the owner isn't gonna rebuild. But we lost almost everything. It's just gonna take a while for my mom to regroup." He pulls his mouth into a smile. "Maybe a week or two. No big deal. We actors love our drama, right?"

"Right." But it's not. It's so wrong. All this time I hadn't thought about the fact I actually go to school with people whose homes were damaged or destroyed in the tornado. I've gotten so caught up in my new life of comfort and security. But I know what it's like to have nothing, to not have a place to call your own.

Okay, God. I'll go on the spring break mission campout. But it's for Jeremy. Not for me . . . . and not for you.

At four o'clock rehearsal begins. Chelsea does her opening scene alone, then Jeremy and I enter for scene two.

We sisters trade insults and jabs at the lowly Cinderella. Though it's all in the script, I hurl my venom at Chelsea like it's straight from my own heart. And it feels awesome. I especially love the part where

I get to step on her toe.

"Ow!" Chelsea rubs her foot. "That was too hard," she growls.

I smile. "Just following the script."

Thirty minutes later we begin the ball scene. While Cinderella glides across the stage in her prince's arms, her two ugly stepsisters stand with their mother in a corner. My script says I am to glare.

Mrs. Hall calls from below. "Excellent facial expression, Katie! We can feel your anger. Very real."

Mid-waltz a Beyoncé song blasts from Cheslea's pocket. "Oh, gotta get that. Hello?"

With a collective groan from the cast, practice screeches to a stop.

"Chelsea, get off the phone. You know the rules—no phones during rehearsals."

Mrs. Hall charges onstage.

Cindrella holds up a hand. "This is important. I have to take this call." And she exits stage left.

Our teacher looks around and her eyes connect with mine. "Katie—" She holds out a script. "Read for Chelsea until she gets back. Take it from the top of the waltz. Miss Parker, I do mean now. Don't just stand there."

Gulp.

On heavy legs, I move from the back of the crowd to the front. Next to Trevor. From my peripheral vision I see him hold out his arms.

"You're gonna have to look at me if we're going to waltz."

My head shoots up, and I'm greeted with his knowing, wry grin. My brain shifts into overdrive, desperate to analyze his expression. Is he laughing at me? Is he being kind? Is all forgiven?

I lay my right hand in his and settle my left on his shoulder.

Mrs. Hall consults with another cast member, and I take advantage of the moment. "I just wanted to say I'm really sorry for Friday night. I had no idea that was going to happen."

He nods, and I watch his dark hair move over his forehead.

"Could've been a better night. I had big plans for us."

I blink. "You did?"

"Maybe another time."

Wait, I want to cry. What does that mean? Tell me!

"Sorry people at school are all over you. I'll see what I can do about that."

I nod. "Thanks. That'd be nice."

The music starts and he lures me into a waltz.

"Chelsea's boyfriend got pretty bent out of shape over it."

My feet stumble and Trevor pulls me in tighter. "Yeah, I guess. Don't worry about it though."

He laughs. "I'm not worried about him at all."

Trevor twirls me around and draws me back. I was so close. This strong, tall, hulking piece of yum could've been mine.

"I still have your plant, you know. With the science fair coming up, I think you're gonna need that."

"Oh, yeah. My plant." I hope no one drowned him in Bud Light. "Maybe you could bring him to school tomorrow?"

"Or you could come and get it."

Trevor delivers his next few lines as we dance. Clutching the script with my hand on his shoulder, I read for Chelsea. This so should've been my part. I was robbed.

We continue to dance as the other cast members react to Cinderella and her prince.

"You want me to come to your locker and get my fern?"

"No. I thought maybe you could ride home with me after school, and we could get your plant. Then I'll take you home." He grins. "And you can assure your parents my mom will be home."

I look out into the seating area and see Maxine dancing her own solo waltz in the aisle, waving her wand through the air. "Let me get back to you on that. I don't want my foster grandma to come after me again. Next time she'd probably bring the fire department. You have no idea what she's capable of."

Trevor follows my stare. "I think I have an idea." With toes pointed, Maxine leaps from side to side. "You just let me know tomorrow. I could bring your fern to school, but . . ." He shrugs. "You don't want to risk it getting hurt, right?"

Charlie and I do have a massive grade on the line here. "No . . . I really wouldn't want that to risk that." My heart thrills at the thought of Trevor wanting to see me. The In Between Community Church sings a "Hallelujah Chorus" in my head.

Is it possible? Could things actually be turning around?

Chapter 30

IN ENGLISH CLASS Wednesday morning I give the girl next to me a nudge. "Hey, do you have a pencil I can borrow?"

"Don't expect to get it back, Sarah. Katie tends to keep the things she *borrows*." Behind me Angel Nelson cracks herself up. I shoot her a withering look. Right now I wish I had some of the superpowers of the X-Men. Freeze Angel over. Cause a wind tunnel to carry her out of my sight. Use my Wolverine blade fingers to give her purple Mohawk a buzz cut.

"Nice to see you could make it to school today. I heard you took Monday off."

I swivel to face my nemesis. "That's right. I did. And what a horrible day it was. I hung out at home, took a nap, went shopping, got some ice cream, watched some movies. I don't know how I got through it all, but I did." I give her my oh-you-silly-little-girl laugh. "I guess I should *not steal* more often because it sure was a good time."

"Your good times are only beginning," she spits.

I heave a sigh. "You bore me, Angel." I stand up and grab a hall pass.

On my way out the door, I hear Angel's psycho voice. "You won't be bored for long."

I quietly shut the classroom door and head down the hall toward the bathroom. Something about getting that close to Angel makes me want to wash my hands.

"Don't tell me you got sent to the office again."

Trevor stands at the end of the hall. How does he do that? Sometimes it seems like that boy is everywhere I am. He lounges against the wall like he owns the place. His arms are crossed, and his playful grin sends a tiny tremor tickling down my spine.

"Hey." I smile back, desperate to play it cool. But seriously, how lucky am I this boy is talking to me again? Flirting with me again? Yet here we are—face to face, hall pass to hall pass.

"I waited for you after rehearsals in the parking lot yesterday. I thought you were gonna come to my house and get your plant."

I shrug and feel my cheeks warm. "Yeah, well, yesterday was a little stressful, my first day back after being expelled and all. So I just went straight home. My foster dad picked me up." And there was no way he was gonna let me go home with Trevor. "I do need it back though. The science fair is coming up soon, and I have a few more experiments to do."

Trevor laughs. "You don't take that stuff seriously, do you? The science fair? Come on, that's for total geeks."

My smile droops. "No, it's not. Charlie takes it very seriously. And so do I."

"Yeah, see, if Charlie's all into it, then you know it's lame." He puts a hand on my shoulder.

Without thinking I flick his hand away. "Charlie is an all-star athlete. He's a starter on the football team and he's only a sophomore. I don't think that's too lame. And he's brilliant on top of that. He's the furthest thing from being a geek." Ugh. I sound like a stinkin' infomercial for Charlie Benson. Why do I have to open my mouth? Why can't I just bat my eyelashes and do something all Paris-Hiltony?

Trevor throws up a hand. "Hey! Okay, okay. Calm down." He touches the tip of my nose. "If this science fair is that important, then all the more reason to get your fern. I'm not exactly experienced with plants, so every day it's in my possession is another day you're risking its life." He winks and the tense mood dissolves.

"I'm going home with Frances after school. Maybe I can talk her into swinging by your house."

"Or maybe you can ride home with me, and she can pick you up later?"

Frances? My guard dog of a friend? "Yeah . . . I doubt it. It's gonna be a miracle if I can get her to drive anywhere near your neighborhood." *Oh, yeah, FYI, my best friend can't stand you.*

Trevor pushes off from the wall. "I'll take whatever I can get. See you after school? You remember how to get to my house?"

I nod. "I think so." *I saw every piece of it on the back of a bicycle, remember?*

His hand slides up my arm, lands on my shoulder and squeezes. "I'll be waiting."

By the end of the day, I am still working on Frances to agree to take me by Trevor's.

"Puhhh-lease?" I clasp my hands and show her my pouty lip.

Frances starts her station wagon, and a plume of smoke announces our departure. "I just don't think it's a good idea."

This is definitely progress. Earlier today it was "No, are you nuts? I'd gouge out my own eyeballs before I'd drop you by Trevor Jackson's house."

"Frances, if I don't get that plant back, Charlie is gonna strangle me. And then his snippy little girlfriend will be all like, 'I told you she would mess this up, Charlie.' And then she'll tell me I'm single-handedly responsible for knocking him out of the running for valedictorian."

Frances cranks up the radio to her favorite station. KPOK. Playing all your polka hits. "First of all, *I'm* gonna be our valedictorian when we graduate, so he doesn't even need to worry about that. And second, what do I get out of this? Tell me one thing you are going to do for *me* for putting you in the hands of that . . . that total male hoochie."

"I'll . . . um . . ." I am losing this battle.

"Fine, here's our deal. We'll pick up your plant on one condition."

"Name it. Anything."

"You go to the spring break mission campout." Frances takes her eyes off the road long enough to gauge my expression.

I shake my head and compose my face in to the most serious of frowns. "I don't know Frances. That's asking a lot." *Yes! I am so home free.* "But for you . . . I'll do it."

She squeals and claps her hands on the steering wheel. "Yes! We're gonna have such a great time. You'll see. You won't regret it."

Five minutes later, with a wave at the guard, we drive through the gate and navigate through the golf course to Trevor's house.

"You have to stay in here," I say, and Frances's hand freezes on the door handle. "Please? Just give me five minutes."

Her ebony eyes narrow. "Five minutes? Do you know what could happen in that time?"

"No, but I think I'd like to find out."

"Katie, you're playing with fire here. This guy is . . . is . . ."

"Don't blow this out of proportion. I'll be right back." I slam the car door and all but skip up the steps.

Trevor answers the door. He's changed from his jeans and button-down into shorts and a Nike t-shirt.

"Hey, hotness, come on in."

I look behind me. Is he talking to me? Oh, my gosh. Trevor Jackson just called me hot. And I have no witnesses.

"It's in my bedroom. Come on up."

His room looks like a wing of the NBA Hall of Fame museum. Like ESPN threw a party and didn't clean up. A basketball hoop sticks out of one wall. Framed pictures of athletes, signed to Trevor, decorate the wall beside his bed.

"Kick off your shoes. Stay awhile."

Since his chairs are full of clothes, I sit down on the bed. "I can't stay. Frances is waiting for me."

"Plant's in my bathroom. I'll be right back."

He disappears around the corner just as his phone vibrates next to me on his bedside table. I check the screen.

Chelsea Blake.

"Here it is. Safe as promised."

I startle at his voice. "What? Oh, thanks. He looks good." Trevor places the fern in my hands.

"Oh, I have a message." He picks up his phone and scrolls through. "Chelsea calling to discuss the play." His eyes flick to mine.

I force a smile. "That Chelsea . . . she's so . . ."

"Committed?"

Could we commit her? Some place far, far away.

"Does she call often?" My face is as serene as one of Millie's meditation sessions.

Trevor sits on the bed next to me. Right next to me. "Let's not talk about Chelsea." He tucks my hair behind my ear. "In fact, let's not talk at all. It's kind of overrated."

I scoot out of arm's reach. "I like talking. Talking is good. You know what else is good? Dances. Yup, dances are so—" He moves closer. "Fun." I swallow as Trevor's hand plays with a lock of my hair. "Are you going to the spring dance?"

I feel his breath on my neck with each word. "Do you want me to go?" And then his lips.

My eyes squeeze shut. I should be enjoying this. *Why* am I not into this? I have *the* Trevor Jackson's lips on my neck. Girls would kill to be in my place.

"Yeah. . . I'd love for you to go."

His lips kiss a trail across my cheek and move closer to my mouth. "Uh-huh. I'll go."

"You will?" I breathe.

"Whatever you want."

I throw my arms around Trevor and allow him to pull me close. My mouth meets his, and I kiss him with all the joy I can barely contain. I have a date for the dance. I have a date for the dance. I'm the luckiest girl in the world.

Trevor's hands cradle my face and he deepens his kiss. I sigh into it and—

The door crashes open, and I jump out of his embrace.

"Katie Louise Parker!" Frances stomps into the room, hands balled into fists. "Your five minutes are up."

"Frances, I—" That is not even my middle name.

She throws up a hand. "Save it. My wagon is leaving in sixty seconds. Are you going or not?"

I pick up my plant and mumble a quiet apology to Trevor. Again. All I do is apologize to this guy. "I'll see you later."

Playful wickedness shines in his eyes. "No problem. See ya tomorrow, Katie. Good luck with the science project. Later, Frances."

"Yeah, see ya." She jerks her head towards the door, and I follow her downstairs and outside.

When we get in the car, I check the time. "That was only four minutes!"

Frances shrugs. "Whatever. Four minutes too long, I say." The car sputters to life, and my fuming friend drives us out of the ritzy neighborhood. "He had his hands all over you. What were you thinking?"

Mmmm, who was thinking? "He didn't have his hands *all* over me."

"One more minute and he probably would have. I do *not* like that guy."

"Well, you don't have you like him. You just focus on Nash."

Frances frees one hand from the steering wheel and grabs my arm. "Nash is going to the mission campout!" She shakes my arm and squeals.

"Cool."

Her face snaps back into a scowl. "Quit distracting me. We were talking about you. Ever heard the word *boundaries*? I mean that guy was all up in your space. So not cool, especially given the short amount of time you've known him."

The radio blasts out "She Thinks My Tractor's Sexy," the accordion version. I turn it up to drown out Frances. "I have boundaries, thank you very much." Don't I? It's not like I would've let that mini–make out session go any further. "Excuse me for paying attention when Gladys gave her lesson on kissing."

We drive in heavy silence, passing Gus's Getcher Gas, Bubba's Asian Cuisine, and the diner where Maxine will be eating before church.

"So was it the same?" Frances turns the radio down a notch.

"The same as what?"

"Kissing the orange. Is it the same kissing Trevor?"

I laugh. "Not even close."

After a loud and crazy meal at the Vega house with Frances and her family, we all pile in the family minivan and ride to church.

Pastor Mike greets us at the doorway of the youth building. "Hey, it's two of my favorite girls. How's it going?" He sticks his meaty fist out, and I tap my knuckles to his.

"Katie has something she wants to tell you," Frances says.

My eyes widen. I am *not* about to confess any make out sins here.

Frances crosses her arms. "About the mission camping trip?"

"Oh! Right. Yeah . . . I . . ."

"You've decided to go with us." Pastor Mike slaps me on the back. "I knew you would. I've been praying for you, Katie, and I just knew you'd have a change of heart."

Sorry, Pastor, but this week of spiritual outdoorsy-ness isn't about me. I'm only going for Jeremy.

He points a finger in my face. "I know you're meant to spend spring break with us. I really believe it's where the Lord wants you."

I nod and clear my throat. "Well . . . good." Yeah, what do you say to that? I got nothing.

Frances and I walk into the room. As usual there's some rockin' Christian music playing on the stereo. The small stage up front is decorated with white candles of varying sizes. And the room is filled with wall to wall teens.

All these people here and my eyes are drawn to one in particular. Charlie Benson.

No. I'm totally into Trevor. *Stop it, Katie.*

Before I move my gaze, Charlie spots me. His eyes catch mine, and we share a smile. Then Chelsea tugs on his arm, and he turns his head to give her his full attention. I feel a strange twinge in my heart. I've never been a Chelsea. Never gonna be. And it's never bothered me—'til now. Just once it would be nice to be the prettiest. The most popular. Have the best hair, the best smile. Have that indefinable quality that attracts the boys like the newest game system.

The house band takes the stage and leads the room in a few worship songs. As always, I'm aware of Frances, so at ease and comfortable with totally getting into the moment. She lifts a hand in praise and closes her eyes, singing every word like a love song to God. Though it makes me a little uncomfortable, it is kind of cool how personal God is for her. Like they're friends or something.

Pastor Mike jumps on stage and welcomes everyone. "Guys, tonight I want you to just kick back and relax. You are among friends here."

He must not know Chelsea Blake is in the house.

"Lately we've been talking about faith. About believing in God no matter what. Trusting him with everything you've got, even when it looks like your situation is hopeless."

My mind drifts to Jeremy, and I wonder if he's saved. What's he hanging on to? Nearly everything he owns went up in a twister. What gets him through?

"God wants you to lean on him fully. To lay all of your burdens down at the cross of Jesus, and just . . . let go."

Is that what Millie did? (Aside from her kooky new herbal-meditative-organic chicken phase.) Did she just give her cancer up to God? How can you not hold onto it and let that worry eat at you? Maybe I worry enough for me and Millie both.

The pastor reads for a few minutes out of his worn Bible. "In

Jeremiah, God says he will *fully* satisfy the weary soul. And he will revive every worn-out and sorrowful person." His eyes scan the room, but I would bet money they rest on me longer than anyone else. "Is this where you are tonight? Are you tired? Totally sad? Do you need some rest? Do you need God to tell you it's time to give that sadness up? To release that fear?" Pastor Mike holds up his Bible. "Because that's exactly what He's saying."

How can I? Everything is a mess. Millie has major cancer. Angel is harassing me. And I just don't know I'm ready to trust you, God. Where have you been? I've needed you. Where were you?

"Are you ready to let God satisfy your soul? Are you ready to give it up? Because the way you're doing things now—how's that going for you?"

Not so hot, thanks for asking.

"One of the ways God works is through us." Pastor Mike nods. "That's right, he wants to use every one of you. We've got a lot of people in this town who need some God—who need some replenishment and lifting up. We have the opportunity to do just that over Spring Break. I need you to prepare your hearts and get prayed up. Make this coming week about ministering to others and be totally amazed at what God will teach *you*, how God will speak to *you*."

Is that what you want to do—speak to me? I've been here this whole time. Why haven't you spoken to me yet? I waited for you, you know? How am I supposed to see you in all of Millie's cancer business? In my own ragged past? Do you really expect me to believe you were there in all of that?

"Next week lives are going to be changed, guys." Pastor Mike sets his Bible down. His eyes lock onto mine, and his words shoot straight through me. "Will yours be one of them?"

I don't know, God.

Will it?

Chapter 31

"THANKS FOR COMING with me to get my dirty PE clothes, Hannah. I need to wash them before tomorrow. Maxine's now on laundry duty and says if I bring home any more stale, stinky t-shirts, she's gonna start torching them."

We round the corner into the locker room.

"Hey! My jacket's gone."

And find Robin Martin, a fellow PE classmate, digging in her locker. With Angel right beside her.

Angel swivels around at our arrival. "Well, well. Look who's here. What a coincidence. Robin's jacket is missing, and here's Katie Parker now. You know, Katie, don't you, Robin? She's the one who was suspended for *stealing*." Angel moves in between me and Hannah. "Anybody seen Robin's jacket?"

Hannah looks at me and twists her long hair around her finger. "Did you happen to see it?"

I stare at my friend's doubtful face. "As in did I see it when I took it?" I shake my head and shove past Angel to my locker. "Thanks. Thanks a lot, Hannah." With shaking hands I punch my gym clothes into my bag and throw it over my shoulder.

"No . . . um, I just meant—"

"I know what you meant." Could someone just stick a hot poker in my eye? It might be less painful. "You *know* I didn't steal anything. This is the first time I've been in here today."

Angel stomps up behind me. "Parker—"

"Not today, Nelson. I don't have time for your drama." I'm only a whisper's distance from Angel. "You and I both know I didn't steal anything. At any time. And we both know who *is* taking things."

Angel laughs and every head that wasn't already pointed in our direction swivels our way. "I believe the evidence would tell a different story." She holds up her hands. "I wasn't caught with the goods. You were."

"Yeah, and I wonder how that could have possibly happened?" I can hear my own pulse pounding in my head. "I'm not done with this. I *will* get to the bottom of it. And when I do, you're going down, and everyone in the school is gonna know you for the deceitful loser you are."

Our shoulders connect as I shove past her.

"You can't leave!"

"Watch me."

"My mom will tell Mr. Wayman."

"Tell him Katie Parker says hi."

Angel's angry voice becomes a blur as I race out of the locker room and shoot through the gym doors.

The school day now officially over, I dig into my backpack and whip my cell phone out.

"Hello?"

"Charlie, it's time to move on your Angel plan."

"What Angel plan?"

Boys and their one-track minds! "The plan you said you'd come up with. Remember? You were gonna help me?"

I hear a muffled sound and another voice. Chelsea.

"Katie, I'll have to call you back."

"You're bailing on me, aren't you?" *Why* did I think I could count on him? "You didn't come through with a plan to get Nash and Frances together, and now you're worming out of this." I end the call and walk outside.

Five seconds later the phone vibrates in my hand.

"What?"

"It's me. Don't hang up." Charlie's voice is so low, I can hardly understand him. "Meet me at the Burger Barn after drama practice."

"Why?"

"Just do it. And bring Frances. I'll have Nash with me. We'll discuss the science fair."

"I don't *want* to discuss the science fair."

"And my idea to redeem your good name."

"Do I hear you laughing, Charlie Benson?" Some of my anger drips off like PE sweat. "Because I *did* have a good reputation before all of this."

"Whatever, Mother Teresa." He snorts. "Just be there."

"You are *such* a jerk." Yet when I close the phone, I'm smiling.

And twenty minutes later, when Trevor walks into the Valiant, I'm glaring.

The boy, whose lips were on mine just yesterday, saunters into the theater with his arm around Pamela Gillham, a.k.a. Woman At Ball Number Four.

His eyes widen for a split-second when he sees me. But then he sends his custom wink my direction, shares one last laugh with Pamela, and turns her loose. I guess this is what it's gonna be like to date the school flirt.

I wish I could give it right back though. I look at Jeremy, sitting next to me. Maybe I should throw my arm around him, lean in close, and—

"I got a new prosthetic nose off eBay." Jeremy sticks his new snout in my face and breathes through it like an asthmatic Darth Vader. "What do you think?"

I think wrapping my arms around you right now would be so counterproductive.

"Students! Students, attention please!" Mrs. Hall, in something that looks like a gypsy Halloween costume, steps onto the stage. "We only have two and a half more weeks until the play. I need you focused and ready. Every rehearsal should be your best. I hold you to high standards . . . just like I held my soon-to-be ex-husband to high standards. Do *not* disappoint me. Like he did. I expect you to not miss your cues. I expect you to be where you are supposed to be when you are supposed to be there. And sure, some people, like Mr. Joel Hall, call that whining and harassment, but I hope, unlike *him*, it won't lead you to loose morals and overly bosomed tarts."

The stage lights hum and whine above.

"All right, then. On with the show." Our teacher climbs down from the stage and takes her seat in the middle of the first row.

"I'd give my eye teeth to meet an overly bosomed tart."

I roll my eyes at Jeremy and pinch his nose. "Keep dreaming."

Jeremy and I walk onstage when it's our cue. We practice the scene in which we toss our gowns on Cinderella so she can fix them for the ball.

"Don't throw it so hard next time, Katie," Mrs. Hall calls from below.

I smile. "So sorry."

"Iron my dress, you lazy girl."

"Katie, dear, don't smile when you say that."

Two hours later, I stand on stage next to Jeremy, my sister in ugliness, and the girl who plays my mother, as we put the finishing touches on the final scene.

"We've skipped it until now, but Trevor, the script says you are to kiss Cinderella." Mrs. Hall clasps her hands. "You've just discovered your soul mate . . . for whatever that's worth. Claim your princess."

Kissing? He can't kiss her! Ugh. Can't. Look.

The cast hoots and whistles as Trevor pulls Chelsea to him, dips her slightly back and plants one on her.

Shouldn't there be an awkward moment here? Like that whole moment of my nose will go left, you go right? That kiss went way too smoothly. Like they'd been practicing.

But that's just silly.

Okay, seriously, come up for air. This is Cinderella, rated G. Not the Cinemax version.

They're just acting though. What am I worried about? He's on the verge of dating me, right? I mean he asked me to the spring dance. Not Chelsea. Or Prince Charming's mother. Or Woman At Ball Number Four.

. . . At least I think he asked me.

Mrs. Hall claps her hands. "Yes, that's good. I think you've got it."

"Wow," Jeremy whispers.

"What? It's in the script," I scold.

Chelsea clings onto Trevor for a more moments as the two share a twittering laugh. I grit my teeth. *Yes, your making out was hilarious. Loved it. Encore. Autograph my program.*

Trevor catches up with me after rehearsal. "Hey, Katie, a group of us are going to the movies tonight. Want to go?" Chelsea is all but plastered to his side.

I paint on my best smile. "I'd love to, really I would." I lay my hand on his arm for all to see. Take *that*, Cinderella. "But I'm meeting some friends at the Burger Barn."

Chelsea bows up like a wet cat. "Charlie's meeting Nash at the Burger Barn."

"Yeah," I say, not sure where to tread. "We're gonna work on our science fair projects. It's coming up pretty quick."

The blonde bombshell holds up her BMW keys and gives them a jangle. "I'll see you there, then." She casts a pouty look at her prince. "Sorry, Trev. I guess Charlie forgot to mention this wasn't a boys night out. I know he'll be upset if I'm not there with him."

Yeah, I can see him sobbing over his triple-decker Burger Barn combo meal already.

She pats his arm (the one I had just touched), and clicks away in her dainty spiky heeled boots, cell phone pressed to her ear.

"So . . ." I nod slowly, hoping for divine inspiration and some witty banter. "Nice, um . . . rehearsal."

"Yeah," Trevor grins. "It was a lot of fun today."

Oh, I'll just bet it was.

"A blast." Can't. Hold. Smile. Much. Longer.

"So how's that plant doing?" Trevor speaks to me, but his eyes travel the room. He waves to Pamela and Woman At Ball Numbers Five, Six, and Seven.

"Leafy is doing well. You took good care of him," I purr, trying to reclaim his attention. "I really owe you."

He finally focuses solely on my face. "Yeah . . . I guess you do." He wraps an arm around me, and we begin to walk out of the theater. "Whatever could you do to repay me for my plant-loving generosity?" He pushes open the exit doors, and I follow him out to the parking lot.

I tug on his letterman jacket to slow him down. "We could get dessert before the dance. My treat." I hope that didn't sound suggestive. Oh, my gosh, did that sound suggestive? For the record, I am *not* the dessert.

"Yeah, um . . . about . . . Hey! Quincy! David!"

Suddenly I notice we're practically surrounded by Trevor's loyal followers from In Between High. Wonderful. Maybe we can reminisce about old times—like that one time I was publicly humiliated in front of nearly all of In Between at a party.

"Whatcha guys talking about?" His refrigerator-sized friend Quincy slaps Trevor on the back. Trevor's mouth opens, but nothing comes out.

"The dance," I say. "We were just discussing the spring dance." I smile up at Trevor. Who does not smile back. Quincy must've hit him too hard.

"Awwww," drawls David Higgins. "Is Trevor taking you to the dance?" Though the question is directed at me, David's attention is on Trevor. Sheesh, is *every* male in this town born with ADD?

"Hey," Quincy yells. "Trevor's taking Katie to the spring dance." Laughter erupts through the group.

Um . . . and this is funny because . . .?

Trevor frowns. "Don't worry about them. But, Katie, about the dance, I—"

Quincy butts in between us. "He'll pick you up at seven. Isn't that right, Trev?"

Trevor stares at the ground. "I—"

Honnnnk! Honnnnnk!

"Oh." I spot Frances in her station wagon. "My ride's here. I gotta go." I don't hide the fact I'm trying to read his expression. "Trevor . . . is everything good here?" *With you? Me? Us? Your psychotic friends?*

Trevor nods and briefly draws me to him with one arm. "Sure. See you later."

More cat-calls from his oaf posse. With an uncertain look back, I get into Frances's car.

"What was that about? There's more testosterone in that parking lot than at an NFL game."

My eyes hold onto Trevor as we drive away. "I don't know. Boys are so weird."

"Closest things to alien life form I know."

Then Frances ambushes me with a million questions about our rendezvous with Nash and Charlie.

"Frances, calm down. Breathe, for crying out loud. We're gonna have some burgers, talk about our science fair projects, and then Charlie will tell me how to nail Angel to the wall."

"Sounds like fun." Frances nods. "And I can do this. I can."

"No choking this time."

Frances steers the wagon through downtown to the Burger Barn. It's literally a partially fixed-up barn with a flashing neon sign and a drive-thru window. On Saturdays the owner's son has to dress up in an anorexic cow costume and shake his hoof at the passing cars. You know he's gonna grow up to have some issues.

I wave at the guys as we walk in. Chelsea is already there, draped across her boyfriend. Ew. Like I needed to see this before I put down a totally awesome, greasy, drippy, overfried burger?

"Hey, dudes . . . er, guys . . . boys . . . Cash . . . Harlie . . ."

I nudge the sputtering Frances. "Hey." I scoot into my seat and grab a menu.

Charlie shrugs off Chelsea's arms. "So—bad day today?"

"Oh, it was horrible. First my flatiron wouldn't heat up." Chelsea flips her perfectly straightened gold locks. "Then I had to eat two percent milk on my cereal this morning instead of skim. I specifically asked my mother never to bring two percent into our house again. And then—"

"Actually I was talking to Katie." Charlie pats Chelsea's hand and turns to me.

I watch Chelsea consider having a meltdown. "Yeah, could've been better. More stuff was stolen in PE today." I shut my grease-caked menu. "You do have a plan, don't you?"

"Yeah, I think I do. I'm working on it." His *not now* look has me changing the subject.

"So . . . Nash, are you excited about playing for the mission project campout?"

"Totally, dude. I am so there. Really excited about it. How 'bout you, Frances?"

I push her menu down so her face is visible.

"Yeah, very, very excited. Thank you very, very much for asking. It was a pleasure to answer your question, Nash." And the menu pops back up.

I smile like my best friend isn't totally insane. "Frances was telling me you have a new band member, Jessi White. I think I have a class with her."

"Yeah, totally righteous bass player."

Frances pipes up. "I'm sure she's the righteous-est."

I continue with my prodding. "Is she going to play next week on spring break?"

"Nah, she's not really ready for that yet." The waitress comes and Nash gives her his order.

"It's cool to play the guitar. Is that your type of a girl? The rocker-chick Jessi type?"

Nash frowns at my question. "I dunno. I'm not really into types."

I stare a hole through Charlie. *Help me.*

Charlie takes a drink of his Coke. "So are you interested in Jessi?"

Beside me Frances is humming the Chihuahua fight song and beating out the rhythm with her silverware.

Nash studies his fizzy drink. "I don't like to mix business and my social life."

What about self-proclaimed nerds and your social life? Do those mix?

Chelsea sighs and grabs her boyfriend's hand. "I have an extra rehearsal tomorrow night."

My face pinches in a frown. "We have an extra rehearsal?"

Chelsea's glossy lips snarl. "No, Ugly Stepsister, *I* have a rehears-al."

"You and who else?" I ask, my inner sensor on alert.

She picks up her napkin and twists it around her finger. "Trevor and I. We're having some problems with a few scenes and want to clear it up before spring break." She melts into Charlie. "You understand, don't you? You know how important this play is to me."

Charlie just smiles. "Yeah, sure."

Conversation turns to the science fair, and all of us but Chelsea pull out some notes to swap and discuss.

"Your data looks good, Nash."

I beam at Frances, proud of her for completing a sentence all by herself.

I squint my eyes to get a better look, but I would bet my strawberry shake Nash is blushing. Could it be? Is it possible Nash likes

Frances? Or maybe he's just a sucker for compliments on the scientific process.

The waitress brings our food—a heaping tray of burgers, fries, and shakes. And one lonely salad, dressing on the side.

"My fork is dirty." Chelsea holds it up for the waitress's inspection. The woman apologizes and removes the offensive utensil from Chelsea's grip.

"Who wants to pray?" Nash asks.

I disconnect all eye contact and choose a spot on the far wall to stare at. Hmm, nice moose head. Didn't know you could catch moose in In Between, Texas. Very pretty Christmas ornaments hanging on his antlers too. Especially lovely this time of March.

"I will." Charlie bows his head. "Dear God, thank you for our friendships here. Thank you for our opportunity coming up to serve you in our own town. We pray you give us servants' hearts and really open our eyes to what you need us to do and what you want to teach us."

God, just teach me how to survive next week.

"Lord, we pray for our science fair projects, and that it goes well tomorrow, the big due date. Help us to do the best work we can. No disasters, no mishaps."

Hey, what's a two letter word for disaster and mishap? Me.

"We pray for Katie. Lord, she's under attack at school, and we ask for your hand to be over her. Guide her and protect her. Give her the help she needs."

Or just remove Angel Nelson from this planet.

"And we ask for total healing for Millie Scott, God. In Jesus' name we pray, amen."

The waitress appears at our table as our heads rise. "Here's you a new fork, hon."

"Keep it," Chelsea hisses. "That one is bent. Is it really that hard to bring me a decent fork?" She looks at us and laughs. "I guess I should've brought one with me. I didn't know it was gonna be this hard."

"You can have mine." With an apologetic face, Charlie thanks the waitress and takes the bent fork. Chelsea eats her salad with her Cruella DeVille smile.

An hour later I slurp the last of my shake. "I think we've got it all down."

Frances picks at her mutilated, uneaten burger. "I think we're ready for the science fair."

"It's gonna be great." Charlie finishes off a piece of chocolate pie and shoves his plate aside.

Chelsea's designer bag beeps. "Oops, that's for me." She pulls out her phone and reads it. "Gotta go." She leans in and kisses Charlie on the cheek.

"Where are you going?" He stands up and helps her with her chair.

She smiles prettily and holds up her phone. "Emergency practice called for the play."

I open my mouth.

"No." She holds up a hand. "You don't need to be there. Gotta go."

"Call me later." Charlie sits back down, his brow wrinkled in a frown as he watches her leave.

"I really should be going, too. I told James and Millie I would be home by seven-thirty." I look at Frances, who is openly staring at Nash like he's a triple banana split.

We all pay, then Charlie puts a hand on my arm to stop me from walking out. "Nash, walk Frances to her car. I need to talk to Katie."

"Uh . . . yeah, sure." Nash holds the door open for a petrified Frances.

"I've been thinking about this stealing business." Charlie watches our friends walk out of the restaurant to the parking lot.

"I do believe you mentioned something about helping me."

He smiles down at me. "Yeah, I believe I did." He digs into his backpack and pulls out a small gadget. "Know how to work one of these?"

"I don't even know what that is."

"It's a video recorder. Got it from my uncle who's a P.I. in Dallas."

"Keep talking."

"Do you know anyone who could let you in the gym locker room before school starts to hide this baby?"

I shake my head. "Well, you know, Mrs. Whipple probably would've, but I borrowed her favorite apple vest last week and didn't return it. She hasn't spoken to me since."

He laughs and puts the camera in my hands. And for a moment our fingers intertwine. *I like Trevor, I like Trevor, I like Trevor.*

"What about Mrs. Hall? She thinks a lot of you."

I clutch this idea and hold it close. "She does?"

"Don't you know that? Katie, you really gotta work on your self-confidence."

"What, are you channeling Oprah?"

"Seriously, I think if you explained to Mrs. Hall about what's going on, she would help you. We need someone with some keys to get you into the locker room so you could set the camera up."

I hold the camera to my chest. "Thanks, Charlie. You didn't have to do this."

He places his hand on my shoulder. "That's what friends are for."

I just stare at him and nod, Frances-style.

"I'm glad you're going on the camping trip too." Charlie drops his hand.

"Yeah. It'll be fun."

"Fun? Yeah, probably. Life changing?" He holds open the door. "Most definitely."

Chapter 32

RIDAY MORNING AT six-thirty, Mrs. Hall and Charlie meet me up at the school. Mrs. Hall lets us in the building and into the girls' locker room. I thank her for the millionth time.

"It's no problem, Katie. You should've come to me sooner with this."

Charlie turns a full circle among all the girl stuff. "Wow. I'm standing on sacred ground here. Do you know how many guys would pay to be able to say they've had an up-close-and-personal tour of the girls' locker room?"

I snap my fingers in front of him. "Focus, would you? And quit looking for stray bras to stare at."

Mrs. Hall's bangles chime as she lifts her hand and yawns. "I cannot believe anyone has accused you of stealing. Preposterous! I know guilt when I see it. And I know a rotten liar when I see one. Hmph! I lived with one for—"

"Thanks, Mrs. Hall. I really appreciate it." I open my locker and peer inside. The jacket wasn't there at the end of the day yesterday, but I wouldn't have put it past Angel to plant it in the middle of the night.

"Still no jacket, right?" Charlie pulls his camera out of the case. "Did you get Hannah's locker combo?"

I pull a small piece of paper out of my pocket. "Got it." After practically accusing me of theft, Hannah was more than happy to share her combination so we could plant the camera in her locker, which is directly in front of mine, giving us a bird's eye view.

I recite the numbers for Charlie and the locker in front of mine snaps open. He sticks his hands inside, then stops. "Maybe you should set the camera up. I don't want to . . . touch anything."

Despite my fatigue, I laugh. "Such the gentleman." I take the camera and with Charlie's guidance, set it up just right in her locker. It's so tiny, it's not hard to hide it among some PE clothes.

Charlie nods. "Perfect. We have up to eleven hours of battery life in that thing, so if anything happens today, the camera will get it."

"Yeah." I sigh. "If anything does happen."

Mrs. Hall lays her arm across my shoulders. "Honey, you've done all you can do right now. If this doesn't work then I'll help you think of something else. I'll do whatever I can to help."

Anxiety gnaws at me the rest of the day. What if Angel doesn't place the jacket in my locker? What if we have to do this every day for the next month until we catch her? What if we never catch her? It's bad enough to be Party Ruiner Katie, but to add Kleptomaniac Katie to it is just more than I can bear.

Seventh hour descends on me like a two-ton weight. I take a deep breath of reality. I mean, seriously, what am I getting all worked up for? The odds we caught anything on tape are slim to none. This is probably gonna take weeks.

I walk into the gym, watching my reflection on the shiny wood floors. Funny, I don't look like a big chicken.

But I am. I turn around and head back to the lobby to change in the bathroom. If Robin Martin's jacket is in my locker and the camera missed it, I will have to deal with that all spring break. And I can't. I just can't.

Five minutes later I stand on the gym floor with the rest of my sisters in misery, ready to receive our torture sentence from Coach Nelson.

Tweeeeet! "Listen up, ladies. Today I have something new for us."

My heart soars at the thought of some variety.

"Instead of doing fifty push-ups like we usually do on Fridays, today we're gonna skip that."

This is awesome news.

"No, not gonna do fifty push-ups. We're gonna do thirty one-armed push-ups. Now go!"

My soaring heart sinks to the floor. It flops pitifully once or twice before giving up like a dying fish. Is she crazy? Whoever came up with the idea of PE should be tortured. Coach-Nelson style.

After we struggle through some push-ups, we run the rest of the class period.

I grab my backpack from the gym floor and drag my limp body into the shower. It's everything I can do not to run to Hannah's locker and grab the camcorder.

When I step out, clean and sweat-free, I meet the cold stare of Angel in the mirror. She combs through her short hair.

"You know the principal is gonna be checking your locker today."

I wrap my hair in a towel. "So?" What if they find something? I feel disaster looming. It would so be my luck. "They didn't find anything yesterday."

I feel my blood pumping pure heat as she laughs. "Your stealing's gonna catch up with you."

I believe this moment calls for a classic line from a timeless and inspirational cheerleader movie. I step in her space. "Bring it on."

I stomp past her and move toward Hannah. I try to waste time, hoping Angel will leave so I can sneak the camera out of Hannah's locker. Ten minutes into Angel doing hamstring stretches in the middle of the floor, I know I can't stall any longer. I won't be leaving with the camera.

With my hand already punching buttons, I have Charlie on the phone before I hit the parking lot.

"It's me. I couldn't get the camera out. What do I do?"

"Let me take care of it."

Call me crazy, but I think that's the hottest thing I've ever heard. *I like Trevor, I like Trevor, I like Trevor.* "Um . . . yeah, sure."

His voice vibrates in my ear. "I'll see you at your house in an hour. We'll see what we've got."

"Okay." I wave at James, waiting for me in his truck.

"And Katie?"

"Yeah?"

"Don't get your hopes up, all right? This plan could take some time."

I nod like he can see me. "Right. Of course. I'm not expecting anything." Who am I kidding? I'm expecting everything.

"How was your day, kiddo?" James's smile takes up his whole face, as I climb in the truck. "Was your early morning rendezvous successful?"

I shrug and strap on my seatbelt. "I dunno. I'm not gonna worry about it."

His eyebrow lifts, but he doesn't pursue it. "Hey, Millie bought a wig today. You know, for when she starts chemo. She'll want to show it off, so I wanted to warn you."

Translation: don't freak out.

"Millie's gonna wear a wig?" That's gonna kill my foster mom, who's never without makeup, never a hair out of place.

His smile doesn't falter. "Yeah, just part of the chemo. She'll start that in a few weeks."

"What'll happen?"

"She'll be fine. The doctor says she'll just get a little run down and tired." He smiles. "Maybe that means fewer soy bean casseroles."

We pull into the drive and Rocky rounds the corner to greet us as James and I get out of the truck.

James pets the mongrel on the head. "Whatcha doing outside, Rocky? You're usually stationed in the kitchen when Millie's fixing dinner."

"Hey, there!" Millie stands in the doorway. "I hope you guys are going to be hungry later. We're going to have a special meal for your last weekend home before the camping trip."

I walk into Millie's arms and give her a hug. Both her arms wrap around me. "Heard you got a new do today. I hope you went with something different, like a some dark J.Lo locks or maybe some Whoopi Goldberg dreds."

"It looks just like my own hair. I asked for the Jessica Simpson style, but they were all out."

The four of us move into the house and we follow Millie toward the kitchen.

"Um . . . Mil, what is that smell?" James frowns at the scent.

"Pizza." Millie goes to the fridge and pulls out the tea pitcher.

I brave another sniff. "Pizza? Are you sure?" Maybe the cancer has affected her brain.

"Tofu bean sprout pizza. It's gonna be so good for you."

I cover a laugh and shoot James a quick look. "Wow, Millie, you shouldn't have gone to all that trouble. Ordering delivery would've been so much easier."

"Nonsense. Do you know what's in that stuff?"

No, but that's what makes it so good.

Millie shakes her head and highlighted blonde curls bounce. "Preservatives and trans fats."

"Mmmm. I love those." I breathe through my mouth to avoid the stench.

My foster mom pours me a glass of tea. "Don't be silly. We're not eating a toxic diet anymore. So get used to it."

I glare at James as I lift the glass to my mouth. "*Blech*!" I rake my sleeve over my face. "What is this?"

"Organic herbal green tea. James, would you like some?"

I smirk at my foster dad "Yes, he would. Hey, where's the sugar, Millie?"

"No sugar."

"Sweetener?"

She lifts her eyebrows. "Kills rats."

"I'm totally fine with that."

"And I threw all your diet sodas out."

I set my tea down with a thud. "Do you know what you've done to—"

"Greetings!" Maxine bursts through the kitchen, wearing a full-length formal.

James chokes on his green tea. "*What* is that?"

Maxine does a wobbly pirouette. "Mrs. Hall and I are having a little dispute over my costume choice as the fairy godmother. This is my latest creation." She picks up a corner of her skirt. "I think it says sophistication and worldliness."

James scratches his stubbly cheek. "That's not what it's saying to me."

"Mom, you better change if Sam's going to eat with us tonight."

"Yes, Maxine, time to get out of your play clothes." James shoots a wink my way.

An hour later, we all sit down to the table for dinner. Or as James whispered, "The meal that will precede a few bowls of cereal."

"Katie, are you excited about your week of mission work?" Sam passes the salad.

"Yeah, sure." I guess. I don't know. It's my first churchie event, so I'm kind of nervous. I still don't even know where all the books of the Bible are yet. What if somebody we're helping says, "Quick! Find Leviticus!"

"I think you'll have a great time." Millie smiles and hands me the organic carrot and bean medley. Again. "It's perfect, really." She turns her attention toward Sam, and I brush my veggies into my napkin. "They sleep in tents on the church campus. They'll do reconstruction and cleaning in the community during the day. Then at night it's a church service for those in the shelters and the kids get to cook for them."

"Marvelous opportunity. I'm so pleased you're going. So pleased."

Maxine spears a bite of pizza with her fork and sniffs it.

"No more slumber parties in my room when I'm not there, Maxine. Last time you did that I found three pair of knee highs, one orthopedic shoe, and a Depends in my room."

Maxine clutches Sam's hand. "None of those things belonged to me."

Millie inspects my plate. "Katie, you're not eating much. Too excited about Monday?"

"Uh-huh." Yes, that's it. Because normally when I'm handed a plate of organic vegetarian goo, I just *can't* stop eating.

"Well, I have a surprise." Millie rises from her chair. "Guess what we're having for dessert?"

"Tofu cupcakes?" Maxine bites her lip. "Soy soufflé? Green bean smoothies?"

Millie frowns at her mother and disappears into the kitchen. "Your favorite!" She comes back out carrying a loaded tray. "Homemade chocolate brownie sundae. Just like at that restaurant you love."

Millie scoops some ice cream over my still warm brownie and drizzles hot fudge sauce over the top. "Here you go, sweetie."

The doorbell rings.

Who would interrupt this sacred moment, this reunion of girl and oozing, melting sugar-filled chocolate?

"I'll get it." Maxine bounds up from her chair.

I swallow my bite. "The back of your skirt is tucked in your hose."

Without missing a step, she yanks it out. "Thought it felt a little breezy."

James leans towards Sam. "You marry her, and that can be yours every day of your life." He wiggles his eyebrows. "I could perform the ceremony right now."

"James—" Millie scolds.

"Could have her packed up in two minutes."

"Look who I found." Maxine enters the dining room with her

arm around Charlie Benson. "He looks familiar." She claps his chin in her hand and pulls his face close. "Where do I know you?"

"Church?" Charlie searches the room for help.

"Nope. Where else?"

"Last fall you came to visit at my grandmother's house."

Maxine scratches her head. "Not ringing any bells."

"You sent Katie up in a tree to spy on Sam and she fell into my grandma's pool."

"Well! Nice of you to come by. Wish you could stay. Tell everyone good-bye." She claps him on the back and turns him toward the door.

"Wait." Charlie digs in his heels. "I have something special for Katie."

"She's not that type of girl. Shoo!" She gives him a big push.

"Mother! My goodness, let the poor boy come in and sit down." Millie pulls out an empty chair. "Join us, Charlie. We were just having dessert. Have you eaten dinner yet?"

Behind Millie, I nod my head in frantic jerks.

"Um . . . yes, ma'am." He eyes the pizza blob with curiosity.

"Well, then you just sit down and have some dessert. James, get this boy a spoon." Millie dishes out more brownie sundae for Charlie. I don't know that I feel close enough to him to share *my* going-away super-special dessert.

"What do you have there?" James inspects the bundle in Charlie's arms.

"It's my video camera." Charlie's metallic gray eyes stare into mine. "Mrs. Hall let me back into the school about thirty minutes ago. He digs into his bag and pulls out his James Bond device. "It's got some pretty interesting footage."

James pushes out of his chair. "Bring your bowls and follow me."

We crowd into the den. I chew on a fingernail as Charlie plugs the thing into James's laptop.

Millie pulls me into her side. "Even if we don't get it this time, you know we will clear your name soon."

I wrap my arm around her and breathe in her comforting Millie scent. She smells like . . . a mom.

"I watched part of it already. Check this out. The counter says it's eleven forty-five, right before lunch." Charlie pushes a button and a blurry image of the locker room pops on the screen. Charlie begins to narrate. "Right here." He points to the lower corner of the screen. "You can see the shape of someone standing in front of your locker. She's pulling something out of her pocket."

Maxine springs from her chair. "Let's go get her!"

Everyone ignores her as Charlie continues. "Now she's opening the lock."

"It's my combination. That's what she has on the piece of paper."

James nods. "She had to have gotten it from her mother or from watching you get into your locker. The problem though is you can't even see her face. We have to prove beyond a doubt it's her."

"Her mom keeps a record of our combos somewhere in her office. But if that's Angel, how is she getting the stuff out in the first place? She's never out of my sight in PE, and yet that's when things are being taken."

Charlie shushes me. "Right here. It's a little hard to make out, but she puts something in your locker and covers it up. She shuts the door and . . . there. Right there!" He taps on the glass. "Did you see that?"

I shake my head. "Rewind it."

"I'm gonna slow it down. Watch for it." The images reverse and then begin again.

A hand spins the dial on my locker and the intruder slowly turns around—her face turned to the camera.

"It's her!" I jump up and down. "It's Angel! It's Angel!" I grab Charlie and hug the breath out of him. "You did it." I step away and clear my throat. "Thank you."

"Yes, thank you, Charlie." James claps him on the back. "This is priceless."

"Glad to help." Charlie blushes, making his cute dimple stand out. "I'll leave the camera with you." He unhooks it from the TV and hands it to James.

"Let's call the fuzz. I know a few guys who work for the FBI."

Millie rolls her eyes. "Mom, that won't be necessary. But we will take care of this."

"I guess it will have to wait until we come back from spring break. There's nothing we can do now." I have to sit on this for a whole week.

"Oh, my dear." James's mouth turns up in a sly grin. "You don't know the lengths to which a determined parent will go." One brow lifts over his glasses. "I believe your principal is due for a home visit from the pastor of In Between Community Church."

We watch the video three more times, and my stress lightens on every viewing. Free at last. Thank God for technology, I'm free at last.

After his second helping of my dessert (I actually offered him the next round), I walk Charlie to his car.

"Thank you, Charlie. You didn't have to do that for me, but I'm glad you did."

He shrugs and opens his door. "Like I said, that's what friends do."

"I'm glad you did." Why is this awkward? Boy just saved my behind, and I can't even put two sentences together.

"I'm glad you decided to go to the campout." His eyes meet mine and we just watch one another for a brief moment. "Well, I gotta go." Charlie shakes his head and climbs into his car.

"Yeah, see you on Monday morning." I wiggle my fingers in a small wave. "Thanks again."

His eyes never leaving mine, he waves back, and shuts his door. I stand in the driveway and watch his car rumble out of sight.

Okay, God. I look skyward to the canopy of stars hanging overhead. *Thanks.*

I push open the front door. "Can you even believe that? I can't wait until—"

Four pair of eyes stare back at me, wide and unblinking. Millie steps forward, her fake smile wobbling.

"What's wrong?" Ice blasts through my veins. "What?"

"Katie." James stands next to his wife and puts his hands on my shoulders. "Iola Smartly just called."

No, no, no! I am *not* going back. They can't make me. I will throw myself in front of a moving bus of sumo wrestlers before I go back to Sunny Haven. "She can't come and get me. Millie's gonna be fine. You said you were gonna be fine."

"It's not about Millie." James squeezes my shoulder. "It's your mom, Katie."

My mouth opens but nothing comes out.

"She's been released."

Chapter 33

Dear Mrs. Smartly,

What do you mean my mother's case got overturned? She got caught selling drugs. What part of the evidence was tampered with? I was there, am I not evidence? Who did this? I want names.

It's not that I don't want my mom out of prison. I do. But now is not a good time. Millie needs me. I have to stay here in In Between—at least for a little while longer.

James said you mentioned you and mom might come to my play. It's just a minor part. No big deal. Nothing worth driving six hours for. Well, actually, I am pretty fabulous in it. Minus my glue-on nose. But I'm sure I can send you two a DVD of the performance. I've heard the camera adds ten pounds, but I'm willing to risk that to save you some wear and tear on your old Sunny Haven minivan.

I better go. I have thirty more minutes until I leave for church camp, and I still have to eat breakfast. Yes, that's right I said church camp. Me and the churchies. Doing church things. For five whole days. And yes, I wrote my name in my underwear. I will go to any lengths to protect my Victoria Secret undies. I'm sure you understand.

Or maybe not.

Much love,

Katie

I fold the letter and stick it in a pink polka-dotted envelope.

I cannot believe my mom is out of prison. My head pounds from my lack of sleep. Questions and thoughts did battle in my head all night, and this morning I woke up certain of nothing. Except that I needed some Tylenol. If Millie hasn't thrown it out.

Mrs. Smartly told the Scotts Mom was released last week. Why hasn't she called me? Maybe she's forgotten she had a daughter. That's nothing new. She can't take me away from the Scotts yet, can she? Shouldn't I get a say in it if she tries?

And then when I'm not raging with anger and fear, I'm swimming in guilt. This is my mom. I should *want* to go home. I should be happy she's out and free. I should be thrilled at the idea of returning to life with her. But I know our trailer is gone. My cat—gone. And it's not like I had been in my old school long enough to make many friends. The old me—is there anything left of her?

And I can't figure out if that's good. Or bad.

Knock. Knock.

Millie pokes her head in the door. "Katie, are you up?"

At six o'clock in the morning only Millie Scott would be in full makeup.

"I'm up." I lick the envelope and scribble Mrs. Smartly's address.

"Time for breakfast." She glides across the room, her steps muffled by the white shag rug. James follows in behind her and sits down on my bed.

Millie drapes her arms around my shoulders. "It's gonna be okay. You'll see."

I blink back tears. "We're talking about my life. *Nothing's* ever okay."

Her soft laugh tickles my ear, and she kisses my cheek. "Don't worry about anything until we get more details, all right?"

James swabs his glasses with his polo shirt. "You just go to camp and have a good time."

I turn in my desk chair and grab onto my foster mom. "I don't want to go."

"Oh, honey, it's just until Friday night. And we're only five minutes away. You know we're gonna call you every night."

"Nooo." My voice breaks. "I don't want to live with my mom."

"Oh." Millie pulls away and smiles down at me. "We're not at that point yet, all right? You're not going anywhere right now." She brushes away my tears with her thumb. "Except for camp. And you don't want to be late. Lots of people in In Between depending on you."

Me and all my misery join the Scotts and Maxine downstairs at the breakfast nook table.

Millie slides something out of a skillet and onto my plate. "Scrambled tofu."

I sniff. "Thanks." I'd even eat this to be able to stay. I push my plate aside. Just not today.

A lumpy mixture falls out of the pitcher as Millie pours her concoction into my glass. I raise my brows in question.

"Guava juice." She pats me on the head.

Oh, to be like normal kids and drink Sunny Delight for breakfast. And have a mom who hasn't done time.

Maxine, her head cocked, blows on her coffee and stares at her plate.

"I'll pray for us." James eases into the chair on my left. "Dear Heavenly Father, Lord, we praise you for this day. Thank you for Katie, and for her willing heart to serve her community and spend time with the church youth. We pray you would keep her safe. Lord, we ask you would speak to her this week. Give her guidance as well as assurance. Let her see you this week and see where you need her to be. Give her comfort, for we know all things work to your glory. We trust her to you, God, and pray you'd bless her. In Jesus' name, amen."

My head lifts, but my heart still sags.

Maxine gets up and shuffles into the kitchen, sticking her head in a cabinet.

"Mom, if you're looking for your secret stash of Fruit Loops, I tossed them yesterday."

I can see Maxine's eye twitch from across the room. I laugh despite the fact that my world is spinning out of control and about to implode.

Later I hug Maxine good-bye in the driveway and crawl into the Scott's backseat. Anxiety pounds on my head as we drive to the church. The car lurches to a stop at the youth building entrance, and we bail out.

"Well, here we are." Let the party begin. Whee. "Millie, if you guys need me just—"

"We won't." Millie puts her hand on my cheek. "We'll give you all the details of the week when you get back Friday night. I promise." She holds onto me for a few seconds before I'm released, only to be picked off the ground and squeezed by James.

"I'm putting two Pop-Tarts and a can of diet soda in your pocket right now," he whispers.

I've never had a dad. Until now, never knew I wanted one. But as we share a grin, and I pat down my lumpy coat pockets, I know I've been missing out all this time. This guy braved Millie's wrath to bring me processed foods and an acidic, artificially sweetened, chemically-loaded beverage. I couldn't ask for more.

James unloads my suitcase and sleeping bag from the car, and we walk into the youth building.

"Hey, Katie! Glad you're here." Pastor Mike's wife Laura checks my name off her clipboard. "It wouldn't be the same without you."

With a final good-bye to James and Millie, I watch them walk away, the door shutting behind them. *Don't run after them and make a total fool of yourself. Eat your Pop-Tart and think happy thoughts.*

"All right, guys. Just put your stuff against the wall. We're gonna head out into town and get started." Pastor Mike checks his watch. "We'll come back here at noon for lunch and pitch our tents. Then go back out and work for a few hours, start the shower rotation while we prepare dinner, feed some folks, and have our evening service. Any questions?"

Silent, sleepy stares are his only response.

"So today we're working on a house that was badly damaged. Some guys from the church repaired the roof and hung new sheet-rock last week. And today we're cleaning and painting." He waves us onward. "Load up on the bus."

I sit next to Frances, who's sipping on a mocha despite the jos-tling ride.

"Did you have a good weekend?" She asks, strategically slurping between bumps in the road.

"Good doesn't quite describe it."

The brakes screech in protest as we jerk to a stop on Marshall, one of the hardest hit streets in town.

We file out, and Pastor Mike leads us to the yard of a small, yel-low home.

"Half of you will come with me and work here, at Mr. and Mrs. Dobbs's house. The rest of you will need to follow my wife to that home." He points across the street. "And she'll put you to work."

Too tired to take the ten extra steps across the road, I stick with Pastor Mike's group. Frances joins me as we walk into the house.

"Welcome!" A small, stooped African-American woman greets us at the door. She shakes every hand that passes by her. I hold her gnarled hand in mine and feel her fragile bones. "I'm Sarah, and this is my husband, Elmer." She gestures to a man sitting in a sheet-covered chair, breathing into an oxygen mask. "I'll be popping in and out to help, but Elmer's going to visit the neighbors, aren't you dear?"

Elmer, a man probably in his early eighties, nods his bald head and smiles. "Praise the Lord." He continues nodding. "I sure do praise the Lord for you."

Pastor Mike gives us the ground rules for painting then turns us loose.

I follow Frances into a small kitchen and inspect the paint cans.

"Sunshine yellow, that's right." Mrs. Dobbs hobbles in behind me. "Isn't that a lovely name for some paint?" Her rusty laugh fills the room. "Lord knows we could use some sunshine in this old house."

Frances hands me a paint roller and smiles at the woman. "When do you expect to be back in your house, Mrs. Dobbs?"

"Oh, child, you call me Sarah." She pushes a stray piece of hair out of her eyes. "Well, we've been living with the neighbors for over five weeks now, but we'll be able to move back in when you children get done and the fumes clear out a bit. But we've waited this long, we can wait some more. No hurry." Mrs. Dobbs pats me on the back. "It's all in God's timing, isn't it?"

"Yes, it is." I nod like I mean it. "Do you have family here?"

"No, our family's all gone, except for Elmer's brother in Ohio. The Lord didn't bless us with children, so it's just me and Elmer." She grins toward the living room. "But God gave us good neighbors and a good church. He always provides. Yes, indeed. Don't you agree, child?"

My head lifts as I realize she's directing her question at me. Again. "Um . . . yeah."

She leans in closer. "I didn't get to be this old without knowing what I'm talking about, you hear what I'm saying?"

I swallow. "Yes, ma'am."

"When you paint my walls the color of sunshine, you think about what the Lord has brought me through. Would you do that for me?" Mrs. Dobbs pats my shoulder with her bent hand. "This wasn't my first tornado, you know what I'm saying?"

She waddles away, chuckling to herself.

I've said it before, but I'll say it again. Christians are a weird species.

"Hey, guys." Charlie walks in carrying two brushes and some

painter's tape. I see he brought his attachment, Chelsea, who, for whatever reason, wears ballerina flats, a denim miniskirt, and some rich girl shirt that was probably seen on the red carpet just last week.

Frances and I grab a roll of the blue tape and help Charlie tape off the room. Chelsea leans against the kitchen table and watches.

"I think that should do it for now." Charlie surveys our work. "Let's get started. Chels and I will detail, and you two use the rollers."

I paint in small areas like I've seen on HGTV, and soon the wall looks cleaner and brighter. Like sunshine.

"Are you kidding me?" Chelsea shrieks and holds up her dainty hand. "I can't get this paint off my fingernails."

I try not to laugh but totally fail. "It's not permanent. It'll wash off with soap and water."

She curls her lip. "I just got my nails done. So no, I don't think it's just going to wash off." She gazes mournfully at her fingers. "I'm gonna have to leave and get this fixed."

Charlie puts his brush down. "Chelsea, it's not that big of a deal."

Her mouth drops. "Not a big deal? Going like this—" She sticks her hand in his face. "For five days is *not* a big deal?"

"This is a mission trip—a working mission trip. What did you think you'd be doing when they said we were helping tornado victims?"

Her gum crackles in her mouth. "I don't know, Charlie. Dusting? Baking?"

Baking. Yes, a tornado tore their home apart, and what they want more than anything is some cupcakes.

"Would you rather paint with the roller?" Frances asks patiently.

Chelsea rolls her eyes. "Forget it. I'm fine." She looks at Charlie, who clearly is not impressed. "I'm sorry. I didn't have my latte this morning, and you know how I get."

Psycho? Whiny? Obnoxiously annoying?

"I think we need some more help in here." Charlie stands up from his spot on the floor.

I look around, proud of our progress. "No, we don't."

His eyes widen for a millisecond. "Yes, we do. I'll be right back."

Paint fumes getting to him, I guess. I dip my roller in the tray and continue splashing on the yellow.

"Look who I found." Charlie pulls Nash into the kitchen. "I was hoping you'd help me tape around the cabinets."

"No problem, dude. I am here to help." Nash greets everyone and goes to work.

I catch Charlie's eye and give him a thumbs up.

"So . . ." I scoot closer to Chelsea. "How was your rehearsal Friday night?"

Her forehead wrinkles. "Rehearsal?"

"Yeah. You know, the one you said you had with Trevor. That the rest of us weren't needed for?"

Her eyes drop to her brushstrokes. "Oh, yeah. Of course. It went fine. Just a few rough spots to work out. We have very challenging parts."

Frances snorts behind us.

"Which part do you find such a challenge?" I ask.

Chelsea huffs and her brush stills. "I'm a perfectionist. I'm not content to just memorize some lines and sleepwalk through a production."

"No, of course not." I bite back a grin. "Everyone knows what a strong work ethic you have."

She forces a smile. "Exactly. Now if you'll excuse me I need to go text my manicurist."

Thirty minutes later Chelsea is still blissfully absent, and Charlie has maneuvered Frances over by the cabinets next to Nash.

"Nicely done."

Charlie picks up Frances's discarded roller. "Thanks. I hope you don't still think I'm letting you down on all my promises."

I raise my nose a few inches. "The jury's still out."

Charlie's eyes fuse with mine. His hand raises slowly and inches towards my face. Maybe he thinks hard work is sexy on a girl.

"You have some paint on your nose." His fingers brush the tip of my nose, his gray eyes holding mine.

"Thanks. For everything." I should look away. But I can't.

"You're not so bad, Charlie Benson."

"Wow, from you that's quite a compliment." Those captivating eyes twinkle.

"Oh, that is looking marvelous. It's like a new kitchen already in here." Mrs. Dobbs bursts into the room, breaking the spell. Charlie and I both take a step apart.

She shakes her gray head. "Elmer will be tickled to death when he sees this. This looks so good it's bound to make my cookin' taste better." She laughs and the noise travels through the tiny house, like her joy won't be contained in this small space.

Mrs. Dobbs studies each one of us before her gaze settles on me. "Yes, indeed, Elmer and I huddled up in the living room. I couldn't get him to the bathroom to take cover, so I just said, 'All right, Lord, if the living room is as far as I can go, then I'm gonna trust you to take care of us.'" She stares through me like she's reliving the night. "And that mean old twister came and dipped into our house. There's not a sound like it. And I knew it was hitting us, but me and Elmer, we kept on a praying. And do you know what?"

Forgetting everyone else around us, I look at Mrs. Dobbs. "What?"

"Our giant oak tree in the backyard crashed into our house. The only room that wasn't hit was—"

"Your living room." Chills tingle up and down my paint-splattered arms.

"Do you think that was luck, child?"

I slowly shake my head. "No." And tears pool in my eyes. Why on earth is this making me weepy?

"No, it wasn't luck. It was the Lord. We got a big God. Sure enough. He's so big he can take care of the both of us."

"You and Mr. Dobbs?"

"Him too." Her wrinkled eye lid drops in a wink. "But I meant you." Her shoes click on the linoleum as she walks away whistling a happy tune.

Chapter 34

IXING A BOWL of Frosted Flakes is about the extent of my meal preparation abilities. And right now I'm listening to the youth pastor's wife explain how we're going to cook for over one hundred people. No problemo.

"So you just add water and butter and stir. And in a few minutes, you have mashed potatoes. Got it, Katie? . . . Katie?"

"Huh? Oh, yeah. Stir, pour in water, and put in some . . . um, more water."

Frances pushes up her tiny glasses and squints. "Weren't you listening?"

"Sure I was." I caught at least two or three words. My body hurts from stretching in ridiculous positions to paint the Dobbses' walls today. And then Sarah and Elmer won't get out of my head. And I wonder what my mom is doing right now. Is she thinking of me? Is she wishing things were different? Making plans so things will be better? Knowing her, she's probably propped on the couch, a beer in one hand and a cigarette in the other, screaming at Pat Sajak for a vowel.

"You okay?" Laura pulls me to the side, away from the food prep.

I nod and look down, totally uncomfortable. "Yeah. Seriously, I'm fine."

"Sarah Dobbs is a pretty cool lady, isn't she?"

"Uh-huh." If I had just listened to the potato making instructions,

I wouldn't be having this conversation right now. Was I supposed to add milk?

"That woman is amazing." Laura shakes her head and her blonde ponytail sweeps across her shoulders. "It's like she can see right through you, you know?"

"I dunno." But I felt it too.

"It's like God whispers in her ear exactly what to say to someone." Laura shrugs. "Oh, well, maybe it's just me."

An hour later I have whipped up my last batch of instant mashed potatoes. Like my arms weren't already about to fall off. Maybe all this arm work will boost my bust line. "Hey, Katie, how'd you get those new and improved boobs?" "I made mashed potatoes."

"Have you guys seen Chelsea?" Charlie wipes his hands on a towel then drapes it over his shoulder.

"Yeah, she's over there icing our sheet cakes." Frances points to a far-off corner in the activity center.

He mutters something under his breath and heads in her direction.

"She's been icing the same cake for forty-five minutes." Frances chops into an onion and blinks at the powerful smell.

"Well, it's hard to talk on the phone, text, file your nails, *and* spoon out icing."

"Frances, the salad is ready for the onions."

Frances shoves her bowl of onions at Pastor Mike. "Good riddance." She wipes at her tearing eyes.

A half hour later the first of the dinner guests arrive. Mr. and Mrs. Dobbs, holding hands like high school sweethearts, lead the line.

"Hello, children. My, it smells wonderful in here. Doesn't it, Elmer?"

"It sure does. Not as good as anything from your kitchen, but I do believe it smells good enough to eat." Mr. Dobbs grabs a plate and hands it to his wife.

Frances gives everyone a piece of fried chicken, placing it on their plates like it's a masterpiece. When they have all their side items, they come to my station for their dessert.

"This is the most important part of the meal, I say." Mrs. Dobbs grins. "I might even eat my dessert first."

Chelsea butts in behind me. "I made it."

"You did, did you?" Mr. Dobbs nods in appreciation.

"Yes, she put the canned icing on this cake all by herself." Oops, did I say that out loud?

"Well, we've all got our role here. And I think the cake looks beautiful."

Feeling Mrs. Dobbs not so subtle chastisement, I cut extra big pieces for the couple. They thank me and move on.

I slice another piece and ease it onto the next plate held out.

"Thanks, Katie."

Before I even raise my head, I know this voice. "Hi, Jeremy." My cheeks flush, and my brain overloads with the awkwardness. "I like your nose."

He touches his face. "What?"

"Er, I mean the one you brought to rehearsal last week. I liked it. It was your best one yet." In some part of my brain it registers I'm friends with someone who collects noses.

"Oh, thanks." Cheeks pink, he looks down when a little boy with orange hair like his scoots beside him, plate wobbling.

"Help your brother." Jeremy's mom balances a baby girl on her hip and her own plate of food.

"Mom, this is Katie. She's my ugly stepsister." Jeremy's eyes light up as he laughs. A sharp contrast to his mother's expression. She wears a look of weary that is so set in, like it's tattooed on and never coming off.

"Nice to meet you." She glances at me for a second then walks away, pushing her middle son ahead of her.

"Well, I'll see you later. Thanks . . . um, for the . . ."

"I'm glad you're here, Jeremy. And if you want extra dessert, I've got connections." We exchange smiles, and he joins his family at a table.

"I didn't know Jeremy was poor." Chelsea appears at my side and inspects her handiwork again. Her voice oozes revulsion.

"You don't have to say it like that. I happen to be poor."

She laughs and rolls her eyes. "No, you're not. I've met your foster parents."

"Yeah, *foster* parents. Wanna know where I came from before the Scotts took me in?"

"Not especially."

"A trailer park. And I don't mean the nicely decorated modular home variety. Ours was orange and white. With green shag carpet. And if your next question is did we have tires on our roof, the answer is yes." Though honestly I never knew why. "And before that? We lived in our car for a few weeks. And before that—"

"Chill out." Chelsea's glossy lip rises in disgust. "*What* is your deal?"

I set the cake server down with more force than necessary. "My deal is you. We're doing mission work here, not let's count how many people we can look down our noses at."

"I'm not looking down my nose at anyone."

Oh, that's right, because if you did that, you'd have to actually stop and really look at people. I take a deep breath, remember I am supposed to be nice to Chelsea. I so deserve a medal. "I just think you and I are here for two different reasons."

"Really? And what exactly *is* your reason for being here, Katie?"

"To help some people, and to—" My mouth snaps shut.

"To what?"

I don't know. Or at least, I'm not sure. But I think Pastor Mike was right. I'm starting to feel like I'm supposed to be here too. "Never mind." My eyes skim the crowd, and I see Charlie playing with Jeremy's brother, but watching Chelsea and me. "I'm sorry, Chelsea. I hope you have a good week here." Ouch. That little piece of niceness hurt.

Much later the lights dim when Pastor Mike climbs the stage and opens his Bible. He reads from the book of Hebrews, listing people in the Bible and things they've gone through.

"Look at all you've overcome. Each one of you here. God wants the opportunity to be your ultimate rescue."

I doodle on a piece of paper stuck in my Bible as he wraps it up and begins the invitation. The God Wads set up behind him and begin to play at a low volume.

A guy standing behind the pastor softly sings. Nash picks at his acoustical guitar and harmonizes with the lead singer. Words are thrown up on a screen. My eyes scan over the lines, and I find myself humming along.

Then quietly, hesitantly . . . singing.

For the first time since coming to In Between Community church, I do more than stare at the words. More than wordlessly move my lips. I am singing.

The words about amazing grace wash over me like the shower that took away all the yellow paint. And I get it—this grace stuff. I glance at Jeremy and at the Dobbs, and I see myself. If not for some serious grace, I could be right where they are. And in some ways, I actually am. Like them, I'm depending on people for help. Before I came to the Scotts, I had nothing. No home, no real family of my own, few people to care about me, and life was bigger than any homework assignment a teacher would throw at me. And like these people here, things are still totally up in the air. I don't know when or if my mom is gonna show up. And I don't know with one hundred percent certainty Millie is gonna be all right. And I still go to bed each night in fear Rocky will crawl into bed with me and drown me in drool. But the Scotts have given me grace. And so much more.

The words to the song ring in my ears. I'm not lost anymore. I am found. Millie and James Scott picked me up and asked me to trust them. And they haven't let me down yet.

Is that what you're asking me to do? Give you blind trust?

That's so not my thing though. Until Mrs. Smartly and until the Scotts, no one on this planet had come through for me. No one. And now I'm just supposed to free-fall into faith like God's gonna be there to catch me.

But can I? The Scotts are there—I can see them, touch them. Bum money from them. But God? How can He be that real to me?

I really want to believe you're there.

A few rows over Mrs. Dobbs raises up her hands and sways to the music. Her eyes closed, her head tilted back, she sings her heart out to the Lord. God is that real to her. Is it really just that easy?

Through many dan gers, toils and snares . . .
we have already come.
'Twas grace that brought us safe thus far . . .
And grace will lead us home

It's not like it could hurt. I mean, I'm Katie Parker. Disaster sits in my back pocket and follows me everywhere. I could use the insurance. It seems to have worked for the Dobbs. That woman sat in her living room and prayed, fully expecting God to take care of her and her husband. And he did.

I need you to take care of me. And Millie.

Pastor Mike continues talking as the band sings the first verse again.

A movement to my left catches my eye. Jeremy, my friend and cast-mate, places himself in front of our youth minister. Pastor Mike puts his arm around Jeremy and pulls him close, speaking in his ear over the strains of music. I see Jeremy nod a few times and brush at his eyes with the back of his hand. Minutes pass before Pastor Mike signals for the band to close.

"Guys, tonight I want to introduce you to Jeremy. His family was hit by the storm, and they lost nearly everything they had. Jeremy's been trying to make sense of it all ever since. Tonight it's not about logic, it's about what God's put in your heart. Following his lead. Jeremy, are you ready to let God take that lead?"

Jeremy nods, his eyes fixed on the pastor. "Yeah."

"It's that easy, guys. It's trusting that God is big enough to carry all you've got to throw on him. It's believing Jesus died on a cross for you. Nobody understands pain more than him."

My heart speeds up watching Jeremy stand there with my pastor. Do I have it in me to do that—just accept it all and surrender? Can I do this? Should I do this?

"Preacher, I'd like to testify, if I could."

I frown in confusion as Mrs. Dobbs stands up. Testify? Like what you do before Judge Judy yells at you?

"Go ahead, Miss Sarah."

"Just as sure as I know the Lord was in my living room that night, I know He's here." As Mrs. Dobbs casts her eyes over every single person, the band resumes their quiet chorus without the words.

"The living room was as far as we could go. And that's where He met us." Mrs. Dobbs pauses and watches us all. A pressure builds in my chest as I feel the weight of her stare on me. "No matter where you are when you cry out to him—that's where you'll find him."

"Amen," Elmer shouts from his chair.

"And if a tornado tore apart our home for no other reason than to see someone come to the Lord, then I say . . . you bring on another twister."

I once was lost, but now I'm found.
Was blind, but now I see.

With tears streaming down my face, I grab Frances's hand. "I think I'm supposed to go up there."

She leans in close. "What?"

"I think Mrs. Dobbs is talking about *me*." I can hardly hear myself over the blood rushing to my head. The pressure to do what I need to do battles with the dread over laying myself open in front of all these people.

OK, God, you can have me. I don't know what's coming for me, but I want to be in a safe place when it does.

"Katie, what are you trying to tell me?"

I rub my hand over my nose. "I get it, Frances." I meet her dark eyes and nod. "I get it."

My best friend—the only one I've ever had—squeezes my hand, her own eyes pooling. "Are you ready to do this?"

My throat stings with tears, and all I can do is nod. Nod and sniff. I close my eyes, battling the voice that tells me to stay seated, and I stand to my feet.

Frances grabs my arm and tugs. "No, Katie."

I stop.

"Your days of doing things alone are over." She puts her thin arm around me much like Millie has a hundred times before. And we step across legs and purses until we reach the end of the row and walk the aisle towards an awaiting Pastor Mike.

"Hold up."

Ten feet away from the front, Charlie Benson stands at the end of his row and waits.

For me. He steps to my other side, places his hand at my back and grins.

And together, the three of us take the longest walk of my life. Stepping in time to the words of grace, I walk toward music, toward Pastor Mike.

And you know who was waiting there for me?

God.

Chapter 35

"**S**URPRISE!"

"Congratulations!"

"Finally, you're saved! I bet Myrtle May Higgins, and she owes me five bucks."

I walk into the house on Friday night to streamers, confetti, party horns, and a sign hanging over the entryway that says *Katie+God 4EVS*.

Maxine lays a hand on her chest. "I made the sign."

I laugh and give her a big hug. "Never would've guessed."

"We're so proud of you." Millie's blue eyes glisten. "We've been praying for this since day one."

"Oh, I remember that first day." James sets my bag down and shuts the door. "You told us you had a boyfriend named Snake, and your favorite class was shop because you liked to play with sharp objects."

We all laugh. That seems like a hundred years ago when Mrs. Smartly dropped me off. I'm so far from that girl who stood in the Scott's driveway, totally alone, utterly scared.

"Guess what I've got for dinner?" Millie claps her hands like a cheerleader. "Pizza!"

"Oh, wow, Millie, it's only been five days since we had your tofu pizza. I want to savor the memory a little longer." Plus I need to call the Food Network and report my foster mother's crime against the basic food groups.

"No, I'm talking pepperoni, gooey mozzarella cheese, crispy crust—"

I smash Millie in a fierce hug. "Who are you and what have you done with my foster mom?"

With three slices of artery-clogging heaven sitting on my plate, I sit at the table surrounded by my family—James, Millie, Maxine. Oh, and that stupid dog, of course. In between bites, I toss out all the random questions about God swimming in my head. Though the pieces are starting to fit, there's still so much I don't know. And James says that's just fine.

"So you wouldn't tell me over the phone about your conversation with the principal. How did that go?" I grab the packet of fake Parmesan cheese and sprinkle until my pizza is totally blanketed in unnatural goodness. Millie frowns her disapproval, but doesn't say a word.

James pushes up his glasses. "Saw your principal Saturday afternoon. Invited him to a round of golf, then pulled out my phone and sprung the video on him." He nods and grins. "Best game of golf I ever played. Mr. Wayman couldn't seem to keep his mind on the game. Not only will he and Mrs. Whipple be apologizing to you in person, but they will also make a public apology to you Monday."

"Cool." Though it pains me, I set my third piece of pizza down, half eaten. Perhaps I should wrap it up and keep it so I can remember what the real stuff looks like. "Thanks for doing that, James. I really appreciate it."

"Kid, I'd go to bat for you any day."

I raise my lips in a smile, but my conscience tugs it right back down. I have yet to tell them about going to Trevor's party. About deceiving them. And about the alcohol. I get that all my sins are forgiven, but it doesn't seem right to hold on to this one.

After dinner I heave my tired, overworked body upstairs. I cannot wait to kick off my shoes, flop on my bed and—

"Maaaaxiiiiine!" I stand in horror at the sight before me. Leopard print. Everywhere I look. My white rug—gone. Lying under my feet a fake bear rug—complete with fake bear head. A giant tiger poster hangs over my bed. An enormous stuffed lion sits in the place where my cushy bean bag chair once was.

"What are you yelling . . . Oh."

I swivel and face my roommate. "'Oh? *Oh* is *all* you have to say for yourself?"

"Well, I was going to ask you how you like our matching cheetah comforters, but you didn't give me a chance."

I march over to my bed and rip off the insult to bedding. "Where is my hot pink quilt? My retro pillows? My bean bag? My white rug?"

She backs up a few steps. "Now, Sweet Pea, calm down."

"Don't tell me to calm down. My room is . . . is a jungle!"

Maxine sniffs. "I would think anyone would find this beautiful."

"Yeah, if you're a chimpanzee."

"Now, just a minute—"

"I leave for five days and you do all this?" I pace the room, finding new wildlife in every nook.

Maxine plants herself in my path and halts me with her hand. "Let me push rewind for you, little girl. I distinctly remember us having a little deal. Am I correct?"

Still furious, I nod.

"And in exchange for my silence on your certain misdeed, you agreed to a list of items in return. Still with me here?"

My nostrils flare with my every breath.

"And you said I could add a few personal belongings to this room."

"I never said—"

"Ah-ah-ah." She holds up a finger. "Don't interrupt me, my little apple dumpling. Per our agreement, basically anything I say goes." She walks to the door and pulls it open. "By the way, I have a friend coming next week to paint a mural on the walls. I came up with the design myself. I call it 'Maxine Runs With the Tigers.'"

I catch up with my foster grandmother on the fifth step down, nudge her out of my way, and skid to a halt in the kitchen.

Millie looks up from her place at the sink. "Is something wrong?" She hands James a dish to dry.

Here goes nothing. "I need to tell you something."

Maxine appears behind me and pokes me in the back. "You really should think this through," she hisses.

I shake my head. "No, I really need to talk to you guys."

"Silly child is obviously exhausted from her mission work." Maxine puts her hands on my shoulders and pushes. "I'll get her to bed."

I dig in my feet. "Two weeks ago I—"

"Fell and bumped her head." Maxine clucks her tongue. "Poor dear."

I shoot her a look hot enough to sizzle bacon. "You two were at the hospital. It was your last night. And I went—"

"And played hide-and-seek with the chickens."

"No! Would you be quiet?" I step back, my foot landing not so accidentally on Maxine's toe. "I was mad. At you, at your daughter, at myself because—"

"The darn chickens found her every time and—"

"I went to a party! There was alcohol! It was at Trevor's, and his parents weren't home." My voice rattles the cabinets.

Millie hands James another glass. He swabs it out with a tea towel, inspects it, then passes it back. "You missed a spot."

She smiles and nods. "Thank you, dear. I believe you're right." Millie returns the glass to the sudsy water.

I move in closer. "Did you hear what I said?"

"Here you go. All clean now." Millie reaches for a salad bowl. "Yes, I heard you. Did you hear her, James?"

My foster dad picks up a fork and rinses. "I think all of Dallas, Houston, and San Antonio heard what she said."

They clearly are not comprehending. "I went to a party. I took a drink of beer. And Maxine caught me and hauled me back home."

Millie rests her rag on the counter. "We know."

"I know you know. I just told you."

"Nah," James says. "We've actually known a little bit before to-night."

From my peripheral vision I see Maxine slowly backing out of the kitchen. "If you value the Justin Timberlake scrapbook collection you keep under your bed, you will stop right there."

Maxine freezes. She turns back around, her face glowing with innocence.

I return my attention to Scotts. "Exactly how long have you known?"

"Would you say ten minutes after Mom brought her home or closer to fifteen?"

James purses his lips and stares at the ceiling, his brow wrinkled in concentration. "I . . . believe I would say ten minutes. Yes, I'm gonna have to go with ten."

I pounce on Maxine. "You," I growl. "You have totally taken advantage of me. I washed your unmentionables. I brought you breakfast in bed. I picked all the seeds out of your oranges. I fluffed your pillow every single night." My hands clench and unclench at my sides. "For *you* I fluffed!"

"Now, Katie, dear. There's no need to get upset." She pats my head. "Grandma loves you!"

James barks with laughter. "Katie, you brought all this on your-self."

"I have to admit, it's been a fun two weeks waiting for you to come clean. Especially that day I saw you ironing mom's pantyhose."

James snaps his fingers. "Or the time she had to stand outside the bathroom and read Shakespearean sonnets to Maxine while she soaked in bubbles."

Soon everyone dissolves into chuckles.

Everyone but me.

"I'm glad you guys think this is so funny. So glad I could entertain you."

Millie swipes at her mascara and levels her gaze on me. "You could've ended it any time."

I glare at Maxine. "Believe me, lesson learned." I pull out a seat at the bar and rest my cheek on my fist. "How long were you gonna let this go on?"

James pats me on the back. "We knew we wouldn't have to wait long."

"What made you think I would tell on myself?"

He sits down next to me. "Because it was the right thing to do."

"And we trusted you to make the responsible decision," Millie says.

"You're saying you trusted me?"

James nods. "Yes."

"And you trusted me to be honest?"

"Yes."

"And you knew I would tell you the truth, despite how hard it would be?"

"Yes."

"And since I clearly have passed this moral test, you have decided not to ground me?"

James hops off his stool. "Not on your life."

My hands fumble with the wet tea towel James used to dry the dishes. "I'm really sorry I let you down. It was a miserable night."

Millie pushes a strand of hair behind my ear. "Despite the fun we've had at your expense, Katie, you know the reality of what you did isn't humorous at all. We have rules, and they are to be followed. We expect more from you."

"Yes, ma'am."

"Through you've suffered enough at the hands of Mom, you are grounded. And James and I have decided that includes the spring dance."

I open my mouth to protest. It takes all my inner strength to shut it once again and bite my tongue. No spring dance. No Trevor picking me up in his Hummer. No flowers at the door. (What? A girl can dream.) No discovering "our song" as we swayed on the dance floor, gazing into one another's eyes. No opportunity for Trevor to say, "Katie, I'm just a shell of a guy. Make me complete and wear my class ring." Not that the Scotts would let me within ten miles of him anyway.

Hours later I roll over in bed for what must be the millionth time. I plump my pillow and jam it back under my head.

God, where is my hope in this? I want to be positive and accept my punishment with some maturity. Give me some encouragement. Something to hold on to.

I sigh and stare at the ceiling.

"Would you *please* go to sleep?" A drowsy voice calls from the other side of the room. "If I have bags under my eyes tomorrow morning, grounding will be the least of your punishment."

And then it hits me.

I toss my covers off my legs and bound out of bed.

"What do you think you're doing?"

I feel my way across the room, find the door, and scoot my hand over a little more to the left.

And flick on the light.

"Augh!" Maxine jerks the covers over her head. "Are you crazy?"

I put a foot on her bed and hoist myself up. "No, actually I'm brilliant." I balance myself on her mattress and rip her velvet picture down with a fierce jerk.

She gasps and bolts to a sitting position. "How *dare* you!"

"Grandma," I drawl. "Jesus won't be sipping mochas in *my* room *any*more."

Chapter 36

"IF YOU'RE INTERESTED in trying out for cheerleading for the next school year, please attend the meeting today at lunch in the gym lobby."

I twirl my pencil between my fingers in English class as the school secretary reads the announcements.

"Since the bubbles have been removed from the pool, the swim team tryouts have been rescheduled for Thursday after school."

I hope it didn't shrink anyone's Speedo.

"The Powder Puff football game will be held April third. Girls will play football and boys will cheer. Please sign up if interested. Team captains, please make sure your cheerleaders wear underwear this year. That is all. Conduct yourselves as befitting the Chihuahua!"

Ms. Dillon stands up. "Turn in your books to page—"

The speaker overhead crackles and whines. "You go first. You're the principal!"

Everyone in the classroom stops and looks up, like someone's going to crawl out of the overhead speaker.

"It's Mrs. Whipple," someone behind me says.

Next we hear a deep, exaggerated clearing of the throat. Ew.

"Students, this is Mr. Wayman. Er . . . your principal."

The class bursts into laughter.

"I would just like to say . . . That is, I would like to take this moment to . . . Well, on behalf of Mrs. Whipple and myself, I would like to humbly . . . er, deeply, truly, um . . . seriously apologize to Katie Parker. And . . . now here's Mrs. Whipple to explain why."

Everyone swivels in their seat to watch me. Angry whispers filter though the speaker then the sound of the phone exchanging hands.

"Oh, all right. *Ahem*, yes, students, I, too, would like to apologize to Miss Parker. There seems to have been an unfortunate misunderstanding. Really, anyone could have made this teeny, tiny mistake. And it may come as a surprise to you, but Mr. Wayman and I are not perfect."

The class erupts in more laughter.

"We make mistakes too. And we are sorry for wrongfully accusing Katie of theft at In Between High. She has been completely cleared of any charges and accusations. I believe that is all, so . . . What?" The overhead speaker crackles with static. "No, Mrs. Beasley, I don't think that is . . . oh, very well. To make amends for our grievous error, Mr. Wayman and I will be buying Miss Parker ice cream in the cafeteria for the rest of the month."

Mr. Wayman's voice booms out of the speaker again. "We need to see Angel Nelson in the office immediately." Click.

The class erupts in excited chatter, and I field the hundred or so questions thrown my way.

Angel stomps down the row and knocks my book onto the floor.

I reach for the literature book, but Ms. Dillon's voice stops me. "Miss Nelson, you are going to pick that book up right now. Then you're going to apologize to Katie. And then you're going to march yourself to the office."

Angel turns to face me, her face red, her pupils dilating. I can tell she's weighing her options. *Please don't pick the one that says, "Hey, I have nothing to lose at this point, I think I'll ram this book down Katie's throat and pull it out through a nostril of my choice."*

Angel schools her features, bends down and pick up the book. She tosses it on my desk, her eyes shooting lethal daggers.

"And you will apologize," Ms. Dillon repeats.

Angel squares her shoulders and turns her body so she is totally facing me. "I'm sorry." Her voice carries to the back row. A leering smile grows on her face, and she drops her voice a decibel. "This is *not* over."

At lunch I sit among the churchies and other friends. I feel like I got promoted or something. I belonged before, but now more than ever I feel a part of my church friends. And soon, even *I* will know where Leviticus is.

"Thanks for the ice cream, Katie!" Hannah toasts me with her push-up.

"Yeah, this is awesome. The whole month." Frances licks her fudge pop before it drips.

Nash approaches our group and holds out a hand for his. "How did you get all these?"

"I picked out fourteen from the ice cream freezer and charged them to Mr. Wayman. He said he'd buy dessert. He didn't say I could only have one a day."

"Did you find out anything more about Angel?" Frances asks, her eyes looking everywhere but at Nash.

"Yeah, actually Mrs. Beaseley told me Angel had made copies of her mom's locker room keys, including the one to the back door. She'd pass it on to one of her friends, and while Angel was in PE, her friend would sneak in the back way and take stuff."

"Then Angel would go in later and plant it. Dude, that's crazy." Nash sits in the only seat available—the one next to Frances. "Hey, Frances, you like fudge bars too?"

Frances grabs a napkin, blots her face, and picks up her tray. "I gotta go. Talk to you guys later."

I try to catch her eye and read her face, but she looks down and charges through the lunch crowd.

Nash frowns. "What did I say?"

My eyes meet Charlie's across the table.

"Did something happen on the mission campout?" Charlie asks.

Nash shakes his head. "Absolutely nothing happened. Every time I tried to talk to Frances last week, she did just what she did right now—clam up and leave." He peels his ice cream wrapper off and takes a sad bite. "Maybe she heard I was gonna ask her to the spring dance and doesn't have the nerve to tell me no."

Our table freezes and my Oreo bar lodges midway down my throat. "What? What did you say?" My eyes jerk to Charlie, but he shrugs, totally clueless.

"Yeah, I know I'm not her type. She's made it very clear lately I'm not the sort she wants to hang out with." Nash's head droops. "But ever since I pulled her out of her cousin's birthday cake . . . I can't get her out of my head."

"Her cousin Esther?"

I send my elbow into Charlie's ribs. "Frances, you dork! He likes Frances. All this time he's *liked* Frances!" I jab my finger into his chest. "Why didn't you know this? Are you telling me this entire time you didn't just ask Nash how he felt about Frances? You never once tried to initiate some guy talk about her?"

Charlie removes my hand. "I didn't know what to do! Do you think I match-make on a regular basis?"

"No, but I would think Mr. Four-Point-Oh could figure it out. One of the basic rules to setting people up is to find out how the other person feels. We *knew* how Frances felt. But did—"

"Wait." Nash holds up his dessert. "What do you mean you knew how Frances felt?" He looks around then locks his eyes on mine. "Has she ever mentioned me?"

Charlie's cheeks explode as he leans back and laughs.

"What are *you* laughing about? This is not a funny situation. Frances has totally given up. Didn't you see her just now?" I clutch Nash's jacket sleeve and jerk. "If you like her, you have to tell her. Now."

His eyes round and he shakes his head. "No. I can't tell her. She can't even bring herself to talk to me. Are you saying she liked me at one time?"

I nod. "Yes. But it's not too late, Nash." If this were a Disney movie, I'd totally break out in song. "You've got to talk to her."

He grabs his food and slings his backpack over his shoulder. "Nah. It's too late. She made that clear over Spring Break. She obviously doesn't want anything to do with me. She's a shiny, polished flute. I'm a banged-up, out of tune, used Gibson guitar." Nash walks off. The opposite way of Frances.

I smack Charlie on the shoulder. "Good job, Einstein."

"What? How could I possibly know?"

Boys are so stupid. I mean seriously, Charlie's good friend likes my best friend, and he didn't even know it. Why did I ask for help from a guy whose first pick for a girlfriend is Snobby Barbie?

"Where is Chelsea anyway?"

Charlie checks his watch. "She's rehearsing."

"I didn't have a rehearsal—"

"She said it's not for the entire cast."

My eyes narrow. "Just for her and Trevor." Speaking of Trevor, I have to figure out a way to tell him I can't go to the dance with him. I've avoided him all day. Well, I was *going* to avoid him when I saw him, but actually I haven't run into him a single time.

"So when you were talking about English class earlier, you mentioned Angel saying to you that it wasn't over."

I ignore Charlie, still fixating on this secret rehearsal. How many rehearsals does it take to do a little waltzing, a little shoe fitting, and one big kiss?

"Katie, what do you think Angel meant by that?"

I snap my attention back to Charlie. "I don't know. You're the brainiac here. You figure it out. It's not like I have anything left to lose. What's she gonna do, steal my fake rubber nose before the play? TP my house?"

Charlie slaps the table. "The science fair."

"What?"

"We set up for the science fair in the gym, right? She could easily get in and sabotage our project."

"Angel got expelled today. She can't be on campus."

Charlie rolls his eyes. "Yeah, like that's gonna stop her." He grabs my hand. "We've got to stop her."

"Nothing's gonna happen. Why are you so paranoid?"

"Just humor me."

I am. I'm letting you hold my hand. Which, by the way, do I tell him he's still got my hand? Do I remove it? What exactly are the rules for non-boyfriend hand-holding? What's the protocol for hand-holding in a moment of scientific passion?

"I think we should hide out in the gym and watch for her."

"Charlie, that's crazy. Besides, I have play rehearsals."

He looks down at our hands. And drops mine like a football with a penalty flag. "It's not crazy. Katie, we have worked for weeks on this project. Can you honestly sit there and tell me you are one hundred percent sure there is no way Angel would try something like destroying our project?"

"No, I can't say with one hundred percent certainty, but—"

"Then it's settled." Charlie jumps up from his seat and stacks his trash. "I'll take the after school watch. Then you come over after play practice."

"No. Look, I'm grounded as it is. I can't get in anymore trouble."

"Our ferns need you." A hint of a smile plays at his lips.

"I can't. If I *could* break into the school and hide out in the dark gym with you, risking expulsion just to stare at science fair projects no one is gonna touch, I would. But I can't."

"I CANNOT *BELIEVE* I let you talk me into this. By the way, Mrs. Hall says we can only stay as long as she's in the building. Something about getting fired would make it hard to pay for the PI she's hired to tail her husband."

I sit under a table, my body scrunched into a ball next to Charlie.

A sheet covers our hideout just a few tables down from our science fair project, but still allows for us to make out any human forms coming to torch our data or kidnap our plants.

"I knew you'd cave." I hear the smile in his voice and find myself smiling back in the dark. "Nice of Mrs. Hall to bring you over after practice."

"It's *rehearsal.* Practice involves Gatorade and jock straps. What we do is art."

"You sound like Chelsea."

I gasp and ram my elbow into his ribs. "I do *not!*" Okay, cozy moment over. I now feel the need to hurl.

"Just kidding."

"What do you see in her anyway?" Wow, turn off the lights, throw a sheet over my head, and I'll say anything.

His shoulders, pressed warmly to mine, lift in a shrug. "I don't know."

"That's romantic. So you saw her across a crowded room and thought, I have absolutely no opinion about that girl. I think I'll ask her out."

"No, I mean . . . I don't really know anymore." Under the table our eyes meet. "It's not the same. I'm not the same."

So many comments pounding at my head for release, all of them involving Chelsea insults, but I shut them out.

"What about you and Trevor?"

I force a laugh. "What about us? There really *is* no us. He asked me to the dance—well, sorta. And now I can't go because I'm grounded. I kept trying to tell him tonight at rehearsal, but I couldn't. I want to go to that dance so bad." I rest my head on my bent knees. "You should see my dress. It's the prettiest thing I've ever owned in my entire life."

The gym makes creaking noises as it settles in the silence. "I know you'd look great in the dress. There will be another dance."

"Maybe not for me. Not here. Who knows where I'll be next

month. Next year."

"That dress would've been wasted on Jackson anyway. The guy's a jerk. You're too good for him."

This doesn't fire me up like it once did. In some part of my brain, am I starting to buy this? There are tons of red flags where Trevor's concerned. But doesn't every guy come with warning labels?

"You're not gonna get grounded for being here, are you?"

"Nah, the Scotts know we're with Mrs. Hall." They just don't know exactly what I'm doing.

Forty-five minutes later my body is screaming in protest. "I can't move my neck," I whisper.

"I know. I lost all feeling in my legs."

I really regret not bringing snacks. "Charlie, do you give up yet? She's not gonna show. I think even Angel has her limits."

"Just give it time. I have a feeling."

"That's just your butt falling asleep." I roll my shoulders and try to readjust in the small space. "Angel would have to sneak out of her house to get here. I'm sure her mom is watching her like a—"

Creeeeaaaak!

Charlie and I freeze like statues as a door slowly opens somewhere toward the front of the gym.

No way. Angel wouldn't be that stupid.

I put my mouth next to Charlie's ear. "It's probably Mrs. Hall ready to go."

He lays a finger over my lips and shakes his head.

The wooden floor groans with each step as someone crosses the gym and gets closer and closer. Charlie removes his finger from my mouth, but I continue to hold my breath. My heart hammers in my chest, and I close my eyes. Why am I here? Why did I agree to this? What if it's not Mrs. Hall? Even worse what if it's not Mrs. Hall and it's not Angel, and this someone sees the outline of two idiots sitting under a gigantic model of the solar system, and we get hauled to jail for stalking science fair projects?

Charlie nudges me, and I lift my head and open my eyes. He nods and points.

Sure enough, my eyes focus, and I can make out the tell-tale spike of Angel's hair. My ears perk as I hear her unzip a bag and rummage through it. Maybe she's just impressed with our scientific findings and wants to take a picture.

I see the outline of two hands reach for our plant, lift it overhead and—

"Stop!"

Ready to spring, my body jerks to a halt at the cry of a fourth person.

I lift the sheet. "Mrs. Hall?"

The lights shutter on, and my drama teacher eases out from behind the bleachers and steps forward. "Set the fern down, Miss Nelson. Nice and slow." Mrs. Hall catches our shocked expressions as Charlie and I climb out from our post. "What? You didn't think I was going to let you hide out in here alone, did you? I have too much experience in spying and covert operations to leave you to fend for yourselves."

Angel looks from Mrs. Hall to me and Charlie. Then back to Mrs. Hall.

"I said *drop it*, Angel." The teacher pulls out her phone and punches in some numbers. "Mr. Wayman? I need you to meet me at the gym pronto. Yes, this is Mrs. Hall. What? No, I didn't get my scarf stuck in the door again." She shuts her phone and walks toward Angel.

I stretch and follow Charlie toward our table.

"You were right, Charlie." We stand in front of Angel, and I lock my eyes with hers. "I said she wouldn't sneak in and destroy our project, but you were right." I pin her with my cold stare. "And to think I gave you the benefit of the doubt."

She rolls her eyes in disgust.

"Would you let it go?" My voice echoes off the wood floors.

"Whatever it is you are so freakin' mad about, it's not about me. Don't you get that yet?" You'd think the girl had never seen a single episode of Dr. Phil. "*You* talked *me* into that theater last fall. I didn't ask you to deceive me into tagging along for your little joyride of destruction. And *I'm* the one who worked my tail off fixing all the damage you and your friends did. You just had to do a little community service. Why are you still so mad at *me*?"

Angel's reptile eyes narrow to slivers. "You were supposed to be one of us. I took you in. *I* was your friend when no one else would be."

"In the short amount of time I've known you, you've broken into a theater, nearly destroyed it, got me hauled to the police, you've stolen things and planted them in my locker, and now this." I wave my hand over the table. "And I should want to be friends with you because . . .?"

Her eyes tear up. "You don't even know me. Don't stand there and judge me."

"Ten seconds ago you were about to kill my plant *and* demolish our science grade. I'm way beyond the point of reserving judgment."

Angel turns her head and stares at the floor. Her fury radiates like the stink from the composting experiment three tables down.

"That's all you and your friends do—judge people like me. You're so high and mighty."

I move closer. "I'm just never gonna have a big enough rap sheet for you, am I? You're gonna spend your whole life waiting for the world to hug you back, but it's not going to. I've been there. *This* is not how you make things better."

"Oh, maybe I could go to church and then my life would be perfect," Angel sneers.

"If things are that bad for you, there are options," the drama teacher says. "Have you talked to the counselor?"

We all gape at Mrs. Hall.

"Right. Well, maybe you could talk to our junior high counselor."

Angel takes a few steps back. "Save your advice. I don't need it. I don't need any of you."

"You walk out that door, young lady and—"

Angel ignores Mrs. Hall's commands to stop and bolts out of the gym and out the doors. The three of us chase after her, sprinting into the parking lot, but it's too late.

Her car peels out, her tires screeching, and she races away in a plume of smoke.

Charlie digs in his jacket for his keys, but Mrs. Hall's hand on his forearm stops him.

"No, don't go after her. We've done our job." She retrieves her phone again. "I know people who know people . . ." she nods and quirks a brow, ". . . who can find her."

Overcome with a crazy impulse, I throw my arms around my teacher. "Thank you." I pat her back and let her go. "Thank you for . . . everything."

"Anytime, Katie." Her face glows. "We drama queens have to stick together, right?" She glances at her watch. "Speaking of that, I have a few calls I have to make for the play, then I'm out of here. I have another stakeout, er, meeting with Mr. Hall across town. You kids head out; I'm gonna lock up and wait for Mr. Wayman."

Charlie and I shower her with praise and appreciation until she closes herself back into the gym. The sun sets in pink and lilac brush strokes in the In Between sky as my coconspirator opens his truck door.

"Can I give you a ride?"

"Nah, I'll just call James." I unzip my backpack and search for my phone with my hand. "Augh. Are you kidding me?" I mutter aloud. "I must've left my phone at the Valiant."

Charlie walks around and opens his passenger door. "Hop in. We'll call the Scotts on our way and tell them you'll be home soon. Can we get into the theater?"

I shut my door and enjoy the scent of Charlie all around me.

"Yeah, I know where the spare key's hidden."

Charlie drives us through down and straight to the Valiant. We jump out, and I grab the key under the fourth largest rock in the front landscaping and wiggle it in the lock.

"That's odd. It's unlocked. Oh, well. Sam's probably cleaning up."

We chat at mach speed, sailing through the lobby, laughing and talking over one another as we rehash the evening's events.

"This night just could *not* get any crazier." I giggle and yank the heavy theater door open. And stop.

Charlie crashes into the back of me.

We both stand, rooted to the spot.

Silent.

On stage, intertwined, are Chelsea and Trevor, making out like it's their last moment on earth.

"Well," I say. "*That's* definitely not in the script."

Chapter 37

"KATIE, WOULD YOU listen to me? Open this door."

Outside Trevor bangs on the women's dressing room door on opening night. Woman at Ball Number Four slinks toward it.

I throw out my arm and block her. "You touch that door, and I will not be responsible for my actions." She doesn't look too alarmed. "I used to be friends with Angel Nelson." She disappears.

The pounding continues.

"Oh, would you just open the door! I have a headache."

I glare at Chelsea Blake. *Sister,* you *are a headache.*

I shove past Chelsea and the Evil Stepmother, jerk the door open a crack, and stick my nose through. "What do you want?"

Trevor strikes a pathetic pose. "Can I come in?"

"Yeah, I bet you'd like that. You could pretend to talk to me while you ogled a room full of half naked girls."

"We need to talk."

My teeth clench. "No, we don't. I think the kissy noises you and Chelsea were making Monday night said enough."

"Katie, look, I don't want this bad vibe between us to affect the play. There's a college recruiter out there from the—"

Slam!

More knocking. I fling open the door. "Leave!" I shout.

Frances blinks. I grab her hand and yank her inside.

"I wanted to tell you that I know you are going to be fabulous."

"Thanks, Frances."

"And I think you are going to wow the audience."

"Thanks, Frances."

"And Nash Griffin asked me out today."

Then we clutch each other and jump up and down, screaming like the girls that we are.

"Charlie drove up in my driveway, pushed Nash out of his truck, and then drove around the block for ten minutes. By the time he had made his twentieth lap, Nash had asked me to the dance." She squeals again then stops, her face falling. "Oh, I'm sorry."

"No, hey, it's totally cool. You go and have a great time tomorrow night. I'm so excited for you."

With some final words of encouragement, Frances skips away, drunk and delirious on love.

While I shut the door and try to calm my quaking nerves. I need to clear my head. Calm down and refocus. I grab my costume and lock myself in the bathroom.

And sit on the floor. Just like I did when I became Juliet in this theater last fall.

God, what a ride it's been, huh? Tonight, I just want to be the best I can be. Help me to forget everything else. Help me to block out the image of Chelsea and Trevor lip-locked, even though it's seared into my brain. Give me the strength to be totally in character, though I will be dying to scan the crowd and check for my mom. And help me to be the greatest ugly stepsister ever. Amen.

I step into my hoop skirt then pull on my blue brocade gown. I have to admit, blue is one of my colors. I turn in a circle and smile at myself in the mirror.

Knock! Knock!

"Open up, Sweet Pea. I got something you need."

I open the door to Maxine, wearing a lavender ball gown that goes from toe to neck.

"Nice turtleneck." I move aside so she can come in.

"Shut your yapper. This was not my idea."

"No, really?"

"Mrs. Hall seemed to think all my ideas showed too much cleavage." She huffs. "I'm not sure what she has against me displaying a little bit of the good Lord's bounty."

"I think you look nice." In a nun sort of way.

"Well, thanks, toots. Now, Jeremy said I was to help you with this." She holds up a giant nose. "Bend down."

"No way. I'm not wearing that thing. I can't breathe with it on."

"You should try this corset." Her blue eyes cross. "Anyway, I've got all the supplies here, so squat down and get your new beezer."

Minutes later as Maxine helps me with my hair, Chelsea sweeps in, looking elegantly beautiful and regal. Even though she's in a ragged old brown dress.

She stifles a giggle when she spots me. I ignore her.

"You look lovely, dear." Maxine cuts her cat eyes at Chelsea. "Quite fetching for a girl who cooks and cleans chamber pots all day."

Chelsea flips her hair. "Just because Cinderella works hard doesn't mean she has to be homely. I want her to shine with dignity."

"You'll definitely be shining with all that glitter spray in your hair." My voice comes out in muffled honks through the filter of my rubber nose.

Chelsea blasts a scathing look in my direction. At least I think it's in my direction. This stupid nose is obstructing my view.

"You know, Katie, there's no need for you to be mad at me. It's not like I stole Trevor from you. Did you know he never intended to go to the dance with you?"

Ice water poured over my head could not have chilled me any faster. I want to brush her off and act like I don't care. But I can't. "What do you mean?"

"You assumed Trevor was going to go with you. I think his friends egged that on, if I have my story straight. But . . ." She shakes her long, blonde waves. "He wasn't taking you. He had been trying to find a way to break it to you."

Maxine chortles and takes a hair pin out of her mouth. "Oh, she got the message. What a classy moment *that* was." She continues to laugh to herself as she arranges my hair. "Cinderella, you better watch yourself. Just because he looks like a prince and kisses like a prince, don't mean he ain't a toad underneath it all."

Chelsea and her haughty stare disappear from the bathroom, and I take a deep breath. Maxine pats me on the back.

"Girl, you are gonna be great. You just put all of this out of your mind."

I nod slowly and pull my lips into a smile.

"Now, I've prayed for you. I hope you're praying for me." Maxine's brows knit together. "In the closing scene when all the cast gathers, I fly across the stage, but we've only practiced it twice with those wire contraptions." She shakes her yellow head. "I'll deny it if you repeat it, but I am too old to be flying through the air by a few pulleys and a harness between my crotch."

"Thanks for that visual."

From outside the door, Mrs. Hall calls.

"All right, Sweet Pea. Showtime!" She tweaks my prosthetic nose. "Show 'em what you're made of."

I grab her hand. "You too. Break a—"

"Uh-uh." Maxine shakes a finger. "Hon, don't ever tell someone my age to break a leg." She pats me on the tush and shoots on by.

I walk out of the dressing room and steer myself toward the left wing where Jeremy waits.

"Katie?"

I turn, keeping one eye on Chelsea, who's taking the stage for her opening scene alone.

"These are for you." Woman at Ball Number Six thrusts a

wrapped bouquet of roses into my hands.

I stare at Jeremy in confusion.

"Open the card," he whispers. "Hurry."

I sniff the flowers, a collection of varying shades of pink, then tear into the card.

You'll always be the brightest star to us.
We love you,
James and Millie

I pass the flowers back to Number Six and thank her.

"Don't tear up now. You'll ruin your mascara. And we're almost on." Jeremy grabs my arm and pulls me along. "Here we go, sis. After those flowers, do you think you have it in you to be mean and nasty?"

My eyes zone in on Chelsea, sweeping near the fireplace. "I think I can manage."

The play zooms by. I only flub up one line, but Jeremy recovers for me. My gaze draws to the crowd during the party scenes in which the cast is supposed to simply gaze at the lovely couple. Yet I can't see a thing past the first three rows for the glare of the lights. My mom could be out there. Watching me. Me and my crooked, pointy nose.

The next to final scene opens with the great reveal. Trevor slides the glass slipper onto Chelsea's foot, as Jeremy and I cling to each other, sobbing hysterically.

Chelsea rises from her chair, smiling into the eyes of her prince. Trevor takes her hand and kisses it. He then turns his attention to Cinderella's stepfamily.

"My father will return. And when he does, he will hand down a punishment for the cruelty my future princess endured."

The scarlet curtain falls, and we all scramble to our final spots.

Seconds later, the curtain rises on our frozen tableau. Jeremy and I stand huddled with our mother and watch in horror as Cinderella and the Prince recite their vows. The girl playing my mother cries loudly into a handkerchief. I contort my face into varying looks of disgust. No acting skills needed.

Trevor leans in to kiss his bride, and I look away.

And see Maxine flying out of the ceiling.

"Aughhhhhhhhh!"

She swings by.

Then comes back again.

"Auggghhhhhhhh!" Her body twists and turns as she sails past us, spread eagle. "Some . . . body . . . stop . . . this . . . thing . . ."

We dart out of her way as the wires lower her closer and closer to the stage. My eyes bulge when I realize she's gonna hit someone. I leap out of my spot.

"Trevor, move, she's—"

Pow!

"Gonna hit you."

Everyone in the house wears the same expression—jaw dropped, eyes wide—as Trevor goes catapulting backwards, clutching onto Maxine, who is still airborne.

Her voice echoes through the theater as they soar back again. "Let go of me, you player! I will not be one of your conquests!"

They swing through again, this time with Jeremy and the king chasing after them.

"Oh, no. No, no, don't drop me! Nooooo!"

I remain glued to my spot, transfixed in terror as Maxine grabs onto Trevor with all four limbs.

And crashes to the ground.

The crowd shoots to their feet.

The cast runs to center stage where Trevor lies heaped over the fairy godmother.

"You have two seconds to get off me or I'm sticking this wand—"

"I'm up!" Trevor scrambles to pull himself off and brushes dirt from his black pants.

The collective sigh of relief is so loud, the theater seems to tremor.

Trevor holds out a hand for Maxine. "Are you all right, Mrs. Simmons?"

Concerned, I move in closer. Maxine bats his hand away, rises up on her elbows then pushes herself up, her body shaking in fury.

The crowd goes wild. Their shouts and applause fill the room and bounce off the walls.

My foster grandmother turns around slowly at the concert of cheers. A slow smile graces her face, and then she waves to every corner of the room. The applause reaches a crescendo as the retired dancer from Las Vegas claims her stage once again and soaks up every bit of her moment of glory.

The curtain flutters down on the cast as we take our bows.

And *Cinderella* is over.

I follow a limping Maxine into the lobby as the cast gathers for the receiving line. Though I'm totally pumping with adrenaline from the calamity that the final scene almost was, my heart weighs heavily as I watch the door and scan every face as the audience files out.

Not my mom . . .

Not my mom . . .

Definitely not my mom . . .

James and Millie break through the crowd and pull me into a three-man hug. A Scott sandwich.

"Thanks for the flowers." I crane my neck and peek around them. "Is she here?"

James smiles. "She sure is."

My foster parents step apart, and there before me stands Mrs. Iola Smartly, director of the Sunny Haven Home for Girls.

She squeals with glee and pulls me close. "You were marvelous! Wonderful! And this—" she flicks my nose "—is a lovely addition."

"Thanks." I stand back and take in her familiar polyester, paisley-print dress and her fuzzy, salt-and-pepper bun sitting crooked on her head. "Where's my mom?"

Iola glances at the Scotts. "Sweetie . . . she's not here."

My heart plummets, and I blink back the tears. I guess I really did want her here. To see me on stage. Mostly I just wanted her to *want* to be here.

Mrs. Smartly places her giant hand on my shoulder and gives it a brisk rub. "I know you're disappointed."

I shrug and look down. "No. I shouldn't be surprised."

"She's just not ready yet."

Not ready to see her own daughter. The tears drop, and I watch them plop onto my shoes. "Yeah, I understand." I sniff and wipe my nose. "I gotta go back stage. Maybe you could stick around for the cast party?"

Iola nods and her giant glasses slip down her nose. "Oh, I'd love to. And Katie?"

"Yeah?"

"I'm so proud of you."

My throat closes and suffocates any response. I bob my head, leave the three of them with a watery smile, and dash off to the dressing room.

I toss off my gown, sigh with relief when I zip into my favorite jeans, and rip out the hairpins.

Bending over to tie my shoes, I notice my bouquet of roses by my bag. I pick them up and the card shimmies to the floor.

I snatch it up and read it again.

You'll always be the brightest star to us.
We love you,
James and Millie

I sit down and read it over and over, letting the words pour over me and sink in.

God, tonight didn't go how I wanted it to. And I don't mean Maxine flying out of the ceiling. That was actually a highlight.

I don't understand. Why wouldn't my mom want to see me? All I want is to be loved. What have I ever done that I don't deserve that?

My eyes are drawn to the card again. And the flowers.

And as I sit there looking at the perfect petals, the events of my life in In Between dance through my mind. Millie making me smiley-faced pancakes. James teaching me to drive—and not yelling at me when I crashed into a light pole. Maxine hauling me out of the party on the back of her bicycle built for two. Millie's excitement when she bought me all new clothes on my second day in town. A wink from James at the pulpit.

I dash away my last tear and stand up.

You know what?

I am loved.

I *am* loved.

Maybe not how I wanted, not how I expected, but it's more than I've ever had.

Clutching my flowers, I fling open the door and run out. I've gotta catch the Scotts before they go to the cast party.

I round the corner, dropping a few petals behind me. "Millie!" I speed my walk into a jog. "James!" *Please be here.*

I race through the theater and up the center aisle. Bursting through the doors, I push through the thinning crowd.

"Millie! James!"

I stop a man in a black jacket like James's, but it's not him. I search the faces, but none of them belong to the Scotts.

My shoulders sag as I turn around and walk through the lobby again, ready to collect my stuff from the dressing room.

The heavy doors inch open, and I use my foot to shove it away from my body. The stage sits there alone, washed in lights.

And on the second row waits James, Millie, and Maxine.

My family.

My foster grandmother stands up, rubbing her hip. "You sailed out of here like your pants were on fire. Didn't even notice us."

I follow the carpeted trail down the center of the theater, gaining speed with the slope of the floor. By the time I get to the second row, I'm almost sprinting.

Millie rises and a smile grows on her face. "You didn't think we'd leave without a good-bye, did you?"

I shake my head. "No. You would never do that." And I launch myself into their arms. I pull them close, this family of mine. My perfectionist foster mother, my scholarly yet sarcastic foster dad, and my insane and aerodynamic Maxine. "I love you guys." And now I'm blubbering, spreading tears and stage makeup all over them. "I mean it. I love you."

And they pull me in.

Closer. Tighter.

No matter what happens, whether my mom shows up tomorrow or next year, these people are mine.

And I'm theirs.

And I know, as we stand in the glow of the spotlight, this is right where I'm supposed to be.

Chapter 38

THE CICADAS CHIRP their spring conversations as I sit on the back porch swing, pushing myself with my toe. The toe that happens to be in heels. As in the heels that match my spring dance dress.

Yes, all right, I'm feeling a wee bit sorry for myself. I fan the shimmery pink skirt out and watch it catch the light.

I wonder if Trevor is there. Dancing with Chelsea. Or the cheerleading squad. Or the girls' basketball team. Or—

"I think I like you better with the big nose."

I jerk back to reality at the sound of Charlie Benson's voice. He leans against the corner of the house and watches me from his spot in the dark. He pushes off with his foot and ambles my way.

He smiles as he takes in my dress, my shoes. Okay, and my updo. And my handbag. Fine, and my painted nails.

"You look really pretty, Katie." He steps onto the porch and into the light.

My heart adds a few beats at the sight of him. "I hear I have you to thank for getting Nash and Frances together." I grin. "Finally."

"You don't call me Einstein for nothing."

"I also hear we got an A on our science fair project. Thanks for that too. Sorry we didn't win." My pulse skitters a crazy beat. "I hope I didn't bring us down."

"I don't think you've ever brought me down." His eyes sparkle in the glow of the back porch light. "It's a shame you're all dressed up with nowhere to go."

My face burns a nice shade of embarrassed. "When I opened up my closet tonight, my dress just seemed so lonely."

"And the purse?"

"It too." My heels tap a nervous beat on the deck. "So I thought, why wait until the next dance? Who knows if there *will* be a next dance for me here in In Between." I raise my eyes, daring him to laugh. "So I just put this on. Why wait?"

Charlie digs into his coat pocket. "I totally agree." He pulls out his phone. "Why wait?" He punches a few buttons then sets it on the grill. A familiar slow song pours out.

"Katie Parker." Charlie holds out his hand. "Would you like to dance?"

I tilt my head back and laugh, the sound rising to the night sky. And with my gossamer dress swishing around me, I stand up and place my hand in his.

And we dance.

He twirls me around the deck floor and pulls me back into his arms.

"Just so you know . . ." I stare into his face. "I don't normally kiss on the first date."

"Just so you know," he drawls, "I wasn't gonna try."

He gives my fingers a squeeze and I smile. "This is pretty sweet though."

"Are you considering an exception to your rule?"

I press my lips to his cheek. "I'll let you know."

And under a canopy of stars and one giant Texas moon, I attend my very first dance.

With my very own Chihuahua.

Can't Let You Go
A Katie Parker Production Novella
Summer 2014

Katie Parker is now a twenty-three year-old college graduate, fresh from a year of performing on the great stages of London. When she runs into old flame Charlie Benson in the airport, both of them are bound for In Between, brining their baggage and more secrets that can be stuffed in an overhead bin. A flight mishap throws the two together, and Katie finds she can't escape Charlie when she returns to their small town. But does she even want to? Katie's returned to mend a broken heart and figure her life out, but when she discovers what has really brought Charlie back to town, she's thrown in the middle of an all-out battle.

Can she risk her heart again for a guy whose kisses make her weak in the knees, but whose secret could destroy all that she holds dear?

Chapter One

"What do you mean my bags aren't here?"

I lean over the counter at the O'Hare airport, fresh out of patience and smiles. The TSA employee's fingers clickity-clack on his keyboard, his generous brows knit together like an escaped wooly worm.

"I'm sorry, Miss Parker. Something apparently went very wrong, and your luggage seems to be on a flight to Reykjavik."

"This is unacceptable. Who goes to Iceland?"

"Apparently your bags do."

I want to slap my hand on the counter and yell until Mr. Brows makes this all okay. Because I just can't handle one more catastrophe. My bottom lip quivers, and I hear the pitiful words tumble from my lips. "My whole life is in those bags."

"Surely not everything," says a voice behind me.

That voice.

One I haven't heard in years, except in my dreams of home and heartache.

I turn around, pushing my tired, limp hair from my flushed cheek. Suddenly all the exhaustion of a ten hour flight evaporates, the weeks without sleep, the homesickness. All that I left behind in London. "Charlie Benson." His name comes out of my mouth like a sacred whisper as he stands there smiling.

I immediately burst into tears.

"Hey," Strong arms wrap around me, and I'm taken right back. My head pressed to Charlie's chest, I inhale his achingly familiar scent, and I'm no longer this broken, exhausted twenty-three year old, who just spent a year studying abroad, the pieces of my heart, my only luggage that followed. I'm sixteen, back in my hometown of In Between, dancing with one sweet Charlie Benson on my back porch underneath the Texas stars.

"How are you here?" I dash at the tears and take a much-needed step back. I take in the boy before me. Can I even call him a boy? He stands tall, shoulders broad, as if now carrying not just muscle, but some of the world's responsibility. With his dark dress pants, white button down, and navy tie, Charlie looks all man. And a professional one at that. "Are you traveling for work?"

"I live in Chicago now. Got out of a meeting only minutes ago. I'm on my way to In Between. You?"

I gesture to the desk. "I was trying to track down my luggage. I flew in from Paris, but had a terrible layover. I'm finally headed home as well." To my mom and dad, my crazy grandmother, to people who love me.

"You were studying in London this year, right?"

Don't think about it. Don't think about it. "Yes."

"My mom keeps me updated on In Between. She said you were in some plays on the West End." At my nod he smiles. "She says you're kind of a big deal."

Glad someone thinks so. "Just lucked into some good roles, I guess."

"*Flight 247 for Houston will now begin boarding our first class passengers. . .*"

Rain pelts the wall of windows at the gate, and I wonder if the crew has noticed.

"Are you on this flight?" he asks.

"Yes, you?"

"Yep." He reaches out, runs his hand down my arm, his head tilted just so. "Are you sure you're okay?"

"What, me? This?" I gesture to my mess of a face. "Jet lag, you know? And then the airline losing my stuff." I give a laugh so genuine, the Academy should FexEx me an Oscar. "I'm sorry. I'm a little homesick, and when I saw you—" I shake my head and smile. "I guess you were just a sight for sore eyes."

His lips tip in a grin. "Last I heard you were engaged."

Another announcement for our flight cracks across the speakers, but it sails over my head. "Wow. Word travels fast."

"You can't beat the small town communication system."

"You mean my grandma?"

His laugh swirls around me, settling somewhere in the gray recesses of my heavy heart.

The garbled voice comes across the speakers again.

"Time for me to board," Charlie says. "Where are you sitting?" He holds out a hand for my ticket, and I fumble in my bag to find it.

"It's here somewhere." I dig through the outer-pocket, coming up with a nail file, half a Snickers, two pieces of gym, and ten wads of used Kleenex.

"Hey." He steps nearer. "You're shaking."

I shrug and continue digging. "Fatigue."

He takes my worn leather messenger bag, looks in the middle compartment, his eyes never leaving mine, and pulls out my ticket. "You're still afraid of flying, aren't you?"

The things people remember. One senior class trip to Miami Beach with me trying to storm the cockpit demanding two forms of identification from the pilots, and everyone thinks you have a full blown neurosis.

Please. I've grown up since then.

"Final boarding call . . ."

"It's been incredible seeing you today." Charlie pulls me in for a hug, and I just breathe him in. The warm, the familiar, the safe. "We have more catching up to do," he whispers near my ear. "Are you going to be okay?"

"Definitely. I haven't had a flying meltdown in such a long time."

It's been at least three hours.

Clutching a water bottle and my wrinkled ticket, I follow Charlie as we board the sparsely populated plane. He stops off in row seven, while I schlep to the very back of the cabin. Next to the bathroom. How these odiferous seats don't come with a discount is beyond me.

I squeeze my bag in the bin above me, then settle into the window seat, hoping the two empty seats on my right remain that way. Buckling in, I check my phone one last time. I quickly respond to a text from my mom, two from my dad, and five from my grandma that consist of nothing more than her fish-lipped selfies with the message "My face misses yours!"

And then there are those voicemails I immediately delete.

Fifteen minutes later, we taxi down the runway. I sit in my blissfully empty row, push my breath in and out, and pray to the Lord Jesus to spare me one more day. I'm not afraid of what comes after death. I'm just a little terrified of the actual dying process. Especially if it involves crashing, flames, and wasted drink carts.

I'm just promising the Holy Father my favorite mascara and first born when a shoulder bumps mine, as someone throws himself into the seat beside me. I continue to whisper my beggar's prayer when a hand covers my clenched fingers.

I look up.

Charlie smiles. He brushes my damp hair from my face like he's done it a million times before. His strong hand pulls one of mine into his. And he just holds it.

"I'm not afraid to fly," I say.

"Of course not." He gives our fingers a squeeze. "It's the fatigue."

Thunder cracks outside. "Do you think it's safe to fly?"

"I do."

"But I read this report that when it storms, your statistical chances of—"

"It's perfectly safe."

"But sometimes lightning can be magnetically attracted to the wing and—"

"Nearly impossible."

"And then there's the possibility of—"

"Katie?"

My heart beats wildly, and my bones ache with exhaustion. "Yes?"

His gray eyes hold mine. "I won't let anything happen to us."

"Promise?"

With a smile as safe as church and sweet as sun tea, he slowly nods. "Always."

Chapter Two

I was practically raised on the streets. By twelve, I had a rap sheet, knew how to steal to eat, could pick a lock with just paper clips and spit, and could deflect the advances of my druggie mom's boyfriends with one well-placed knee.

I was fearless.

And now here I sat in my cushy, cramped plane seat, a half hour into the ride, tremoring slightly, and noticing I'm still clutching Charlie Benton's hand like it's all that's holding us upright.

I let go and give a small laugh. "Sorry." Nothing like reuniting with an old friend by welcoming them into your neurotic phobia. "Takeoffs make me nervous." And the part that comes after—the whole driving in the sky thing, hanging by clouds, winds, and various gravitational whims. His piercing gray eyes soften, and I remember all the times as a teenager I'd stare into them, sure there was a God, and He had baptized this boy with a benevolence of genetic blessings that resulted in one beautiful, intelligent boy who had routinely taken my breath away.

"I love to fly," Charlie says. "I've put in a lot of miles in the last year. I love the rocking of the plane, the hum of the engine. Some of the best sleeping conditions."

"Right." I would have to be drugged unconscious. "So tell me about your job." Charlie had gone to college in Chicago, leaving the town of In Between, while I had stayed behind, doing junior college, then university.

His gaze leaves mine, and he looks down the aisle toward the flight attendant pushing a cart. "Nothing exciting. I interned for this company my senior year. They hired me right after graduation."

"What do you do?"

"I'm very entry level," he says. "I'm kind of a glorified paper pusher right now."

"I know that won't last long. What company did you say you're with?"

"Would you like a beverage?" The flight attendant brings her silver cart to a stop by us, her red lips smiling.

I request a diet soda, and the woman pops the top on the can and pours it over ice.

"You probably want to give her the whole can," Charlie says. "I think Katie here could use the stiff drink."

"Would you like me to pour in some complimentary tequila?" the flight attendant asks.

I nod vigorously. "Yes, please."

"I was just kidding." She laughs and pushes her cart down the aisle.

More cruelty delivered mid-air. Thanks, lady.

"You're fine," Charlie says. "The hard part is over."

"Maybe you could keep talking." I snuggle my side into the chair, facing my old friend. My old boyfriend. "Keep my mind off our imminent doom."

He laughs. "Tell me about you. You haven't been too present on Facebook the last year. Hard to tell what you've been up to."

Images of the last six months flash through my mind. Some of them amazing. Some of them. . .not worth thinking on. "I finally graduated." I take a bolstering swig of diet soda, enjoying the way it burns going down. "Then I got selected to go work in London." Had that been a blessing or a curse?

"My mom said you were in some pretty impressive productions."

I'd forgotten how intense his gray eyes could be. So focused, like I'm the only person he wants to be talking to. Those eyes were older now, still full of mischief, always reflecting an intimidating intelligence, but now there was something more looking back at me. Something darker, maybe a little bit heavy. Like Charlie Benson might have some sadness and secrets of his own.

"It was an unforgettable experience," I finally say.

"And now you're back for a visit?"

"Yes." I leave it at that, clutching my arm rest as we hit a few bumps of turbulence. "And you? What's bringing you back?"

He lifts his drink and absently swirls it, studies the dark contents. "I want to check on my dad. Spend some time with him."

"I thought he was in remission." My mom had told me last year when Charlie's dad had been diagnosed with liver cancer. The whole In Between community had rallied around the bank president with prayers, well-wishes, and many a foil-covered casserole.

"He is. And things are looking good." Charlie looks past me and out the window over my shoulder. "My company gave me some time to come home and be with my family, so I took it."

I want to ask more, but one turn of mercy deserves another, and I let it drop. God knows I don't want to talk about what's really dragging me back to In Between, and given the set in Charlie's jaw, this topic is not a welcome one.

"You dated that Tate guy for a few years," Charlie says. "What happened to that?"

The plane makes a sharp jerk to the right, and I slap my hand on Charlie's. I frantically look around, but neither of the flight attendants seem concerned. The person across from us reads a *People*, while the couple a row ahead amiably chats.

"Um. . ." *It's okay. We just hit an air pocket. Calm down.* "Tate, yeah. He's now a missionary in Uganda. We're still friends." High School Love Number Two and I had simply moved in different directions.

Lightning cracks outside, and I jump as it feels close enough to touch us. Charlie's fingers slid back and forth over mine. "We're fine," he said as the plane dipped, sending my stomach to my feet. "Just a storm."

And just how many more of those did I have to endure?

I look at my hand captured in his, and I knew Charlie was just being nice. That's just who he was. But the rhythmic strokes of his fingers calmed my frayed nerves as nothing else had on this voyage home.

The plane began to shake and rattle like the busted glove compartment on my old Toyota. Only I couldn't turn up the radio, sing my car solos, and drown out the noisy vibrations.

"Why do you think we didn't work out?" I ask.

Charlie doesn't startle. Merely lifts a dark brow as he inclines his head closer to mine. "Where did that come from?"

"Was it me?"

"I—"

"Is there something about me that pushes guys away? That asks to be dumped?"

His hand on mine stills just as a flight attendant gives a staticky report. "Ladies and gentlemen, the captain has turned on the seat belt sign. We're hitting a brief patch of turbulence with this storm, but we'll be out of it in no time. Food and beverage services will be resumed as soon as we get the all clear."

"That can't be good, right?" I sit up as straight as my seatbelt will let me, frantically taking in every detail around me—the location of the flight attendants, the body language of fellow passengers, the reassuring presence of the wings that still seem to be blessedly attached.

Charlie pours more drink into my icy cup. He's probably regretting sitting by me. He probably wishes I'd drink my diet soda and happily pass out in a carbonated coma, so he could go back to his own seat and read his *Wall Street Journal* or whatever it is a calm, brainiac would read.

I need medication.

"Here, eat some of these." Charlie reaches into the leather bag at his feet and pulls out a box of M&Ms.

I snatch them out of his grip and down a handful. I chew vigorously, savoring the sugar and chocolate on my tongue. What if this is the last time I taste such heaven?

The plane, deciding the shaking was just its opening act, brings on the full-on quaking, jumping up and down like a Pentecostal with the Holy Ghost. My butt gains some air, and I turn my frightened gaze to Charlie. "What's happening?"

"Turbulence." He lifts a shoulder in such a lazy fashion, you'd think he didn't notice the way his hair bounced on his head from the aeronautical shenanigans. "You were asking me why we didn't work out."

"I was?"

His smile is soft, slow. "Why do you think we didn't make it?"

I tighten my seatbelt, trying not to wonder at the age of it. "Because you had your eye on some blonde Barbie who I could never compete with."

"That's not true."

"That you didn't have your eye on Chelsea Blake?"

He has the decency to look guilty. "That you couldn't compare. You were prettier and smarter than her any day."

Men in shimmy-shaky planes will say anything. "But you dumped me to go after her."

"I believe it was a mutual break-up."

"Because I knew what was coming."

"It was you I took to the senior prom." He squeezes the hand he's still holding and gives me a look that zings right to my weary core. "And you and I spent most of the night camping with on a blanket under the stars."

"At the lake." He'd built me a fire, made a pallet on the rocky ground, tucked me into the crook of his arm, and pointed out every constellation he could find in that April sky while I rested my head on his chest and listened to the crickets and the cadence of his heart.

Then we graduated. And Charlie Benson, of the lingering kisses and spell-binding astronomy, had moved away.

Rain and wind battle outside my window, and I utter a quick litany of prayers. Prayers that beg for calm skies and fifty more years of life.

"Guys don't stick around though," I say, watching a bolt of lightning slash the sky. "Eventually they find someone else, something better."

He leans close. "Is that what you really think? That you weren't good enough?"

"It's hard to argue with history." I hold up a hand to stop him from interrupting. "I'm not trying to be pitiful. I just want to get to the bottom of it. I'm tired of making mistakes, wasting my time." Being tossed out, left behind.

The plane takes a leap north then dips back down. My breaths catches in my throat. "I want off this thing," I say. "I want off this thing right now."

"Please put your seats in the upright position," announces the flight attendant. "Return your tray to its proper place."

The pilot takes his turn next, giving instructions and saying God knows what (probably Last Rites). But I can't hear a thing for the rising noise around me. An overhead bin to our left flies open and a bag torpedoes into a grandma and her knitting needles. Somewhere up front a baby wails. Nervous chatter gathers like tornado winds.

"What's the pilot saying?" My heart beats a crazed staccato, and I want to both cry and laugh at the insanity of it all.

"He said to stay calm that we'd be out of this storm soon." Charlie takes quick stock of the situation around us, then turns his attention back to me. "You were telling me why you broke my heart our senior year."

"I did not."

I expect him to smile, to follow up with a joke.

But Charlie says nothing.

He captures my other hand, prying my fingers off the arm rest, then pulls me closer, resting his forehead on mine. "I don't think you remember the events of those last few months accurately."

I swallow then lick my trembling lips. "You left." Just like they all do.

"I cared about you."

"You had a funny way of showing it."

"Katie, I—"

His words die as light and fury explode around us.

The flash of lightning.

Screaming.

Fire.

Falling.

Plummeting.

Spinning.

Screaming.

My world goes dark as Charlie throws his body over mine. "We've been hit," he yells in my ear. "Hang on. Just hang on to me."

I can't breathe. Can't drag in enough breath.

Please God, save us.

I utter the plea silently.

Aloud.

"Charlie?"

"I'm right here. I'm not letting you go."

His arms encircle me and hold my tight. He mumbles words of assurance, broken prayers, and other utterances the terror swallows whole.

"Charlie?" I shove off his hands, his body. "Charlie!" With all my strength I push him away, only to grab his face, his stubbly cheeks in the palms of my hands.

He finally lifts his head, his eyes wide, unfocused.

"I love you, Charlie." I pull his face to mine, blocking out the shrieks around us and the spin and tilt of death. "Do you hear me? I never stopped loving you."

"Katie, I—"

Then I press my mouth to his, holding Charlie Benson to me, knowing these lips will soon draw their last breath.

And I don't want to waste these minutes, seconds.

Then Charlie Benson's kissing me back. His lips cover mine. His hands cradle my head.

The world spins.

The plane falls.

And I just hold on.

"I've got you," I hear him say again. "I'm not letting you go."

And after all these years, I believe him.

Just when it's too late.

About the Author

Four-time Carol award-winning author Jenny B. Jones writes romance with equal parts wit, sass, and Southern charm. Since she has very little free time, she believes in spending her spare hours in meaningful, intellectual pursuits, such as watching bad TV, Tweeting deep thoughts to the world, and writing her name in the dust on her furniture. She is the author of romantic comedies for women such as RITA finalist *Save the Date*, as well as books for teens, like her *A Charmed Life* series. You can find her at www.JennyBJones.com or standing in the Ben and Jerry's cooler.

CPSIA information can be obtained at www.ICGtesting.com
Printed in the USA
LVOW07s2154110515

438050LV00006BA/1103/P

5